# WHEN VILLAINS RISE

*USA TODAY* & *WSJ* BESTSELLER

giana darling

When Villains Rise

Anti-Heroes in Love Duet. Book Two.



Published by Giana Darling

Edited by Jenny Sims

Proofed by Sarah Plocher

Cover Design by Najla Qamber

Cover Model Beto Malfacini

Formatting by R Holmes

*This one is for every single woman who was taught she will never be enough. The simple act of being you inspires me. The strength and tenacity of the female spirit is unconquerable.*

*And to Michelle Clay.*

*The woman who always champions and cheers for other woman.*

*"It is as inhuman to be totally good as it is to be totally evil."*

*– Anthony Burgess*

# PLAYLIST

"Come Back For Me"--Jaymes Young

"So It Goes"--Taylor Swift

"Come Away With Me"--Norah Jones

"Naked"--Ella Mai

"Power"--Isak Danielson

"Far From Home"--Sam Tinnesz

"Flames"--Tedy

"Love Don't Hate It"--Duncan Laurance

"Devil Devil"--MILCK

"Musica Per Vino"--Italian Instrumental

"Turn Me On"--Norah Jones

"Goddess"--Cobi

"Secrets and Lies"--Ruelle

"Woozy"--Glass Animals, Jean Deaux

"Kingdom Fall"--Claire Wyndham

"Rival"--Ruelle

"You Belong To Me"--Cat Pierce

"Start A War"--Klergy, Valerie Broussard

"Play With Fire"--Sam Tinnesz feat. Yacht Money

"I Shall Rise"--Karen O

"Soldier"--Fleurie

"No Time To Die"--Billie Elish

"Count On Me"--NEEDTOBREATHE

"Boom Boom"--2WEI, Jon, Bri Bryant

"Touch"--HAUX

"Buon Natalte"--Nat King Cole

"Brooked"--Amos Lee

"Work"--Charlotte Day Wilson

"Falling Water"--Peter Oren

"Call Out My Name"--The Weeknd

"Walk Through Fire"--Zayde Wolf

"Scars"--Boy Epic

"Sweetest Devotion"--Adele

"Build It Better"--Aron Wright

# PART ONE: NAPOLI

# CHAPTER ONE

## *elena*

Loving him wasn't the end of everything.

It's funny they always make it seem that way in the books and movies.

Loving him was just the beginning.

In a way, it was the death of me.

The woman of before, the cold, calculating, stubbornly moral lawyer with a layered life and carefully constructed personality, was buried six feet beneath the earth in New York City.

This new being, born from the ashes of a fire ignited by one man, was reborn on a plane somewhere over the mid-Atlantic Ocean.

I was newly born, as blank as a white sheet of paper, my future hovering over it like a poised pen.

I only knew three things.

Fleeing the country with a known criminal made me a felon by association, so for the first time in my life, I was officially on the wrong side of the law.

We were returning to my homeland, a place I had sworn five years ago that I would never go back to willingly. More than that, we were going into the belly of the beast. Naples. The stinking cesspool that was the heart of the Camorra mafia. The villains of my entire youth.

And thirdly, most importantly, I was indisputably and irretrievably in love with a mafia Don, a man who could and most certainly *had* killed people with his big, bare hands. A man by the name of Dante Salvatore. A man who had changed my entire world.

It was the only positive thing on my short list, yet it seemed the most all-consuming, the only true thing that mattered.

I was in love with Dante.

I'd loved before.

So, why did this feel so different, so strange?

Even at the height of my affection for Christopher and Daniel, I'd felt solidly independent, removed enough from my emotions to operate logically and efficiently.

With Dante, I felt my edges blurring, my whole being smudged like a watercolor painting into the edges of him and his.

I didn't want space or logic.

*Dio mio*, I'd fled the country and my entire life to be with him. Clearly, I wasn't thinking logically.

But that was the craziness of it all.

I didn't care if I was acting outside of my own interests, that I was being impulsive and reckless and passionate to a fault.

I didn't care so much I felt like roaring with giddy, manic laughter.

I was unhinged, ripped from the caged structure of my previous life by Dante's ruthless grasp.

I felt free.

So free.

For the first time *ever.*

*"Lottatrice mia."*

The low purr of his British-Italian accent hooked through my gut and pulled my focus from the oval plane window and the night ocean beyond to the very man I was thinking about.

Dante sat in the butter-soft leather seat the way he sat in anything, big body sprawled out, thick thighs spread, heavily muscled torso sunk deep into the plush cushions. He should have looked lazy and even insolent in such an easy pose, but it somehow only served to make him look more powerful. As if that relaxed façade could coil and strike at only a second's notice.

With his ink dark eyes pinned on me, it was impossible to take him for anything less than the predator he was.

"Your loud thinking is disturbing my peace," he had the audacity to tell me with one of those Italianate shrugs that was barely a twitch of one shoulder. "If you cannot sleep, Elena, perhaps I can find something else to occupy your busy mind."

I'd fallen into an emotionally exhausted slumber almost as soon as I'd buckled into my seat to take off, and I'd only just woken up to the calamitous riot of my thoughts. Trust Dante to know I was awake and brooding even while he was busy conducting business on his phone.

I leveled him with a haughty look, but inside my chest, something like joy bubbled up. "Excuse me for disturbing your peace. You're right. It's completely unacceptable that I'm stewing over the fact I just effectively destroyed my life in New York to chase after a runaway felon fleeing to a country I abhor. How selfish of me."

There was the faintest twitch in his full mouth, but otherwise, he only continued to give me that thousand-yard stare over steepled fingers. "Frankie?"

"Yeah, Boss," his second-in-command called from the rear of the main cabin where he was doing something on two computer monitors.

"Get out," Dante ordered.

Without another word, Frankie powered down his application and got up. He shot me a sly wink before turning on his heel and disappearing into the back room.

Suddenly, my mouth was entirely parched.

I watched wide-eyed as Dante uncoiled that massive frame from his seat, straightened his cuff links idly, then moved across the space between us to loom over me. I could see the bandage taped beneath his left collarbone through the white shirt. Frankie had stitched up the bullet wound, but the sight of it scoured through me. He'd taken that bullet for me. Put his entire life at risk *for me*. That such a powerful man would gamble his kingdom and livelihood for little old me made me feel nothing short of a queen.

His eyes pinned to mine, he bent his torso to brace both hands on my armrests, effectively caging me into my seat.

My heart raced with a curious mixture of fear and excitement.

It was Dante's unique charm that convinced you he might as easily kiss you as kill you.

"Perhaps it would help if I reminded you why it is you gave up everything you know to be with me," he purred in that rich, dark voice

I wanted to eat off his tongue like dark chocolate.

I was aroused; there was no denying it. A second pulse beat between my thighs, growing more and more insistent. My nipples were pebbled beneath my silk camisole despite the heavy cashmere cardigan I wore over it. The airplane air was cool, but every inch of my flesh itched with heat.

Yet I felt nervous, awkward, and almost irritated.

I wanted to play this game of seduction, but how in the world did I compete with the raw sexual magnetism of this man?

I *felt* when I had spent so many years quelling every emotion.

I trusted that, the feeling.

Even if I was wary of where it would take me.

So, I sucked in a bracing breath and raised my hands to slide my fingers around his warm neck into the short hairs at the back of his head.

"Show me," I told him, barely above a whisper. "But I don't need reminding. I could never forget why I left it all behind. I could never forget you."

A growl worked through his throat as he dipped down to capture my mouth in a savage kiss. It was all tongue and teeth, a dance of ownership. I didn't back down to his possession, desperate to show him how much I wanted to possess every inch of him too.

"Kissing you is the sweetest agony," he murmured against my damp lips as one big hand moved to my throat. The feel of him collaring me that way should have been deplorable. Instead, it felt like the most exquisite necklace, one I wanted to wear with pride forevermore. "I never want to stop kissing you, at the same time it makes me hungry for more."

"Don't stop," I implored him, fisting my hands in his shirt collar so I could tug him harder against my mouth. "Kiss me."

"Oh, I intend to spend the next hour doing just that," he promised darkly even as he pulled away from me.

A noise of protest rose unbidden in my throat. He chuckled at me as he dropped to his knees before my seat and moved close, forcing my thighs wide apart to accommodate his bulk. A little shiver of discomfort tangled with desire moved through me.

Instinctively, my hands moved to stop him as he reached for my cashmere lounge pants.

He quirked an eyebrow at me, his expression entirely unamused. "Elena, do not try to keep me from your beautiful *figa*."

My beautiful pussy.

A blush poured down my front.

"I-I don't really like it when…when people do that to me," I admitted awkwardly.

"Why the hell not?"

It was a good question, but it was also one I didn't want to answer. Dante didn't know about Christopher. He didn't know that I'd been groomed and used by him for years then finally, in the end, flat-out abused by the man.

He didn't know every time a man tried to go down on me, I had Christopher's voice in my head telling me it was dirty.

Sensibly, I knew he had been hypocritical and most probably *wrong*.

He'd forced me to fellate him often enough.

But I still couldn't shake the anxiety that seized me as Dante gently brushed my hands away and tugged at my pants. I held my breath so I wouldn't strike out at him as the fabric moved down my legs and off. He tossed them blindly over his shoulder, then shocked me by placing his right cheek against the inside of my thigh. His hot breath wafted over my silk-covered sex.

I shivered almost violently, sick with lust and shame.

"*Sei bella,*" Dante told me in an intimate murmur as he stroked a thumb over the top of my groin. "You are beautiful, Elena. From your red hair to your endlessly long legs, your velvet gray eyes and your elegance. Even, and especially, your pussy. This"--he dropped a chaste kiss to my covered clit that made me gasp--"is beautiful. Do not deny me the pleasure of kissing you here. Of tasting you straight from the well."

His thumb edged under the silk and swept over the delicate skin at the crease of my thigh and groin. I was bare beneath the silk but for a strip of carefully groomed hair over my clit, and the sensation of his rough finger against the tender flesh was almost absurdly arousing.

When he looked up from watching his hand move over me, his eyes were hot as freshly poured tar. "I want to be the one to make you lose control. I want to watch you bend and break beneath my hands so I can glue you back together with pleasure."

Desire lodged in my throat, making it impossible to get words past my lips. Instead, I loosed a conflicted groan.

Dante took it for the frightened consent it was and bent his head to seal his hot mouth over my clit through the silk.

My head rocked back against the leather seat as the heat of his tongue flicking over my flesh seared through my entire groin.

*"Dio mio,"* I whispered, a prayer and a benediction to some higher power to forgive me for my sins.

Because this was sinful.

The slide of Dante's tongue through the silk, the wet fabric providing a delicious friction on my sensitive nub, the breath hot then cold against my flesh. Even the sight of Dante, so big and broad wedged between my slim thighs, his dark head against my pale flesh. It was all too decadent to bear.

I squeezed my eyes shut, trying to focus on the beauty of this man and not the trauma of my past.

*"Lottatrice mia,"* Dante rasped between kisses. "Watch me worship this pretty pussy, hmm? I want you to see how the taste of you undoes me."

I couldn't breathe properly, so I started to pant as I forced my eyes open and fixed them on Dante. He locked gazes with me, then slowly drew his tongue over my wet seam through my panties and hummed at the flavor of me.

"Sweet and salty," he told me before hooking his fingers at the silk crotch of my underwear.

And then he tore them brutally from my skin, the fabric rending with a quiet gasp that echoed from my mouth.

He growled as he looked at me spread wide and bared for him. I thought he'd never looked like such a beast, ready to devour me whole.

"There has never been another man for you," he said fiercely, eyes flashing up to mine and filled with primal possession. "I am the only one to touch you this way, to bring you this pleasure. Forget the past, Elena, because I am the only man in your future."

Before I could say anything, he bent his head reverently, as if in prayer, and sealed his mouth over my sex.

I choked on my gasp as I threw my head back. Pleasure rooted deep in my gut and spread through my blood from there, warming every inch of me inside and out.

Instinctually, my hands found their way into his thick black hair and clasped him tighter to me.

He groaned in approval, lashing his strong tongue between my folds. The illicit sounds of his wet mouth against my increasingly wet sex made me flush even as they heightened my pleasure. It was almost impossible to feel my old shame when Dante was so completely unapologetic about his enjoyment of my body.

His brazenness was like a key in the lock barring me from my own self-satisfaction. His thumb played at the entrance of my pussy, then slowly sank inside and turned to hook against a spongy spot that made me see stars.

"*Dio mio, Dante,*" I chanted as my head thrashed at the intensity of sensation building at my core. "Oh my God, Dante, *more*."

He banded his arms around my writhing hips, anchoring my bottom to the seat and my pussy to his ruthless mouth.

"Come for me," he ordered roughly, his ruddy mouth slicked with my wet. "And Elena? Say my name when you do."

I shivered as he wrapped his lips around my aching clit and sucked hard, two fingers working their way into my tight channel at the same time. Air wouldn't fit into my constricted lungs, and my blood seemed to boil too hot beneath my skin.

"Dante," I almost sobbed, still frightened by the sensations. My womb clenched almost painfully, and then seconds later, I cried out as everything in my body went tight and hard, clenched like a fist, only to explode open swiftly afterward.

"Dante, Dante, Dante," I called to the ceiling of the plane as my fingers spasmed in his hair and my pussy spasmed against his fingers, clit throbbing on his tongue.

"That's it," he purred like a conquering warrior reveling in his spoils. His fingers pumped gently inside me, wringing out every ounce of pleasure to be had. "Look at you coming all over my mouth and fingers like that. So fucking beautiful and all mine."

While I was still trying to catch my breath, Dante swiftly undid his belt and black trousers, pulling his thick, veined cock from his boxer briefs. The head was flushed and swollen and purple as a plum, and when he jacked it hard and slow, a pearl of precum beaded at the tip. I wanted to do something with that cock, something licentious and wrong like rubbing the warm, hard flesh all over my face, burrowing my nose in the short hairs at its base to scent his male musk, then suck at the tip until he rewarded me with more of that salty juice.

But Dante didn't give me time to cave into those base desires, and a small part of me was glad for that. I didn't feel totally ready to act the wanton, even with him.

Watching him act that way, though, was an entirely different story.

I groaned raggedly as he stood, roughly pushed my camisole up to my neck to bare my breasts, and said, "Hold it there."

I did without question.

He raised one foot onto the armrest of my chair, which brought his large body looming over my own, his thick cock trained at my exposed chest. It should have been demeaning, but I loved the dynamics of this big man pinning me to my seat with the threat of his form. Because he would never hurt me. Never debase me. He was so turned on by my orgasm he couldn't restrain his heathen impulses.

Dante Salvatore, the educated, sophisticated Duke's son, wasn't before me now.

This was the mafioso. The Don. The Devil of NYC.

Using the sight of my languid, sexed-up body to get himself off.

The rush of power that ignited in me made me light-headed.

"You see what you do to me?" he demanded in a war-torn voice as he fisted his cock almost viciously and jerked off inches from my face. I was transfixed by the sight of his strangled head moving wetly in and out of his grip. "Only you, Elena. Only with you do I feel like fucking you, marking you, owning you with my body and my cum. I'm going to paint you with it right now so you know you're mine. Mine to fuck. Mine to cherish. Mine to love."

"Yes," I hissed, licking the drool that pooled in the corners of my mouth as I watched his boxed abs contract and twitch with the force of his pleasure. "When I watched you that night in the office, and you came so much all over yourself...well, I wanted to be the one you jerked off on."

Dante snarled as he fell forward enough to place his free hand at my throat, pinning me still so he could twist his fist over his cock right above my swollen breasts. We both panted, eyes fixed to the sight of that dick leaking precum down the shaft.

"Tell me, *donna,*" he bit out. The tendons strained in his neck as he beat himself to climax. "Tell me you want my cum on this classy skin."

"I want it," I admitted, feeling weak with longing, my skin already tingling in anticipation. "Come for me, my capo."

"*Cazzo,*" he shouted gruffly seconds before his hips snapped forward, and he started to come.

I hadn't forgotten how much he was capable of coming. The sight of him covered in his own spend was forever branded on my conscience, but I was still shocked and deeply aroused as spurt after spurt of hot seed striped my chest. Without thinking, my hands went to my lower breasts to cup them in offering to Dante.

His groan rattled through his chest as he squeezed the last of his cum from the head and finally released his softening organ. He stared down at his handiwork with blazing eyes, then slowly, deliberately, he reached out to smear the wet into my skin.

"You wear my cum with pride," he said in a way that was half order and half question.

I appreciated the tone of both. He wasn't the kind of man to ask explicitly for my consent because he knew the trappings of my mind. If he asked, I'd feel forced to disagree because that was how I'd been trained.

But these subtle half-questions, the words written in the screens of his ink-black eyes, and the slight hesitation in his hands when he pushed me past my boundaries all spoke to his awareness of my hang-ups. He respected them even as he fought to demolish them.

"Yes," I agreed with a firm nod, locking our gazes. "I wear it with pride."

His smile was blinding, slightly crooked from exhaustion as he tucked himself away and did up his trousers.

"*Excellente,*" he praised as he bent to collect me suddenly in his arms.

"Dante, you're injured," I protested as he lifted me, turned us both, then settled himself in the chair with me in his lap.

He repositioned me until I was laid across his lap with my head tucked in the crook of his neck and shoulder, my shirt rolled down over my sticky breasts. "Please, it's barely a bug bite."

"What is with Italian men insisting on the Mr. Macho routine?" I demanded, pushing off his right side to glare at him. "You're a big, strong man who just came copiously all over my chest. I think your masculinity and virility can rest easy, Dante. It's your stupidity that's rearing its ugly head carrying me around as if you don't have a bullet wound to the chest!"

Dante threw his head back into the cushion as he roared with laughter, the beautiful sound moving through his entire body into mine. I couldn't help the small smile of awe that seized my mouth as I watched his face crease with mirth, his eyes squeezed shut at the force of it. When he finally tipped his head down to look at me, his eyes still captured the effervescence of his humor.

"Clearly, I need to work harder at leaving you comatose after a climax if you still have the ability to berate me for my foolishness after I've made you come on my tongue."

I sniffed primly. "I wouldn't hold your breath."

Again, he laughed, just a chuckle that was somehow even more intimate because he hugged me gently to him as he did so.

"My fighter," he acknowledged, but it wasn't a put down the way it could have been.

It was a compliment, one that warmed my chest like brandy.

I let myself snuggle closer, my fingers playing in the chest hair exposed by the open buttons of his shirt. The silence between us was warm and familiar. Before Dante, I'd never known there could be such language between two bodies. The way he held me said everything about his contentment in having me with him on this new adventure, about having me as his woman. I hoped almost desperately that he could feel how I felt about him in the way I rubbed my nose against the hollow of his throat, in the way I traced my fingers lightly over his quilted chest.

"It won't be easy," he said finally, but he didn't sound daunted. "We won't be able to hide away in a villa in the countryside without being noticed."

"Why did you choose to go back to Italy then?" I asked. "I would think it's the first place the police would look for you, and they have an extradition treaty with the States."

Dante snorted, playing with a lock of my hair absently as he spoke. "The government of Italy may have an agreement with the US, but the country is truly run by *le mafie*. Do not worry, Elena, my own people will not turn me over to the authorities. That is not why this is dangerous for us both."

I frowned, trying to understand what risks there could be. "Surely, the Camorra of Naples will support you. You're the Don of the most successful outfit of their operation in America."

"How much do you know of the Camorra structure?" he asked me. "It is not like the Cosa Nostra or the movies in America. The Camorra is a collection of 'families' or groups with their own internal hierarchy. The capo, the consigliere, the underbosses, and soldiers. Each capo is the head of a unit." He paused, his voice dropping so low I felt it through my skin more than I heard it. "There is always a *capo dei capi*, Elena, but what do you think happens when you put the capos of each family in a room together, hmm? We are like wolves in a new territory, and we rip each other to shreds for a chance to lay claim to that land, *capisci?*"

"Too many alphas in one room," I surmised, shuddering a little at the idea of ten Dantes in one room together. "How did you get anything done as an organization?"

He laughed. "This is a very good question. It led to a lot of problems before technology gave us a better solution. In the old days, we had to meet face-to-face. Now, we rarely meet in person. It's riskier. The feds or the carabinieri in Italy are always monitoring known or suspected members. We have…digital channels available to us that make everything much more difficult to sniff out."

"So, why are you going back to Naples?" I reiterated, anxiety prickling under my skin. "Amadeo isn't in charge anymore. Is the local *capo dei capi* even friendly with you?"

Dante's full mouth compressed into a flat line. "Not exactly."

I blinked at him. "Okay…Is there a way to turn the plane around?"

He chuckled, leaning close to brush his nose over mine in a gesture that was achingly sweet.

"You are with me now, *si*? You are mine as I am yours. I told you once, I am the most honest man you will ever meet so do not ask questions you do not want the answers to." He paused, his black eyes all-consuming. "So I'm asking you, how much do you want to know?"

Unconsciously, I picked at a hangnail as I considered his question.

I could physically feel the conflict inside me, the sharp edge of jostling swords and the agony of pierced flesh. My body was a battle zone for the thoughts raging in my head.

I didn't want to be a bad person. I never had, which wasn't to say I'd succeed in that.

I'd been bad.

But I'd always had this fairy-tale ideal of good and bad, pure and evil. I'd assumed I would always be on the "right" side of the law and morality. But when one contradicted the other, I found myself at a crossroads.

And Dante was asking me to pick one path and journey down its shadowy corridors alongside him. I wasn't naïve enough to think I could be with Dante romantically and not become entangled in his underworld dealings.

The truth was, it had already happened.

I'd unwittingly become the right-hand woman to his *consigliere* when I took on his RICO case. I'd befriended his closest associates and overheard information in passing that could make the case I was an accessory to criminal activity.

I'd shot a man.

Seamus Moore was dead because of me.

But then...hadn't I already been embroiled in the mafia and crime because of that same man? The father who sold my youngest sister into sexual slavery at the age of eighteen in order to repay his gambling debts? The same father who brought Christopher into our lives and consequently into my bed.

It was ironic in a way, to think that I'd eschewed all things morally gray and certainly criminal because my father was a deplorable human only to meet a man who was both of those things yet the best person I'd ever known.

It was mind-boggling, and I couldn't sort the threads of my thoughts well enough to give Dante an eloquent answer.

"I want to be with you," I promised solemnly as I cupped his jaw, running my thumb over the jutting bone and the sharp stubble there. "I just don't know what that means for me. If I stand beside you the way you might want me to, it means I could never be a lawyer again. You have to understand, the dream of being a lawyer has tethered me all my life. It-it would be difficult to give it up."

Difficult, but maybe not impossible.

I had to re-examine why I was a lawyer, and if there was some way I could do good in another capacity.

Dante's laughter was hard and hollow, a spent casing clicking against the floor. "We are going into the belly of the beast, Lena. I'll do my best to shield you from the brunt of it, but I can't make any guarantees. If people know you are my woman, they'll assume you stand at my side."

"Don't most mafioso's wives and girlfriends stay one step behind them?" I quipped lamely, trying to pull the frown from between his thick brows.

He blinked at me solemnly, those long lashes absurdly thick over those fathomless eyes. "I'm not most mafiosos. I thought we had already established that."

It was my turn to blink hard, this time on a wince.

I didn't mean to continue to judge him, but a lifetime of carefully constructing my own moral compass made it difficult to curb my impulsive reactions.

His sigh wafted over my forehead, stirring my hair. "You are here with me when I never thought you would take such a risk. For now, that is more than enough."

"I don't want to let you down," I admitted even though it hurt, the words torn straight from the fabric of my heart. "I've let my loved ones down all my life, and I can't bear the thought of doing the same to you."

"Then don't," he said simply, palming my throat and dipping down to kiss my brow. "But Elena, you should know, I have never met a woman with such *coraggio*. And I have no doubt that whoever you felt you let down in your past let *you* down as well, *si?*"

I thought about Daniel and Giselle, but the sour tang of bitterness and remorse didn't wash over my tongue the way it normally did.

"You give me too much credit," I murmured, avoiding that penetrating gaze that seemed capable of X-raying more than just my bones.

His fingers slid into the hair over my ear, tipping my head so that he could feather a kiss over the bruising my father had left under my eye when he hit me. When he pulled back, his eyes were soft as suede. "No, you do not give yourself enough."

And just that easily, Dante convinced me once again that abandoning everything I knew just to be with him was the best choice I'd ever made.

Dante placed his head on my shoulder. "Based on the way you are staring at these clothes, I thought you were trying to crack open a safe or discern the meaning of life."

I snorted softly. "Close. I'm trying to decide what to wear to meet your father figure."

"You've met Tore before."

"As your lawyer, not as your…" I hesitated, scrambling to define what this gorgeous man was to me and me to him. "As your partner."

He turned his head so that his hot breath wafted over my neck, his lips tickling the thin skin over my hammering pulse. "Partner? Mmm, I don't think so. I like the sound of… my lover, my woman, *innamorata mia, amora mia.*"

My love, my heart.

I shivered as he clamped his teeth around the side of my neck and sucked in a way that would leave a bruise. Hickeys were tasteless marks, yet I found myself leaning into the suction, gasping at the sensation and the knowledge that everyone who looked at me with him would know I was *his*.

I'd never yearned for possession the way I did with Dante. I was a woman who valued my independence fiercely so I'd always thought that the idea of belonging to someone else was a direct contradiction to my independence. I'd been wrong. Owning the heart of a man like Dante Salvatore didn't make me weak, it made me strong. I was proud to be seen as his because I was proud of the man he was and the woman he helped me to become.

"We land in twenty minutes. Come sit with me," he said as he pulled away. "You look beautiful."

"I look like I spent ten hours on a plane," I argued. "And before that, I spent hours locked up in a basement in Brooklyn."

"I don't like the bruise that *bastardo* put on your face, but no one will judge you for that, least of all Tore."

"My outfit is part of my armor," I told him even though it exposed a vulnerability. "I'll be out in two minutes. Just give me time to change."

"You don't understand this yet, but you do not need your armor all the time now. Not when you have me." He lipped the edge of my jaw all the way up to my ear, where he spoke his next words on a purr. "I will be your sword."

Before I could gather my scattered thoughts enough to respond, he squeezed my hip in his palm then moved away, the door clicking behind him.

Love hadn't suddenly made me naïve.

I knew no matter what, Dante and I would continue to face adversity. I would need his sword and my shield both if we were going to survive Naples.

But I couldn't ignore the way my heart seemed to float in my chest, filled with a joy so effervescent it couldn't be contained.

*I will be your sword.*

I shook my head to ground myself again, then went into the bathroom to fix my curls and apply a fresh coat of Chanel lipstick in the shade 'Gabrielle' that made my mouth a bold, sultry pout. I settled on a tight black, high-waisted pencil skirt and a sheer black blouse that hid the scabbing wounds at my wrists from when Seamus had zip-tied them, feeling instantly more at ease when I looked in the mirror at the respectable image I formed. I didn't wipe the dried cum from my chest even though it made my skin tight.

Something in my gut delighted in the sinfulness of wearing it there while I looked otherwise suitable.

When I returned to the cabin, both Frankie and Dante were seated for landing. The former whistled low as I took my seat, laughing when Dante shot him a raised brow glower.

"She's beautiful, D. What do you expect?"

"I expect respect," he countered. "You treat her like a piece of meat, *amico*, and I'll let her treat you the same."

When they both looked at me, I raised a haughty brow at Frankie. "Next time 'you look beautiful, Elena' would suffice better than a catcall, Francesco."

He bit the edge of his smile as he saluted me. "Aye aye, *Donna*."

I took the seat across from Dante and smiled when he extended his leg so that our shoes were pressed together. He leaned forward, forearms on his thighs, to dip his fingers into a bag on the floor.

"I have a present for you, *lottatrice*."

"Oh?" I asked, unable to curb my excitement.

I could admit to being a material girl. I loved gifts.

He chuckled at me. "This is not the kind of gift you are used to, I think. This is more...practical."

My eyes widened comically as he pulled a small silver gun from the bag and held it in the palms of his big hands. It seemed oddly innocuous there, too small in his grip, but there was no doubting the threat of the weapon.

"Surely, I don't need that," I whispered even as my fingers reached out to touch the cool metal. "You'll keep me safe."

His features softened slightly, but he still shook his head. "No. Only a very foolish man thinks he will be able to protect his loved ones at all times. You're a good fighter already. I will teach you to be good with a gun. I won't have my own egotism be a chink in your armor."

I swallowed past the lump in my throat. "I know I shot Seamus, and I don't regret it, but I don't want to make a habit of killing people."

His lips twitched with morbid humor. "No, I don't want that either. But it never hurts to be prepared to defend yourself, does it?"

"No, I suppose it doesn't."

"Have you ever held a gun before the other day in Brooklyn?" he asked, already moving to place the weapon in my limp hand, molding my fingers to the grip. "This is light and small. The recoil shouldn't jar you too badly. This here is the safety. Press it in when you want to fire. You cock the top like this to reload the chamber. There is a makeshift range at Tore's villa we can practice at."

I stared at his hand over mine on the gun and wondered why the sight was so powerful. "I'll learn if it will make you feel better. But you should know, I never settle for mediocrity. If I'm going to learn to shoot, I'll probably become a better shot than you."

I knew he'd laugh, but the sound still impacted me just the same. It moved me like piano music, like fine Italian wine. I wished I could record it and listen to the sound whenever we were apart.

"I look forward to seeing you try," he said with a wink before pulling back to hand me a small black holster from the bag at his feet. "This is a thigh holster." I swallowed thickly when he moved to his knees in front of me again and ran his rough fingers up my calf to my thigh. He held my eyes as he wrapped the contraption around my right leg. "Wear this here whenever we are outside the villa, *si*? I had meant to give them to you back in New York. You are lucky I am a sentimental man and brought them with me now."

I nodded, struck mute by the unexpected eroticism of Dante rucking up my skirt to fit the gun in the holster. He lingered, gaze as hot as his fingertips on my delicate skin.

"Still have the taste of you on my tongue," he murmured just for me. "It's not enough. When we get to safety, I plan to lay you out on the bed and feast for hours. Could you handle that, Elena?"

I shuddered.

His lips curled sensuously as one hand gripped my thigh above my knee in a hard squeeze that shot sensation to my core. "It doesn't matter if you can't. I'll tie you to the posts and eat my fill."

My mouth opened at the force of my quickened breath. "Dante..."

He arched a brow in challenge, knowing I wanted to protest even though the idea made me hot and tingly all over. "*Si, lottatice?*"

"I don't think I would like to be tied up," I breathed, but the words were more of a question than conviction.

"I disagree," he said easily, dropping a kiss to my knee that burned like a lit cigarette. "But I would never make you do anything you did not want. Do you understand that?"

Jerkily, I nodded. "It's not you I'm afraid of really. I don't...trust myself with how much I want you."

He cocked his head, confusion creasing his broad forehead. I couldn't curb the impulse to hesitantly reach out to run a finger over the indentation there. "I wonder if you trust yourself at all sometimes. *Non ti preoccupare,* do not worry, I will teach you to trust yourself as I trust you."

"You want to get a concussion before we even land?" Frankie called as the plane noticeably swooped lower in descent. "Sit your big ass down, Boss."

Dante shot him a look over his shoulder. When he looked back at me, his eyes were hot and solemn. "In New York, you were my champion, hmm? My lawyer and my advocate striving to keep me safe. Well, Napoli is *my* courtroom. Put down your weapons, relax your shields. For once in your life, you do not have to fight all your own battles. I will fight for you. Here and now, I will be your champion. Do you trust me?"

Was trust the same thing as love?

Because I loved him.

Lord knew I loved this man with the olive-black eyes and golden heart better than I'd loved anything else in my life.

But trust? I hadn't trusted anyone new in so long, I wondered if I even had the capacity for it anymore.

I sucked in a deep breath through my teeth and nodded slowly. "I trust you. *Io sono con te.*"

*I am with you,* I said, echoing the words he'd spoken to me during that horrific car chase on Staten Island. And I was. For better or worse,

I was with Dante Salvatore, mafioso and wanted fugitive.

Now, I just had to discover what that made *me*.

"*Bene*." His face broke into that broad, magnificent grin that stole the breath from my lungs.

Satisfied, he got back into his seat, attached his seat belt, and turned to speak in low Italian with Frankie.

I tuned them out, staring down at my thighs where the strap of the holster was barely discernable through the fabric. The cold metal of the gun was warming slightly against my flesh. It should have made me nervous to have a concealed weapon on my person. It was illegal in the States, and I'd never in my life had a weapon stronger than pepper spray on my person.

But the weight of it felt good.

I was heading into the lion's den, and I needed all the weapons I could get. Not just to defend me, but to defend Dante, even to defend Frankie and the rest of the ragtag team of criminals in Dante's crew who had become something like family to me over the past few months.

Dante's love had razed me to the very ground of my soul, demolishing all my preconceived notions of right and wrong, even of my own identity and desires. I was going to step off this plane a new woman, and for the first time in my life, I was excited by my lack of foresight and structure.

So, when the plane landed smoothly on a private runway outside of Naples, I took Dante's offered hand with a wide smile that made him blink.

I was still smiling when the attendant opened the door, and I stepped into the blinding sun of a midmorning winter's day in my hometown. It was that very same sun that blinded me for just a moment.

At that moment, I heard a series of mechanic clicks like locks sliding into place.

I frowned as I blinked away the sunspots, but Dante was already pulling me hard back into his chest, then slightly behind his body.

Finally, I understood why.

The clicks weren't a series of locks turning.

But a series of guns loading.

*"Ciao, Don Salvatore!"* someone called warmly in Italian, a man who stepped out from the congregation of armed *soldati* to stalk toward the stairs leading up to the plane.

Dante didn't move a muscle as the short, portly man with diamonds in both ears lumbered up the stairs and came to a stop before us. He had small dark eyes, wet black hair like an oil slick and just as greasy. With a jovial grin, he lifted a massive handgun in his left hand and pressed it as high as he could reach on Dante, right on the soft underside of his chin.

*"Benvenuto a Napoli."*

Welcome home.

# CHAPTER THREE
# DANTE

Rocco Abruzzi was a typical Made Man. In it for the cash, the girls, and the power. He had two ex-wives and a current one, each younger than the last, as well as two mistresses he kept housed on opposite sides of town. One was classy, the other trashy, a staple of Piazza Garibaldi where the seedy side of the city thrived. He'd grown up in deep poverty the way many Camorra soldati did, but the reason he thrived and rose in the ranks when so many didn't was because Rocco had a mean streak a mile wide. He loved to hit his wives, see out his own hits even though Dons never carried out their own kill orders as a rule, and he was known as "Rocky Rocco" by his street thugs because he'd been known to beat a man just for looking at him wrong.

He was dangerous, not because he was clever but because he was *not*.

He was bad-tempered and quick to react as a startled rattlesnake. He was feared, not revered, but in Naples, that was enough to secure you a fuck ton of power.

When Tore and I left for New York, we'd promoted "Bon Bon" Flavio Marconi as *capo dei capi*.

Two months later, Bon Bon was at the bottom of the Bay of Naples and Rocco Abruzzi, a capo known for his cruelty and profitable gambling operation, was the sudden king of mafia kings.

This was not good for me.

Rocco never liked Tore. He thought he was soft because he tried to protect the Lombardi women from Seamus's gambling debts and resulting punishments.

Rocco hated me.

I was younger, fitter, and next in line for the underworld throne. Once, years ago, Rocco had put a cigar out on my hand during a poker game. I'd been twentysomething, young and still wet behind the ears after joining Tore's operation.

I hadn't flinched, and I hadn't snitched.

Instead, I beat Rocco at his poker game and left with a circular burn mark in the meat of my thumb to remind me of another debt he would pay one day.

I still intended to extract my retribution, but my entire plan hinged on getting Don Abruzzi's good favor.

So when he pressed a gun to my chin and smiled like a madman up into my face, I didn't snap his neck for threatening me and frightening Elena the way I wanted to. Instead, I let my hands fall from Elena's tense form and moved forward slowly but deliberately to kiss Rocco on one flaccid cheek and then the other.

"*Ciao, fratello mio,*" I murmured to the older man as I respectfully greeted him. "It is a pleasure to be back on Italian soil. What a warm greeting you've arranged for us."

Rocco's eyes narrowed so they nearly disappeared under his sagging brow. "You mocking me, Salvatore?"

I blinked innocently. "I'm many things, Don Abruzzi, but an idiot has not been one of them for a number of years."

He studied me for a long moment, then looked over my shoulder at Elena, his features going slack at the sight of her beauty.

"Who do we have here, huh? A present for your host?" he dared to ask.

I forced a deep breath through my nose, my hands shaking with the urge to throttle his fleshy neck. "No."

"Not gonna introduce me?" he demanded, his look souring as his gaze swept back to me. "I got a right to know who's in my territory."

There wasn't time for deliberation. I cursed myself for not talking about it with her on the plane, but I hadn't wanted to overwhelm Elena when the last forty-eight hours of her life had consisted of being abducted, shooting her father, and running away with a fugitive.

This was why love could make a man weak.

I had put her comfort before her safety, and now I was paying the price.

"My wife," Frankie asserted from behind me.

Shocked but schooled enough to hide it, I turned in time to see him sling an arm around Elena's waist and press a kiss to the very hickey I'd put on her neck only minutes before. Elena's eyes were pinned to mine, but she let Frankie touch her.

Smart girl.

One slipup and we'd be dead on the hot asphalt beneath the plane.

"Thought you married a Sicilian girl," Rocco muttered skeptically, staring hard at Elena's dark red hair. "The girl barely looks Italian."

*"Te assicuro che sono Italian,"* Elena promised in fluid Italian, her voice distinctly Neapolitan. "Frankie got rid of the old bitch and traded up for me."

Rocco let out a hard, little laugh, his eyes glazed with desire as he moved closer to me in order to get closer to her. "Fiery thing, aren't you?"

"Touch me and you'll find out just how much," she purred, leaning into Frankie provocatively even as she kept her eyes pinned on him.

The entire charade was ridiculous. I wanted to pick the Don up by his fat neck and break him over my knee like a feeble stick. A man like him didn't deserve to even look at Elena. The difference was almost blasphemous, a sinner looking on a saint.

I wanted him to die for wanting her, and he hadn't even tried to touch her yet.

He would.

I knew it as surely as I knew the sun would rise in the sky every morning. He was a man ruled by his impulses, and his gut cried out to take Elena's strength and overpower it with his own. He didn't understand a woman like her. He wanted to break her to prove his machismo, not understanding that a true man stood beside a woman like that and was made more powerful by her own strength at his back.

"I worried for a moment," he said slyly, shooting me a beady-eyed look. "If you were married, you would be of no use to me."

"Oh?" I didn't give him the benefit of genuine curiosity. Instead, the word fell like dead weight to the ground between us. I checked my cuff links and adjusted the golden crest on my right sleeve that spoke of my first life in England.

He growled. "You wanna find a home in Napoli again, Salvatore, I got a home for you. But it's in the bed of Mirabella Ianni. You remember her? The woman you were supposed to marry?"

I fought the crushing desire to shoot Rocco with the gun he'd dropped to his side. Of course, the *figlio di puttana* didn't entirely trust that Elena was Frankie's woman and not mine. Just in case, he'd thrown a grenade at us, hoping for maximum impact.

Elena didn't say a thing, and I didn't dare look over my shoulder to see her reaction, but I trusted that her impeccable poker face was in place.

My own was not.

A muscle in my jaw spasmed as I ground my teeth.

"I'm not here to marry some country girl, Rocco." He flinched at my disrespectful use of his first name, but I was beyond caring. He flinched again when I took a step down the stairs so I could loom over him. His gun raised between us, the butt pressed right to my heart, but I didn't shy away from it. I was a man who only feared one thing, which I was learning was infinitely more dangerous than a man who feared nothing.

I would not lose Elena.

Not for anything.

Not for my bloody kingdom and stacks of crisp bills.

Not for my honor or my family, my Italian ideals.

She was it.

Mine.

Forever.

And if Rocco wanted to test that, I'd show him what happened to people who tried to come between our love and wedge us apart.

"I'm here to negotiate like men. I'm here to propose a change to the New York outfit that will mean millions more in cash lining the pockets of your Armani suits, *capisci?*"

He stared up at me, fury seething in the depths of those dark eyes. His breath was heavy between his lips because he was getting old, and he'd always been unfit. Because he was scared of me. There was no denying my physical dominance over him, and I knew he would do everything in his power to make me feel small so he could feel bigger and better than me.

I wasn't intimidated by the prospect.

In thirty-five years of dangerous living, no one had gotten the better of me yet, and Rocco wasn't clever enough to do what no one else had.

So I smiled down into his face, the expression slicing my face in two like the sharp edge of a blade.

"You wanna play, Rocco?" I whispered just for him. "Or you wanna make this as easy as possible for the both of us?"

Unsurprisingly, his eyes darted over my shoulder to peer at Elena briefly before reaffixing to mine. He canted his weak chin in the air, and with one simple sentence, he declared war.

"Come and meet your future wife, Dante. She's missed you. While you are getting reacquainted, I will entertain the lovely Elena."

Rocco lived five minutes from *Spaccanapoli*, a main thoroughfare in Naples. The villa was flashy, sticking out like a sore thumb from the more modest pastel and sun-baked buildings on the rest of the street.

Stupid for a mafioso.

The kind of prideful senselessness that decimated numbers in both the New York and Italian Camorra in the last few decades.

Not to mention, it wasn't particularly safe. Most high-ranking members of the outfit had well-protected, isolated homes in the countryside where they could spot an intruder or the police from a mile away.

Obviously, Rocco thought it made him seem fearless to live his life amid the masses. It made him feel even more untouchable.

No one was untouchable.

And I'd prove that to him before long.

He ushered us into a wood-paneled dining room filled to capacity with a massive, ornately carved table that seated twenty. Every seat but two were filled with a variety of Made Men. His capos, all focused exclusively on me as I entered the room behind their *capo dei capi*. This wasn't New York. Even though most of these men raked in serious cash with their schemes for the Camorra, many of them wore old sweaters and stained tees. The ones who tried to impress had gaudy gold jewelry nestled in their chest hair and on their furred knuckles and the hanging lobes of their ears. If you wore a multi-thousand-dollar suit the way Rocco and I did in this city, you'd likely get mugged, even if you were a capo.

I recognized some of the men from Tore's reign as king, but most were new faces, their expressions tight with bitterness.

Ah, so Rocco had replaced those loyal to the old king and told some stories about me in my absence to the new recruits.

This would be harder than I'd imagined.

To make matters worse, the door across from us swung open as I took the seat Rocco gestured for me to have, and a familiar woman walked into the room.

Mirabella Ianni was a local beauty. Not the way Cosima had been, her name taking on a mythological cast because, for some inexplicable reason, Don Salvatore had forbidden anyone to touch her. But she was known from puberty as premium wife material. She was full-figured, her lush chest swelling over the edge of her neckline, the flesh damp with sweat probably from laboring in the kitchen for these men. Her thick hair curled from the humidity around her heart-shaped face, and those big brown eyes, thickly lashed, were limpid as they snagged mine across the room.

"Dante," she breathed softly, an exhale more than a word.

Her fingers trembled as she lifted her hand to clutch the small golden cross at her throat. The men around us chuckled at her reaction, thinking she was a romantic girl overwhelmed by her reintroduction to a lost love.

I knew the truth.

She trembled because she feared me.

She always had.

After a brief hesitation, she moved around the table to serve espresso to each of the men from a tray on the sideboard. When ordered, she carefully balanced the tray on one hip to cut a spiral of rind from a lemon for the men to rub on the lip of their cups or offered the small bottle of Sambuca to add a splash of licorice liquor to the bitter contents. She handled her subservience deftly, with an ease that spoke of lifelong ritual. It was as beautiful as it was sad.

I'd spent too long in America where the women were fierce and entitled, always climbing, grabbing, scratching. I'd learned to find the beauty in their tenacity and verve, and I'd forgotten the gentle loveliness of women who yearned for less.

"Mira." I inclined my head at her before I cut her out of my thoughts. "Don Abruzzi, gentlemen, if you have a place Elena could wait while we discuss business, let us proceed."

"No," Rocco decided with a mean little grin. "The girl stays."

"This is a conversation for men," I appealed to their deep-rooted misogyny. "Women cannot be trusted."

Behind me, standing with Frankie, Elena's heels clicked as she shifted her weight, and I knew she was struggling to remain meek. It was not in her nature to be as mafia women were raised to be. Elena was fire encased in a hard shell of ice. One wrong word and her cutting tongue would reduce a man to ribbons; one wrong move and her flames would raze him to the ground.

I could feel her heat rise at my back.

"Come here, pretty one," Rocco called sweetly to her, patting his thigh as he made room for her between the table and his lap. "You can sit with *Zio Rocco*, huh?"

Anger sizzled through my blood. "Do not disrespect one of my men, Rocco."

"Frankie doesn't mind, does he?" Rocco asked innocently.

"I do, actually," Frankie drawled casually, but his words were laced with poison.

"I am showing you hospitality. It is only fair that you return the gesture," Rocco insisted in a tone that was not to be debated. "Signora Amata, *vieni*."

Without hesitation, Elena went.

I watched her move around the table with that inherent grace I'd never seen in another woman, her shoulders squared, chin canted high, legs rolling easily on those absurdly high heels she loved so much. She was a queen walking into the arms of a grubby monster.

Rage seethed and boiled beneath my skin. I was volcanic with it, and only years of practicing iron-clad control allowed me to keep my seat as Elena elegantly perched on Rocco's fat thigh.

He chuckled with satisfaction, leaning back in his chair in lazy triumph. "This is how all meetings should be conducted, eh, *fratelli*?"

On cue, his men laughed.

I studied them, looking for the difference between those who thought like him and those who were ruled by fear of him. It was the latter I would collect into my own keeping.

"So, Don Salvatore, what brings you back home?" An old Don, Pietro Cavalli, asked me in a warbled voice. "You fucked things up in the New World? I always say, the young have no respect for tradition."

"Then you will not like what I'm going to propose, Don Cavalli," I admitted easily, shifting my gaze to the younger men around the table. "Because my plan is rather radical."

"Radical?" Paulie Gotti's eyes cut fierce lines into his thick-skinned forehead. "I guess we shouldn't be surprised. You and Tore were always radicals."

I inclined my head, accepting it as a compliment rather than a flaw. "I've heard that *la Cosa Nostra* are using the money funneling in from their American drug smuggling ring to get a leg up on our stronghold in Campania."

There was conspicuous silence. A new capo I didn't know shifted uneasily in his seat, eyes scuttling around the table like a beetle. I made a note to talk to him privately.

"It's nothing," Rocco stated with a wave of his hand. He settled it on Elena's hip when he was done gesturing. Subtly, Elena reached over and removed it from her person. "We have it under control."

"I'm sure you do," I placated. "But I have an idea that will remove the issue entirely."

Don Cavalli snorted.

I ignored him, letting the beast overtake the gentleman as a savage grin seized my face. "Gentlemen, I'm asking for your support to wipe out the di Carlo family of New York City. I have things in place to sustain this plan without your support, but of course, I want the consent of my Italian counterparts to move forward."

"War," Rocco declared flatly.

In his lap, Elena straightened, her eyes alert on me as her mind whirled.

"War," I agreed with a minute shrug, opening my hands to the heavens as if violence was no big thing. To these men, it was not. Aggression and death were as noble to them as God and wine. "They have been pushing for it, so it only seems right we give them what they want."

Rocco scowled, slapping his fat hand to the table, his damp flesh leaving a wet mark on the wood. "We do not go to war without reason, Salvatore. Did your *zio* Tore teach you nothing?"

"He taught me everything," I countered coldly, cutting him off when he would have ambled into a long-winded speech. "He taught me that the only way to wash the family honor clean is with blood. *La Cosa Nostra* has disrespected our family here *and* in New York for too long. It is time we showed them what happens to enemies of Napoli."

There was a smattering of murmured agreement from the men at the table, a tangible current in the air as the energy roused between them.

Italians were easy to rile up. Their passions made them easy marks but horrific enemies.

I was counting on both to lend themselves to my case.

"The di Carlo brothers are fighting with the deceased Don's *consigliere* for leadership of the family in the States. We used that to cleave the outfit in half. There only has to be minimal bloodshed. The vast majority of the action will take place in cyberspace." I gestured to Frankie, who smiled cruelly. "We will attack their accounts, make it seem as if one party is stealing money for themselves. As if the other is siphoning funds to mount an attack on the other. It's easily done."

It wasn't.

Only a man as talented in the dark web as Frankie could make such a plan work, but confidence and ease were key to making the plan seem like a shoo-in success for these lazy, entitled fuckers.

"And here?" Paulie demanded. "You got a plan for Napoli?"

"I don't want to hear it," Rocco interjected, his jowls quivering and flushed as anger overtook his better sense. "You come in here like some hotshot when you've been gone six years and don't know a thing about Napoli today? We're doing just fine here without the Salvatores. Anyone who says different is a lying bastard. Now, you want sanctuary here because you fucked up in New York? I could see fit to grant you that out of the goodness of my fucking heart. But if you want more than a vacation in this town, you remember who is Don here now. *Me.* As for this half-baked plan? We can talk about it the moment you agree to wed Mirabella Ianni and not one fucking second sooner. You get me, Dante?"

In his lap, Elena stiffened, her eyes flashing like light on the edge of a sharp blade.

"As for Elena," he continued in a lower register, one hand creeping over her thigh to stroke at the line of her muscle beneath the skirt. "You wanna have her stay with me for a while, I might rethink your options."

I was the only one who saw the gathering of energy in her long, slim form. She was a woman and a slight one at that, unintimidating despite her height. They never would have suspected what would come next, and honestly, if I'd been a smarter man, I would have stopped her before she could show them the biting edge of her anger.

But I couldn't resist watching the glory of the moment unravel as Elena Lombardi smoothly pulled the gun from between her thighs and leveled it with two steady hands around the grip at Rocco, right on the plump underbelly of his chin.

Right where he'd leveled a gun at me on the airport tarmac.

Around her, the capos sat frozen for one long second, utterly shocked by her masculine audacity.

"It was so pleasant to meet you, Rocco," she murmured in low, liquid Italian, her blood-red mouth brushing his cheek as she spoke intimately to him. "Do not ruin it by insulting my people, mmm? I belong with my man as much as he belongs with me. No one will take him from me, not God or the devil himself. Not even you, the mighty *capo dei capi* of Napoli."

Rocco stared up at her for an interminable moment, his eyes hot and cold with desire and wrath. He was shocked by his own arousal—to want such a bold woman seemingly went against his nature. He didn't know, as I did, that he wanted her the way a leech wants a host, to suck her power straight from the source until he was plump with it.

"You dare to talk to me like that?" he asked gruffly, not as authoritatively as he might have liked.

I maintained my slightly slouched posture in my chair because some of the more astute capos were staring at me, but beneath the table, one hand dipped into my pocket around the folding knife I always kept on my person. Rocco had taken my gun, but he'd been too stupid to search for anything else.

"I dare many things," she admitted in a husky drawl as she drew the gun down his neck, past his chest, to the seat of his pants where she tapped at the bulge there. "Most of which, Don Abruzzi, I do not think you'd like."

"Try me," he bit back, his grin feral with rabid lust.

This wasn't a game he'd played with an attractive woman before, and the perverseness of his nature made her all the more appealing. I knew he was already imagining how he could break her. What she might look like with tears in her eyes as he beat her or fucked her.

A growl built in my chest, fingers tightening around my knife. But Frankie caught my eye and stilled me with a subtle jerk of his chin.

The three of us would be dead if I acted on my jealousy and rage, and that would ruin everything.

"Abruzzi," Pietro Cavalli snapped, the oldest man at the table taking umbrage with the entire situation. "Release Frankie Amato's woman and let us get back to business."

Rocco licked his lips as he took one long last look at Elena's mouth, then patted her hip to release her from his lap. "Go with the women. I want to speak with your husband and his capo a moment more. But, beautiful, I am very glad you have come to my home. I promise to be a warm host."

Elena didn't hesitate. She stood from his lap without ceremony and walked through the doors Mirabella had disappeared through minutes before.

She didn't even look over her shoulder at me as she went.

It wasn't only Rocco, the stinking *bastardo,* who was aroused by Elena's display of power, but it was easier for me to move on from it than the slightly panting Neapolitan Don.

Because I knew that the moment we left this place, Elena would be mine to do with as I pleased.

As she pleased.

And suddenly, the idea of her trailing a gun down my body was hotly erotic.

"You heard me, Dante?" Rocco demanded. "I won't have you thinking you're the boss when you got no say here, understood?"

I smiled at him, a wolf hiding in plain sight among the sheep. "Of course, Don Abruzzi. I am merely a humble visitor."

He stared at me suspiciously but was quickly distracted by another capo who questioned if I would be invited to the funeral of a local capo.

He wondered why I was not properly insulted, effectively put in my place. How could I be so cool and self-assured when he had all the power, and I would only exist here by his own grace?

He didn't understand, as I did, that power wasn't solely in action. It was in the timing of that action and the reason for taking it. He didn't understand that he was showing his hand too soon, that now I knew just how unwilling he was to ever support my plans.

He didn't know yet that his gauntlet had been properly thrown down, and I was just waiting to pick it up when the time was right.

And then, he would know just how much power I had and how willing I was to wield it.

It was about more than just the politics of the Camorra.

He'd made it about Elena.

There was an old Neapolitan saying that perfectly suited the situation.

*Chi vuole male a questo amore prima soffre e dopo muore.*

*Whoever is against this love suffers and then dies.*

# CHAPTER FOUR
# DANTE

It was hours before the discussion finished.

Rocco wanted to posture, waxing fucking poetic about how much money he'd made in the years of my absence, how ruthlessly they'd gone after those who couldn't pay their debts or refused to genuflect to his authority.

It was boring as hell.

But also helpful. This was what happened with thugs who rose to power. They prioritized bragging rights over mystery.

Mystery was what had kept me alive for thirty-five years despite the risks I took every day in my position as the New York City *capo dei capi*.

Frankie stood against the wall with a few other lower-level men, practically rolling his eyes whenever he could get away with it. Another mistake by Rocco. He tried to crush other men with power and ambition instead of cultivating them to strengthen his own objectives.

He disgusted me.

I kept that disgust from my face even when he gestured for me to kiss his damp, fleshy cheeks in goodbye.

"You'll be in touch regularly," he advised me as if I was some wayward nephew.

"Of course."

"And the girl, bring her around," he ordered, his eyes gleaming with lust and calculation as he assessed my response.

I shrugged coolly, checking my Patek Philippe watch because I knew it would annoy him. "She has a mind of her own."

"She needs a strong man to rid her of that bad habit."

My brow hiked. "And you're the man for the job? I think Frankie would take umbrage with you absconding with his wife."

Rocco shrugged, but there was too much interest in his eyes. He was old-school. Women were things, commodities to be traded in marriage for political gains or used for pleasure, housekeeping, and child-rearing.

It was almost impossible not to laugh at the idea of Elena willingly consenting to any of that to the detriment of her own independence.

"Where is she?" Rocco asked. "I would like to say goodbye."

"I think that's enough for today," I countered. "I'll collect her, and we'll be on our way. Thank you for your...warm welcome, Don Abruzzi. It is one I won't soon forget."

He inclined his head like some king to his subject, but I was already turning on my heel to walk out the swinging door into the kitchen beyond where the women had congregated.

Only, Elena wasn't among them.

Mirabella sat at a small, scarred wood table peeling potatoes with a woman I recognized as her elderly aunt and another younger girl barely out of adolescence.

"Oh," she said, her mouth a round expression of shock.

I tipped my chin at her, irritated as I'd always been that she was terrified of me simply because of my size and position. Growing up, I'd only ever been kind to Mirabella, if slightly disinterested. She was pretty, with breasts that ripened before the rest of her could catch up, but I'd always found her meek and uninteresting.

"Mira, where is Elena?"

She blinked.

I bit off the end of a sigh. "It's been a long day. A long *few* days. Please, tell me where Signora Lombardi went off to."

"The bathroom," the younger girl said boldly, shooting an annoyed look at Mirabella as if she too found her slightly pathetic. "She needed to touch up her lipstick."

"Thank you," I said, even though I was impatient to find my woman and get the hell out of there.

"D-Dante?" Mirabella cried softly as I moved to the door to the hallway.

I hesitated but didn't turn around.

"I-I don't want to marry you either," she had the guts to tell me.

So, I took the time to turn around and catch her wide, frightened gaze. "I can't say I'm surprised when you can hardly look at me without fainting."

The younger girl snorted, and Mira's aunt cuffed her lightly on the back of the head.

"Are you in love with her?" Mira had the surprising audacity to ask. When I didn't answer, she nodded slightly and looked down at the half-peeled lump of starch in her hand. "Rocco isn't as dumb as you think he is. Be careful."

"And you? You can't have been careful if you remain unmarried all these years later, and Rocco is determined to fob you off on a foreigner he doesn't even like."

She flinched slightly, staring at that damned potato like it held the answers to all of life's questions. "I was meant to be married, but it… it didn't work out. Now, my uncle is ashamed to have a spinster niece with no prospects. We all have our crosses to bear."

"You won't be one of mine," I promised her without waiting for a response, pushing out the other swinging door into the hall.

I wasn't willing to leave Elena alone in this viper's den for any longer than necessary.

My shoes clacked against the burgundy ceramic tile as I stalked down the hall, peering into open archways and behind half-closed doors.

No Elena.

Finally, there was a single locked door at the end of the hall before the stairs. I knew she was behind the wood barricade the way a seer knew what lay behind the opaqueness of a crystal ball. I could feel her.

Without preamble, I pulled the folded knife from my pocket, jerked it open with a flick of my wrist and angled the blade between the door and the wood frame. A moment later, the blade found the edge of the latch mechanism and the door popped open with one thin voiced creak.

Elena didn't flinch as I appeared in the frame.

Her eyes were pinned on mine in the reflection of the massive, ornate gilded mirror over the sink basin. They were a dense, quilted gray like rolling storm clouds, sparking with crackling lightning that threatened to eviscerate.

Even filled with wrath, Elena was pure beauty.

"Were you going to tell me you were engaged?" she asked in a low, seething voice that slunk toward me like elongating shadows.

I leaned against the doorjamb insolently and crossed my arms as I contemplated the curved edge of my knife. "And you? You've never spoken with me about Daniel Sinclair."

There was a sharp sound as she sucked air between her teeth. I watched as the long line of her body coiled tight with controlled rage.

I settled in, excited about the prospect of watching her rage burst free of its cage.

"Daniel isn't relevant right now."

"He isn't?" I feigned surprise. "The man you lived with for four years. The one you thought you'd marry and adopt a child with. The same one that you couldn't get over until you met me?"

"You are such an arrogant *bastardo*," she snapped, whirling around to face me with color high in her cheeks. "You think you just magically made everything better?"

"No," I retorted, pushing off the frame, shutting the door with one hand before stalking across the small room toward her. "Not everything. We still have to work on some things…" I backed her into the sink until she was bent backward over the porcelain, her chest heaving with the strain of her irritation and burgeoning desire. I palmed the skin above her breasts and slid my rough palm up until it collared her neck. The kick of her mad pulse against my thumb made my cock jerk in my pants. "I still have to teach you everything there is to know about pleasing me. With your hands, with your red mouth, your sweet cunt, and your little arse."

"M-my arse?" she parroted, her eyes as wide as silver dollars.

I laughed huskily as I gathered her hands in one of my own and pinned them behind her back so she was forced to arch against me. "*Si, lottatice,* your tight little arse. Has anyone ever taken you there?"

"Absolutely not," she snapped, the flush in her cheeks deepening and spreading down her neck and chest.

I followed the path with my lips and tongue, lapping up the heat of her skin. "I think you'll like having me there. Do you know why?"

Her breath was a harsh rasp in my ear as I used my free hand to ruck up her skirt. I palmed her silk-covered pussy without foreplay. A fierce shudder rocked through her, a shocked exhale blowing in my hair as I pressed a kiss to her thrumming pulse.

She liked it when I was less than civilized and didn't give her a chance to use that big, beautiful brain to overthink every nuance and expectation.

She wasn't ready to admit she liked it, but soon, she would be.

Soon, I'd have her hot and wet, pliant as warm wax in my hands. She would tell me in detail, in the language of her people she'd once loathed, how much she wanted me inside her, against her, owning her.

For now, I was happy to do that work myself.

"You love it when I worship your body," I breathed against her ear as I cupped her sex and ground the heel of my hand gently into her clit. "When I use everything I am and everything I have to make you come spectacularly for me. Did you know, *cuore mia,* there is nothing more beautiful to me than the sight of you breaking apart with pleasure?"

Her only response was a throaty little purr as I sucked on the hickey I'd left on her neck earlier.

"No woman before you matters to me. They are *insignificante.* They are dust," I growled as I released her hands and turned her to face the mirror once more.

Together, we studied my effect on her body—the heavy-lidded eyes, the parted lips, the flush that glistened beneath her pale gold skin. I reached around her body to cup her throat in my palm. It was a collar as much as any leather or diamonds could be, one of my own flesh and blood that was infinitely more intimate.

"Just as any man before me for you was nothing," I continued, my eyes pinned on her in the mirror. Her face was swathed in the dim light from the Moreno glass fixture above the frame while mine was cast entirely in shadow. "I've told you, Elena, whatever you and I are made of, it is the same. No one exists for me but you. No one makes you come alive but me."

"Yes," she admitted, reaching back to cup my erection through my pants. She squeezed hard, her nails pinpricks of pain around my shaft. "No one for you but me."

*"Si, Elena, mai più,"* I agreed gruffly as I used my free hand to wrench her skirt up over her pert arse.

*Never again.*

Never again would I want a woman the way I wanted her.

She possessed me like a scientist with some great unanswerable question. I knew no matter the length of our lives together, I would never know Elena Lombardi in all her iterations. She would continue to surprise me, impress me, and test me. For a man who had been bored by the human condition for years, it was the greatest gift I could have ever possessed, so of course, it made sense that it should possess me in return.

Elena's hand deftly undid the zipper of my trousers, bypassing the belt entirely. I hissed as she carefully fished inside the open material to grab my cock.

I pushed her hand away, threading my steel length through the gap with minimal pain. As soon as it was free, Elena's long fingers wrapped around the shaft and pulled.

"You need me inside you, don't you, *lottatrice*?" I coaxed darkly, pushing her slightly over the basin so she was forced to grab its edges in both hands to brace herself.

I wrapped my own fist around my cock, pulled her panties down those slim thighs to expose the gleaming pink of her slit, and ran the hot head of my dick up and down that silken pass.

"Oh my God," she breathed, long nails clacking on the sink as she tightened her grip.

"You speak in Italian when I play with you," I ordered her in a soft, flexible tone so she wouldn't rebel.

There was a brief hesitation.

Pressing myself just inside her entrance, I felt the hot clasp of her pussy pulse around me, greedy for more.

*"Dio mio, Dante, dai mettimelo dentro,"* she panted impatiently, slightly irritated with my demands and teasing but too aroused to stall any longer.

*My God, Dante, I want you inside me.*

The smile that overtook my face was victorious. Without warning, I rocked my hips hard, seating myself to the root inside her clutching folds. She gasped, swearing softly in Italian as she fought to maintain her grip on the sink. Always the gentleman, I wrapped the length of her thick hair around my fist to help pin her still while I fucked into her. Her head was canted back, but her eyes stayed on the mirror, the gray blown away by the black of her dilated pupils.

"You love this," I muttered in her ear over the sound of my thighs and balls slapping against her arse. "You love watching what I do to you. How you melt into such a gorgeous wanton for me."

"Never," she murmured, her frown knotted, her eyes almost desperate on mine in the reflection. She needed that connection, to watch me watching her. To see the evidence of my unmitigated lust for her and her alone. If she couldn't see it, I knew it was harder for her to believe in it. "Never before you."

"I know," I soothed, moving my free hand around her waist, up between her breasts so I could pull the fabric of her bra and blouse under the swells, plumping them up in the ruched material.

Her nipples pebbled in the cool air, begging for me to pluck at them with punishing fingers. Every time I pinched those furls, her tight pussy rippled around my driving shaft.

"I'm going to make you come all over my cock with our enemies just down the hall," I told her, watching as her mouth parted wider, her tongue peeking out as if to taste the filth of my words. "You're going to suck on my fingers while you orgasm so they don't hear your pretty cries."

"*Capo,*" she gasped, her skin vibrating beneath my hands, her muscles quivering like a horse at the gate about to explode into motion.

"*Si, Elena,*" I agreed, squeezing my hand at her throat just slightly, just to watch the shock widen her eyes and the desire tremble harder through her form. "Your capo. There is no one else. Only me. Only you. Only us."

A high, keening groan built in her chest and leaked through her red lips as she thrust her hips hard back against my groin, impaling herself almost brutally on my length. I moved my grip high on her throat so I could slide the tips of two fingers into her open mouth, her lips closing around them automatically, sucking fiercely as she moaned. Her body went stiff as a wood plank in my arms and then broke into quaking pieces around me. She tried to thrash, but I pinned her with that hand in her hair and the other at her throat, forcing her to take every ounce of pleasure.

Magnificent.

There was no other word for the way Elena climaxed for me.

It had so much to do with that damp, sucking mouth and the shimmering red hair cascading between us, but it was more than that too.

It was knowing the great walls around her heart, and the ones she carefully erected between her elevated mind and visceral gut were in ruins at our feet.

Because of me.

Because she trusted me to take her where she had never been before.

The power of it seared through me like a hot blade as I held all that glory in my hands. Unable to contain the savageness of my attraction, I released my grip on her hair, covered her back with my entire body, and sank my teeth into her neck over the mark I'd put there earlier that day. My hips punched brutally into that wet, velvet cunt, still trembling with aftershocks that wrenched my orgasm closer and closer to the surface.

*"Vienimi dentro, capo mio."*

At first, the words didn't register. I was so transfixed by the smooth, tight glide of my cock inside her, chasing my orgasm, that I didn't hear the words, and then, when I understood them, I thought I'd misheard.

Elena was all class and elegance, tightly wound conservatism.

Getting her to melt for me, to pant for me, took work. Getting her to talk dirty took coaxing and sexual coercion.

But she was telling me in that breathless yet demanding whisper, *come inside me, my capo.*

And that was it.

The beast inside me burst free of its shackles and ravaged her. I held her down ruthlessly as I pounded into her hot pussy, my panting breath in her ear as I grunted and groaned at the ferocity of the pleasure boiling inside me. Seconds later, pleasure singed down my spine like a lightning strike, and I exploded inside her, dick kicking hard against the tight vise grip of her cunt, filling her with spurt after spurt of hot cum.

She shivered as I filled her up, canting her hips up so I was locked deep inside her, at the very entrance to her womb.

Which reminded me, suddenly and shockingly, that we hadn't been using protection, and we hadn't spoken about it.

"No condom," I grunted, capable of only that as I pressed my face into her neck and breathed in the scent of her Chanel Number 5 perfume and a fragrance beneath that was entirely sex, Elena and I mixed elementally.

"No," she agreed, but her voice was soft, almost tender. Gently, almost shyly, she placed a hand over my loose one still banded around her throat and the other around mine at her belly, and she hugged me to herself. "It's okay. Pregnancy is still a long shot for me, unfortunately."

"And if it happens?" I demanded as something painful twisted in my gut. "If we make a baby? Because, Elena, I do not intend to stop fucking you and filling you with my cum."

She shivered again, her light eyes catching my dark, shadowed gaze in the mirror. "I don't know... I used to want to be married first with the white picket fence American dream kind of life. But now...now I don't know. All I do understand is that your world, maybe *our* world now, is a dangerous place to bring a child into."

"*Si,*" I agreed, linking our fingers together at her neck, dragging our twined thumbs over her slowing pulse. "But not for a baby of ours. Not when he or she will have you as their shield and me their sword."

Emotion flared so bright in her eyes it blinded me like sunlight on steel. She tried to cover it, blinking and lowering that expressive gaze to the sink as if it was vastly interesting.

I used our joined hands to tip her chin up, forcing her to look at me. "There is no shame in anything between us, *lottatice mia*. I will not have you feel embarrassed of your emotions with me. Embarrassed of the dreams I hope you'll come to share with me. Most people have reason to fear me. I'd end them without blinking for even a slight offense against me or mine. But you?" I brushed my nose up her elegant neck and pressed an open-mouthed kiss to her cheek. "You have nothing to fear in me, *capisci*? You have had enough to fear in your life and I will break apart the entire universe if it dares to harm you again. Do you understand me?"

She bit her lip, the lipstick worn down to a pale red smudge. "It's not you I'm scared of so much as I'm afraid of myself. I have the tendency to ruin every good thing I've ever had. And you are undoubtedly the best of them."

I pulled my softening cock out of her slowly, moving my hand down to cup her drenched sex. Our mingled cum leaked between my fingers, sliding a lonely trail down the inside of one thigh. I cupped her there and at her throat as I looked into those storm clouded eyes and made her a promise I never intended to break.

*"Tu si l'azzurro dò mare sì duci e si amar,"* I told her. *You are like the sea, sweet and salty*. "A sailor does not leave the sea because it storms, and it does not begrudge the ocean her moods. I have no intention of giving

up on you, Elena, because there is no part of you I do not find worthy and fascinating. If this ends, it will be because you choose to end it, and you refuse to let me fight to win you back."

"I don't want that," she whispered, so quietly it was barely sound.

"Then I am with you," I promised, sealing the words with a kiss to that full red mouth.

And when I broke away, she pulled me back fiercely, speaking the words into my parted lips like a gardener planting a seed. "*Io sonno con te.*"

# CHAPTER FIVE

## *elena*

Naples was a city of contrasts. They said a person was molded by their place of birth, by the city they were raised in, so in ways I was both ashamed and proud of, for better and for worse, it made sense that Napoli was my home.

We passed through the streets of the city in a long, low Lamborghini Aventador that had appeared outside Rocco Abruzzi's downtown villa sometime while we'd been locked inside. Dante took the keys from a pimply-faced youth wearing an S.S.C. Napoli soccer jersey and six gold chains around his thin, almost fragile neck. It was impossible to look at him and not imagine Sebastian at the same age if he'd given in to the pressure of the Camorra and joined their ranks.

Dante caught my little shiver but didn't say a word as he helped me into the low car and shut the door behind me, calling out to Frankie, who was climbing into a black Range Rover lingering in the middle of the street despite the honking traffic wedged behind it.

In fact, we were both oddly silent as we traveled through the streets. Maybe he was as mired in memories as I was, though it seemed surreal to me that Dante could have existed in the city at the same time I had. It was romantic and foolish, but I felt certain I should have felt him in the atmosphere, a magnetic force drawing us together across the stuccoed walls and chain-link fences.

It was obvious from Rocco's ostentatious villa and the sleek Lambo we were currently cruising through the streets in that Dante's experience of the city was vastly different than my own.

When we crossed into Forcella, the Spanish district, I finally recognized my hometown. There were countless *bassi* there, one- or two-room poor houses with direct access to the street or clogged into alleyways that were the arteries of the city. A man slept facedown on the ground outside the *Ascalesi* hospital, using a bag of old lemons as a pillow. Prostitutes lingered in open doorways partially veiled with swathes of brightly patterned cloth, and kids tumbled through the streets, running errands for their parents while kicking soccer balls off the walls and into the street where they wedged under old, abandoned cars.

This wasn't the glamorous Italy, the tourist's Italy.

This was *my* Italy.

My chest ached as I passed swiftly through the streets. It was a strange and unsettling realization to see how far I'd come from my childhood, sitting there with a Made Man in a hundred-thousand-euro car on our way to what would surely be another opulent villa the likes of which tourists and daydreamers always envisioned as quintessential in my country.

I'd seen a luxury car once or twice in my youth, the yellow paint gleaming so much brighter than the chipped urine-toned stucco on our little house outside the city. Don Salvatore had been in that car, visiting us the way he had sometimes at Christmas or on birthdays. As soon as one of us kids spotted the car in our cracked asphalt driveway, Mama told us to scram so she could talk to the capo herself.

"A penny for your thoughts," Dante offered as we finally broke through to the outskirts of the city, and he gunned the engine, zooming onto the highway that took us south. "They are so loud, I can almost hear them."

I snorted softly, my fingertips on the windowpane as if I could touch the passing scenery. "Just remembering."

"Bad memories?"

I shrugged one shoulder weakly. "Mostly. We were pretty happy sometimes, though. Mama struggled with work and four children, with Seamus and her own depression, but she loved us. She would sing while we hung the laundry in the back yard and chased the twins around endlessly because they always had so much energy. She was always cooking for us, standing in the kitchen chatting about our days while she rolled dough like a master sculptor with clay. It was where we congregated at the end of every day. Even Giselle and I were close when we were young, but she doesn't seem to remember that."

"We all have different relationships to the past. Sometimes, we cancel out the whole to rid ourselves of a few bad parts."

"Mmm," I hummed because I thought he was right, but I'd never entertained the idea. "How did you get so wise?"

He slanted me a look. "Would you believe me if I said I was born this way?"

I laughed, some of the clotted poison in my veins dissipating. "No, I absolutely would not."

He shrugged easily. "It's the truth. I'm a very special man."

I shook my head at his antics, wondering how it was possible he could charm me even when I was sunk deep in confusion and bad memories. Even if I wanted to, there was no denying that he was indeed a very special man.

"So, what's our plan, then, capo?"

He darted a quick look at me as he revved the engine to pass a slow-moving car in the fast lane. "That sounds good."

"What?"

"Our plan, you said, like we are a team."

Anxiety spiked through me, but I took a deep breath to speak through it. "Aren't we?"

"We are," he agreed firmly, reaching a hand over to squeeze my thigh. "But this is new territory for us both. I don't think I have to tell you that traditionally, women are kept in the dark about Family matters."

"It's a good thing you and I aren't traditional then, isn't it?" I was still hyper aware of the heaviness of the gun strapped to my thigh. "When Rocco had dared to insinuate that I could be taken from you…" I shivered. "I realized that I need to stop being a passive participant in my own life. I think I've been the victim too long. I want to be the kind of woman who fights for what she wants. And I've never wanted anything as much as I want you."

Dante turned his hand over on the gear shift, beckoning me to lay my own on top. When I did, he threaded our fingers then turned them over to palm the stick and squeezed. I stared at our joined fingers, how it seemed as though we were driving the speeding car together, and I understood his unspoken symbolism.

If I wanted to fight with him, he would let me. No arguments or caveats. Dante was a powerful man because he didn't fear other powerful people. He collected them like flowers for a bouquet, and now, somehow, he'd decided I was worthy enough to be a part of his world.

His crew.

"Thank you for trusting me," I whispered through the sudden thickness in my throat.

He shrugged one quilted shoulder. "Elena, I trusted you before I blackmailed you into moving into my house. Do you think I would let any old lawyer into my home?"

"No," I admitted. "But I think you forced me to live with you because you wanted in my pants."

*"Certamente," of course,* he said with an arrogant smirk. "I could have had you anyway, but this sped up the process."

"Arrogant," I chastised, but there was no true censure behind the word.

The truth was, if Dante hadn't been so self-assured, so tenacious in his pursuit of my heart, I didn't think he could have succeeded. I was so resigned to being alone the rest of my life, I was almost ludicrously determined to remain that way.

"I don't want you to worry about my plans," Dante surprised me by saying as we moved farther inland into the rolling hills of vivid green vegetation punctuated with citrus orchards and scrolling lines of cultivated grapevines. "Ignore Rocco Abruzzi. I have no intention of marrying Mirabella Ianni, and I never have. Can you imagine? She is not the kind of woman I would fuck. She's the kind of woman a man like me eats for breakfast."

He startled a laugh out of me. "Little Red and the Big Bad Wolf."

His grin was entirely canine, his incisors white and glistening between those ruddy lips. "Yes. And the only woman I want to eat for breakfast is you. Spread your legs."

I blinked at him, caught off balance by his abrupt change in topic. "Excuse me?"

"Spread your legs, Elena." It was an order wrapped in velvet, a request with the subtle implication that aggression might be implemented if I didn't follow his heed.

"You're driving," I pointed out helpfully even though a little thrill zigged down my spine at the taboo idea.

"I've been driving since I was thirteen. I can multitask."

I blinked again, but before I could censure myself, my thighs were parting.

Impatient, Dante lightly slapped the inside of my left thigh, prompting me to spread them wider.

"Enough business," he declared in that arrogant manner of a mafia Don used to getting his way at all costs. "We may be fugitives, but we won't live like that. I know you hate it here. I know it cost you everything to leave your world behind. Let me remind you why you took that risk."

"I'm still wet with your cum," I admitted dryly even though a flush flared up my cheeks.

He chuckled, proud and aroused. "Good. Take off your underwear."

I hesitated, but he didn't rush me. He continued to weave the sports car in and out of traffic, his left hand on the wheel, the tendons in his wrist flexing, revealed by the rolled-up cuffs of his button-up shirt. There was a large silver watch on his wrist, a Patek Philippe he'd told me once had been a gift from his brother, Alexander, when they were younger, before they'd fallen out over their mother's death. His body was too big for the car, dwarfing the leather seat he sprawled in, his thick thighs cramped in the small space.

He was so beautiful, so masterfully crafted of dense muscles and big, roughly carved bones, I couldn't look at him without feeling wetness pool at my center.

I spread my legs even wider, the muscles straining in my thighs, the fabric of my skirt stretched too taut. I pulled the material up my legs so he could watch as I shimmied off the soaked panties I wore beneath it. Carefully, I removed the gun from my thigh holster, checked the safety, and put it in the glove compartment.

"Have you touched yourself to orgasm yet, *bella*?" he asked me in a low, sultry tone that hummed just louder than the engine.

Since my surgery, he meant. It still wowed me to think that two months ago, I hadn't been able to orgasm at all. I was forever indebted to Dr. Taylor for fixing me physically and to Dante for helping me fix myself emotionally and mentally.

I shivered, biting my lip to keep from gasping at the shock of arousal his dirty talking sparked in me. "No."

"Do it for me now," he declared, his eyes still on the road, but his mouth tipped in a challenging grin. "I want to see you come all over the leather seat."

"I don't know if I can do it myself. I mean, without you touching me," I confessed, but the cool air-conditioning on my wet sex, still swollen from Dante's fucking just an hour before, felt sinfully good.

It embarrassed me, but the more he fucked me, talked dirty to me, used me, and taught me in equal measure about sex and sin, the more I longed for it. There was this overfull lockbox stuffed with sexuality I'd never allowed myself to explore until Dante fit his key in the lock and sent it spilling open. The more I explored, the more there was to mine.

"Touch yourself softly, just a fingertip drawing circles over your clit. *Si, bella,* like that," he praised, daring to look over at my tentative display. "When I touch you, it's rough and biting. You like being bent and formed in ways that please me, that suit my need to fuck you hard. But when you touch yourself, you do it like this. You tease those tight folds until they bloom open and your fingers slide into the wet warmth of your pussy."

A stuttering sigh slipped past my lips as I worked those feathering circles over my nub. My thighs were starting to strain and quiver. I wanted more. Harder, stronger, faster.

But I wanted him. I wanted Dante to be the one to please me.

There was something…difficult about doing it myself.

The pleasure was there, but there was a buzzing hum in the back of my mind like static on a television with poor reception.

"Relax, *lottatrice*. You don't need to fight or strain to find this pleasure. Just ease into it like a warm bath. Close your eyes and listen to your capo's voice. You're going to make yourself come for the both of us. Because I want to see your thighs clench. I want to hear your soft, keening little cries as your tight cunt clenches around your fingers. Then, when you're finished, you and I are going to take turns licking the cum from your hand."

*"Dio mio, Dante,"* I murmured, head lolling on the seat as the heat built in my core, deep as burning coals. "Please, can I have more?"

"So sweet when you melt for me," he murmured, and then his hand was on my thigh, drawing circles on my bare knee in tandem with the ones I drew over my clit.

The dual sensation shouldn't have been so impactful, both touches so light they were just a tease of sensation, but my entire body tightened around the lust emanating through my belly.

"Put one foot on the dash," he ordered next.

It was so dirty, so wrong to splay myself open like that in the passenger seat of a car traveling at breakneck speed down a winding Italian road, but I didn't hesitate.

I placed the heel of my black Jimmy Choo on the glove compartment, my knee falling against the door so my entire pussy was displayed to Dante's gaze and anyone who might look through the window into our car.

A shudder rippled through me so hard, my teeth chattered.

*"Bellissima,"* he hissed as he shot a look over at my prone posture. "What a gorgeous cunt you have, Elena. So pink and glistening like a rose with morning dew. I want to lick all that wet up with my tongue."

"I wish you would," I panted softly.

"Another time," he promised. "Now, I want you to keep those nice, light touches on your throbbing clit and use your other hand to fuck yourself."

There was a wet noise as I did as he told me, two fingers dipping into the well of moisture at my entrance and sliding deep. I was swollen from Dante's driving cock battering my walls, but my fingers felt good, soothing the ache he'd left.

"Think of our stay here like a vacation," he urged me as I churned my fingers inside myself, swirling my fingertip over my clit, and he drew those lazy, agonizing circles on my knee.

He was winding me up like a toy doll, and at any moment, I was going to release in a flurry of movement and sound.

"I'm going to use every day to fuck you so often, you'll want me to stop even as you beg me for more. I'm going to teach you how fucking beautiful you are in every single iteration I can think of. Your pert arse in the air as I fuck you from behind and spank your bottom as red as your mouth. Your breasts when I twist and tease your nipples into aching points. Maybe I'll clamp them when we put the washing out on the line, tie you up like a sheet by the wrists and put clothespins on those red peaks."

I gasped at the audacity of his imagination. He was so dirty, so uninhibited and confident in his desires. So dominant, there was no room for me to question him or myself for wanting to enact those dangerous fantasies with him.

"It's so wrong," I whispered through dry lips as my orgasm tangled all my senses into a single pulsating awareness between my thighs.

"No, Elena, nothing is wrong between us. You spread open for me, playing for me, all of it is only ever right," he declared imperviously.

And then his hand was moving up the inside of my thigh, tickling and tingling. I held my breath, heart thundering in my chest as his touch hesitated at the junction of my leg and groin then went arrowing down to the fingers filling my sex.

"Are you still tight, nice and swollen? Or loose and eager to be filled?" he asked.

I was too out of it to realize we had stopped moving, that he'd pulled off the highway onto a hill and parked beneath a massive, budding bougainvillea shrub.

"Filled," I admitted on a ragged exhale. "I wish you'd slide inside me and fill me up properly."

"*Come vuoi*," he muttered.

*As you wish.*

A moment later, he wedged two thick fingers at my already filled entrance and pressed them in alongside my own.

A wrecked groan shuddered through my chest and filled the car as I slammed my head back against the seat at the overwhelming sensation.

"Yes," he murmured again and again in English and Italian as he set a punishing rhythm, dragging my own fingers in and out alongside his.

"So beautiful like this. So *mine*."

It was the *mine* that broke me.

All I'd wanted my whole life was to be seen and loved all the way to my bones.

And there he was, this big beast of a brutal man who was everything soft and kind for me, and he was teaching me something I'd never really known.

Pleasure.

Mind-boggling, body-bending pleasure that made every self-loathing, critical thought I'd ever had evaporate in the steam of the flames erupting at my core.

I groaned and gasped and chanted Dante's name the way most Italians prayed to Madonna and God. He kept touching me, gentle twists of the fingers inside me, increasingly light circles over my clit because I'd stopped the movements during my climax. He wrung my pleasure from me like wet from a towel until I was utterly boneless in my seat.

"That's my girl," Dante praised, his voice thick with lust and pride as he collected my tired hand and brought it to his mouth.

I watched from under heavy lids as he carefully cleaned each of my fingers with his mouth. His tongue curled over every digit, his full lips wrapped tight around me. My tired, lightly aching pussy spasmed at the erotic sight.

"You taste like the sea," he told me on a growling hum when he was finished meticulously cleaning me off. Then he took my hand and pressed it to the iron length of his erection trapped in his trousers. "Feel what you do to me. I've been this hard since the moment you spread your legs for me."

"Only for you," I muttered, some part of me still uncomfortable with what we'd just done.

It was easy enough to understand where my internal slut shaming came from. Christopher had always made sure to tell me I was a sinner, a deviant. That he was helpless against my temptation, my need for him to take me and use me. It wasn't his fault. It was my own as if my sexuality was something that lured him like a siren into dangerous waters.

I was a girl, so I had no sense of my own sexuality beyond a burgeoning curiosity about male and female bodies. I was a blank slate Christopher had graffitied with his crass, poisonous point of view, and until then, sitting satiated in a car with the first man I'd ever truly trusted, I realized how much of his ink still stained my thoughts.

Tears pricked the backs of my eyes as I fought to take a deep, steadying breath when suddenly, all I wanted to do was cry.

Dante, being Dante, noticed my shift of emotion immediately. He didn't hesitate. One second, I was sprawled in my seat, and the next, he was coaxing me, half-lifting me over the console and onto his lap. It was a tight, almost ridiculous fit in the small car, but we made it work, my legs draped on either side of the gear shift, my back against the driver's side door, and my face tucked into his neck.

He smelled bright and masculine, like fresh squeezed lemons and sex. I realized he smelled like Italy, like the south with its citrus groves and ocean brine, its musky men and sweet breezes.

He smelled like home but gave it a new definition. And for the first time since I got on the plane with him, eschewing my old life for an entirely unknown new one, I felt at peace about our future.

Dante was home, so no matter what, I would never be homeless. I'd have his shelter, his protection, and his love to guide me through the worst of life and the worst of myself.

I only realized I was crying when I rubbed my salt-itchy cheek against his wet collar.

"Sorry," I muttered on a sniff.

"You don't need to apologize," he assured me, stroking one big, strong hand over my head and down my back. "Do you know how good it feels to have you vulnerable in my arms? To know it is a gift you only give to me?"

I hadn't ever thought of it that way. "I always feel like a burden when I get emotional. It shouldn't be anyone's problem but my own."

He made a pained noise in his throat, then ran his nose from my forehead down the bridge of my own until he reached my mouth where he spoke the words like a secret. "It is a *privilege,* Elena, to know you intimately. To know what makes you hurt and what makes you blush. To know what your demons are so I can slay them for you when you don't have the strength or watch you overcome your own nightmares because I love to watch my fighter conquer everything in her path. It is an honor to know you, and I won't ever take that for granted."

I laughed wetly. "How do you always know what to say? Seriously, did you take a class for that?"

"No," Dante said solemnly, running his rough fingertips over my cheek to collect my tears. One by one, he brought his wet fingers to his mouth and kissed off my tears. "I just know what it's like to be hated, to feel alone against the world, to feel like a villain. I told you before that we're not so different."

"No," I agreed, rubbing my thumb along the hard cut of his stubbled jaw. "I think we see the world the same way."

"In black and white?" he teased.

"And red," I supplied with a smile that broke my face into two clean halves.

"*Bene,* because you're about to meet your new family," he told me after pressing a kiss to my forehead and levering me back into my seat.

"I've met Tore before," I reminded him as he had reminded me earlier that day.

His smile was dark, an expression of ownership. "Yes, but he and our men here haven't met you as you are now."

"As yours?"

"Not just as my woman, but theirs. The woman, *la Donna,* they will be expected to lay down their lives for just as I would," he said almost casually, factually, as if he wasn't altering my entire world again. "You aren't my lawyer anymore, Elena. *Tu sei la mia regina.*"

*You are my queen.*

# CHAPTER SIX

## *elena*

Villa Rosa was nestled at the top of a hill an hour and twenty minutes outside of Naples in Parco Regionale Monti Picentini near the small town of Sieti. Lush green mountains dominated the landscape, but the villa itself had a riot of carefully cultivated plants in beautiful bloom even though it was December. I held my breath in awe as we wound up the ribbon of asphalt leading to the house, the drive lined by towering cypress trees.

"It's like something out of a dream," I breathed, shocked by how beautiful I found the typical Italian scenery compared to the dingy Naples neighborhood I'd grown up in.

When the house came into view, I gasped a little. It was a traditional *casali*, a farmhouse big enough to host the landlord's family and the families of the field hands. The large structure was made of off-white stone turned rose gold in the light of the setting sun, the tiled roof red as blood. The arched windows and doorways were covered in creeping bougainvillea and vines so that the structure seemed to have burst from the earth like a plant, something organic and timeless.

I loved it.

It felt like a home at the same time it felt like a palace.

And standing in front of it, in two long rows on either side of the colossal wood front door stood its occupants. I knew from reading books and binge-watching *Downton Abbey* with Beau that this was how $18^{th}$ century servants used to greet their lord and lady on their return to the family estate. Twenty-five people, mostly armed men clothed in black even though it was warm, stood at attention as we pulled to a stop in the circular drive.

"*Sei pronto*?" Dante asked.

*Are you ready?*

No.

Not really.

How did one prepare to meet a group of criminals that would suddenly be responsible for keeping you safe? How did *I* meet men who I'd thought my entire life were the very scum of society and not feel ashamed for the way I'd judged them?

"Stop thinking, *cuore mia*," Dante ordered, but there was a gentle humor in his voice as he pulled my gaze from the window to his face. "Embrace *la dolce vita* and enjoy these moments with me, *va bene*?"

He collected my hand and planted a kiss on my palm. Without thinking, I curled my fingers over it, protecting it.

"This is my home more than any place has ever been before. I spent almost every summer here as a boy with my mother, Alexander, and Tore, then I lived here for years after she died. It's my sanctuary, and I hope it will be yours too."

"I feel like all you ever do is give to me," I told him quietly, forcing myself to communicate the tangled knot of emotion clogging my throat. "I was meant to help you, and now, you're only here as a fugitive because of me."

*"Ferma,"* he said, *stop*. "Having to leave the US was always a possibility I planned for, and quite frankly, I could have left Addie, Frankie, Marco, Chen, and Jacopo to save you back in Brooklyn, but I chose not to. We all make choices, Lena, don't let them haunt you when what's done is done."

I laughed a little. "You know, I'm always telling other people that, but I have the hardest time applying it to myself."

"I'll help you," he offered simply.

And I loved him then even more fiercely than I had the moment before that. Because that was who Dante was. He was a dangerous man with the biggest heart I'd ever known, and he never hesitated in offering his love, guidance, or protection to those in need.

"I love you," I told him for the first time since I'd first declared it on the tarmac in New Jersey.

Why did it feel like the most dangerous thing I'd done all day was say three teeny, tiny words people usually said every day of their lives?

I love you.

It was almost absurd how language could so neatly parcel up such enormous emotion.

*"Ti amo, cuore mia,"* Dante responded instantly, so easily I almost envied him that capacity.

He leaned across the console, and in front of everyone gathered before the car, he clasped my face entirely in his huge hands and kissed me. He kissed me languidly, sensuously parting my lips with a stroke of his tongue before diving inside to stroke over my own. I moaned at the taste of him, at the rough bite of his stubble against my smooth skin and the sharp pain as he took my lower lip between his teeth and tugged. When he finished, he pulled away only far enough to lean his forehead against me.

"You are with me now, Elena. Let me welcome you properly to my world."

I nodded, nerves still low in my belly but quieted by the press of love exploding throughout my chest. "Okay."

"Okay," he agreed with a boyish smirk that belied his eager enthusiasm to claim me in this way.

He was moving away and out of the car in a flash, walking around the hood with a ringing, "*Ciao!*" to the men gathered to welcome him. They called out in an uneven chorus in return as Dante reached my door and pulled it up and open for me. I took his offered hand, looking up at him as he winked at me.

"*Raggazzi,*" he called in a jovial shout that carried easily across the large yard. "It's good to be home."

There was a resounding shouted response. Amadeo Salvatore broke free of the formation on the right side and made his way toward us. He wore a white linen shirt undone to his sternum, revealing a thicket of black chest hair and a simple gold cross necklace. In loose pants, sandaled feet, with his deep olive-brown tan and tousled black hair threaded only lightly with silver at the temples, he looked like some wealthy vacationer, not a ruthless mafia Don.

"Welcome home," he greeted with a broad grin that cut creases into his cheeks beside his eyes. It made me realize just how handsome he was and, once again, how rare it was to see such truly golden eyes. I'd only ever known Cosima and Sebastian to have that yellow gaze, and it tugged something loose at the back of my memories I resolved to study later.

For now, I let Dante usher me forward to his pseudo-father.

"*Tore, come stai?*" Dante asked him as they clasped each other by the shoulders and exchanged smacking kisses to either cheek.

Tore didn't release his grip on Dante when they stepped back, squeezing the taller man's shoulders as he beamed at him. "Better, much better seeing you free and well."

"You were right," Dante said cryptically, both of them casting a sidelong glance at me. "From the start. I was always going to change everything for her."

Tore clucked his tongue, but there was more humor and happiness in his expression than I'd ever seen before. The brooding, often angry man I vaguely knew in my youth and the stoic, careful Don I'd come to know slightly better in New York was replaced entirely by this vivacious, warm host.

"You aren't the first man to change your life for love, and you won't be the last." He turned his tiger-eyed gaze to me and opened his arms. "Elena Lombardi, welcome to you. I hope you come to love it here as much as my son and I do."

I hesitated slightly, years of hatred and judgment stopping up my joints like rusted hinges. There was a flash of something in his eyes then, a shadow over that sunny gold. He looked…*devastated.* It was such a strong emotion, but it was there in the tightness beside his eyes even after he controlled his response.

Something tender in me reacted to that sight. I was used to rejection, to judgment, and I didn't want to be the cause of that for Dante's stand-in father.

So, I shook off my reserve and stepped forward to embrace the older man myself, pressing warm kisses to each of his creased cheeks. "Thank you for having us here, Salvatore."

When I stepped back, both Dante and Tore were smiling at me. My man looked proud, and the latter looked properly chuffed. He pressed a hand to his cheek where I'd kissed him, then laughed a deep, chest-rumbling laugh.

"It's me who should be thanking you. I never got used to America and the cold. Winter in the south here is exactly right, cool enough to wear a sweater at night, and that is it." He shuddered. "There was snow on the ground in New York when I left. I only just arrived from Rome and already my bones are happier."

"Your old man bones can't take the cold, huh?" Dante teased.

Tore shot him a withering look. "I'll show you just how young I am tomorrow when we spar. I heard from Frankie that you've slowed down."

Dante searched over his shoulder for Frankie, who stood by the SUV that followed us from Naples with a wicked grin. "I'm coming for you tomorrow."

Frankie shrugged. "If Elena doesn't keep you in bed."

A blush fired up my cheeks as Dante and Tore laughed, but I forced myself to relax when Dante tucked his arm in mine.

"Ignore Frankie," he ordered loudly so the man could hear him.

I tipped my chin up. "I usually do."

He and some of the men lined up to meet us laughed again. It made something in my chest loosen to make them chuckle.

"Come meet our Italian family," Dante told me as he led us to the left side of the line. "First, my cousin and our Italian right-hand man, Damiano Vitale."

A huge man with gorgeous dark skin glistening under the sun like ebony stepped out of line to greet me. He smelled warm and musky as he bent to give me the customary kisses and when he stepped back, his white smile was one of the most beautiful I'd ever seen.

"Hello," he said in lyrical Italian, the hint of a different accent in his speech. "I've heard much about the fierce lawyer Cosima forced to represent our Dante. The rumors of your beauty don't do you justice."

"Stop hitting on my woman, Damiano," Dante muttered darkly. "You have enough women."

"Three mistresses is hardly too many," he argued with a wink to me.

I smiled at him because his roguish charm reminded me of Dante. "As long as they are all aware of the situation and they've consented to it, I don't see a problem."

Damiano's eyebrows cut into his smooth forehead before he laughed robustly. "Dante, you didn't tell me you have such a progressive Italian woman. Maybe I will steal her away."

Dante made a low sound in his throat that could have been mistaken for a growl as he slid a strong arm around my hip and tugged me right into his side. "*Attento, Dami.*"

*Careful, Dami.*

A little shiver zipped up my spine at his show of possessiveness. I never would have guessed that Dante's animalistic displays could be so sexy, his protectiveness and over-the-top possessiveness, his growled threats and displays of violence, his rigorous fucking…it was all out of the realm of my experience, yet I found myself wholly entranced by the dark magnetism of it.

I placed a hand on Dante's chest and beamed at Damiano. "He gets a little grumpy when he's tired."

The black man laughed again with tears in the corners of his eyes. My man only shot me a cool glance, eyebrow raised.

"If I'm tired, *bella mia,* it is only because you kept me up most of the plane ride." He gave a beleaguered shrug at his cousin. "She can't get enough."

"Dante!" I snapped, but there was laughter bubbling up my throat instead of the usual shame.

"A woman who keeps you busy," Dami said with a wicked grin. "I approve. I think you and I will be good friends, Elena."

"I hope so," I said genuinely.

Adriano, Chen, Marco, Jacopo, and Frankie had taught me not to judge mafioso the way I had as a girl.

Speaking of which, I gasped when I saw the man next in line, an all too familiar face from my childhood.

"Nico," I greeted with a wide smile. "It's been years."

"They've been good to you," he said with that big, boyish smile on his brutish face. When I kissed him on both cheeks, he smelled just the same, motor oil and licorice. "I am happy to see you again."

"Me too." And I meant it. "Are you married now?"

"Cosima wouldn't do me the honor, so I never settled down," he said with a chuckle before sobering. "Don't tell her husband that."

Dante and I laughed. "No, I would never. Find me later. I would love to talk."

He nodded, but before we could move on, he reached out to touch me. Dante caught his wrist with a firm look. Nico cleared his throat and nodded awkwardly, shifting his weight on his big feet before looking up at me through his lashes.

"I'm glad you're well," he said quietly. "I'm glad you all got out of here okay."

My heart burned at the sweet words. Nico was not very bright, but he'd always been a good friend to our family even though he'd joined the Camorra at eleven while my brother, his good friend, had not.

*"Grazie mille,"* I murmured.

Nico nodded, a flush in his cheeks as he ducked his head.

Dante ushered us forward, introducing me to the rest of the men who guarded the house and worked for Damiano and, therefore, the Salvatore men. They were all gracious, well-mannered, and slightly reverent as if they were meeting royalty and wanted to be on their best behavior.

When I whispered that to Dante after we finished the introductions, he kissed me. "*Regina mia,* Elena, it's not something these men take lightly. I've never introduced a woman to them this way before you."

Pride washed through me, cleansing me of my preconceived notions, of my terrible past with the Camorra. I wasn't some little kid with a horrible father indebted to the mob anymore. I was an intelligent, grown woman with a mafia Don's love and protection.

"I'd like to be respected because of who I am, not just who I sleep with," I added coolly because I was tired of feeling vulnerable all the time.

Dante's lips twitched as he guided me into the house. "I have no doubt they will if you give them time."

The lobby of the villa was a two-story affair bracketed on one side by tiled stairs with a wrought-iron scrolled railing and on the other by massive arches leading into a living room and down a hallway that probably led to the kitchen. The color palette was all creams, yellows, oranges, and reds, warmth and light saturating every inch of the house.

It suited Dante much more than his black and white apartment in New York, and I found, somewhat to my surprise, that it suited me.

"I need to meet quickly with Damiano and Tore, but I'll show you around after, *va bene?*" Dante spoke into the hair over my temple before pressing a kiss there.

I nodded, already wandering down the hall, waving my hand at him. "I'll be fine. Go ahead."

"Elena," he called when I turned away, waiting until I looked back to smile and say, "You've made me happier than I've ever been before. You had the courage to follow me here and I won't ever forget that or stop striving to be worthy of it."

"Just you saying that proves you already are," I murmured softly, the smile on my face almost unfamiliar, tender and aching.

We beamed at each other for a second before the men started trailing in from outside. I nodded to him, then turned back down the long hall. Family photos hung on the plaster walls, images of Salvatore, a young Alexander, Dante from his youth as a gangly kid with unruly thick hair to a robust teen and finally, the handsome, enormous man he was today. I touched my fingers to an old framed photo of Tore, Dante, Alexander, and who must have been Chiara and Noel. Much to their chagrin, the boys took mostly after their father, particularly Alexander with his golden coloring. Noel had been a large man, unusually tall and thickly muscled for a British peer of the realm, and utterly intimidating even just in the photo. He stood stoically at the edge of the happy little group, Chiara's hand tucked tightly in his own.

He didn't hide his ability to be more monster than man very well.

I knew from stories that Alexander did it a little better, and Dante hid it the best.

But there was an echo of darkness in all their gazes as they stared at the camera.

Even Chiara, who was so beautiful and Italianate she looked like a model from the 1950s. She had her hair back with a scarf, but the dark strands tickled her bare shoulders as she bent slightly to put an arm around Dante. They shared the same black hair and dark eyes, and the slight indent in the firm chin. The silver chain Dante now wore was visible around her neck, disappearing into the black dress she wore on her slim frame.

A gorgeous family until you looked a little closer.

I swallowed thickly before I moved on, feeling slightly intrusive even though the photos were clearly displayed for anyone to view.

I was about to move on into the kitchen when I noticed a final image, a Polaroid tucked into a simple black frame. It was faded as if it had been handled too often and exposed to the hot Italian sun. But I could make out the woman sitting on the edge of the causeway in the Bay of Naples because I'd spent most of my life looking at her.

Mama.

She was so young, beautiful, almost identical to Cosima, but with Giselle's lushly curved body. Her smile was wider than I'd ever seen it, her head thrown back to the sunny sky, hair a cascade down her back as she relished in whatever joy had just been handed to her. So carefree in a way I'd never had the privilege of seeing Caprice.

I knew Tore had a history with our family, but I'd always assumed it had more to do with mafia dealings and Seamus than Mama.

Now, I wasn't so certain.

Beside it, there was a larger photo of Dante, Tore, and Cosima. My sister was in the middle of the two men, bracketed by their arms around her and their big bodies angled into her as if they were protecting her and showcasing her at the same time. There was no darkness in their smiles, only pure, beaming light. After everything Cosima had been through when she was sold into sexual slavery by Seamus, she deserved that happiness and those two men's protection and affection.

Still, that wicked voice in the back of my mind hissed at me, reminding me that I wasn't the first Lombardi in this world, that Cosima and even Mama had come before me. I tried not to let it diminish how special I'd felt being introduced as Dante's woman, as his *Donna*, but loneliness seeped in around the edges of my forced conviction.

My old friend melancholy roosted once more in my gut.

I felt suddenly and horrifically alone standing in that long, empty hall in a house of memories I wasn't a part of and didn't truly understand because I didn't actually know that much about Dante's past yet.

I stared at the photos for a long time, unspooling tangled theories until I was caught up in a mess of threads.

As if summoned by my thoughts, the phone in my purse started to vibrate.

I'd had it on airplane mode for the entire trip, and when I flipped on the data, there were messages from Mama, Sebastian, Cosima, Yara, Beau, and even Daniel.

**Daniel:** *I had a concerning message from Dante Salvatore. Just checking in to see if you're okay, Elena.*

I stared at the text and tried to decide if there were any lingering feelings for him in my crowded heart.

There was still the bitterness of betrayal, which I doubted would ever fully go away, and the echo of my own shame that I hadn't given him a proper chance to explain his sexuality to me. It was my fault as much as his that our relationship hadn't worked out, but I still wished he hadn't fallen in love with my little sister.

There was just so much history between Giselle and me. At this point, I wished them all the best, I really did, because they clearly made each other happy, and I wanted that for them both.

But even as in love with Dante as I was, falling more and more into it every day, I didn't know if I'd ever be close with either of them again.

I didn't know if I had the strength to face the demons both of them represented as individuals and as a unit.

My phone rang again in my hand, and Mama's name popped up on the screen.

I hesitated.

Mama was my confidant as much as Beau was. She had stood by me through the entire Daniel and Giselle affair. But I could realize, especially as I stared at the Polaroid of her on Tore's wall, that I hadn't been the same confidant to her.

It made me want to keep my own secrets from her.

It was spiteful and unhealthy, but that was my instinct.

Only Sebastian's voice in my head talking about the distance all our secrets had caused between our family members made me pick up her call.

"Mama," I murmured as I moved out of the hall into the kitchen. It was a gorgeous, rustic space, but I didn't linger. The massive glass doors to the patio were open, so I moved through them to the warm, citrus-scent air of the back garden.

The fragrance reminded me of Dante and made me smile.

"*Lottatrica mia,*" Mama said warmly. "I read in the paper Dante has run away. This is bad, no?"

I bit my lip as I went to the round, worn wood table under the trellis and took a seat in a cushioned chair. "Well, if he was to return to the country, he would go to jail for bail jumping. They could let him off with a fine and/or community service, but the prosecution wants him too badly to agree to that."

"So he has left forever?" She sounded deeply morose about the idea, which surprised me. To my knowledge, Dante and Mama hadn't interacted more than a handful of times over the years.

"I don't know," I answered truthfully.

"What does this mean for you?"

I chewed my lower lip, noticing a deliberate scar in the wood table. My breath caught as I leaned closer to read the symbols there "*EDD.*" Edward Dante Davenport. I could imagine Dante as a young boy sitting in this exact chair carving his initials into the table to make a permanent mark on a beautiful memory.

My fingers itched to join my name with his.

"As his lawyer?" I asked even though I knew Mama was too shrewd to be waylaid.

"No, Lena. This man, he is *right* for you. Do not tell me you are not with him."

"With him romantically or with him as in with him on the run?" I stalled.

She blew air through her lips and clucked her tongue. "*Lena mia,* I may be an old woman now, but do not insult me, hmm?"

I sighed. "Okay, then yes to both, I guess. We're in Naples together, at Salvatore's house."

There was a pregnant pause, static with things unsaid on both ends of the phone.

"*Villa Rosa*?" she questioned softly.

"Yes, we're staying here until we figure out a game plan."

"You left the law for this man," she murmured, almost sounding awed. "I am so happy for you."

"What?" I blinked at the lemons rattling softly in the wind across the sloping green yard from me.

"This pleases me," she repeated, clapping in the background. "You have a need for a man like Dante, you understand? Daniel Sinclair was looking for peace, *figlia mia*, but you? You were always looking for chaos, *si*? Someone who makes you feel alive."

*So alive I burn.*

I blinked unseeing at the table, my index finger tracing the outline of Dante's initials. "I didn't know that was what I needed until, oh, I don't know, two days ago. How did you know?"

"I am your mother," she stated firmly, then sighed. "I have not done many things right in this life of mine, Elena, but being your mother has always made me so proud. You are fierce and strong. Nothing pushes you to the ground for long. You are a lawyer. You like adversity. Dante, he gives you this conflict and the power to overcome it, yes?"

*Yes.*

She was utterly and completely right.

"He's a criminal," I pointed out, just to make sure she understood the situation completely. "And not some two-bit shoplifter, but a man probably wanted by Interpol and the entire United States government now."

"Yes," she said gravely. "This is a problem, but you like problems."

"I do," I admitted.

"If anyone can fix this, it is you," she stated so matter-of-factly it was as if she was reading the constitution, something historical everyone took as absolute. "You will find a way to bring you both home."

"I'll try," I promised.

Until then, I'd been playing catch-up. The events of my life in the past few days were shocking and irreversible. I hadn't gotten around to thinking of the consequences, let alone how to rectify them.

"Seamus is dead," I confessed to her softly.

Without hesitation, she said, "*Bene.*"

"Really? He was your husband. The father of your children. I hated him, Mama, *loathed* him, but I'm still disconcerted by his death," I admitted, though it was a little different for me.

I'd been the one to kill him.

It could have been Dante, but increasingly, I had the feeling he'd only shot Seamus in the face to absolve me of the responsibility for his death.

"Your father was a bad man masquerading as someone good," she said softly, the words waterlogged with timeless sorrow. "I had a chance once to choose a good man in a bad life, and I chose wrongly. I am happy for my daughter that she is not so afraid as I was."

"*Coraggio,*" I murmured. "Dante makes me feel brave."

"As he should," she declared. "Now, I can sleep well knowing my daughters have found good men."

I laughed. "Maybe 'good' is a loose interpretation. I think Alexander, Daniel, and Dante have all been considered villains at some point in their lives."

"There is peace in the balance," she said, and I could picture her as Osteria Lombardi rolling pasta dough as she doled out sage advice, at once domestic and eternal, every Italian Mama and their wisdom embodied in her single form. "I think with Dante, you will find your balance too."

*"Ti amo, Mama,"* I murmured, cradling the phone as if it was her cheek. "Thank you for always believing in me even when I gave you reason not to."

"I did not do as I should have and protected you when you were a girl." Her voice was thick with tears, with a regret that would never die no matter how many times I told her I didn't blame her. "The least I can do is support you now, *lottatrice,* and know that you will always make your mama proud."

My tear ducts stung with tears, but I pressed my index fingers to both to stem the flow. Apparently, falling in love turned me into an unstoppable crying machine.

"Does he know about Christopher?" she asked tentatively.

"No."

"Lena...you should tell your man. He is not the type to take such a thing well, I think."

"Exactly, so I am not going to tell him."

"You and Daniel kept secrets from each other. Do not repeat the cycle," she advised.

My entire body moved with the heaviness of my sigh. "I don't want him to see me as some victim, Mama."

"No one, knowing you, could think that. No one loving you would ever entertain that even just for a moment." When I didn't respond, it was her turn to sigh. "Okay, *ragazza*, you do what you feel is right. I send my love to you and to Dante, *va bene*? When you come home, he comes over for Sunday dinner, *si*?"

"*Si, Mama*," I agreed, suddenly homesick for her like a child taken away to overnight camp. "*Ti amo*."

"*Sempre*," she murmured back.

*Always.*

After we hung up, I decided to respond to Beau's text but left the others, too exhausted to deal with explanations or drama.

**Elena:** *Met D's Italian family. They greeted us like royalty. It was...odd.*

**Beau:** *Damn straight, they did. Queen Elena. Now, that's a name I could get behind. Do best friends get royal privileges too?*

I blinked at the phone, my lonely heart warmed by the reminder that no matter what, even an entire ocean away from them, I still had a few beautiful people who would always have my back.

And when the tears pushed again at my ducts, I didn't wipe them away.

# CHAPTER SEVEN
# DANTE

I was in a deep sleep, the kind where dreams were so vivid you could taste them, feel them on your fingertips. In the dream, it was deep night, the shadows thick as spilled ink, and Elena was there wearing a traditional Italian lace veil over her head. In the dark, I couldn't tell if it was the white of a wedding covering or the black of a funeral shroud. I tried to get closer—walking, then running, and finally sprinting toward her with a portentous feeling crushing my chest. All I knew was that if I didn't get to her right then, she would die, or she would never again be mine to have.

Both options were disastrous to me.

I woke up with adrenaline coursing through my veins, my muscles coiled tight beneath my skin even though I didn't move a muscle. Elena was in my arms, her warm, sleep-heavy body pressed the entire length of mine, her lips parted over even, soft breaths that fanned against my face. The sight of her black silk eye mask and ear plugs made my lips twitch with mirth and warm intimacy. I tried to relax, to let the sight of her beauty soothe me like some lullaby back to sleep, but there was a lingering prickle of dread creeping up my spine that I couldn't shake.

I'd just closed my eyes again when there was a faint creak, soft as breath.

My lids flew open, and my entire body turned to stone.

I stopped breathing.

Seconds later, there was a sharp but muted *crack* near the locked doors to the patio.

Slowly, with infinitesimal movements, I rolled onto my back away from Elena, careful not to jostle her awake. There was a gun in the nightstand, but I didn't dare reach for it when I couldn't be sure if the intruder could see me from his or her vantage point. If they caught movement, they could fire indiscriminately, and I didn't want to endanger Elena.

So, I waited.

My pulse thundered in my ears, but I strained to hear every shift of air beyond it.

Finally, after a long moment, I caught the *shush* of soft soled shoes against the wooden floor.

They were crossing to the bed.

I risked slating one eye open, peering through the low lid to gauge the distance.

He was twenty-five feet away, close to the doors. I could just make out the entire door handle on the floor, knocked out with quiet tools so they could swing the door right open into our room.

How they knew where to find us in the colossal house spoke of resounding betrayal.

Someone had turned rat.

Anger transmuted my blood to magma, but still, I held still and waited.

That was the predator's most powerful weapon—not their ability to attack but their ability to wait out their prey, to strike exactly when the moment was right.

Twenty feet.

Fifteen.

Ten.

The dark-clothed intruder wore a ski mask over their face, muffling their breathing and obscuring their face, but it was obvious from the size of them that they were male.

And strong.

Only a few inches beneath my six foot five and a dozen or so pounds lighter than me.

It would be a fierce fight.

But there was no doubt in my mind I would win.

This *bastardo* wasn't just messing with me.

He was threatening my woman.

My Elena.

The woman I was just coming to make my own.

There was a gun in his hands, a long silencer attached to the end and trained on me.

They wanted me dead but found in the morning like a message scrawled in blood for Tore and our allies to beware.

Italians could be so unnecessarily dramatic.

Five feet.

Three.

I closed my eyes, peace coming over me as I felt him take the last step at my bedside. There was a faint *click* of the safety.

My cue.

I knifed up from the bed, curling forward under the level of his arms to tackle him mid-gut. The force of the maneuver took us both to the floor with a muted thud. I felt his lungs compress under my weight, my knee colliding sharply against the ground, but I didn't hesitate. The gun was flung to one side, loosely clasped in his hand, and I went for it with both hands. His grip tightened as I went to wrench it from his grasp. His other hand landed a wild punch to my jaw that burst with bright pain. I blinked away the hurt, focusing on the gun. If I could disarm him, he'd be done.

He tried to leverage his weight against the ground to get the torque he needed to toss me off his torso. I moved one knee high to pin his right bicep and successfully wrenched the weapon from his grasp. The metal was warm from his hands, the barrel still hot from a loosed bullet. Somewhere on the property, a guard lay in a pool of his own blood.

Fury moved through me, adding strength to the muscles I honed for exactly this every single day. I used the butt of the gun to hit him across the face, the crunch of bone loud and satisfying in the still room. Blood sprayed from his nose in a wide arc, catching me across the face.

The pain seemed to galvanize the *stronzo,* though.

He knocked me in the temple with a powerful fist that made constellations of stars wheel in my vision. His foot kicked me in the chest as he began to crawl out from under me. The breath left my lungs in a whoosh, the gun falling to the floor as my hand automatically tried to catch me from falling. He collected the weapon just as I regained my equilibrium, standing to train it on me again.

I shook my head hard, grinding my teeth as I lurched to my feet and lunged forward to grab the chamber of the gun from the side. He fired a shot, the bullet flying through the open patio doors without incident, but my hand on the chamber obstructed the casing from discharging. When he went to fire another shot, this one aimed at the shoulder I'd already taken a bullet to when I'd saved Elena from the Irish mob, the gun clicked but didn't fire.

I grinned wickedly at him just before I swung my elbow at his face, catching his left cheekbone with the edge of my bone. His head snapped to the side, his body going limp as he staggered. The gun fell to the floor, but I didn't go for it.

Instead, I stepped behind him and took advantage of his disorientation to catch him around the neck with one arm, the other bracing around his head. He struggled against the sleeper hold, but I was bigger, stronger, and more determined than the *figlio di puttana* who was there on someone else's orders.

So, I waited. Feet braced, the muscles in my arms flexing so hard they burned, the bulk of my bicep cutting off his airway.

It only took fifteen seconds.

Any longer and I would cause irreparable damage.

I didn't want that.

I wanted this sack of shit alive and fucking alert so he would feel every one of my punches and knife strikes as I tortured him for information.

When he was out, I looked up to find Elena standing in front of us. The wind blowing in from the broken patio doors shifted around her, tossing her red hair like a pennant, her black silk nightgown plastered to her body.

But that wasn't what held me transfixed.

It was the sight of the misplaced gun in her hands, raised high and level at the chest of the intruder. There was no fear in her gaze, no tremble in her posture.

She held the gun as if it was a gavel, the weight of righteous justice in her steady gaze.

*"Tranquillo, lottatrice mia,"* I murmured calmly. "Steady, Elena. Don't shoot him."

"Why not?" she asked, her words clinking together like ice cubes.

She didn't lower the gun.

"We do not want him dead."

"He came in here while we were sleeping to *kill* you, Dante," she said in a reasonable tone contrasted entirely by the dark gleam in her eyes.

It was deeply inappropriate, but laughter bubbled up through the fury in my chest and I was forced to swallow it back. Elena would not find the situation as amusing as I did.

But look at her.

No matter the adversity, I could always count on one constant.

Elena Lombardi was a weapon.

And she was *mine.*

"Put the gun down, *cuore mia,*" I coaxed, letting the comatose man drop unceremoniously to the floor so I could go to her. She kept the gun raised, almost frozen with her determination to protect me, until the barrel was pressed to my stomach. I put my hand over the weapon and released the chamber so it fell into my waiting hand beneath. Then I carefully untangled her fingers from the grip and used my free hand to sink my fingers deep in her hair, angling her head to take her mouth in a possessive kiss.

Instantly, she melted. All her dangerous resolve dissolving on my tongue like fucking candy, sweet and addictive. I ate at her until she trembled. Unable to resist, I used my other hand, still cradling the dismantled gun, to palm her sex. It was as wet as I'd known it would be, her juices slick on my fingers, on the weapon that had been intended to kill us both.

When I broke away, she clutched me close, her breath as harsh as mine.

"No one will take you from me without a fight," she whispered vehemently. The nails of the hand she had curled around my neck sank into my skin, so I hissed.

"Anyone who tries to come between our love will suffer then die," I swore to her, kissing her again because I was high on adrenaline, on the scent of her damp pussy in my nose and the victory of a fight won in my blood.

I almost took her right then and there, my cock hard as stone in my boxer briefs, but I knew the intruder would wake at any second, and

I wasn't going to take chances on her safety. So I stepped away with effort, leaving her hands clasping at air, her breath stuttering through her swollen lips.

"Later, *lottatrice*," I promised as I went to the chair near the doors and collected the sash from Elena's robe draped over the back. Crouching beside the man, I rolled him to collect his hands behind his back and secure them in a handcuff knot. "Let me question this *figlio di puttana,* and then I'll finish what we've started, *va bene*?"

She studied me with the body for a moment, something dark working behind her gaze, and then she moved to my side. I watched slightly stupefied as she bent to pick up the intruder's feet.

When I didn't move, she raised a cool red brow at me. "Well, come on. The sooner you find out who sent this asshole, the better."

A hard bullet of laughter exploded past my lips, but I swallowed my amusement down when Elena scowled. Fuck me, but she was perfect.

Not for everyone.

Fuck that.

I didn't want some generic girl who'd bore me in three days.

Elena was perfect for *me* and only me.

Unflappable under pressure, an unbroachable vault for the secrets of the Family, passionate beneath that cool exterior, and smart enough to give me whiplash.

A dream come true.

No, I'd never even thought to dream of such a woman. My imagination was incapable of forming the complicated layers of Elena Lombardi, but I'd happily spend the rest of my days carefully unearthing them like an archeologist.

"Dante?" she probed when I just stared at her.

I lunged forward to stamp a hard kiss to her unpainted lips. "*Sei magnifica.*"

A little grin whispered over her lips before she nodded curtly at me to pick up the man's torso. "You can prove to me just how much after we deal with this *stronzo*."

"Be still my heart," I joked, clutching my chest as I staggered back toward his head.

She rolled her eyes.

And as we carried the body of a man who had just attempted to assassinate us to the basement of Tore's villa, I laughed.

I laughed and I laughed because what a fucking adventure life was with Elena at my side.

His name was Umberto Arno.

He couldn't have been more than twenty-four years old, but then, in his profession of contract killing, not many men lived longer than that.

Tore had recognized him instantly as one of Rocco Abruzzi's men, though he was also a favorite of Pietro Cavalli.

I stared at him impassively as he choked on a sob, blood bubbling out of his mouth and sliding down his chin into the saturated fabric of his black sweater. His right eyebrow was split, his mouth broken open like an eyelet pattern by the force of his teeth cutting through the skin when I hit him.

Perhaps I'd gone a little overboard.

But then again, the *brutto figlio di puttana bastardo* hadn't just come for me. He'd put Elena in danger.

On a long sigh, I reared my torso back and brought the crushing weight of my fist down on his right cheek. It crumpled beneath my force.

Umberto let out an animal wail.

I wiped the blood from my knuckles in his sweat-dampened hair.

"I told you," he panted, leaning limply forward in the chair I'd tied him to. "No one sent me."

"And I told you," I said amiably before I wrenched his head back with a fist in his hair. He squinted at me through the sweat and blood. "I don't believe you. You had a reason for coming here tonight."

He glared at me, one eye nearly swollen shut.

I considered him, irritated that Made Men in Italy were made of sterner stuff than their American counterparts. I snapped my fingers at Nico, who lingered in the corner with Frankie and Tore. He left the room immediately to do my bidding.

Umberto's eyes followed him, then shot back to me.

"Don't worry about him," I suggested as I pulled a chair over the tile floor just in front of him and sat down in it, leaning forward in faux comradery. "Worry about yourself. You're young. Maybe you haven't heard of me. I've been known by a lot of different names in my life, Umberto, but in Napoli, they called me '*principe ereditario dell'inferno.*'"

The Crown Prince of Hell.

"Do you know why they called me that?" He didn't respond. Blood dripped into his left eye and turned it vampiric. "Because I was an aristocrat, but I much preferred using my silver spoon to carve out my enemy's eyes and shove them down their throat."

Perfectly on cue, Nico reappeared through the door holding a blowtorch and a grapefruit spoon with a serrated edge.

Umberto's eyes widened just slightly at the sight before they flicked to me.

I nodded somberly. "You might know a few of the men I left blind and broken before I moved to America. Danny 'Greaser' Ricci, Alessandro Tedesco, Thumper Greco." I paused, took the spoon and torch from Nico, and flicked on the gas, flame bursting out of the nozzle between my face and Umberto's. "You'll live, but I hope you took a good long look at your wife or mother before you left home tonight. It's the last time you'll ever see them."

Behind me, the door creaked slightly.

"*Vaffanculo a chi t'è morto,*" he cursed at me to fuck my dead family members.

Rage sparked deep in the heart of me.

It was the worst insult in Italian, one that infuriated any local because family was sacred in this country.

But it made me see red.

Because my mother, Chiara, was dead. Murdered before her time by my psychopathic father because she'd dared to threaten to go to the authorities about murdering his long string of mistresses.

No one--*no one*--spoke about my mother like that.

Swiftly, I held the spoon to the flame just long enough to sear the pure silver but not warp it, and then I lunged forward, grabbing Umberto by the hair in one punishing hand. He kicked out, struggling in the chair, but I had him paralyzed in my hold. My right hand was steady as I brought the smoking metal to his left eye and dug the edge into his tear duct.

His cry pierced the room, vibrating the old, dusty chandelier Tore had never bothered to take down from the ceiling. The chiming sound was almost as pretty as this bastard's cries.

"*Bene*!" he screamed as I dug deeper, catching the edge of his eyeball. "*Fermata!*"

*Okay, stop*, he begged.

So, I did, the spoon hovering an inch from his bleeding socket.

"Yes?" I coaxed.

His breath heaved through his lungs as if he'd run a marathon. I waited a moment for him to catch some air, then lowered the spoon again.

"Wait, fuck," he called out again in Italian. "You crazy bastard."

"This is nothing," I said with a humble shrug, twirling the spoon between my fingers. "Now, tell me why you came for me."

He glowered at me, but the effect was somewhat ruined by the pulpy mess my fists had made of his face. "You think you can just come back to Napoli and slide right back into your old role?"

"Ah, so you do remember." My smile was smug, and I felt a resounding pang of triumph in my chest.

The truth was, validation was important to me. I'd grown up the second son of a powerful man, the spare to the prodigal heir. No one had their eyes on me, and it chafed more than I cared to admit. I was shaped by that need for glory, so much so that it was entirely too easy to settle for infamy in the place of fame.

I'd wanted to make a name for myself in the world and I'd done it.

There was no shame in being Dante Salvatore, ruthless mafioso, the Devil of NYC, the Mafia Lord, or the Crown Prince of Hell.

I'd forged him like a weapon from the ashes of my old life as Edward Davenport, parentless, with a brother who hated me and no home to return to.

So, it pleased me deeply to hear that my name still echoed through the alleys and underground backrooms of Naples.

"You think you're entitled to whatever you want just because you're some hotshot capo in America? You're all soft and weak. *Porci.*"

*Pigs.*

"No..." The word slid from my mouth on a hiss. "We are crafty and relentless. Where you would have shot me dead in my bed, I have you here about to confess all your plans like a talking toy with a pulled string. Who, may I ask, is the weaker man here?"

He tried to spit at me, but there was only sticky blood in his mouth, so the effort failed.

I sighed wearily and tensed my fingers in his hair again, yanking his head back for a better angle for my spoon.

"*Che palle,*" he cursed. "Okay, you bastard, no one sent me because I came myself."

This was a surprise. I studied the younger man again, but I was certain I didn't know him. When I looked up across the room at Tore, who leaned against the wall with his arms and legs crossed casually like he was waiting for something as mundane as a bus, he shook his head.

We didn't know this man for him to hate us enough to kill us.

"Why?" I demanded, dropping the spoon because I was bored.

Umberto sighed in relief until I grabbed the abandoned torch and lit it an inch from his eye.

When he finished screaming, I repeated myself.

"Because I love Mira!" he shouted hoarsely, too loud and forceful, the tendons in his neck straining.

It was the look and sound of a man at the end of his rope.

This pleased me.

"You're in love with Mira?" I asked, vaguely surprised that the meek woman could inspire such passion that this *stronzo* would risk his life trying to take mine in my own home.

He clamped his mouth shut truculently, but before I could light the torch again, a soft, lilting voice spoke in a language that I wasn't used to hearing from her.

"In love with her? No, you love her, though, don't you?"

I sucked in a deep, steadying breath before I looked over my shoulder at the woman who could seduce me and infuriate me in equal measures.

She was still in her damned nightgown, the silk so thin it molded to her every curve. For modesty's sake, she'd donned the robe, but I had taken the sash, so the entire length of black silk gaped open and made her look even more inviting. Angry as I was, she still took my fucking breath away standing there with all that red hair mussed, her face bare of makeup and all the more striking for it.

In an entirely different outfit, in an entirely different space and she still reminded me of some heathen goddess of sex and war.

"Elena," I began on a low growl, hyper aware of the blood sprayed across my face, the swollen, cut open knuckles on my bloody hands, the blowtorch dangling between my fingers.

This was not how I wanted Elena to see me.

She was too smart not to know what a mafioso got up to in the shadows. How a Made Man might punish someone for trying to take away his life. She knew what I was on trial for. She'd read the FBI files about my supposed crimes front to back more than once.

But she didn't need to *witness* it. Let alone *me* doing those deeds.

She was a lady.

She deserved diamonds and silk and lace, manners and galas in velvet dresses.

Not basement rendezvous at midnight with a man's cries still ringing against the walls.

Not even Cosima had ever seen this side of me, the ruthless, seething darkness I had inside me. I'd never shown her even though she was married to my brother who was often more monster than man.

I hadn't trusted her, or maybe I hadn't trusted myself.

Either way, standing over a man I fully intended to send to hell with the woman I would move heaven and earth for was a deeply fucking unsettling scenario.

She ignored me, her gaze pinned on Umberto. Without hesitating, she walked toward us, her bare feet catching in the blood splatter, tracking red footprints on portions of the clean tiles.

When she was in line with me, she stopped even though she didn't acknowledge my presence. I was irritated but also curious. What was my sharp-minded *lottatrice* thinking?

"You love her," she continued in that liquid Neapolitan accent of dropped vowels and shushing *S*'s that couldn't be taught, only learned from birth. "You love her, but not as a lover. As a sister? Ah, no, maybe a beloved cousin?"

Umberto blinked, but an uncanny twist to his mouth confirmed Elena's suspicions.

"I know Mirabella is afraid of Dante," Elena continued smoothly, sitting in my vacant chair primly, legs crossed, hands loosely clasped like she was in a holding room at a New York jail interviewing a client and not in the basement torture room of an infamous mafioso. "But he wouldn't be a bad match for her, would he? He's affluent and respected in the community. I don't believe you'd kill him just to get your sister out of an arranged marriage. There's another reason."

Umberto's lips twisted tighter, a valiant effort to cap the bubbling emotions bursting inside him.

Elena sighed, leaning forward earnestly. "You don't seem very attached to your sight, Signore Arno."

Taking her cue, I sparked the torch in my hand, the hiss of flame loud in the quiet room.

Umberto swallowed thickly. "My sister deserves to be happy."

"Yes," my woman agreed easily. "Everyone does. Whether or not that's feasible is another case entirely. Have you thought that perhaps Dante doesn't want to marry your sister either?"

"So he can marry you?" he snarled in heavily accented English. "Some American whore?"

Elena didn't say a word as I grabbed Umberto by the throat and squeezed, his face plumping, reddening like an overripe fruit on the vine about to burst.

"Say another word against her, and I'll take your eyes *and* your balls."

He wheezed painfully after I abruptly released him and stepped back.

"This isn't about me," Elena continued calmly as if I hadn't just strangled a man for insulting her, but I could see the way her thighs squeezed together, and I wondered with sudden heat if she liked my heathen aggression. "This is about Mirabella. You want her to be happy. Maybe, Dante can make that happen."

Umberto scowled fiercely at her for a long moment before something in his twisted mouth softened just slightly. His eyes flickered to mine in a gesture that was all question marks and reluctant hope.

"*Forsa*," I drawled, *maybe*. I grabbed the spoon from the floor and used the serrated edge to scrape some dried blood off my palm. "But this *bastardo* tried to kill me. I don't take that lightly. He endangered you, *lottatrice*, and that means he needs to be punished properly."

"So take his eyes," Elena said with a little shrug, but there was that calculating gleam in her eyes.

I felt a surge of pride watching her, sitting prim like a *principessa* with the mind of a fighter, using her skills as a lawyer to manipulate this man into giving us what we wanted.

This was the magic of my woman. Her mind was just as arousing as her gorgeous body.

"Wait," Umberto asked. "*Cazzo*. Fine. What did you have in mind?"

Elena looked up at me then, wickedness tucked between her full, smiling lips and trust shining from those gray eyes. "I'm sure Dante has a plan."

At that moment, I didn't think I'd ever felt such profound love and gratitude for another human being. It was heady to know that a woman as smart and capable, as careful and thoughtful as Elena trusted me wholeheartedly. I'd dragged her into the underworld, and instead of being resentful, regretful, even scared, she was boldly walking at my side, holding my hand in support and offering her love without judgment.

Fuck me.

I'd never been a lucky man.

A serial-killing psychopath for a father. My mother stolen too young. My own brother turned against me.

I had been fundamentally alone most of my life before Tore took me under his wing, but even then, he had his own kids and preoccupations.

I'd never had someone who was just wholly and happily *mine*.

For the first time ever, I wanted to eschew my duty and bury myself in her warmth. Fuck her for hours until she was swollen and soaked, every inch of her possessed by every inch of me.

Instead, I shot her a burning look that promised I'd fuck her into oblivion at the next chance and turned back to Umberto.

"I have the beginnings of a plan," I agreed. "And if you don't like it, you can find out what it's like to be a man without balls."

# CHAPTER EIGHT

## *elena*

I was the kind of little girl who didn't dream about the future so much as I planned for it. No one had ever told me I deserved the best or that anything close to that was attainable, but I'd had this deep-seated conviction that if I worked hard, anything could happen. I could get out of the stinking hell that was Naples, move to some civilized city like London, or Toronto, or New York, and become the kind of woman I read about in books and saw in magazines.

That seed was planted in the fertile soil of my heart, but no matter how I watered it and tended to it by achieving dream after dream––a long-term partner in Daniel, a job at a top law firm, a beautiful home I could be proud of––that seed didn't sprout into more.

For years, I'd wondered if something was wrong with me. If I lacked the inherent ability to be satisfied with life. With myself. I was intrigued by everything I thought I wanted but satisfied with nothing. My happiness was a façade I grew to wear so well, I forgot the mechanics of what went on beneath the mask.

And now I knew.

I didn't know how to grow because I'd numbed myself to the point of intolerance. I didn't allow myself to feel or experience life. It had hurt me so much, I didn't trust myself to survive it anymore. It made my life bearable but hollow.

To think, for so long I'd never known true happiness. How foolish I'd been to think I could carve life up into parts and parcel them into neat little boxes on a shelf. I'd massacred any hope of joy, slaughtered newborn happiness before it could ever grow legs and stand tall. I'd condemned chaos, thinking it was the antithesis of everything a proper young woman should work for. Yearn for.

How wrong I'd been.

Dante had dragged me into the dark depths of his anarchic life and shown me the pleasure to be found in the shadows, the exhilaration of living on the knife's edge of danger, and the headiness of power unfettered by morality or laws. Those tidy boxes of emotion and memories I'd kept so neatly organized came tumbling down, and among all that disorderly chaos, I found that seed again.

I'd found it because finally, after so many years, it had sprouted and grown leaves. It was still such a small, fragile thing in my chest, this new hope and direction after moving around blindly for years. But it was there, and it was so beautiful it made me want to cry.

But it also made me feel fierce and powerful, totally unafraid.

I was a lawyer, curiosity was my trade, so of course, after helping Dante move the body of the intruder down to the basement, I'd snuck back down to see what he would do with him.

The sight of Dante with a blowtorch in one hand and a spoon in the other, a detached, almost feral grin on the same mouth that spoke such beautiful words to me and did such wonderous things to my body did strange things to me.

I wasn't horrified.

Oh, I knew I should have been. Watching my lover torture a man was a scenario I'd never thought up for myself. I'd always wanted a quiet, steady, wealthy lover who worked a quiet, steady job.

Not a mafioso who was astoundingly creative with his torture techniques.

I tried to remind myself how awful it had been for me when Seamus returned home broken and pulled apart by the Camorra for his unpaid gambling debts. How scared and upset I'd been.

But it didn't have the same bearing anymore.

Now, I couldn't forget that Seamus had somewhat deserved such treatment. He'd continually borrowed money from the outfit when he had little luck and no backup plan. The only thing that got him to pause his activities for any length of time was the particularly brutal beatings they doled out every once in a while to remind him that they weren't afraid to take payment in the form of his life.

If Seamus deserved it, then didn't this Umberto Arno deserve it now?

He'd blindly decided to assassinate Dante because he hadn't like Rocco's plans for his cousin. It was sheer instinctual idiocy. If he'd used his brain for a moment, he could have questioned Dante's motive in the scheme, wondered if the visiting Don would be happy about the idea of marrying some local Italian girl with a tarnished reputation.

But no.

Men.

Always acting as swiftly as they reacted.

So, I didn't respond the way I would have even a month ago.

Instead, I felt the heat of desire and righteous fury flow through me as thick and hot as magma. I enjoyed watching Dante scare him the way most people might have enjoyed watching a well-acted play. I was engrossed and more than a little proud that that man, the one with all the power, the diamond-bright and hard-cut mind, and massive, threatening physique was all *mine.*

But then, watching wasn't enough.

If he was mine, then I was his.

And didn't that mean being at his side?

Fighting along with him.

When Umberto made the comment about Mirabella, I saw my opening. I knew what Dante didn't, that he was protecting her not because of some transient passion but a deep, abiding love and respect that spoke of family.

I knew this because I knew Sebastian, if put in the same position, would have risked his life to get any one of his sisters out of the same place Mirabella found herself in.

It was risky to involve myself.

Dante said he wanted me by his side, but thought and action were two very different things. Most mafia wives and women were kept in the dark, meant to stay willfully blind and happy that way. I wasn't most women, and Dante wasn't most men, but we still lived and operated in that society.

So, I was nervous as I stepped out of the shadows, but no one stopped me. Not Nico, a familiar face from my childhood, or Frankie whose keen eyes told me he'd known I was outside the door all along. Not even Tore, who watched me with a steady, implacable expression as I crossed the floor, my bare feet sticking in cooling pools of blood as I went to Dante's side.

And Dante?

He surprised me the most.

He wasn't happy for me to be in that position. It was obvious by the twist in his wide mouth, like he'd swallowed a lemon. But he didn't stop me, not even when I took a position of power and started to interrogate the *stronzo* myself.

Every day, even every hour, he proved to me that he was better than any man I ever could have dreamed up. He was real, raw, and as powerful as lithium.

When we finished planning with Umberto, Tore, and Frankie, Dante took me by the hand, his own crusty with dried blood, and led me from the room.

I followed blindly.

Not because I was traumatized by the violence.

But because beneath my skin, I was *sizzling*.

When we reached our bedroom, Dante had barely shut the door before I was on him. I pushed him hard into the wood, his breath expelling in a grunt as I tore off his black T-shirt.

"Elena," he said, almost just to say my name, not because he wanted to stop me.

Which was good because I couldn't stop.

I was possessed with need, my entire body shaking with it as I dropped into a crouch to drag his sweats down his thick thighs. I left them bunched at his feet, liking the idea that he had to stay exactly there or risk tripping.

"Elena," he said again, this time on a moan as I rubbed my face at the furred junction of his leg and groin.

He smelled rich and masculine, like a man brined by a dip in the Tyrrhenian Sea. I loved the rough texture of his trimmed pubic hair against my cheek almost as much as I loved that heady smell. I breathed deeply, canting my face so I could look up at Dante as I inhaled, his cock swelling rapidly to full erection beside my forehead.

His eyes were twin black holes, sucking up every thought in my head that didn't center around him.

"You're so sexy," I murmured in a voice I'd never heard before, an almost guttural tone. With a little shock, I realized I was speaking Italian to him. "I want to show you what you do to me."

*"Non hai idea di quanto sei sexy,"* he told me as he raked those strong fingers through my hair, collecting it in one hand so he had a clear view of my lips nuzzling the base of his dick.

*You have no idea how sexy you are.*

I didn't care.

That was the secret to Dante's sexual power over me. Every single aspect of his person robbed me of thought, of the ability to self-criticize.

My habitual voice of doubt and loathing was drowned in his scent, in the rough scrape of his deep voice against my senses and his skin on my skin. I was lost in him, less myself and more myself than I had ever been.

I loved that he thought I was sexy. I was usually too elegant, too studied, too cold to be called that.

But this wasn't about me the way every sexual experience between us had been before.

I wanted this to be about him.

About paying homage to this big, brutal, and beautiful beast of a man.

"Put your palms flat on the door," I told him as I wrapped my fingers around his thick base, loving my pale flesh against his dusky length, the vivid red of my nails scraping just lightly up the shaft. "Don't move them."

"Giving orders?" he asked in a low, tight voice that spoke of his barely leashed control.

He wasn't the kind of man to submit.

I didn't even want that from him, couldn't really imagine it.

"Yes," I said truthfully as I lapped once, kittenish, at the bottom of his plum-shaped head. "But only because I want you to see how mad I am for you. Only because I want to do things to you I've never even dreamed of before meeting you, and I won't have the courage to try if you take control."

Without hesitation, Dante pressed his palms to the door behind him and braced his legs farther apart, straining the sweatpants around his ankles, the big muscles in his thighs popping dramatically as they tensed.

My mouth actually watered.

"Am I allowed to tell you how good you look on your knees for me?" he asked in that smoky mixed accent that turned each word into an exotic song. "Am I allowed to tell you how fucking hard it makes me to know you want me in that red mouth?"

"Yes," I hissed before I couldn't stand it any longer.

I placed his weeping head on the tip of my tongue, mouth wide, eyes locked up on his smoldering gaze, and slowly, I impaled my mouth on his thick cock. Wet raced to my eyes as I fought the urge to gag when he touched my throat, then wedged inside the tight channel.

I'd done this before, my gag reflex just a passing instinct, but not in a long time.

I closed my eyes and hummed as I held him deep inside my mouth, feeling the veins in his shaft throb on my tongue.

"*Cazzo, e' incredibile,*" Dante grunted as one of his fists slammed back against the door.

*Fuck, you feel incredible.*

I sucked a breath in through my nose, then pulled off his length, inch by languid inch until he was resting on my tongue again. My own licentious thoughts surprised me as I fisted his base and rubbed his hot head over the flat of my tongue, then sucked it hard into my mouth. I wanted to rub his length against my cheeks and lips, suck it down my throat and sit there filled with him, swallowing around him until he came like a geyser down my gullet. I wanted to take his length between my breasts and fuck him that way, smearing his precum over my nipples and licking it off his length whenever he thrust close to my mouth.

I told him this in low, liquid Italian as I jacked his steely cock, lapping at the head between sentences.

Dante grunted and groaned, his breath laboring through that barrel chest. His hands slapped and thumped against the wall as he fought to control himself from taking over, and fuck if that didn't make me wetter than I'd ever been before. All that leashed sexuality and dominance tethered by my simple request to let me have my way with him.

But this was Dante. He was never passive, and the only way I'd given him to express himself was with words.

So, he gave them to me.

"*Si,*" he said. "I'll fuck your tits, Lena. I bet no one has ever done that to you. But you know it's not me degrading you. You know when I do these dirty, delicious things with you, it's only sex and pure fucking beauty."

Then, "*Inarcha la schiena.* I want to look at your sweet arse as you fuck me with your mouth."

*Arch your back.*

And, "One day, I'm going to keep you beneath my desk while I work. We'll make a game of it. If you make me cum before I finish my task, you win, but if I have you begging for me to bend you over the desk and finish in your needy cunt, I win."

"What does the winner get?" I panted before taking him straight to the back of my throat again, setting a rhythm that made me breathless and Dante quake.

*"Cazzo,"* he growled loudly, his head banging against the door, his thighs trembling under my braced hands as I thrust my head over and back on his length. "The winner gets to come again."

"Mmm," I hummed around him.

One hand found his balls, and I rolled them across my palm.

*"Sto per venire,"* he ground out.

*I'm going to come.*

*"Bene,"* I told him as I pulled off his shaft, spit trailing from my lips to his head. I licked it up with a little smile as I looked up at him. His face was ravaged with lust, jaw muscles jumping, lips pressed into one tight line like a bulging zipper. "I want you to come for me. I want all that cum I saw that day in your office in my mouth. Sweet and salty," I told him, repeating and twisting his words from the day before, "like the sea."

*"Guardami,"* he ordered through his teeth.

*Look at me.*

I did.

I watched him as his hands came off the wall and twined in my hair, holding it back so he could see every inch of his cock slide in and out of my lips.

"So beautiful. So mine. So fucking perfect. I want to come in your mouth and on your breasts. Take them out for me," he ordered.

I tugged my silk nightgown beneath my breasts with one hand while the other continued to jack him, aiming his dick at my open mouth.

*"Magnifica,"* he practically purred as his abs contracted into fiercely

defined boxes and his thighs shook so strongly I thought he might fall over. "*Si, Elena,* like that. Hard for me, milk that big cock."

"*Dio mio,*" I breathed, squirming as my clit throbbed hard and wet leaked down my thighs to my ass, dampening the heels of my feet where they supported my weight. "You're so sexy. I love having you like this. Love seeing what I do to you."

"You wreck me," he grunted, hips knifing forward to thrust even harder into my hand. "From the inside out. You fucking wreck me."

"*Vieni per mei,*" I begged.

*Come for me.*

Dante squeezed his eyes shut, head thrown back to the sky, and he *roared* as the first spurt of cum lashed out over my cheek and into my waiting mouth. The salt and musk taste of him exploded on my taste buds. Eagerly, I stuck my tongue out as rope after rope of seed painted my lips and breasts.

He chanted my name as I milked him dry, pumping him with increasingly gentle strokes until he moaned and softly pushed my hand away. Even then, I leaned forward to catch the last drop of spend from his tip.

He leaned against the door, torso heaving with exertion, glistening with sweat in the pale dawn light brightening the whole room with a peachy glow.

"*Magnifico,*" I echoed back at him, suddenly overwhelmed with tenderness.

I leaned forward and wrapped my arms around his hips, my cheek to the pulse thudding hard in his groin. Covered in cum and sweat, my own pussy pulsing with unfulfilled want, I seriously considered staying there forever.

Dante had other plans.

He lifted me by the armpits until I was standing, then spun to push me against the door so quickly I gasped.

"My turn," he whispered darkly before bending his head to lick his own cum from my breasts.

My breath left my body in a *whoosh* as I watched him clean me with his strong tongue, suck off his juices from my hard, pulsing nipples until I squirmed against him. It was outrageously hot to watch him lap up his own seed, hotter than my prudish mind ever could have fathomed.

He pressed one hand into my stomach to pin me to the door as he attacked my tits with more and more aggression, sucking and biting until pain bloomed just enough to heighten the edgy pleasure.

He fell to his knees with a thud, already reaching around to cup my ass, arms supporting my thighs. When he lifted me, my hands shot into his hair to brace as he held me suspended between the door and his mouth on my sex.

"Holy fuck," I shouted as his lips wrapped around my clit, and he *sucked*.

He ate at me ruthlessly, like a starved animal having his first meal in months. There was no gentle gathering of tension at my core, no soft ascension. I'd already been so close to climax just sucking him off that the moment he displayed his strength by lifting me against his lips, I was already this close to coming.

"I have to come, Dante, *please*," I begged on a sob as I clutched his hair so hard it must have hurt, holding him so tightly to my pussy he could have suffocated.

His response was a growl I felt vibrate through to the root of my clit and up into my womb.

That was all it took.

The stars wheeling in my vision exploded into a single supernova. Every muscle in my body stiffened, contracting around the burst of energy at my core and then released. Vaguely, I was aware I let out a scream as he ate my cum up, licking and biting at my lips, not slowing or gentling, just driving me so high I thought for one blinding moment, I might actually die.

Only when I went absolutely boneless in his hands, eyes closed, head tipped up like I was drowning and gasping for breath, did Dante finally soften his ministrations. I hummed and squirmed and gasped as he tenderly licked up my swollen folds, cleaning me and soothing my ragged nerves.

When he was done, he shocked me by standing up completely with my thighs still draped over his shoulders.

"Dante," I gasped on a little laugh as I clung to his hair while he walked us to the bed blindly, only familiarity with the room guiding him.

He dropped me onto the mattress with aplomb and watched as I bounced once, then twice before settling. I let my legs fall wide and extended my arms to him, needing his heavy weight on top of me to ground me after that intense experience.

His eyes were all black, brows lowered with lingering intensity as he crawled onto the bed and caged me with his body, rolling us both so we lay side by side, our limbs naturally tangling together like the roots of a single tree.

His hand brushed through the damp hair over my ear as we stared at each other quietly for a long time. It was peaceful. That nasty voice in my head was still beaten into submission by the intimacy between us, and I relished in it. I focused on the way our damp skin connected, on the mingling of our distinctive scents into one glorious fragrance I wanted to wear every day for the rest of my life.

My fingers tangled in the silver chain of his necklace. I looked down, gently pulling the large, ornate cross up into the small space between us. It was solid silver, heavier than I would have expected, and beautifully detailed with a prone Jesus Christ nailed to its surface.

"It was my mother's," Dante offered in a quiet voice, his eyes distant even though he continued to stroke my hair. "Before that, it was her father's, and before that, his father's, and so on and so forth. There was a chapel at Pearl Hall, where I grew up, and she always spent a lot of time in there holding this cross as she kneeled on the altar. I asked her once why she did that when I knew she didn't believe in God. Do you know what she said?"

I shook my head, mesmerized by his speech. It hit me that I didn't know much about Dante's life as Edward Davenport, and I was hungry for information.

"She said she wasn't praying while she sat there in the chapel. She was thinking about her ancestors, all the lives they'd lived and the mistakes they'd made, how it led to that very moment, to her alive and sitting there. She said thinking about life like that made her feel at peace. That no matter where she went, she had them with her, inside her. That no matter where she was going, the decisions she had made meant that Alexander and I were alive and our children would be one day too. She said it reminded her that we don't just live for ourselves. That mostly, we live for our families. I think she found peace in that, even when her own life was horrible."

"That's devastatingly beautiful," I admitted, chest aching.

"It haunts me sometimes," he admitted with a grimace that might have been a grin. "But I wear this for her always and know she's with me."

"She would be proud of you," I stated so strongly it was almost a yell in the close, intimate air between us.

I'd never known her, but I felt sure of my statement. How could a mother not see the man Dante was and rejoice?

He chuckled, the sound wafting over my lips. I stuck my tongue out slightly to taste it and found it sweet. "You remind me of her, sometimes."

"Oh?" I asked, on the precipice of what felt like the best compliment I'd ever received.

"She was a complicated woman, too. She felt everything so deeply that sometimes she didn't know how to deal with it, so she blocked it out completely. It took me a long time to realize that she didn't tell Alexander and me about the abuse and neglect and then about Noel murdering his mistresses because she didn't know how to deal with it herself."

A haunted look came into his dark eyes, a ghost walking an empty house at night. "The truth is, Noel dragged her into his Hell, and she was too soft for that world. It killed her long before Noel did."

"You couldn't have known. You were just a young man."

His lips compressed. "Alexander and I were never just young men. We were raised in the image of our father from the time we could cogitate. He *trained* us. We learned fencing and chess, read *The Art of War* and Marquis de Sade books as boys, attended Eton then Oxbridge with only the best tutors. We were smart and taught to be smarter. We should have known what was going on in our own home."

"Eventually, you found out. Even if both your parents didn't want you to. Your mama was probably trying to protect you, Dante. Lord knows, Caprice has made so many mistakes because of exactly that," I admitted.

His eyes sharpened, peeling back my skin with scalpel-like precision. "What mistakes has she made with you?"

My heart stopped up in my chest, a panicked response that made my skin prickle with knife points of anxiety. "Nothing too bad."

"Tell me."

"No."

"Elena," he growled, constricting around me like a boa making a meal of me. "Tell me. I want to know what you've been through."

"It's nothing really," I said, but the lie scalded my tongue.

I didn't want him to know about Christopher, about the years I'd spent stupidly allowing myself to be groomed and used by him. How he'd turned on me when Giselle was taken from him. How he'd taught me how to hate myself and hate my own sister.

Dante opened his mouth to pry further, but I was exhausted from traveling, from the outrageous events of our lives over the past week. I just wanted the peace only he could afford me and a deep sleep safe in his arms.

"Not now, capo," I murmured, snuggling in close so I didn't see the way his eyes warmed. "I'm tired."

"*Va bene, cuore mia,*" he murmured, kissing my hair and holding me close. "Sleep well, and I'll watch over you."

"I know," I muttered, already half-asleep. "You're the only person who's ever made me feel safe."

And then I fell asleep, not knowing that Dante lay awake for hours holding me with his nose pressed into my hair.

# CHAPTER NINE
# DANTE

I left Elena sleeping in after our late-night interrogation, her long, pale body stretched out diagonally across the bed the moment I left it, seeking my warmth. I watched her bury her face in my pillow, hugging it like it was my torso, and felt a heat balloon in my gut.

Tore was on the red flagstone patio at the back of the villa, drinking a small espresso and reading *Corriere della Sera*. He didn't look up when I walked to his side and plucked a ripe plum from a bowl in the middle of the old, scarred wood table. There was a tiny EDD carved into the soft top that I'd put there as a boy on one of our first visits to *Zio* Tore's home. I traced it with my thumb, wondering at how far I'd come since then.

"You'll do anything to keep her." Tore started the conversation the way he had a habit of doing, starting in the middle as if picking up the thread from a talk we'd already been having. "Even though the smart thing would be to marry Mirabella Ianni."

"Is that the smart thing?" I questioned before taking a bite of the fruit, juice seeping down my chin. "A girl whose reputedly not a virgin anymore, with few important ties and little else to commend her."

"Abruzzi wants it. He's *capo dei capi* here now, *figlio,* whether we like it or not. He could help with the di Carlo situation in New York. You know support from the motherland means everything, even to those arrogant Americans."

"Maybe," I conceded, sitting across from him as Martina, Tore's ancient housekeeper, appeared with an espresso and a fresh, homemade *sfogliatella*. I thanked her before turning my attention back to Tore. "But there's more to this Mira situation than we've been told. Rocco used to love his niece, and now, he speaks of her as if she's an abomination."

"You know they prize virginity here."

I hummed, but something about it still rankled me. "You know I'll do what it takes to keep our family safe."

"And Elena?"

"Always." Anger reignited in my gut as I thought of Umberto endangering her last night. "She will always come first."

"Her safety or her happiness?"

And wasn't that the question.

"I'll do whatever it takes to ensure both," I admitted. "Even if it means sacrificing my own safety and happiness. No one has ever put my woman first, and I am not going to make that mistake."

"So, you won't marry Mira."

I downed my espresso, the bitter liquid heating my gut where a cold, hard kernel of dread sat. "I didn't say that. Marrying Mira might be the only way to keep the New York crew safe from the di Carlos.

You overheard the plan we made with Umberto Arno last night."

*"Non tutte le ciambelle riescono col buco."*

*Not all donuts come out with a hole in the middle.*

An old Italian phrase meaning not everything works out as planned.

I shrugged a shoulder. "Maybe, but I'll find a way to make it work. I just need time. While I take it, I fully intend to make Elena fall in love with her country again."

"And more in love with you so she won't leave when she realizes there is never any end to our troubles?" Tore sighed, rubbing a hand over his tired mouth. "I shouldn't be surprised you've ended up with a Lombardi woman. You're very much like me after all."

"Hopefully, we will have the happily-ever-after you didn't get with yours," I said softly, watching the pain move through his craggy face. It was still as bright and fresh as I imagined it had been decades ago when Caprice broke his heart.

"I love her still," Tore said with a forced faux-casual shrug. "It's not the end. Maybe one day, she'll realize how much better life would be together. I don't hold my breath. Caprice has always been stubborn."

I laughed. "She gave that to her daughters."

"You won't tell her," Tore questioned, almost sheepishly. "About Cosima and Sebastian being mine. Caprice wouldn't want her to know, or she would have told Elena herself."

"I don't like keeping secrets from her. To be frank, Tore, Elena's been made to feel like an outsider in her own family for too long. Secrets are only part of the reason for that, and I don't want to play into it. I respect you, so I won't say what isn't mine to tell. But I warn you, there's a time limit on this."

"Fair enough," he agreed. "I'll give Caprice a call."

"Will she answer?"

He sighed. "Maybe. She has been a little more receptive since Cosima has proven to be so happy with Alexander, but I'm a long way from being out of the doghouse. I don't think she'll ever be willing to forgive me for the part I played in Cosima being sold, even if I did it to save the entire family. Speaking of, Cosima and Alexander are on their way. She called when she read the news." Tore tossed the folded copy of *The New York Times* across the tabletop at me. "She wants explanations."

*The Mafia Lord flees New York*, the headline on the front page read above a photo of me on the steps of the courthouse. In the background of the grainy black and white photo, Elena stood with Yara, her poise regal, gaze tipped down her nose to stare witheringly at the reporters who'd been shouting questions at us. I touched my finger to the flimsy newsprint over her face and felt a pang in my chest, knowing I'd willingly ripped her away from her entire career.

"There's no going back for her," I muttered, rubbing at my chest where the ache emanated.

"Do you regret it?"

"No. I almost wish I did. But I'm too selfish. She was meant to be mine, Tore. I'm just sorry she had to give up everything she worked so hard for in order to be with me. It seems like a poor trade."

"She's a smart girl, so I'm sure she would disagree with that," Tore said, staring at me solemnly over his raised espresso. "There's no mention of her in the article. Yara is covering for her at work, saying she has extended medical leave. The public won't connect the dots, but the di Carlos might. They know you're gone now, Dante, they'll make moves to take over what's ours, and they'll do it by hurting our people."

"Jaco and Chen will hold down the fort. We have good capos in charge of good crews. I have faith in them. And when we give the go-ahead, Caelian Accardi and Santo Belcante are ready to move on the di Carlos."

"Faith in *soldati* is important, but you must not forget that while the cats are away, the mice will play," he reminded me.

"We still have a mole to worry about, too." I'd thought about who could be betraying our outfit almost every day since Mason Matlock confessed to it. "Jaco was acting strangely before I left."

"You mentioned, but Jacopo is your cousin. The first friend you made in America. My heart wants to discount him entirely, but I'm old enough to know the heart is a magnificent idiot," he said with a wry, self-deprecating grin.

"My heart led me to you. To Cosima. It led me back to my brother and our kinship, to Addie, Chen, Frankie, Marco, and Jaco. To *lottatrice mia*. I don't doubt my heart, Tore. I only doubt my ability to keep those in it safe."

We were stretched too thin. Most of my crew in New York City was at risk now that Tore and I were gone. With the head of the hydra chopped off, enemies were left thinking they could take down the whole beast before another head could grow back.

Rocco had proven yesterday with his less than warm welcome that we weren't in friendly territory in Napoli anymore.

It was easy to become overwhelmed in a life like mine. There was rarely peace, rarely an end to the drama and intrigue that made life in the fast lane so dangerous.

I fucking loved it.

But it meant being vigilant at every moment, sacrificing your pawns for the safety of the queen and her king.

And I was only too ready to start my maneuvering on the Italian board.

"First things first," I murmured as I ate the last of my sweet pastry. "We have enemies on this side of the Atlantic to take care of."

When I got up, Tore frowned. "Where are you going?"

"To Rocco," I admitted, doing up my suit jacket. "We have a wedding to plan."

One of the most profitable industries in Italy was counterfeit fashion. Billions of euros in merchandise passed through the Bay of Naples from Europe and China every year, and the Camorra knew how to press that advantage. We had cheap labor houses that employed impoverished Italians, often those with disabilities or criminal records who couldn't otherwise get jobs, to produce trendy counterfeit purses and scarves, replicas of outfits from red carpets and royal photo shoots. Leonardo Esposito was the capo in charge of the operation, but Rocco could be found in one of the largest warehouses by the water every

Monday, walking the lines of workers, shouting over the clap of sewing machines to be heard by his underlings as he surveyed their wares. When Tore was capo dei capi, he had employed an old man by the singular name of *Bello* to oversee production because he'd once been one of the top designers at Italy's most prestigious fashion house, but when Rocco took over, he retired to Malta.

Now, rumor had it, the pieces weren't going for as high a price tag. Some reputable fashion connections that bought the Camorra's work for cheap under the table then claimed it for their own had stopped putting in orders.

So, Rocco was there every Monday, breathing down everyone's necks.

There were guards at the chain-link fence cordoning off the property and more at the entrance to the nondescript building, but they didn't try to stop me from entering.

It seemed Umberto Arno had misled me about my reputation.

It still preceded me into every place I went in Napoli.

I lingered on the floor near the edges of the room, saying hello to some of the workers I remembered from years ago, their gnarled hands still flying over the garments, their eyes permanently squinted from the harsh light. They were happy to speak about how much they liked Leonardo, the same capo who had seemed uncomfortable around Rocco at the table the other day. When I brought up Abruzzi, they were closed-mouth and shifty-eyed.

That said more than words ever could.

There were fractures in the outfit, and I was only to ready to exploit them.

When I was done with my surveillance, I climbed the metal stairs to the second level that wrapped around the walls and left the middle section open to the first floor. Rocco, Leonardo, and a few other men were in a glass room at the back of the building. Even from a distance, I could see Rocco was riled up, hands jerking wildly through the air like dive-bombing birds.

"...pathetic excuse for a capo if you can't get your shit in order," he was shouting as I approached the door and then quietly pushed it open to lean insolently against the frame.

It was a pose I enjoyed because it was inherently condescending.

And it had the desired effect when one of his soldiers cleared his throat, and Rocco trailed off before spinning around to face me, a gun pulled seamlessly from his waistband and aimed at my head.

"You have a bad habit of pointing a gun at me, Don Abruzzi," I drawled.

His lips puckered like an irritated anus. "You have a bad habit of showing up where you don't belong, Salvatore."

I shrugged. "I came to offer something of a white flag, but if you'd rather I leave..."

He scowled then spoke rapid-fire Neapolitan to his crew, ordering them out of the room. Leonardo left with them, but he tipped his chin to me respectfully as he left, another sign he would be a willing ally.

I ignored him because Rocco's beady black eyes were trained unerringly on my face. He rounded Leonardo's desk and took a seat, kicking his feet up on the desk, leaning back to fold his hands on the hard swell of his belly. "Thought you were going to be a dumbass about this, kid. Glad to see you've seen reason. I'm assuming you're here to tell me you'll take Mirabella Ianni off my hands?"

"Maybe." I moved farther into the room, but I didn't take the seat Rocco expected me to across from him. Instead, I loomed over the desk, my body casting a shadow over him in the artificial yellow lights. "I want to know how she went from a diamond in your crown to a lump of coal you can't pawn off quick enough."

His lips compressed, thick and wet because he licked them compulsively. "It's none of your business."

I considered him, cracking my knuckles just to watch his gaze drop and widen at the sight of my big, scarred hands. "Then it will be none of your business what exactly I plan to do to the di Carlos after you give me your support to end them in New York."

We stared at each other like two lions about to battle over territory. I was younger, faster, stronger, but Rocco had an entire militia of Made Men at his disposal in this warehouse alone. If he wanted me dead, it would be done.

I blinked lazily at him and watched irritation flare over his features. It annoyed him to no end that I didn't fear him. Fear was the only tool in his arsenal.

"*Va bene*," he said finally. "But I want you married quickly."

"Whatever pleases you," I demurred.

Suspicion tightened his florid, fleshy face. "I won't have any funny business, Dante. You screw this up, you're done. In the eyes of the Camorra and in *my* eyes."

The veiled threat was threadbare, but I nodded anyway. "I wouldn't dream of it. Now, let's talk numbers."

# CHAPTER TEN
## DANTE

I'd just returned to Villa Rosa, the Lambo purring gently to a stop near the fountain, when Frankie burst from the front door with an expression like thunder.

Instantly, my heart dropped into my stomach.

"*Che cos'è?*" I demanded as I got out of the car and met Frankie in the middle of the drive. There was sweat beaded on his forehead that had nothing to do with the balmy December heat.

His mouth barely moved as he spoke. "They got to Marco."

A chill blew through me straight to the bone. "How bad?"

I didn't want to know.

Not really.

Marco.

He was the sunniest motherfucker I'd ever known, filled with energy and joy even though he was married to a woman with vinegar in her veins instead of blood.

I'd met him two weeks after moving to the city when Jacopo and his father were touring Tore and me around their operation. Marco had been a low-level *soldati* in charge of their chain of pizzerias. When we went into the kitchen of the restaurant in Queens, he'd been at the massive vat of red sauce with the chef, his arm around him, singing "*O sole mio*" at the top of his lungs.

I'd liked him instantly.

But it wasn't until the following year at a meeting with the local chapter of The Fallen biker gang that Marco proved his worth. We'd been ambushed by the Ventura drug cartel, the same one that killed Jacopo's father. The only reason Tore hadn't died was because Marco had thrown himself on top of his capo and taken two hits in the back for his trouble.

And that was it.

Marco became a member of my crew.

Frankie sucked a breath in through his teeth. "It isn't good. They got him outside of Santa Lucia's Pizzeria in Queens." The same place we'd first met. "Two bullets to the chest and two to the gut. He's in the emergency room about to go into surgery."

"*Cazzo,*" I cursed, wanting to wring someone's neck, my hands opening and closing fruitlessly. "Who is with him?"

Frankie winced. "It gets worse."

I stopped breathing.

"Bambi was with him. It seems they were kinda seeing each other on the side," he admitted, knowing I'd fucking hate that because Marco was goddamn married, and that should be taken seriously, but also because I abhorred secrets within my crew. "She was there when it happened, but she wasn't hurt. She was in emergency with him until his wife arrived and caused a scene."

"*Merda.*" I ran both hands through my hair. "They're gunning for us harder than I thought they would. We've been gone one fucking day, and they're already throwing down."

"*Si.*"

"Have Jaco pick up Bambi and take her and Aurora to his house. They should stay with him until we get back Stateside or take down the fucking di Carlos."

"How are we going to do that with half the crew including our capo in Italy? You're a wanted fugitive, D. The second we go back, they'll arrest you for bail jumping and then drag the trial out for years to keep you in jail."

"You think I don't get that?" I said between my gritted teeth. "I'll think of something."

"You always think you can get out of any tight spot," he argued, reminding me of Alexander. "Sometimes, there are consequences we gotta face, D."

"Watching my guys get picked off by the di Carlos isn't one of them. I'm not some uneducated thug, Frankie. You forget I've got a brain, and I know how to use it."

"I'm just saying, you can be smart as hell and still make mistakes, still get busted. *Cazzo,* Dante, you didn't even fucking kill Giuseppe di Carlo, and they're trying to take you down for it. I'm just saying, we got a shit ton of fires to put out here. Some things might get burned."

"I won't allow that," I reiterated in a voice that felt like stone, the words hard and painful in my throat before I said them. “This shit isn’t just my business, Frank. It’s family.”

Finally, his face softened, and he sagged a little. When he reached forward to clasp my shoulder, I did the same to him. We stood there like that for a long moment just taking in air, sending out prayers for our brother Marco.

“Your woman is on the patio being all domestic preparing dinner with Tore,” he finally muttered. “The old man’s laughing with her. It’s a scene I never thought I’d witness. She doesn’t know about Marco yet.”

“Some good today, then,” I allowed as we broke apart and moved in tandem toward the house. “I’ll add it to my win with Rocco.”

“He agreed to back our plans for the city?”

“If I marry Mirabella Ianni.”

“Huh.”

“Yeah.”

“Another fire,” he pointed out gently.

“Not afraid to get burned, Frankie,” I reminded him casually as we made our way into the kitchen at the back of the villa and out the massive glass doors.

The sight of them hit me like a wave, taking my thoughts out from under me.

Elena sat at the round wood table in the seat I usually took facing the citrus grove. She hadn’t curled her hair, the strands loose and wavy beneath a green, white, and red scarf she was using to hold back the mass of it as she bent to cut rounds out of a zucchini. The strap of her white linen dress had slipped off one shoulder, the skin browning in the

Napoli sun. She hadn't noticed me yet, fixed on her task, but her mouth held wide by a genuine grin as Tore told her a story I recognized about my time spent in the villa as a boy.

He was leaned back in his chair with a glass of red wine held in one hand, the other telling his tale in tandem with his voice as it moved through the air in that quintessential Italian manner. His face was creased with the depth of his smile, his aura utterly relaxed.

I couldn't breathe for the beauty of the scene. My two favorite humans, the only two who loved me enough to fight for me, smiling together at the dining table, the rolling green mountains at their back, the soft strains of Andrea Bocelli playing in the background.

This was what I'd wanted since my mother died.

Exactly this.

A family.

A home.

Sensing me, both of them stopped almost simultaneously and swiveled their heads to look at me. My throat closed up as twin smiles broke open their faces.

"Dante," Elena sung happily, more carefree than I'd ever seen her. She opened her arms for me instantly.

*"Figlio,"* Tore greeted in that low rumble, tipping his chin at me.

"I'll do anything to protect this," I swore in a muted whisper to Frankie beside me before I strode across the red flagstones to Elena's side.

When I bent to her, she offered her mouth without hesitation, my conservative girl blooming so fucking beautifully after only a few days of my love and validation.

My heart pounded slow and hard in my chest, each pulse heavy with awe and fear. I'd never had so much to lose and never been so unwilling to lose any of it.

"I missed you this morning," she whispered in my ear after accepting my kiss. The words made her blush, but she powered through. "I ached for you."

I kissed the top of her head and then coaxed her to get out of her chair so I could take her place then bring her down onto my lap. She allowed me to maneuver her and settled naturally in my lap. Something on the table caught my eye, fresh cuts in the wood beside the muted tone of my carved initials '*EDD*.' I leaned forward, taking her with me, to peer at the table and then swallowed thickly at what had been newly cut into the wood.

*EDDS + ECL*

Edward Dante Davenport Salvatore had been joined by Elena Caprice Lombardi.

Emotion threatened to strangulate me.

When I looked up, my gaze snared on Tore's golden eyes, his expression suffused with tender happiness. He liked this for me. Elena for me.

My heart burned.

"I hope you don't mind," Elena said, showing me the knife in her hand, her lips curled on one side in a little smile. "I didn't like the look of it alone."

"No," I agreed gruffly. "This is better."

"I have to talk to you," I told her, leaning in to press a kiss to the hickey still purpling a spot on her neck. "Will you go for a walk in the grove with me?"

She frowned slightly, running a hand in the back of my hair in a way that made me want to fucking purr. She didn't realize it because she thought she was cold, but the way she offered me comfort was automatic and beautiful.

"Of course." She stood, dropped the knife, and wiped her hands on a dish towel. "Tore, I'll finish the chopping for the *ziti* when we get back."

*"No ti preoccupare,"* he said, *no worries.*

We shared a look over her shoulder as I stood and took her hand to usher her away from the house. His face smoothed out and turned to stone, his eyes alive with fire.

He knew what had happened to Marco.

He was just the best actor I'd ever known and had unwittingly passed that trait on to his son, Sebastian, who didn't even know that was where he got the talent from.

So many fucking secrets.

"What's happened?" Lena asked me, her eyes sharp on the side of my face as we padded across the sloping lawn to the rows of lemons trees.

Their scent was thick in warm air, sweet and tangy enough to make my mouth water.

"Dante?" she asked, tugging on my hand so that I would look at her.

She was so beautiful there among the yellow fruit, her classically beautiful features made striking by her remarkable red hair and pale gold skin, by the heavy-lidded eyes that made her gaze unbelievably sultry. For a brief irrational moment, I just wanted to lay her down under the *Sfusato Amalfitano* lemons and fuck her into the dirt. I wanted to bury my sorrow and fear in her sweet body and forget about the weight of so many worlds on my shoulders.

"Marco was shot," I told her instead, telling it to her straight as I took her face in my hands. "He's in the hospital, but it doesn't look good."

"No," she breathed, the word an expulsion of air from a popped balloon.

I nodded. "The di Carlos got him outside one of our pizzerias. The same one I first met Marco at years ago. We have a mole in the outfit, and this fucking reeks of his work."

"A mole?" Her eyes were wide, dark, and textured as wet concrete.

"Mason Matlock told me a few months ago, but I haven't been able to discover who it is," I admitted.

"Mason Matlock has been missing for months…He's presumed dead," she said slowly, that keen mind working.

I shrugged. "We didn't kill him. We gave him back to his family when we were done with him."

"…But at that point, he would be more of a liability than he was worth," she surmised. When I didn't say anything, she cursed softly. "This world of yours is savage."

"This world of ours, *lottatrica mia*. I wouldn't love you so much as I do if you weren't capable of withstanding the savagery."

I watched as my words starched her spine and made her eyes flash. It was only the truth, but it reminded me how little praise she'd received in her life.

"Marco will be okay," she declared as if she had some say in the matter.

It made me smile despite myself. "If anyone could conjure that out of the universe by sheer will power, it would be you."

"I hate that we can't be there for them," she murmured, her eyes sheened with wet even though I knew she wouldn't let herself cry.

"Bambi was there. Apparently, she and Marco have been having an affair for a while. She wasn't hurt, but it's a mess with his wife."

Her face spasmed with something like horror.

"What?" I asked, foreboding rolling through me.

"I…" she sucked in a deep breath. "Bambi came to me a few times in New York. She said she was having troubles with a boyfriend who was getting rough with her. She said she worried about her safety and Aurora's. Even when I pressed, she wouldn't tell me who the man was but now…"

"Marco," I breathed out as her words sucker punched me in the gut. "No, there's no way he would hurt a woman. You know him, too."

She bit her red lip. "I know. I honestly never got those vibes from him. But how else are we supposed to connect the dots? If he kept his affair with Bambi secret from you is it so unlikely he would be the kind of man who would beat his partner?"

"Or become a mole," I muttered darkly, bitterness on the back of my tongue as the piece of my heart that had belonged to Marco burned up to ash.

We were quiet for a long moment, standing under the awning of greenery and sugar-sweet lemons with the knife of betrayal running through both our backs.

"We have to get back," Elena said suddenly, clutching at my forearms, nails digging deep. "Marco could have compromised everyone. What if they took him out because they'd gotten enough from him and now they're going for everyone else?"

"They won't just take out every person in the Camorra," I assured her, though my heart had turned to lead, poisoned, a dead weight in my chest cavity. "They'll go for our businesses first and if there is anyone in the way, they'll take those men out. Addie is still recovering, he'll be careful. Chen and Jacopo are smart."

"And Bambi? Aurora? I don't feel comfortable not being there to comfort them," she admitted. "We haven't known each other long, but Bambi trusts me. If I could talk to her, maybe she would tell me something. Maybe Marco told her what was going on."

"I doubt it. If he was the mole, the shit went deep and he would *not* jeopardize himself by confessing to a woman that close to you. There's a chance I'm wrong. *Cazzo*, more than a chance." I raked my hands through my hair then punched a massive lemon off a limb, the fruit bursting at the impact.

Elena calmly picked a piece of rind out of her hair before collecting my heavy fists in her hands. "I don't want to leave you, but should I go back? I could help."

"You've known these people for four months and you'd go back for them." I ran my thumbs over her cheekbones as I shook my head incredulously. "This from a woman who is convinced she is a villain."

"I'm a terrible person. I'm not afraid to admit I've done some terrible things," she said, as if I didn't understand.

But I did.

I understood that anytime someone attempted to offer her comfort or praise, she shied away. She tried to poison it with the alchemy of her self-hate.

Anger crashed into my chest like a sixteen-wheeler. If I knew who or what had caused her to feel that way about herself, I would hunt it down and rip it into pieces with my bare hands before lighting that shit on fire.

"They say beauty is in the eye of the beholder, but so is goodness," I told her, folding her into my arms, her slightness fitted perfectly to my broad chest, her head tucked beneath my chin. "By my definition, there is no one braver or worthier of love and admiration than you."

"Are you trying to make me cry?" she demanded, shoving away from me as if she was irritated.

But I caught the pleased glow in her cheeks, the curl of that poppy red mouth.

"Never," I swore. "And there will never be a time where I want to be parted from you so get the idea of going to New York alone out of your head. You belong by my side."

She glared at me under a raised brow and fisted her hands on her hips. "Because I'm a woman and you're a man?"

"Because you're Elena and I'm Dante," I corrected. "I belong at your side just the same."

"Then tell me the plan," she demanded, even going as far as to stomp her wedged heel into the ground, releasing a burst of tangy citrus into the air. "And don't tell me not to worry my pretty little head about it."

"I would never," I said, fighting back my smile because fuck, she was captivating.

"Make a choice, Dante. I'm not going to hide out of sight or stay one step behind you. I'm your woman? Then I'll always stand beside you. I know you think that's what you want, but that isn't the world you rule in. Are you really prepared to make me a part of your life in every way?"

"Are you ready to be part of it? There is no going back once you're Made, Lena."

"Can women be Made?" Her eyes were wide, not with shock, but with intrigue.

I snorted. "This is the 21st century, there are female capos though not many of them. The Cosa Nostra even have a Donna who rules with an iron fist in Chicago."

"Then Make me, or whatever," she demanded.

"This is a serious commitment, Elena," I said, a growling edge to my words because she didn't seem to understand. "Just being associated with me put you in danger in New York. Gideone di Carlo, a man known as 'The Butcher,' approached you. Thomas Kelly abducted you."

"Please," she waved her hand through the air in that Italian way and I realized we were speaking Italian again, her voice fluid and lilting. Only two days in her homeland and Elena was already forgetting her diastase for her country. "Seamus abducted me. Don't kid yourself and think you are the first man to put me in danger. Seamus was ground zero. I grew up knowing *exactly* what the Camorra does in the shadows. You don't have to shield me from shit, Edward Dante. I'm a big girl. A smart girl. I can make my own decisions and the most important one I've ever made in my life was getting on that damn plane with you. I left everything to be yours! So do it. Make me yours and never let me go."

The edge of desperation in her voice tore through me. I approached her the way I would a startled mustang, gently, hands up and open. "Lena, I won't leave you. Ever. Even if you stay out of my business."

She glared at me with those stormy eyes, shifting and swirling like gray clouds into angry formations. "Prove it."

"I won't have you goad me into ruining your reputation," I barked, finally losing my cool.

There was too much.

Marco, Bambi, the di Carlos.

Rocco, Mirabella Ianni, the entire fucking Camorra.

I lost it.

"Fuck my sterling reputation," she snapped, the flames of my rage catching on her edges and igniting her entire body. "I worked so hard for that, and it got me nowhere. Unhappy and alone. I don't care what anyone thinks anymore. No one but you and the family we love."

"What about the law? You want law enforcement agencies around the world to know you're an associate of one of the most notorious mafiosos in America?" I demanded, plucking a lemon from the tree and fisting it tight in my palm. The fruit exploded, pulp running down my fingers. "There goes your legal career."

"Mafiosos have lawyers," she retorted mulishly, crossing her arms and bracing her feet like a soldier about to do battle.

My fighter.

*Lottatrice mia.*

Even angry, I had to admire her. "If you're at my side, Elena, those bullets people sling at me could end up *in you*. You want to risk your life to be with me, huh?"

"I'm willing to take a life-altering risk for a life-altering reward," she told me steadily, her flames cooling to ice-cold surety. "I don't know what love means to you, but to me, it means loving someone no matter what baggage they come with for as long as they'll let you love them and as hard as you possibly can. The only risk I fear is one where I lose you. You fell in love with a fighter, Dante. Let me *fight* with you."

We stared at each other under the dappled gold light filtering through the lemon tree branches, the breeze whistling through the leaves, the long grass swaying around our ankles. I could hear both our breaths, harsh and fast with passion.

I wanted to throttle that beautiful long neck for thinking she could get out of loving me alive. I wanted to beg God or whoever might be in charge of fate not to take her from me the way They'd taken my mother. I had seen too clearly what happened to her after being caught up in Noel's dark world.

I couldn't fucking bear it if that happened to Elena.

She read my face, eyes tracking every minute expression until finally, she softened, the starch leaking from her mouth on a sigh. She came to me, wrapping her arms around my torso, pressing her cheek to my chest, on top of the cross necklace beneath my shirt, on top of my erratically thudding heart.

"I'm not your mother," she murmured. "I was born in this world. I might not have liked it as a girl, but now I know it was for a reason. It was so when I grew up and met you, I'd be ready to face the reality of life loving a mafia Don. I *know* what to expect, Dante. The assassination attempts in the middle of the night, car chases across Staten Island, kidnappings. I know, and I'm ready. Because between all of the chaos, there's you. And to me, there's nothing better in this world than *you*."

I stared down at her as she held me tight, her face tipped up so her mercurial gray eyes could meet mine. There was so much honesty in her expression. Her heart flayed open and exposed for me.

How many more times would I make her prostrate herself until she proved to me she wanted this?

Wanted *me*.

Not just the Duke's second son with the money and prestige.

Not just the mafia Don with the edgy dangerous sex appeal.

Me.

Edward Dante Davenport Salvatore.

Realizing that felt like a baptism, a spiritual rebirth. I hadn't even known I felt unworthy and afraid of love until I fell for my fearless gladiator. It was only when she seemed impervious to my flaws, uncaring of my dangers, that I realized I'd been expecting her to run away scared at the very least or hating me at the very worst.

She did none of those things.

Shooting her father, carrying the body of a man I'd knocked out cold into a basement then watching me interrogate him with a blowtorch and spoon, Elena hadn't run scared once.

She'd barely even fucking blinked.

It occurred to me that if she was right about being born for me and the life I could give her then maybe I'd been born for her. Only my history could have prepared me to understand how it felt to be unloved by your family, to be ostracized by them and then to do it to yourself because you wondered how you could possibly be good enough if even your family didn't believe in you?

Maybe every bad thing that had happened to us, maybe every single time we'd been made to feel like the villains of our own life story, we had been moving farther along the path to this.

To us.

Two broken and battered people made whole by love.

Not sweet, sugary, happily-ever-after *cazzato*.

No.

This love was all teeth and claws, fight and passion.

Light was easy to love.

This love was dark. It was night as black as my eyes and as stormy as hers. It was seeing the shadows in each other's souls and being drawn into their abyss. It was knowing we would never understand each other, not fully, and it was loving that challenge as much as the mystery.

This was what happened when two villains fell in love.

And it was as beautiful as anything I'd ever known.

"Say yes."

She blinked up at me, her mouth red as a flower I wanted to pluck with my lips.

"*Scusi?*"

"Say yes," I told her, holding her so tightly I could feel the bones beneath her skin. "I'm going to ask you to trust me because I'm going to tell you a nightmare, but then I'm going to hand you a dream."

"Dante..." she murmured, a wary question.

"*Dimmi si,*" I repeated in Italian this time.

"Okay," she said simply, melting into my arms even further so I was almost carrying her, trusting me with her body as well as her mind. "Yes, Dante."

"There is going to be a wedding between Mirabella Ianni and me," I told her slowly, ready for her flinch. She tried to pull away, but I held her close and let her struggle fruitlessly. "Marco's in the hospital fighting for his life. He could be the mole, and even if he isn't, there is someone out there who *is* helping the di Carlos come for our family, Lena. We have to do something. We won't get support from the Italian Camorra without this wedding. It's how things are done in the Old Country. I don't have to tell you that."

"You're marrying Mirabella Ianni," she said coldly, the ice queen back in such force she was almost too cold to touch. "After everything."

"No." The word was a bullet piercing her through the heart. "No, *cuore mia*, I would never marry Mirabella, but there will be a wedding, and I need you to trust me even though it might seem like I'm betraying you."

"Just tell me the plan," she insisted.

"I can't. *Mi dispiace,*" I murmured against her forehead. "I don't exactly know yet how I'm going to pull it off, but I will. I promise you that."

Her heavy sigh feathered against my neck. I felt her lips there when she finally spoke. "I thought about it a little while ago. If there could be love without trust. And I decided there could be. I loved Daniel, but I didn't trust him. I haven't trusted anyone in so long… not even my family." She tipped her head back, her hair cascading over my arms around her back, her eyes as depthless as the sky above us. "But I trust you. So, yes, Dante. Whatever it is, I trust you, and I believe you when you tell me you're going to give me a dream one day. I haven't had one of those in so long, and I'm happy to wait a little longer for it."

I'd never been a lucky man, but standing there with Elena in my arms in the only place that had ever really felt like home even with enemies all around us, I felt like a fucking god.

# CHAPTER ELEVEN

## *elena*

"I'm taking you out."

I was lying in the sun beside Tore's lap pool on a chaise lounge that felt like a cloud. In my haste to catch Dante's plane, I hadn't packed a bathing suit, but when I mentioned that fact to Dante, he'd disappeared for a few hours and returned with armfuls of shopping bags.

"I got bored so the lady picked out some of it," he admitted as I rifled through the Valentino, Versace, Intimissimi, Prada, and Dolce & Gabanna branded bags. "But I got you three swimsuits I *heartily* approve of."

I was wearing one now, a tiny red number that hardly covered my small breasts, let alone my groin and buttocks. Normally, I never would have something like that, but the way Dante's eyes heated like lit coals made me feel like a goddess in it.

I was reminded of that as I opened my eyes, shading them with one hand so I could squint into the descending sunlight at Dante standing near the foot of the lounge chair.

"Oh?" I asked, raising my foot to run my toes along his inner thigh. "I wouldn't mind staying in."

He growled slightly as he caught my foot, lifting it higher to place a kiss on my arch. "As tempting as that is, I realized we haven't been on a proper date yet. I want to take you out. Woo you properly."

"I followed you to Italy," I noted dryly. "I would say you've done a serviceable job of wooing me already."

"No, *lottatrice,*" he murmured as he sat on the edge of the chair near my hip and leaned forward to cage me in with his muscular arms. His breath on my face smelled of lemons and mint. "I am going to take you to the most beautiful place in the south, water you with the finest wine and the best food you've ever tasted, praise you until you feel like *regina mia,* and then I am going to bring you back home and fuck you to within an inch of your sanity, *capisci*?"

I blinked at him, the heat of his words surpassing that of the sun on my skin. "Well, I have a very busy schedule today, but I suppose I can make time for you."

"*Sei cosi bella,*" he said, almost to himself as he traced a single finger from my ankle up to the inside of my groin. "Should I tell you how I plan to fuck you later, or do you like the suspense?"

I shivered. "Surprise me."

His smile was wolfish, teeth glinting in the light. "*Va bene, bella mia.* I have meetings until six thirty, but I will meet you in the foyer at seven o'clock."

"It's a date," I agreed, feeling like some teenager about to go to prom.

We didn't have such a thing at our school in Naples, and if we had, I'd never been the type of girl to attend parties, but I didn't care.

This was so much better.

I prepared myself in the same way, spending hours soaking in a deep tub overlooking the lemon trees to the green hills beyond, shaving every inch of my body before slathering it in lotion, then doing my hair and makeup impeccably.

I wore a dress Dante had bought me because I knew instinctively, he had bought it with this date in mind. The white fabric was nearly sheer, my nipples a dusky promise beneath the plummeting neckline, the stark color offsetting my deepening tan. It was rare for a redhead not to burn, but even though I had Seamus's pale Irish skin, I inherited the capacity to tan from Mama. Despite the risqué neckline, the simple cut of the long dress was elegant and sophisticated.

With my hair tousled in loose curls around my shoulders and breasts, longer than I'd worn it in a year, I felt beautiful.

That little voice in the back of my head reminded me of my flaws, but it was drowned out by how I imagined Dante might react to the sight of me like this. What he might say.

Beautiful, *magnifica*, mine.

He proved me right when I descended the stairs that evening, his face slack as he took me in.

"So this is how Paris must have felt," he muttered, eyes burning as I neared him. "Knowing he would risk his entire kingdom for the love of one woman."

"Do you think he believed it was worth it, even in the end," I countered as I hit the main level and clicked over the tiles to him on my six-inch heels. "Even while Troy burned?"

He collected my hand and raised it to his lips, flipping it to press his kiss to the inside of my palm. "Undoubtedly."

I sucked in a shaky breath because the power he had over me made my knees weak and my belly flutter. "Where are you taking me?"

His grin was so beautiful that it took a moment for the words to sink in. "Sorrento."

*Sorrento.*

I had been there once before.

A very long time ago.

I was sixteen, my heart soaring as I drove beside the man who would soon be my first lover on La Sorrentina drive, one of the most scenic portions of the coast. Christopher looked so exotic in the rented Fiat, his pale skin pinked by the hot sun pouring in from the windows. His otherness had been so sexy to me then. I remember reaching over and poking his flushed flesh to see it go from pink to white and back, imagining how the rest of his body might look when we undressed later that evening.

It wasn't that the memory of our time in Sorrento that weekend was bad because he had treated me poorly. At the time, Christopher was still deeply invested in our relationship. It was bad because it hurt to know how naïve I'd been, how important I'd let him make me feel just because I longed for male attention I'd never get from my father.

Thinking about it made me feel foolish, something I'd spent the rest of my life trying to avoid.

It killed the happy butterflies in my gut, my belly a graveyard of memories.

"Lena," Dante called as he tugged me closer. "You do not like Sorrento?"

I didn't know what to say.

I didn't want to tell Dante about Christopher for all the reasons I told my mama, but also because we were having a kind of honeymoon here despite the circumstances and I didn't want to ruin it with decades old heartbreak.

"No," I assured, running my nails over his freshly shaven jaw. "I can't wait to go there with you."

The Amalfi Coast was the jewel of Italy's natural beauty. The steep cliffs festooned with brightly colored homes like something in a patisserie display window, the long rows of sun-baked lemons giving off a sweet, slightly tacky aroma on the sea scented breeze, and all that greenery bursting with multitudes of vivid blooms in the long spring and summer seasons. There was a quality to the light there that brought artists through the ages to those craggy shores in droves, but people visited for the food too--the sweet-tart tomato sauces smothering pastas and pizzas and eggplants, the green bite of pine nut pesto, and the lemon liquors thick with cream or sour as biting straight into the flesh like an apple. The people wore their sun-leathered, sea-weathered skin with pride, their bodies agile beyond their years from climbing up and down the countless stairs and hills that made up the topography of that pointed peninsula.

It was a beautiful place filled with beautiful, vivacious people.

And I'd hated it since I was sixteen.

It was filled with memories of the stupid teenage girl I'd been, believing myself in love with a man who had never loved me back. He had used me the way one uses a tissue, carrying me around crumpled in his pocket, hidden and dirty, to pull out when there was a deposit to be made into it.

Disgusting.

Filthy.

The entire affair.

I could think of it now, after years of therapy with less self-loathing. I didn't want to throw myself off a cliff at the realization of how stupid I had been when I thought myself so worldly and wise. Now, I just felt sad when I thought of that time. Then, it had been the happiest period of my life. I'd laughed and danced, I dreamed and played piano as if I was possessed, emotions flowing through me to hammer at the keys. Music spilled from our little house in Forcella at all hours of the day when I wasn't with Christopher.

It was why I avoided music so much after we moved away and left him behind.

It wasn't possible to sit in Dante's Lamborghini as we easily navigated the harrowing turns on the cliffside roads of the coast on our way to Sorrento and not remember the relationship that had poisoned me against sex and love, against Giselle, and against myself.

"No one loves you," he said in English, the words staccato compared to the way my own Neapolitan dialect tended to meld each sentence into one long ribbon of sound. "Do you understand me?"

I shook my head, because I didn't really. English was the one subject in school I struggled with despite my best efforts. I didn't understand the strange, pattern-less rules of grammar, and my mouth seemed incapable of biting off the consonants properly.

But that was okay, because Christopher had offered to give me private lessons. My own father was a native English speaker, but he was rarely home and even when he was, he seldom took an interest in his bookish eldest daughter.

Christopher took a keen interest. He knew Seamus from Papa's few years working at the local university, and they'd stayed friends.

I liked him. He was quintessentially foreign in every way, from his round, faded denim blue eyes and pale face inclined to burn in the hot Napoli sun to the way he drank tea instead of our strong Italian coffee. He was exotic. To a preteen girl with a head stuffed full of escapist dreams, he was utterly tantalizing.

And he knew it.

"No one loves you," he repeated again, this time in Italian. His words were as soft and tender as the hand he passed over my head, down the back of my hair. "Not really. No one except me. You know that, don't you, Elena?"

I blinked up at him, remembering how much bigger he seemed than me as a thirteen-year-old girl. The descending sun backlit his hair, burnishing it so that it shone almost as copper-toned as my own. I wanted to touch it, and his words of love gave me the uncharacteristic confidence to do so. He smiled encouragingly as my fingers rubbed a strand of light brown hair.

"*Capisci?*" he asked again. "This is why you are always so alone. This is why I come to play with you."

It was true. I was often alone in our little house on the outskirts of the city. Seamus owed too much money for Mama to stay home all the time, so she worked at a trattoria in town. Even Sebastian had a job at eight years old, helping at the docks, and Cosima had already begun to model locally.

Only Giselle and I didn't work, though I could and did argue that I worked as the housewife my mother should have been, the one Seamus still expected when he eventually turned up back at home.

I cooked, I cleaned, I did the budget and the shopping—sometimes with Mama, but sometimes alone.

Alone.

Yes, I could admit to Christopher that I was often alone.

"I hate the sound of silence," I confessed to him then and watched as my words seemed to turn some mysterious key in the lock of a door he'd previously kept shut up tight.

His expression grew radiant as he pulled me from my chair over to his, up into his lap so he could wrap me in his arms. He smelled papery, the perfume of a learned man whose office was a library. Eager to learn as I was, the scent was almost heady.

"We will make music together to banish the quiet, *si?*" he murmured in my hair as he fondly held me close.

I hummed in response as I wrapped my arms around him, surprised and awed by how whole I'd felt, how long it had been since my own father had hugged me or treated me with any kind of warmth.

My mother loved me, but her love was worn through at the edges with stress and responsibilities. I was her daughter and her co-parent, her dependant whom she utterly depended on. It had been a long time since she had handled me like a child, and a secret part of me, deep in my heart, missed that.

My sister Cosima loved me too. When she was home, she would sit on my lap while I read a book and have me read it to her. She would touch my hair, in awe of its color, and wax poetic about how beautiful I was to her. She did not resent me, as Sebastian did, for being the eldest and, therefore, the most in control. She did not rebel when I demanded she help around the house or finish her homework. She was happy to please me, happy only to love me in whatever way she could even though I could be terse and unhappy.

She was special, my Cosima.

Giselle might have loved me too, but it was hard to tell. She walked through life with her head in the clouds, completely unaware of the way the rest of the family bent themselves out of shape to protect her from harm or anything that might upset her delicate sensibilities.

Once, when Seamus returned home with four Made Men armed to the teeth, their guns brandished in broad daylight so the acrid yellow sun glinted off them like dangerous jewels, Giselle hadn't hidden like I'd asked her to. She was too engrossed in the chalk art she was sketching into the broken concrete path leading up to our doorway.

One of the goons, I still remembered him for the missing front tooth that punctured his leering grin, had noticed her and moved quickly, with too much interest, up the walkway to crouch before her.

I snatched her under the arms and dragged her back into the shadows of the hot, dark house before he could utter a single word. She'd cried out at my rough handling, at the way I'd broken her precious stick of white chalk, but I ignored her protests and shoved her in the cabinet under the sink in the kitchen before the man could follow us inside to find her.

When he rounded the corner into our little kitchen, followed closely by the others, including a wild-eyed Seamus, he'd asked me where she'd gone.

I shrugged.

I shrugged, knowing that Made Men did not take no for an answer, and they did not suffer impudence, especially not from women, especially not one they barely considered Italian because my father wasn't of the blood.

It didn't surprise me when he backhanded me so hard across the face I saw constellations of stars swirling before my eyes. I fell to the ground hard on my hip, agony singing through my bones, my eyes smarting.

Chip-Tooth shoved me down when I tried to rise with the toe of his leather shoe, a cruel chuckle spitting from his thick lips.

They'd left me there, the local crew and my father, bleeding from a split lip on the cracked linoleum.

When I retrieved the twins and Giselle after they'd gone, Giselle cried to Mama about how I'd broken her chalk.

So, yes, I had family, though a small one by any Italian standard, but I did not have much attention.

And silly, twelve-year-old Elena made the life-altering mistake of equating love and attention as one and the same.

So, when Christopher tugged my head with his hand in my hair to land a soft kiss on my mouth as I sat on his lap that fateful late summer afternoon, I was ready to do what I could to please him so that he would never leave me alone again.

"You're quiet," Dante noticed, reaching over to grab my hand, thread our fingers together and place both back on the gearstick. "Are you unhappy Cosima and Alexander are coming to visit?"

"No," I murmured, staring at our twined fingers; Dante's so thick and rough tipped.

Christopher's had been long and pale, the knuckles knobby beneath the skin. I'd thought them elegant when I was younger until they started to do cruel things to my body.

"Elena." Dante hadn't spoken to me in that tone before, sharp, almost alarmed. I looked over at him to find his eyes dark as pits. "What aren't you telling me?"

"Nothing," I assured.

Too quickly, too cheaply.

"Do I need to pull over this car and force you to tell me what's causing that haunted look in your eye?" he demanded.

"No," I responded, almost mulishly, annoyed that he was so perceptive.

"Then tell me, now. And, Lena, if you even think about lying to me or passing whatever it is off as non-trivial, I will not be responsible for my reaction, *capisci?*"

I sighed, but it released none of my tension. I couldn't look at him as I started to speak, my eyes pinned to the blurred scenery, the rose gold coin of the sun descending into the cerulean sea.

"When I was young, I was with a man named Christopher. I guess you could say he was my boyfriend because even when I was thirteen, and everything really started between us, that's what I called him. My boyfriend." I never called anyone that again after him. It was why Daniel had always been my partner, why I now thought of Dante as my man. Boyfriend had been tarnished with so many other things in that man's wake. "He was Seamus's friend from the *Universita degli Studi di Napoli Federico II*. We all grew up with him around the house, and he was kind to us all. He took a special interest in me when I took English tutoring with him. He said he liked my mind and the way I looked, that my red hair reminded him of home."

My sigh fogged up the window, obscuring the beauty beyond it.

Beside me, Dante emanated a dark, pulsating energy as if he was an imploding star about to transform into a black hole.

"We started to date secretly when I was thirteen, but we came out to my parents three years later. I wasn't that young, and it wasn't that unheard of in Naples for a sixteen-year-old to have a relationship with an older man." This was true. It was a staple of our culture, specifically of *la mafia* and its propensity for arranged marriages. "Seamus and Mama were happy for me."

"He raped you," Dante ground out, his voice savaged by fury.

I swallowed back the bile that rose in my throat. "Not at first, not for a long time. He started to take a fancy to Giselle. I think he was a pedophile, really, and I was getting old for him by the time I turned eighteen. He started to see her secretly behind all of our backs. I guess he didn't want me to be suspicious so he told me nasty things about her, how she was less than me, how she was always trying to make me out to be some *troia*. I was surprised when I found them together one day behind the house kissing in the shade of a Cyprus tree."

I could still remember the hot knife of betrayal sliding into my back.

"It didn't occur to me that Giselle wasn't very willing. She was young and guileless. She didn't know how to say no to him. Cosima found out somehow and sent Giselle to Paris to study so she was free of him."

"But not you," Dante concluded.

I shot him a look, noting how white his knuckles were around the wheel, how fast the car took each curving corner.

I didn't tell him to slow down. The air was filled with an anger so hot it felt as if we had already wrecked the car, the frame on fire and filling rapidly with acrid smoke.

"Not me," I agreed, staring down at my hands. "He asked Mama if I could move in with him, and she agreed. He was still the love of my life even though he'd wanted Giselle. I was so desperate for love and attention that I didn't care I was in second place. But he was angry after she left, and he started to take that out on me. He used me for a few months, so hard I had bruises but always where only he could see."

"How did you get away?" His teeth clipped as he snapped the words between them.

"He asked me to bring him a beer one day. Some imported English *merda* he brought with him everywhere. He'd already fucked me once that day and told me he was the only one who would ever love me, who would ever accept me for being the pathetic bitch we both knew I was."

I shrugged, but the words were an echo my mind never forgot.

"I guess something just clicked because I don't even remember what I was thinking. I broke the beer bottle against the edge of the table and held it up to his neck. I told him I was leaving, and if he followed, I'd tell Mama about how he hurt me, and I'd tell the police. He threatened me, but I think he believed I'd come back at some point, that he'd succeeded in brainwashing me."

"You didn't go back."

"No. Two weeks later, Cosima told me she had the money to send Mama and me to America. I avoided him until then, and then we just took off. I didn't see him again for four years."

"Where is he now?" he asked, his voice a silk ribbon, but lethal, a noose and a trap.

"Relax, Dante, he showed up in New York almost two years ago looking for Giselle. I found him assaulting her and beat him up pretty soundly." I couldn't help the smugness in my voice. "That's why I'd been taking self-defense classes for years, just in case my wildest dreams came true and I ever got to face him again. He's in jail now, serving time for aggravated assault and stalking. He won't get out for years."

Silence descended between us.

It felt like I should say more, maybe apologize for keeping it from him, but my pride rebelled against the idea. I didn't owe him every secret of my past, every mark and bruise I'd ever gotten relived just so I could share it with him.

The quiet was so thick it vibrated the space around us.

His breath was too slow, too controlled through his massive chest. The face I loved for his expressiveness, the creases cut into the skin beside his eyes and mouth that showed his thirty-five years beautifully had turned to unmarked stone.

"Dante, it was a long time ago," I whispered into that clogged air. "You don't have to be so angry for me. I'm fine."

"Fine," he spit, eyes darting to me with unrestrained fury. "You're *fine*. Elena, you've been living like a fucking ascetic for years because this *cazzo di Merda* robbed you of whatever joy you might have been able to scrounge up in your childhood. Is it his voice you hear in your head telling you that you'll never be worthy of love? That you won't ever be better than your sister, good enough to warrant true love and actual respect from a man?"

He was shaking, physically trembling with the force of his rage. I didn't know what to do sitting there, watching him come apart at the seams with emotion stronger than I'd ever seen before.

"Jail isn't enough for this *brutto figlio di putanna*," he growled so harshly it must have hurt his throat. "He deserved to be killed slowly, death by a thousand fucking paper cuts. I'll take his eyes and his balls, his fingernails, then his section of the finger, knuckle by knuckle, finger by fucking finger. I'll pour acid in his wounds until he can't scream anymore, and then, because he won't need it ever again, I'll rip out his goddamn motherfucking throat."

"I don't need you to do that," I told him calmly, trying to use the coolness of my voice to offset the heat in his.

I wanted to soothe him, but there was no comforting a cornered beast, and my history had done just that, caging him in bars of iron wrath.

"You do!" he shouted, startling me even though I knew he wouldn't hurt me. "Don't you fucking see, Lena? You do need me to do this for you so that you'll finally understand what this man tried to make you blind to."

I hadn't realized we'd arrived in Sorrento until Dante stopped at a hairpin turn descending from the Sorrentine Peninsula to the ocean at its feet. He gunned the car passed a trio of Vespas and parked in a tiny space before a stone balustrade overlooking the sea.

He got out of the car and stalked around the hood to my door, opening it and tugging me out before I could gather my senses. After practically dragging me to the stone wall, he lifted me up and crowded me, stepping between my legs to take my face in his hands.

His expression was wretched, a battlefield after war, battle torn and weary, filled with a bitter rage.

It made something in my heart sing a strange song.

"You need me to kill this man to prove to you that you are worthy of love. You are worthy of passion. You are worthy of respect. In all my life of hardships, Elena Lombardi, you are the truest thing that has ever been worth fighting for. You deserve the loyalty and love you give to everyone but yourself, and now I know, this *figlio di cane* made you feel like a beggar when you are a motherfucking queen."

Tears clogged my throat and blurred his face. "I don't know if killing him will make that all go away."

"It's a start," he promised, his hands so gentle on my cheeks even though the rest of his body still quaked with bottled-up fury. "All your life, men have hurt you. I didn't understand until now. Seamus, Christopher, Daniel. None of them showed you how goddamn tragically beautiful you are, Elena. But I will. I'll prove it to you every single day until I die, *mi senti?*"

*Do you hear me?*

I did.

His words scalded my ears, scoured down my throat, and burned in my gut like *grappa*. I felt them, saw them, heard them in every way language could be understood.

He grabbed my hand and pressed it hard over his madly beating heart. "This beats for *you*. It bleeds *for you*. I am yours. Your sword, your champion, your lover, and your home. You don't understand this yet, but I will never hurt you, Elena. I only ever hurt for you because fuck me, you've been through too much already. I will only ever hurt those who hurt you because I love you, and I won't let anyone else ever get away with putting pain in your heart without consequences. *Mi senti?*"

*Do you hear me?*

"Yes," I said through the silent tears that ruined my makeup. "I hear you, Dante."

"I love you, Elena," he said, the words like four punches straight to my chest, breaking through the cage of my ribs to directly impact with my tender, eager heart. "*Mi senti?*"

"*Ti sento,*" I promised him, licking the tears from my mouth. "I hear you."

"You believe me?"

A sob wedged in my throat and moved painfully in my mouth where it exploded from my lips and fell between us, wet and ugly. "Yes," I hiccoughed, clutching at his chest with one hand and his hand on my cheek with the other. At that moment, I couldn't fathom him ever letting me go. "I believe you."

He stared at me like some avenging angel, mad with powerful, vengeful rage, but slowly, breath by breath, he softened until he finally sagged against me, forehead to forehead.

"*Cuore mia,* my heart breaks for you," he whispered raggedly before kissing the tears from my cheeks. "I won't let yours break again."

"Okay," I whispered through my strangled throat. "Okay, Dante."

"Thank you for telling me. I know it was hard."

"It wasn't, actually," I confessed. "I feel better than I have in years. I'll have to fire my therapist if we ever get back to New York."

He laughed because he knew I wanted him to. "*Mia bella lottatrice,*" he murmured like a prayer across my lips before he kissed me.

*My beautiful fighter.*

I kissed him like one. Like a fighter and not a victim. Because I felt for the first time like the victim I'd been could be properly buried and grieved for, moved on from. There would always be a gravestone in my soul where what Christopher had taken from me was buried, but it wouldn't define me.

I wouldn't let it, and neither would this beautiful brute of a man holding me like I was his treasure.

"Should we go home?" he asked because he was just that dreamy.

I sighed, nuzzling into his neck because he smelled so good. "No, I feel okay."

He made a noise of disagreement in his throat, so I pulled back to smile at him. "I promise, I do feel okay. I want to replace all those old memories I have with Christopher with something so much better. With you. Fuck the past. Let's focus on the future."

"I love to hear you curse," he said to lighten the mood.

I kissed him lingeringly. "Wine and dine me, capo, and then later, I can't wait for you to fuck me."

"*Che coraggio,*" he murmured against my lips. *What courage.* "Okay, *lottatrice,* let's go."

# CHAPTER TWELVE

## *elena*

We ate on the quay beside the glittering aquamarine ocean. Dante knew the owners of the small restaurant off the beaten path, around a massive cliff face from the major promenade filled with tourists. We started with Aperol Spritzes and moved on to wine to accompany our fresh seafood appetizers and pasta dishes, the meat course swimming in verdant green pesto, and a bitter espresso to finish it all off.

We laughed.

It was strange to think I could laugh after such a confession and that Dante could smile naturally after being so consumed by rage.

But that was the power of this thing between us.

We made each other come alive, in good ways and bad, everything heightened and poignant.

Dante told me happy stories about his childhood at Pearl Hall and promised we would visit the manor together one day so he could show me all his special haunts. I told him about being eight years old and dropping four-year-old Sebastian on his head. He'd had a massive lump for ages afterword, which was why we all affectionately called him *patatino*, little potato.

When a little local string band started to play after the sunset and the string lights were turned on over the stone walkway, Dante asked me to dance.

I stared at his offered hand, remembering how he'd asked me to dance in New York at the San Gennaro party, and wondered at how far we'd come. From enemies to lovers, from rivals to a single unit locked tight with respect and adoration.

I slid my hand into his big palm and let him escort me into the empty space between the tables on the edge of the causeway and the restaurant tucked up against the cliff.

He spun me into his chest, then dipped me back over his arm, smiling down into my face. "How is it that even with enemies at the gate, I feel at peace with you?"

My heart turned over in my chest as he locked our groins tight, his hand dominating the entirety of my lower back as he pressed us together and led me into a series of tango steps. I followed him easily, drawn up in his gravitational pull.

"Because you and I are the same," I said, and I meant it.

Our entire lives had led us to this moment. I caught the glint of Chiara's cross around Dante's neck through the opened throat of his white button-up, and I knew that she'd been right. Even our ancestors' lives had brought us here.

Dancing beside the cool blue ocean on a hot winter's night in a place that had once been the scene of a nightmare turned dance step by dance step into a dream.

"The men are watching you," Dante growled in my ear as he extended his arm, showcasing me at the end of it as I undulated like a flame to the increased tempo of the jazzy music.

When he curled me back into his body, my back to his front, his words were hot on my neck. "They want you."

I tipped my head back on his shoulder, rolling my hips into the bowl of his groin, finding the thickening ridge of his cock with my ass and grinding into it.

"You like them watching you," he continued to murmur in that sensual commentary, matching me movement for movement, our dance swiftly turning from something fun and frivolous into something deeply erotic. "You like them admiring your beauty because you feel safe. You know I'd never let them have you."

"Yes," I panted as he placed his hands on my shoulder, gently escorting me down into a languid squat where I writhed for a moment before slowly moving upright, my body flush against the heat of his.

"I wouldn't let them get close enough to even smell you." His nose was in my hair, dragging in the scent of Chanel Number 5 and the lingering tang of lemons. "They don't deserve that. They're lucky they even get to look at you."

"And the women?" I countered, spinning to face him, my fingers diving into the sweat-dampened hair at his nape as I straddled his thigh and melted into his torso.

*"Non ci sono donne."*

*There are no women.*

People were watching us. I could feel their eyes on my skin like needle points. I wasn't the type for public displays of affection, but then, I hadn't been the type to do a lot of things before Dante.

So, I gave in to the impulse unfurling in my gut and kissed him.

I brought his mouth down to mine with my hands in his hair and took it the way he'd so often taken mine, owning him with my tongue, teeth, and lips. Our chests were pressed so tightly together, our hips still swaying, that I could feel his heartbeat against my own.

His masculine scent was in my nose, all sweat, citrus, brine, and man. I felt drugged by it, by the feel of his massive, powerful hands bracketing my hips, urging me harder against his thigh so the friction found my clit and set my core to throbbing.

"Are you wet for me, Lena?" he said against my damp lips. "If I moved my hand between your thighs, would you soak my fingers?"

A panting groan was my only answer before he kissed me again. I was so lost in the silken slide of his lips against mine that I didn't notice his hand move subtly between our bodies and down my belly, his fingers curling into the fabric of my dress until they palmed my pussy.

"Hot and damp," he concluded, nipping at my lower lip. "It's time to go home."

"Yes," I agreed. "*Andiamo.*"

The car ride was just over an hour, but it felt infinitely longer. Dante ordered me to touch myself for him again while I slouched in the passenger seat, but he didn't let me take off my underwear this time. The friction wasn't enough for my aching pussy, but his grin was cruel when I begged.

He liked to see me on the edge, needy and wanton for him.

When we finally reached *Villa Rosa,* he didn't lead me inside.

Instead, when I got out of the car, he tugged me off balance and scooped me up over his shoulder in a fireman's carry.

"Dante," I protested, hitting him on the back. "Let me go!"

He ignored me, striding around the house to the back yard and straight to the lemon grove. His face was almost severe with desire when he finally put me down at the edge of the trees between the fruit and the hanging laundry.

"I wanted to take you here yesterday. Lay you down and bury myself inside you until everything else faded away," he told me as he studied the hanging clothes, then pulled a white sheet from the line and ripped a long strip from the end of it.

Only the bright moon and the light spilling from the house lined his features in silver and gold, his eyes twin pools of black darker even than the night sky. He wound the fabric around his hands and snapped it taut as he approached me.

"Hands up, *bella mia,*" he ordered sinuously.

I didn't hesitate.

I was still hypnotized by the pulse of lustful music between us, by the rhythm that had been set between our two bodies. I actually ached for him to touch me again.

Dante's smile glinted menacingly in the low light as he crossed my wrists and tied them in a complicated knot to the wooden trellis that supported the trees sloping down the steep mountainside.

Briefly, anxiety flared through me. Christopher had tied me down a few times, and it was almost impossible to forget those memories. But I resolved to replace them with stronger, positive ones just as Dante and I had done in Sorrento.

*"Che coraggio,"* he murmured for the second time that night as he stepped back to study me.

*What courage.*

Warmed through with his praise, already wet and pulsating, I demanded, "Touch me."

"Like this?" he teased, stepping forward to run his hand down the middle of my chest, following the plunging neckline of the designer dress.

*"Di più,"* I ordered, glaring at him.

*Harder.*

He gently tweaked my nipples through the fabric. *"Va bene cosi?"*

*Like this?*

"No," I ground out, arching my back to get closer. "More, Dante."

"You want me to fuck you hard, my Lena?" he asked darkly, twisting my nipples tight between his knuckles until I hissed. "Because after tonight, I need to fuck you until you feel me on every inch of your skin."

"Yes," I agreed. "Do it."

"In Italian," he coaxed, letting go of my breasts.

*"Scopami, per favore." Fuck me, please.*

His grin flashed in the moonlight. A moment later, both hands found the neckline of my dress, fingers curling into the fabric, and he ripped it straight down the middle. I gasped as the fabric capitulated to his strength, tearing cleanly all the way down to the hem until it gaped open on either side of me.

"*Ottimo*," he growled, palming my naked breasts, rolling the nipples against his palms.

*Better.*

It was so much better.

My head fell back between my shoulders as he stepped closer to bend his head, taking one of my hard peaks into his mouth to suck and nip at it with his teeth. The contrast of the pleasure and pain made my breath stutter.

He held one breast to his mouth as he worked it while his other hand went straight to my sex. His growl vibrated through my nipple when his fingers slid into the pool of wet at my center.

"Fucking drenched for me," he groaned.

My shiver had nothing to do with the cool winter night and everything to do with the way he traced every fold and dip in my pussy like a cartographer determined to map out my pleasure.

"You know, we didn't have dessert."

I watched with heavy lids as he plucked a heavy lemon from the tree and pried it open using just his thumbs. The juice ran down his wrist. He raised his arms to lick up the rivulet of sweet liquid and hummed.

"Do you want some too?" he asked innocently, but Dante was entirely indecent and utterly wicked.

I'd never known lemons could be erotic until I nodded breathlessly, and he brought a morsel of the yellow flesh to my mouth. The Italian fruit was so sweet, you could eat the rind, and I closed my eyes as he fed it to me, little piece by little piece.

"Now, me," he stated, squeezing the other half of the lemon between my breasts.

The cool liquid made my flesh pebble as it traveled down my trembling belly to my groin, then trailed down one inner thigh.

Dante hummed as he got to work, his tongue hot and lashing against my flesh as he licked me clean, tweaking my nipples as he worked. When he dropped to his knees in the grass and collected my thighs to put them over his strong shoulders, I let myself go limp, supported entirely by my tied hands and his broad back.

He licked up either side of my thighs, sucking at the skin until not a trace of sweet lemon remained.

"Honey and lemon is the best combination," he murmured almost to himself before nosing the top of my pussy, taking in a deep breath of my scent.

*Dio mio,* it was sexy as hell that he loved the smell of me like that.

A moment later, he parted my swollen folds and dipped his tongue inside me.

My womb coiled tight like a spring instantly.

"Fuck," I shouted coarsely.

Dante moaned in response, the vibration sweet agony on my clit as he took it between his lips and assaulted it with his tongue.

This was sex.

This was pleasure.

This was what I'd been missing my entire life.

I felt no shame as I rode Dante's talented tongue, as I slid one, then two, then three fingers into my sex and pumped them until I writhed and moaned.

I had been naked before. I had fucked before.

But I had never let another person into my body and mine to fuck them both.

Not until Dante.

He was under my skin and in my blood. His scent was the only thing my nose could scent even in a lemon grove. There was no night sky above me, no ground beneath, not even any gravity except the magnetism exerted by the man eating like a glutton between my thighs.

I was nothing but his, and he was nothing but mine.

It was that thought that alchemized my body from solid to gas, my limbs dissolving into smoke that threatened to carry away on the breeze.

I came and came and Dante ate and ate until all I could do was fight to get breath in my lungs.

When he stood, his mouth and chin glistened with me. He didn't wipe it off when he took my lips in a savage kiss, eating at me as he'd eaten at my cunt.

There was no gentleness left in him, only hot need and fierce aggression. He grunted as he lifted my thighs over his forearms and notched his thick shaft at my center. His sweaty forehead was pressed to mine as we both looked down at where our bodies joined.

A second later, he thrust into me to the hilt.

I screamed, but it felt like a goddamn hallelujah.

He fucked me hard, like I was a vessel and not a woman. Like I was built for this, for him to fuck me and use me and fill me up with his cum.

It wasn't debasing or wrong.

It was so hot, it melted my insides and turned my brain to goo.

"*Dai!*" I urged him. "*Di più.*"

*Harder.*

My teeth clanged as he took my ass in his broad hands, pinning me midair so that he could do as I bade.

He fucked me so hard his cock met my cervix with a bite of pain.

But it was pain that bloomed into bone-rattling pleasure.

I grit my teeth to absorb the shock and fisted my hands in the rope that held me up so I could try to fuck back against him.

"*Cazzo, come sei bagnata,*" he growled over the wet slap of his balls against my drenched core.

*Fuck, you're so wet.*

I was. The sloppy sounds and smooth, liquid glide of his hot length inside me were almost too much to bear.

"I'm going to come so hard," I whimpered, a little scared by the looming weight of my climax bearing down on me.

"Come with me," he ordered, taking my mouth for a moment even though we were both breathing too hard to make it last. "Milk my cock with your sweet, tight cunt."

*Dio mio,* I mouthed on a silent scream as he bent his head to bite at the junction of my neck and shoulder while his cock hit a specular angle inside me that set something off like a powder keg in my gut.

I burst apart with pleasure, coming on his driving dick in a rush that soaked his groin and my thighs. He cursed in Italian as he felt me clench almost painfully all around him, as I bucked my hips fruitless both trying to increase the sweet agony and end it before I died.

Moments later, he seated himself at the very end of me and whispered my name like a final prayer before he came. He came so much it leaked out around his thick cock and dripped down my thighs.

It was messy and loud, utterly filthy.

"That was incredible," I croaked into his damp neck as he held me up though I didn't know how he had the strength.

"*Completamente,*" he agreed on a hoarse whisper.

"Let's do it again," I said, not even sure how much of it was a joke and how much of it was a rabid, reckless wish.

He was my drug. Even after taking a hit, I craved more with an intensity that was next to madness.

His laugh stirred sweat-wet hair. "Do you know how it makes me feel to see you as the ice queen for everyone else and the fiery temptress for me and me alone?"

He pulled back, letting my legs slide to the ground so he could untie my hands. His strong thumbs worked the stiffness out of my joints before he raised each palm to his mouth to place a kiss in the center the way he was making a habit of doing.

"It makes me feel like a king," he confessed.

"A Don," I corrected, gasping as he bent to collect me in his arms to carry me back to the house. It was archaic, but I was grateful because it seemed my bones had melted. "A Don and his Donna."

# CHAPTER THIRTEEN

## *elena*

One week in Italy felt like an entire lifetime.

For the first time since I was fourteen, I didn't have a job to occupy my time, but that didn't mean I was lazy.

To my surprise, Tore ran a business out of his steeply terraced lemon orchard and olive grove. He made boutique olive oil that sold for over one hundred euros a jar and limoncello so bright and creamy, I found myself liking the liquor for the first time in my life. He took me with him to tour the processing house where the olives were pressed, and I helped a group of workers pick Meyer lemons one day, collecting them in old-school huge wicker baskets the women propped on their hips like babies and the men on their hatted heads.

Dante was in and out of the house planning his wedding with Mirabella and taking meetings with Rocco to plan a two-pronged assault on the Cosa Nostra, in America and in Italy. I tried not to think about what would happen if we didn't come up with a plan to pull off the wedding without Dante having to marry her. Mama's words echoed in my ears. If anyone could fix this problem, it was Dante or me.

News from New York was grim. Marco had survived his first week post-surgery, but a number of complications could still arise, and he was still in a medically induced coma. The di Carlos had ambushed another deal with the Basante cartel and set fire to a construction site owned by one of Dante's shell corporations that set them back millions of dollars. I'd FaceTimed with Aurora and Bambi once, but even the little girl seemed tensed and frightened. They didn't say anything about Marco, and when I asked about Bambi's boyfriend still scaring her, she clammed up. I was desperate to get back to the city, but I hadn't figured out yet how to do so without Dante going to jail.

Despite everything, Dante still found time for me, taking me on dates escorted by Frankie in case anyone saw us out together and reported to Rocco. We went to Rome and Ravello, spent a late afternoon in Positano getting drunk on *Aglianico* red wine until Frankie finally told me the whole sordid story of his romance with his wife, Lilianna.

I continued to spar in the mornings with Dante and Frankie, but many of the men joined us too, including Tore. It was amusing at first, to watch my six foot five, packed with muscle lover circle the older man who was still high muscled, but lean and corded next to Dante's bulk. The moment they first made contact, I lost my smile.

They attacked each other like two beasts locked in a cage. Their swinging fists weren't tempered, hammering through the air to impact with the body on a dull, wince-inducing *thud*. They kicked and ducked, punched in a variety of combinations that was entirely too quick to track. Dante was better, but youth gave him his edge where Tore was all experience. He knew when to duck and bend and when to attack relentlessly.

By the time they were done, the mats were slick with sweat, large crystal beads of it rolling down both men's glistening bodies.

They trained like Spartans, like they were headed off to battle the very next day to fight for their lives.

When I told Dante this after the first time I watched them, both of us under the cool stream of the shower in our room, he'd laughed even as he said, "We don't fight often, but when we do, Lena, that's what it is. A fight for our lives."

His words should have chilled me more than the cold shower, but they had a different effect, one I was beginning to understand was my natural reaction to danger.

My whole life, I'd been risk adverse, careful to the point of drudgery.

Now, my bubble was cracked open, and everything was spilling inside, violence and chaos, the threat of death that only proved to heighten every other aspect of life.

I was coming to know myself, and something about that was frightening.

Like meeting the monster you always knew lurked under your bed.

I wasn't all elegance and refined grace.

If I was a shell, there was that pearl of refinement inside me, but it was surrounded by the grit of sand and dirt.

I was baser than I'd ever realized.

Sex was on my brain anytime Dante was in the same vicinity as me. I couldn't look at those densely muscled hands without imagining how his thumb might taste sucked into my mouth. I couldn't sit across from him at the breakfast table without running my toe over the crisp hair of his calf just to have the intense thrill of his skin against my own. I wanted to bite him until bruises blossomed like tattoos of my ownership. I wanted to fuck him until all that power in those muscles and bones melted away, and he was lax and vulnerable with spent ecstasy.

There was violence in me too. Maybe I'd always known that. I'd taken too much delight in beating Christopher when he came for Giselle. I enjoyed the tang of blood in my mouth when Damiano mistimed a punch and hit me on the edge of the chin. The feel of a gun in my hand was becoming natural, an extension of myself that suited the armor I'd honed all these years.

Dante had told me once that one person didn't have to be only one thing.

And I was learning the hard way that I was no saint.

Only Dante's words about being too much of one thing still resonated in my head.

I was done being boring, done trying to fit into this box I'd let society make for me.

With Dante, in Italy of all places, at the house of the capo I'd rued in my childhood, I found myself.

And I was starting to like her.

"Grip it higher." Dante's voice was like smoke, dark and sinuous as he stood behind me and studied my stance. "It will give you better leverage."

I adjusted my right-hand grasp on the butt of the gun and let my left hand find the grooves in the hand already wrapped around the tang, so they felt locked into place on the weapon.

"*Molto bene, lottatrice mia,*" Dante practically purred. "You look like a warrior goddess like this. Maybe you should lose the clothes, hmm?"

"Dante," I said on a laugh. "Don't distract me. I want to hit them all this time."

"I'll make you a wager," he offered in that same sexy tone, definitely trying to distract me. "If you hit all six wine bottles, you can do whatever you want with me." He chuckled when I shivered lightly. "And if you don't…I get to do the same to you."

"Deal," I agreed instantly, my pulse already moving down between my legs.

"You two are sick," Frankie deadpanned, but I knew without looking at him that he was joking, so I didn't take it personally the way I might have before.

"I've overheard you FaceTiming with your wife, Frankie," I pointed out with an arched brow. "Pot meet kettle."

The men laughed, the sound of it calming me even further. Their friendship was what preoccupied me and kept me from thinking about Dante's upcoming wedding to Mirabella or the war raging without us in New York.

I took a deep breath, my hands sweating lightly on the gun because of the high noon sun. Fifteen yards away, Dante and Frankie had set up makeshift targets, a collection of old olive oil, Limoncello, and wine bottles they'd pilfered from Tore's stores. They were staggered across a crumbling stone wall that had once been a sheep enclosure.

There was a light breeze, but nothing to worry about as I focused on the targets. I ran through the instructions Dante had given me the past four days of practice and calmly squeezed the trigger.

There was a loud snapping noise as the bullet discharged and then the crashing tinkle as it impacted with the olive oil bottle on the far right, glass shattering everywhere.

Faintly, I heard Frankie let out a little whoop.

But I had my eye on the prize.

*Snap, crack, tinkle.*

I fired the gun, cocked to reload, and fired again.

Again.

Again.

I only had one bottle left, a squat Limoncello bottle on the far left.

Behind me, the air shifted, and the heat of Dante's body fired the air between us.

"*In boca al lupo,*" he whispered.

*Good luck.*

Or more aptly, *in the mouth of the wolf.*

Only Dante was the wolf who wanted me in his mouth if I failed, and I refused to have that happen.

I sucked in a deep breath, the taste sweet of lemons and the tang of olives on my tongue, and fired.

*Snap, crack, tinkle.*

"*Ammazza*!" I cried out as I discharged the empty casing and clicked the safety, then threw my hands up in the air.

I spun to face Dante, my hips moving side to side in a little victory dance as I began to belt the words to "*O Sole Mio*," a traditional Neapolitan song that locals sang at the slightest provocation on any and all occasions.

Frankie held his belly as he laughed beside me while I started a little victory lap around my man.

It didn't last long.

Dante's long arm hooked around my waist and pulled me into him. I collided with his chest with an *oof,* then was carted up, up into his arms, his hands supporting my bum.

The gun had dropped to the ground so I threaded my fingers in the short sides of Dante's hair and beamed down at him.

"I told you I'd become a sharpshooter," I crowed unabashedly.

"You did." He wasn't smiling exactly, but his eyes danced like a night sky filled with constellations. "I knew you would."

"Because I'm brilliant?" I teased, feeling light as air, so light I could float away if Dante wasn't holding me in his big arms.

"*Si, splendido,*" he agreed solemnly.

I kissed him.

My hands held him still while I bent to take his mouth, the first taste of him making my head reel even more than the victory. He'd been eating freshly made *taralli,* salt and yeast still on his tongue. I tangled it with my own, moaning as his hands flexed on my ass.

"Wow."

The voice was familiar, but I was too mired in everything Dante to recognize it at first.

I angled my head steeply so I could kiss him more deeply.

"I've never in my entire life seen my sister make out with anyone," that same voice, laughing now, mock-whispered close by.

That voice.

Speaking English with that lilt of Italian she'd never rid herself of, a hiccough of British muddling the mix. In a few years, she might even sound exactly like Dante.

I pulled away with a gasp, immediately turning toward the voice.

And there she stood.

My Cosima.

The hot Italian sun burnished her olive-toned skin, still caramel even though she was suffering through a cold British winter, and her long, thick hair hung in inky waves to her waist. She was in one of those beautiful dresses she'd always loved, a floral-patterned thing that hugged her curvy form and let her exposed skin do the talking.

She looked beautiful.

But more, she looked incandescently happy.

The reason for that stood slightly in front and to one side of her, as if we were threats he had to shield from his beloved wife. Alexander Davenport was the scariest man I'd ever known despite his gorgeousness. He had the coiled stillness of a predator always ready to pounce, an alertness to his gaze that never wavered even when he was supposedly relaxed on the couch with Cosima. It was as if he was ready for an attack at any moment, and I had no doubt any enemy of his would suffer and die a quick but horrifically brutal death.

Dante had the same capacity for savagery, but his was buried beneath layers of charm.

Alexander let it be seen in his silver eyes, sharp as weapons. Even though he had a slightly bemused look on his face as he stared at us, he still looked every inch the Duke of Greythorn in his custom St. Aubyn suit.

I could see it now, though, the resemblance that was hard to find between the brothers at first. Dante and Alexander were night and day, light and dark, utterly contrasted in their coloring and then reserved again in their personalities. But they were both massive men, tall and broad-shouldered, though Dante was packed with more muscle. Their features were carved out of marble, strong bones under fine golden skin, and the shape of their eyes when they smiled was similar, I thought, though I couldn't remember Alexander smiling often.

Loving Dante was so new, and my life so utterly different than anything it had ever been before. Quite honestly, I hadn't thought about what my siblings might think about our relationship.

The reality doused me with cold water. I could feel my bones seize up as my thoughts went arctic, how I sat differently in Dante's hold, like he was keeping me captive instead of holding me up. Sensing the change, Dante left me down slowly, inch by inch against his body until I was on my feet but flush against him. He kept me there with a hand anchored over my lower back, his hand reaching all the way around my waist, his fingers curled over the opposite hip.

"This is Napoli. Trespassing could get you killed," Dante said in an oddly mechanical voice, all tone and no subtext. "We have a sharpshooter here that could take your earlobes clean off."

Cosima's eyes danced as she moved closer, rounding Alexander without admonishing him for being stupidly protective. "I am rather attached to my earlobes. Still, I have it on good authority that I'm welcome at *Villa Rosa*."

Dante arched an eyebrow and regarded her coolly. It took me a moment to realize he was channeling his brother, who was affecting the same posture behind Cosima. I laughed a little, then coughed to cover it up.

"What makes you think that?" Dante asked.

"Well, for one, the house happens to be named after my mother," she said with a light laugh, her eyes fixed on Dante so she didn't catch my frown. "And for another, my best friend and sister happen to be here. Obviously…here *together*."

"I'm not asking you for permission if that's what you're insinuating," he countered dryly.

I realized I was holding my breath, that the reason for my tension was the possibility of Cosima's disapproval and censure. I'd had both before, when I hadn't handled Daniel and Giselle's affair as gracefully as I should have, and the memory of her criticism still plagued me.

"I suppose I didn't ask you for permission to date Xan," she agreed easily. "But a phone call announcing the relationship might have been nice. Especially because I had to read in the newspaper that you'd fled the country, D."

We both winced a little. Dante looked down at me then, smiling this little smile that was only for me, more of a secret tucked between his curled lips than an actual expression.

"We've been busy," he admitted, his voice soft, intimate as he looked down at me and pushed a lock of errant red hair behind my ear.

I got caught in those obsidian eyes, drowning in the words he'd written in black ink on black paper so only I could read them as close to him as I was.

He wasn't going to give Cosima a chance to judge us. He was telling her in his own way that we were together. That he loved her, but there was a boundary between them now there hadn't been before, a line drawn in the sand with my name on it.

It was possessive and bullying and bold; all things Dante could be so it didn't surprise me because it wasn't out of character.

But what did surprise me was how much that meant to me.

That he didn't care what his best friend thought because he loved me too much to change his mind now.

That *she* was somehow trespassing on an intimate moment between us instead of me being the third wheel in a relationship that had begun years ago and been through so much.

That he implied *we* were busy, meaning whatever he was doing, I was doing it with him. We were a team, and he was broadcasting that so loudly to Alexander and Cosima it seemed blared from a loudspeaker.

"*Io sono con te,*" he said so softly, lips barely moving, that for a second, I wondered if I imagined it.

But no.

*I am with you,* he'd said.

A reminder. An affirmation that even with his brother and best friend, he still wanted me to come first.

Tears burned the backs of my eyes, hot as the blowtorch Dante had used on Umberto Arno. I didn't let them fall, but I couldn't evaporate them either. So I stared at Dante with glazed eyes and swallowed down a sob.

*"Ion sono con te,"* I repeated quietly.

The fingers on my hip gave a squeeze.

When I looked back at Cosima, she seemed a little thunderstruck by our connection, but she wasn't angry. When she caught my gaze, those yellow eyes melted like butter in a hot skillet.

"Lena, my love," she said, extending her hand. "I've missed you so much."

Those tears I'd been fighting so valiantly to keep at bay surged over my lower lids and fell down my cheeks in two scalding trails.

"Cosima," I breathed as I broke from Dante and stepped forward.

Cosima stepped forward too, meeting me halfway, catching me up in her long, thin arms so she could hold me tight. We were the same height, but where I was slender, almost hollow boned, with smaller breasts and hips, Cosima was all length with the bonus of exaggerated curves. It felt good to be held against her softness. It reminded me of Mama and how much I missed her.

"Hi," Cosima whispered in my ear, her nose in my hair smelling deeply. "Missed you so much, *sorella mia.*"

I clutched her tighter in response even though I wasn't normally so physically affectionate. My tears fell into her thick hair, but she didn't mind. She just held me quietly for a few minutes, murmuring into my hair how much she loved me, how happy she was to see me, how proud she was of me.

She didn't know anything about my life since I'd taken the case, at least nothing besides my infertility procedure, but somehow, she knew I'd been through the wringer and needed her endless love to soothe me.

"Seamus is dead," I croaked through my tears, grabbing a handful of her silky hair because it reminded me of braiding it when she was a girl, of tucking her into bed and reading her stories because Mama was working and Seamus was nowhere to be found. It reminded me of a time when I'd comforted her as an older sister should, but it didn't make me ashamed for needing her now.

She was my sister, and I'd never truly let her be in my life enough to support me when I needed help.

"I'm sorry," I cried softly, hysteria bubbling up through the chaos, turning my stomach into a tempest. "I'm sorry I didn't know what Seamus did, what *you* did to save us all."

"Oh Lena." She sighed, looking over her shoulder at Dante. "Why don't you take Xan inside for a cold beer, D?"

He must have nodded because a moment later, I felt a soft caress on the back of my head and then soft footsteps through the grass as Dante led his brother and Frankie back to the house.

Cosima led me over to a bench at the edge of the lemon grove and sat us both down, curving me into her chest under her arm.

"I'm sorry you had to find out," she murmured.

I pulled away to glare at her. "I'm not. I'm only sorry I didn't know."

"What good would it have done?" she countered softly. "It was you who told me a few days before my eighteenth birthday that the happiness of the few is worth more than the happiness of one. I agreed with you. It was my pleasure to sacrifice for my family, Lena. If you had been in my place, you would have done the same."

"I know I'm not as beautiful, but it should have been me."

"Why? Because you're the eldest?" she challenged. "That's so arbitrary. Besides, you sacrificed for all of us our entire youth. You didn't have friends or go off to uni or do anything a girl growing up should have because you were too busy raising us when our parents couldn't. You'd done more than enough."

I held her beautiful face in my hands and realized I hadn't done such a thing since she was a girl and her cheeks were plump with lingering baby fat. My heart panged for those more innocent days even though I couldn't regret that they were behind us.

"Do you know what made me happy back then?" I asked her as I stared into those melted gold eyes. "Knowing that Seb, Giselle, and you were healthy and as happy as I could make you. It made me happy to know that you were getting to school on time, that I could help you with your homework and make dinner so you could study or hang out with friends. I didn't need my own happiness because I could borrow yours. So, it kills me that I failed you and you had to live through what I can only imagine were unspeakable things."

"You know, at first I was surprised by you and Dante," she admitted, cupping my hands on her cheeks. "But it makes such sense to me now that I think about it. You both have the biggest hearts of anyone I know and the courage to do anything to protect your loved ones."

"That's one of the nicest things anyone has ever said to me," I admitted.

"Now, that makes *me* sad," she countered. "I'm not the only one who's been through unspeakable things, Lena. Don't pity me. Just like you, I've come out on the other side much better for the things I survived."

"Alexander was the one who bought you," I confirmed, trying to keep my voice neutral even though the idea of him buying my sister to use as a sex doll made my blood heat to a vicious boil.

"Yes," she said simply, eyes wide and sincere. "He had his reasons. If you need me to explain the whole torrid thing, I can, but I'd rather let sleeping dogs lie. There is no one in this universe for me, but that cruel and beautiful Lord, and no one else for him but me."

"I feel the same way about Dante," I admitted somewhat shyly.

It wasn't in my nature to divulge personal details or express my emotions.

Dante was teaching me how to love again, and one of the most important lessons I was learning was that verbal affirmation was an essential part of loving someone.

"That makes me happier than I can say," Cosima said, beaming. "No one will love you better than he can, and you deserve that. Who would have guessed we would end up with brothers! Our kids will be more like siblings genetically than cousins."

My heart clenched painfully, the hurt reflected in my eyes for Cosi to see.

She winced, grabbing my hands. "I thought you said the procedure worked? Dr. Taylor told you that you'd be able to have kids naturally one day."

"It's still a bit of a long shot. I have one working ovary and scar tissue on my womb from the ectopic pregnancy."

"But it's possible," she pressed.

"Yes, it is."

Her grin was girlish and slightly indecent, a little sister reading something salacious from an American magazine. "I don't think you'll have any problems. The Davenport men are very…virile."

"Cosima!" I admonished through my laughter, but then stilled, eyes widening.

In response, her hand went to the nonexistent swell of her belly. "It's really too early to announce anything, but this is why Alexander didn't let me go to you when you had your surgery. He's over-the-top protective normally, but now…" She trailed off because the force of her smile wouldn't allow her to talk.

"I'm so happy for you." I leaned forward to hug her, stroking her hair, in awe that my baby sister was having a baby.

"I hope it doesn't trigger bad things for you." Another reason she was so lovable—she was always thinking about others, always in tune with their emotional climate.

"I'm only happy," I assured her. "Mama is going to be ecstatic to have two grandbabies to play with."

She didn't laugh. "One day, she'll play with yours too, Lena."

I shrugged, but my heart burned with yearning. "I hope so."

"I know so."

"Are you two finished?" Dante called from the patio behind the villa holding a bottle of wine in each hand. "I've got news."

Cosima looked at me eagerly, but I laughed. "No, we aren't engaged or anything like that. We just started seeing each other."

She cocked a dark brow. "Dante might call himself Salvatore now, but he's still a Davenport. When they see something they want, they don't only take it, they make it theirs irrevocably in every way they know how."

That sounded like Dante.

My sister got up, waiting for me when I hesitated.

But something had caught in my mind, jostling loose a collection of fragments I'd been collecting since my time in Italy.

"Why did you say *Villa Rosa* was named after Mama?" I asked slowly because the truth was I didn't really need an answer.

Everything was falling into place like a tumbling row of dominos.

Cosima wrung her hands, then caught herself when I stared at the tell.

"I shouldn't have said that." When I only leveled her with a cool stare, she sighed. "You should really ask Salvatore."

"I think I should ask my sister," I said slowly, each word deliberate. "You know, Sebastian came to visit me after my surgery. We had a good talk, and we decided that secret-keeping was corroding this family. I think that stops now, Cosima."

She winced. "You know I can't disobey when you use that voice."

I didn't even blink when she looked at me beseechingly.

"Okay, come on, walk and talk."

I got up, but didn't take the hand she offered me. Old wounds, scars of betrayal, flared up, making my skin hot and cold all over.

I didn't realize I was holding my breath until she started to speak in low, fast, but fluid tones. "Amadeo Salvatore and Mama had an affair decades ago, twenty-three years ago to be exact. Sebastian and I are a result of that."

If she expected me to freak out and throw something like a child with a tantrum, she was sorely mistaken. I only blinked at her behind my icy mask and waited for her to go on.

"It was a brief and passionate affair. Apparently, they wanted to run away together, but one day, Tore's enemies got hold of Mama when she was pregnant with Seb and me. It scared her out of being with him. She stayed with Seamus and never told Tore about the pregnancy. Tore left town and didn't find out about us until years later when he came back to Naples and became *capo dei capi*."

"That's why he interfered with Seamus," I said flatly, everything locked into its rightful place. "You have his eyes, those tiger yellow eyes I've never seen on anyone else. I should have connected the dots sooner."

"It's not exactly something you'd look for."

We had crossed the lawn, but stood at the edge of the stone terrace, speaking in hushed voices while Frankie, Tore, Dante, and Xan set the table for lunch with platters of charcuterie and baskets of fresh bread, red bowls of gazpacho like blood at each setting.

"So, you aren't my sister," I said as I digested the news, my stomach growling then cramping around the weight of the truth.

"I *am*. Of course, I am," she snapped, stepping forward with anger tightening her pretty face. "Do not ever say that to me again."

"I'm not saying it because we have different fathers," I said, watching each word cut into her flesh. "I'm saying it because you've been keeping so many secrets from me, I feel like I don't even know you right now."

"And you?" she countered, fisting her hands on her hips. "I show up in Naples because I've read in the paper my best friend has fled the country, and only when I called Tore did he tell me that *you* were here with him. I may have been keeping secrets longer, Lena, but don't be a hypocrite. You're just as culpable here."

We glared at each other for a long moment. Vaguely, I was aware of Frankie murmuring something about the Lombardi woman stare and shuddering comically.

"You're right," I muttered finally, feeling petulant but knowing I was wrong. My sigh was a long ribbon of sorrow. "Some things are just difficult to tell."

"Yes," she agreed, her face softening with surprise.

I didn't blame her for that. Even six months ago, I wouldn't have capitulated so gracefully to any kind of blame. My defensiveness was almost legendary.

"No more." The words were a promise as I extended my hand to her and linked our fingers. "*Insieme sempre.*"

She smiled at the word we'd used in our youth to symbolize our bond as siblings. "*Insieme, Elena mia.* I am sorry for my secrets, though I meant to protect you. I'm even more sorry that you felt you couldn't tell me about Dante. I want to be here for you always, even if I can't be with you in New York. You are important to me and I never want you to doubt that."

We walked to the table, holding hands loosely. The men were already seated, but Alexander and Dante stood to pull out chairs for Cosima and me.

It was only when his scent was in my nose that I realized what I had forgotten.

I froze, then slowly swiveled my head to look up at Dante, whose own face was carefully, uncharacteristically blank.

"You knew about this."

His slow blink was the most eloquent expression.

I pushed back from the table even though he tried to cage me in.

"No," I growled, ducking out from under his arm and backing away from him as I lifted a trembling finger of accusation. "You *knew* this? How could you not tell me?"

"It wasn't exactly my secret," he tried to explain calmly, opening his palms to the sky in benediction.

But this new Elena was still too tenuous, this thing between us so fresh, we had barely taken off the plastic.

"You lied to me." I wanted the words to be a shout, an accusation, but they fell waterlogged to the floor between us where we both stared at them.

He was a capo. Of course, lying came easily to him. It was essential to his survival. But...I'd believed him when he told me he was the most honest man I'd ever meet because almost every action up until now had proved exactly that.

Now, though, my mind was reeling.

Keeping the knowledge that Cosima was Tore's daughter from me felt like such an obvious betrayal.

My gaze swept around the table, tracking Alexander and Frankie's expressions.

"You all knew," I concluded hollowly, holding up a hand when Dante stepped toward me. "Everyone in this house knew, didn't they? And I've just been wandering around like an oblivious *stronzo*."

"No, do not say that," Dante snapped.

He was coiled with energy, ready to spring at me, to force me to listen to his reason.

I didn't want to.

That old, bitter self-loathing flooded my veins like water through a broken dam.

"What else are you keeping from me?" I whispered, the words too hot in my cold mouth. "Do you really intend to marry Mirabella? You'll just keep me as some mistress on the side because you know I love you enough to stick around? You're wrong, Dante. I could never do that. I won't watch you kiss another woman or have kids with anyone but me."

My voice wasn't hysterical, but every word was increasingly cold, icy smoke like dry ice.

"Elena, do not jump to fantastical conclusions," he ground out. He lunged forward slightly to grab my hand, his grip tender but firm. "I haven't lied to you about anything. I just kept this secret from you because Cosima and Tore asked me to."

"And you put them first. I understand."

And I did.

I thought, for once, I'd found someone who would love me best, but once again, love had proved me foolish and naïve.

Tears burned the backs of my eyes, but they didn't fall. I calmly wrenched my hand from his grip and backed away.

"I need some space. Don't follow me, Dante."

He was opening his mouth when I spun on my heel and darted into the house. By the time he realized I was leaving the property, I was already in the Lambo peeling down the driveway, my capo a fading statue in the rearview mirror.

# CHAPTER FOURTEEN

## elena

I went to church.

The Cathedral of Naples was much grander than the small edifice we attended as children, but I'd navigated blindly into downtown Naples after leaving *Villa Rosa,* and something made me stop at the grand opulent structure dedicated to a God I didn't believe in. It might have had something to do with the fact it was named *Duomo di San Gennaro*, dedicated to the same saint Dante and I had celebrated what seemed like a lifetime ago in New York his first night of house arrest.

I was grateful to be wearing a silk blouse and black cigarette pants instead of one of the skin-baring dresses Dante had bought me, because Italians still took modesty in the house of the Lord incredibly seriously. As it was, no one stopped me from entering the Duomo.

It was quiet, with fewer than a handful of people milling inside. Lunchtime was meant to be spent with family or friends over wine in a piazza or the family home, but a few dedicated worshippers dotted the pews with rosary beads in their hands.

The click of my heels echoed off the marble floors and rebounded against the gilt-painted Baroque ceiling through the purloined archways bracketing the main chapel. No one watched me as I made my way to the main altar and slid into a wooden pew in the first row.

It had been years since I went to church, but my body knew how to fold itself to its knees on the provided cushions, hands clasping, head bowed. I wished I had beads to move through my fingers, counting my sins as well as my blessings like some religious calculator. Better yet, I wished I had Dante's cross, the silver heavy and poignant in my hands.

I had nothing to grasp but my own turmoil.

Seamus was dead because I'd killed him.

Killed a man.

Killed my own father.

Cosima was my half sister because Mama had fallen in love with a Camorra capo and irrevocably changed our lives in doing so.

Would we have been protected from the mafia as much as we had been without that relationship? Would Cosima have ever been sold into sexual slavery without it, though?

The past was a knotted rope, tangled in my hands. I wanted to carefully unwind it so I could begin to understand why the decisions of others had seemingly landed our family, landed *me*, in this particular situation.

If I could understand it, maybe I wouldn't be so hurt by the past.

But I knew even as I sat there until my knees ached and my skin grew cold and clammy from the air conditioning that I wouldn't be able to decipher this the way I could the law or the constitution.

Human beings made messy choices based on instinct and the base urge to sin.

I didn't know what it was like for Mama, raising two young girls without the help of a husband who increasingly didn't return home at night or even in the morning. I didn't know how it might have felt to have Amadeo Salvatore, so powerful and magnetic, take an interest in her, show her perhaps how a man should treat a woman, if only for a handful of nights.

But then, didn't I?

That was exactly how I felt about Dante. How he'd seduced me away from myself and into something better.

Only, I'd had the courage to follow my capo into the dark when Mama had not.

I sighed, scrubbing my hands over my face.

It was possible I'd overreacted.

But it was shocking and disheartening to feel like the only idiot with their head in the sand. To imagine everyone talking about it behind my back.

That wasn't really Dante's fault, though.

Of course, Cosima would want to tell me herself, and she hadn't been able to until now, even though she'd had plenty of time before I took Dante's case to fess up. I understood, even if I didn't like it, that before then, I had no real reason to know because Dante and Tore were nothing to me.

No reason beyond the fact that I was Cosima's sister.

I wanted that to be enough, but when had it ever been?

Giselle was my sister, and she'd cheated on me with my ex-partner.

Sebastian was my brother, and he'd only just confessed his long-time love for not only a married woman but also a man.

Caprice was my mother, but she'd never told me about Salvatore.

We were as fractured as a windshield after a crash, only held together by a sheer feat of engineering that was the Italian family ideal. Stay together at all costs. Pretend to be happy when your neighbors ask how you are, even if your life at home is nightmarish.

It was pathetic.

My knees cracked loudly as I stood, a *nonna* glaring at me as if I disturbed her purposely. I ignored her glare as I made my way into the separate chamber that housed the ruins of the old temple to Apollo. My skin sizzled as I stepped into the hallowed space, my soul connecting with the pagan god where it hadn't with the Christian deity.

Apollo was the god of healing and of music.

A fitting divinity for me if ever there was one.

There were no pews in this chapel, only the altar and the echoing, empty space before it. I planted myself before the painted frescos and made a promise to myself that was almost like a prayer.

I would play music again. Christopher didn't own the pleasure, and I wouldn't allow him to taint it any further.

I would open myself up to my family, crack open my soul no matter how much it hurt and show them its chaotic contents.

I would love Dante to the fullest extent of my soul because he had taught me how to love again by healing my heart with his pure kindness and loyalty. He deserved nothing less.

When I spoke the words under my breath, I didn't address them to God. I addressed them to the ancestors who had led me there and to the Elena I was honing myself into—not a victim, but a fighter.

A queen.

I left the church feeling cleansed and exhausted, my gaze more internal than external, so at first, I didn't notice the lovers twined together in the narrow, shaded alleyway behind the Duomo.

I wouldn't have even paid them any notice at all if I hadn't glimpsed two heads of long, dark hair, two dresses tangled together at the hems into one.

They were women.

Homosexuality wasn't unheard of in Italy, of course, but it was an antiquated society with bigotry still rife in everyday society. I was surprised enough by this courage to make out in public to pause as I passed them, peering into the shadows.

My gasp alerted them to my presence, and my suspicions were confirmed.

Mirabella Ianni gaped at me over her lover's shoulder, her pink mouth still wet from her kisses.

We stared at each mutely, both struck momentarily dumb by the inconvenient coincidence of our meeting.

"*Signora Lombardi,*" she finally whispered, panic suffusing her entire face, giving it an urgency that under other circumstances would have made her placid prettiness fierce with beauty. "Please, do not tell anyone about this."

Her girlfriend moved to face me, glaring at me as if I was the anti-Christ. They held each other still, arms looped around waists, shoulders pressed together.

A unit.

A team.

Just like Dante wanted with me, if only I'd stop fucking it up with my insecurities.

I studied Mirabella with new eyes. There was desperation in her pale brown eyes, a tremble in her fingers as she fidgeted with the sleeve of her lover's dress. She was in love, powerfully so, and she was used to being ridiculed for it.

My heart panged.

"I won't tell anyone," I assured her, stepping closer, something stirring at the back of my brain. "But Mira, what are you going to do?"

"I told Dante I won't marry him," she said, and I could tell she wanted to be fierce, but she was so soft it didn't hold.

Her girlfriend, on the other hand, stepped forward and snapped, "You can't make her do anything."

"No…but Rocco Abruzzi is her uncle and *capo dei capi* of the Napoli Camorra. He can absolutely make her do whatever he wants. Unless…"

Mirabella had long dark hair that fell nearly to her waist. She wasn't slender, but she had the olive-gold skin of southern Italians, and enough height that, in heels, maybe it could work…

"I have an idea," I said slowly, despite the mounting excitement in my blood. "But it's fairly crazy, and you'd have to trust me."

Mira stared at me with those guileless eyes for a long moment. "He loves you."

"He does," I confirmed proudly, feeling the truth of it suffuse me once more. "Neither of us want this wedding to happen. At least come with me now to *Villa Rosa* and discuss things with us. I think we can make this work."

"We tried to run away a few years ago," Mira admitted, clasping her girlfriend's hand so tightly, their fingers went white. "*Zio* Rocco caught us."

Which explained his desperation to pawn her off on Dante before anyone else could find out about his Sapphic niece and have it "tarnish" his reputation.

I sighed at the horrible realities of this world, then remembered how many atrocities I'd witnessed as a lawyer in New York, far removed from the mafia.

There were villains everywhere, but at least in the shadows, I had a better chance of taking them by surprise.

The girls, Mira and, I learned, Rosetta, followed me home in their little Alfa Romeo.

My family was still on the back patio, the conversation terse as I rounded the corner with Mira and Rosetta at my back.

Conversation stopped immediately, Dante's chair scraping painfully across the tiles as he stood and stalked toward me.

I didn't move an inch.

He collected me in his arms and carted me up against his chest, burying his nose in my hair. My hands found the back of his hair and tangled there, holding him to me.

"You leave without a guard again, *lottatrice*, I'll tan your ass so red you won't be able to sit for a week," he growled in my ear before pulling away.

I smiled a little, shifting my hand to his cheek so I could run my fingernails over his stubble. "I think that's fair. I'm sorry I was so stupid. I think I'm so ready to be betrayed, sometimes I manifest it."

"It's understandable," he murmured, running his nose along mine. "But to betray you would be betraying myself. I won't do that to either of us."

"I know." I winced. "I think I just needed to remind myself of that one last time before it got through my thick skull."

He kissed me then, softly, lips wet and silken as rose petals at dawn. I sipped at him, licked at him, hummed when he palmed my throat and slid his thumb over my pulse to feel my heart beat for him.

Because it did.

It always would.

Which was why I'd concocted a mad plan to keep him for myself at all costs.

When I pulled away, I smiled.

"Do you want to tell me why you brought my betrothed over for lunch?" he asked, eyes crinkled with mirth.

I was relieved he wasn't mad at me, harboring righteous resentment at me for taking out my shock and anger at him, that I couldn't speak for a moment.

"This is Mirabella's lover, Rosetta," I explained as I stepped away to gesture them closer. "This is why Mira absolutely does not want to marry you either."

*"Assolutamente,"* she echoed firmly.

Dante didn't miss a beat. He moved forward and kissed Rosetta on both cheeks in greeting. *"Ciao, amica mia."*

Hello, my friend.

My heart almost burst in my chest.

We all moved to take seats at the table, and I squeezed Cosima's shoulder as I took the chair beside her, letting her know I was sorry. She reached up and squeezed my wrist in return, her eyes soft with understanding.

"Okay, so I may be new to all this, but I was a damn good lawyer so hear me out," I started, looking at the face of the family around me, desperate for this to work. "The wedding is next Monday, and if Cosima and Alexander are willing, this is how it will work..."

# CHAPTER FIFTEEN
# DANTE

Elena's plan was good, but it wasn't enough.

Even if it all worked out against the implausible odds, it left our operation in Italy floundering and the war back home in America without its general.

We needed more.

So in the week leading up to the wedding, I set my own plan in motion.

I met with Leonardo Esposito.

With Umberto Arno, still recovering from the partial loss of his sight in one eye.

With Mattia Filoso, a semi-retired fisherman who'd taken the money I'd given him for a job six years ago and started a luxury boat rental company to take advantage of wealthy tourists.

The night before the wedding, I sat on the back patio under the twinkling string lights Elena and Frankie had put up a few days before and drank an over full glass of Sambuca with Tore, Alexander, and

Frankie.

"Everything's in place?" Tore confirmed, taking a puff from the Cuban cigar between his teeth.

"As much as it can be," I said.

"And you're sure?" Alexander asked, his voice so crisp and British it made me nostalgic for my old life and first home in England even though both would forever be tainted by Noel.

"The only thing I'm sure of is Lena. No matter what happens, I won't let her go. I'll kill anyone who tries to come between us."

My brother's golden brows cut creases into his forehead. He looked so much like Noel sitting there in his bespoke navy-blue suit, his only concession to the casualness of the setting a lack of tie at his throat. But he was so much more than Noel had ever been.

He was capable of love, the kind he'd kill and die for happily.

After years of bad blood between us, it felt unspeakably good to share a drink with him. To share my soul with him.

He tipped his glass of whiskey to me. "Lombardi women are worth all the treasure in this world."

"Aye aye," Tore agreed, raising his own glass.

"The only thing I'm not sure about is Elena's reaction to your part of the plan," Frankie admitted with a glint of dark humor in his eyes. "She's not the kinda woman who thinks being duped is romantic."

"We need to get back to New York, *fratello*. Our Family is under attack, and they need their fucking capo to put things to right. This is the only way I can return home and keep her safe."

"Yeah, she's gonna like you turning yourself in even less than what you have planned for tomorrow," Frankie noted.

And he was right.

My fighter would never willingly give me up for anything.

Which was why I was taking the choice from her.

I thought of her upstairs in a guest room asleep beside her sister. She hadn't thought anything of it when Cosima suggested the girls' night, even though she made sure to fuck me in the lemon grove before she disappeared for the night. She had no idea I'd suggested the idea to Cosima so we could adhere to Italian tradition.

The groom should never see the bride the night before the wedding.

"The moment you think you know Elena, she surprises you with more," I told Frankie. "Think about how much she's changed since we first met her. I shouldn't say changed, really, because it was already all there beneath the ice and scar tissue. No matter how angry she might be with me, she'll do what needs to be done when we return home."

"Cosima did the same thing to me," Alexander confessed, staring into the bowl of his glass as if memories were playing out on a screen there. "I never knew what love was until her."

"And she'll never know it again without me," I asserted. "That's why I'm doing this. It might not have happened tomorrow or this year or even the next, but the truth is, none of that fucking matters. Elena became mine the day she got on the plane, and I was never going to give her back."

I told myself that again and again because honestly, I wasn't sure how my fighter was going to take the second half of the plan I'd put in place.

She was independent and strong-willed, and she was also the kind of woman who had been planning the events of her entire life since she was a little girl.

This was definitely not something she could have predicted.

But there was no other option.

If I wanted to stay alive and keep her out of jail, Elena Lombardi would have to become my wife.

# CHAPTER SIXTEEN

## *elena*

The Sunday before Christmas dawned bright and cold, a wind rushing in off the bay that rattled the lemon trees and swirled the garbage in the streets of Naples like snow in a globe. I got ready for the wedding alone in the room I shared with Dante, my lover gone long before I woke up to ready himself for the day.

There was a lot to be done if we were going to pull this thing off.

I strapped my thigh holster to my leg under the red wrap dress I wore, secure in the fact I knew how to yield the weapon if I needed to. I took extra time getting ready, making my lips as red as my dress, curling my hair until it fell in a mess of Chianti-colored waves around my breasts. It was a bold color to wear to a wedding, but I wanted Rocco to see me in the crowd.

I wanted him to think he was safe.

My sink was stained with dye from the night before that I carefully rinsed out before I went downstairs to meet Tore.

He was dressed in a beautifully tailored suit looking every inch the mafia boss as he extended his arm for me to take. When I did, his other hand found my forearm and squeezed.

"I am sorry you had to find out about Caprice and me this way." His eyes were as golden as the gilt scrolling on the shrine to Apollo in the *Duomo di Napoli*. As golden as his daughter's. "I want you to understand, I have loved your mother for most of my life, and I do not see that changing."

"Have you told her that?" I wondered.

His lips thinned. "She knows. She says there is too much water under this bridge."

"Bridges exist to straddle the void," I countered. "Maybe you just need to build a new one."

There was a ghost of a smile in his short beard. "I have your approval then."

"If you need it," I offered, then shrugged. "Though I won't ask for yours with Dante."

"You don't need it," he assured.

I raised an eyebrow, inferring that I felt the same about him. "Maybe a few months ago, I would have judged you and Mama more harshly, but I'm in no place to do so now. If Dante wanted to drag me into the bowels of hell, I'd go with him gladly. Love makes animals of us all, all instinct and heart with no capacity for reason. I won't judge you for loving her or the things you've done in service of that love, just as I wouldn't judge a wolf for slaughtering sheep or a bear for protecting its cubs. It's just in our nature."

"Eloquently said." He patted my hand, then led me out the doors to his waiting Maserati.

"Are you ready for today?" he queried once we were settled into the low yellow car I remembered from my childhood, and the engine roared into wakefulness.

"I'll end the day as Dante's mistress, or we all end it free. Either way, I'll go down fighting."

He grinned as he gunned the car, speeding down the driveway with a roar of the engine like a trumpet announcing our call to war.

*"In bocca al lupo a tutti noi,"* he called over the cacophony.

*Good luck to us all.*

The church was packed to the gills with smartly dressed Neapolitans. Everyone wore black as if it was a funeral and not a celebration, but the women dripped with jewels to show their affluential connections in the mafia, and the men wore sunglasses even though it was a cool, overcast morning and the light inside the church itself was dim.

Tore and I waited in the receiving line to greet the father of the bride, in this case, the uncle.

"Elena," Rocco said, ignoring Tore even though it was extraordinarily rude and therefore dangerous to do so. "You look exquisite today."

"Thank you," I demurred, holding on to Frankie's arm as if I couldn't bear to be separated from him.

The truth was, he'd met us at the church with a distinctly distracted aura and wasn't playing the part of my doting husband very well.

"You will come to the party at my villa after," Rocco asserted, still holding the hand he'd raised to kiss.

"I wouldn't miss it." I gave his palm a squeeze before firmly pulling away from his sweaty grasp. "Frankie and I are taking something of a second honeymoon while we're here, so we might not stay long."

Rocco's beady eyes narrowed.

I smiled placidly at him.

He was smart enough to know Dante wasn't the kind of man who enjoyed being maneuvered into corners, but he wasn't smart enough to guess at how he might strike back at him.

"You'll sit behind me during the ceremony," he announced. "So I can keep an eye on all of you."

"*Va bene,*" I agreed easily. "It will be nice to have a front row seat."

Reluctantly, Rocco gestured for us to move on so he could greet the other attendees in the line. I let out a little breath of relief when we passed into the cool church, my hand clammy on Frankie's suited arm.

"*Tranquilo,* Elena," Frankie soothed in a low murmur as we walked down the flower-studded aisle to the second pew from the front. "Everything will work out."

I nodded, but my stomach was twisted into so many knots I doubted I'd ever be able to untangle my nerves.

Tore reached over to my lap and grabbed my twisting hands, taking one in his own. He had large hands, the same shape as Sebastian's.

It comforted me more than I thought it would.

We waited as everyone settled into their seats, and finally, a hush fell over the proceedings.

From an antechamber to the left of the altar, shoes clicked across the marble floor.

A moment later, the groom appeared flanked by his best man, Damiano Vitale, and the priest. He looked ridiculously handsome clad entirely in his requisite black, but the starkness made his skin startlingly pale.

I doubted anyone would notice because a moment later, there was a clamor outside the doors to the church, and then they swung open to reveal the bride escorted by Rocco himself.

She was a vision of frothing lace, the train extending four feet behind her, a traditional handmade veil draped over her head to partially obscure her face and torso. There was a murmur of approval from the guests at her beauty as organ music played powerfully in the background, her steps timed perfectly to the march.

It seemed to take her ages to reach the altar, but maybe that was my own perception, mottled by the way my heart beat too fast and hard in my chest, mocking the rhythm of the wedding song.

When I was a girl, I'd imagined something like this for my wedding. This was long before Seamus and the mafia taught me to hate my own country. Before Christopher made me hate myself enough to think I deserved a small, civil ceremony or just a common-law relationship like I had with Sinclair.

I dreamed of lace and silk, feminine and almost old-fashioned, like the brides in the magazines Mama had from her youth. I wanted everything traditional, from the *Millefoglie* wedding cake to my future husband buying me my bouquet, a custom most modern brides eschewed.

I hadn't believed in those dreams in so long, they seemed dusty and antiquated when I thought of them then.

Or maybe it was because if I ever married Dante, that wasn't the kind of wedding we'd have. We had hardly been together long enough to have conversations about such things, but in my heart of hearts, I imagined us eloping to some beautiful foreign land, just the two of us.

Not because I didn't love my family, but because our relationship was the center of my new universe, the spoke on which my life revolved.

Loving Dante had made me realize how self-centered I'd been, mired in my own bitterness and misery until I didn't even know how unpleasant I was to be around half the time. He reminded me that life was worth living and love was worth giving.

So, maybe just us, somewhere romantic, but even that didn't matter to me the way it once had.

I'd marry Dante in a back alley or a parking lot if it meant being his legally.

The paperwork didn't matter either, not the way I thought it had when I was with Daniel.

It was about the symbolism.

I wanted to be his *lottatice, regina,* and *moglie.*

His fighter, his queen, and his wife.

Even though we had a plan, it was still disconcerting to watch this ceremony. It made me aware of how little rights I had if Dante was ever imprisoned again. I couldn't be his lawyer if I was his lover and I wasn't his wife.

Tore squeezed my hand as if sensing my inner turmoil, pulling me back to the moment at hand.

When Mira finally reached the front, Rocco handed her off with ceremonial words to Dante, who accepted her hand and tucked it into his arm as they turned to face the priest.

It was all so civilized.

Not for one second did Dante appear to be anything other than a suitably thrilled groom about to marry the love of his life.

Rocco turned to take his seat in the front pew and caught my eyes. His grin was a pennant of victory flying in the face of my hopes and dreams.

*I win,* his sparkling eyes proclaimed.

*Underestimate me,* I channeled back with a tightly curled smile, *I dare you.*

Italian ceremonies took forever, but after a long forty minutes of service, the priest declared Dante Edward Salvatore and Mirabella Ianni, now Salvatore, man and wife.

A famous local soprano appeared on the dais to sing *Ava Maria* as the couple turned to face the crowd and began their walk down the aisle.

It was impossible to watch them walk by without feeling my heart like a lead ball in my stomach. Everything hinged on this wedding going off without a hitch.

Before we could leave the pew to follow the happy duo out the doors like the others were, ready to throw rice in celebration over their heads, Rocco stopped me with a hand on my arm.

"This is the way things work here," he told me condescendingly.

He didn't understand that this wasn't my first interaction with the mafia.

It wasn't even my one hundredth.

He just saw a pretty girl and imagined I'd been sheltered my entire life, that I had no brain in my head and that, because I wasn't born with literal balls, I lacked a spine.

"Arranged marriages?" I asked meekly.

"That," he agreed, but his fingers grew tight on my arm. "And whatever I say goes. It has been this way for years. It was this way even six years ago when I sold your sister to Alexander Davenport."

For one single second, my heart stopped.

I thought Rocco had discovered my duplicity and was letting me know I would pay the price for it.

But no.

The stupid oaf was only bragging about his evil deeds like some villain in a bad action movie. He was trying to rile me up, attacking the woman because he assumed I was the weak link, and a little provocation would reveal whether Dante had a revenge plan for him or not.

I blinked at him mildly, the fire in my soul hid entirely by my icy casing. "*A mali estremi, estremi rimedi,*" I said coolly as if I understood he'd only been doing his job.

Literally translated, it was an idiom that meant "to extreme evils, extreme remedies," or in English, desperate times call for desperate measures.

But I was referring more literally to the evil of the man himself and the upcoming remedies we were putting into place to end his tyranny.

Rocco's grin was smug as he squeezed my hand, patting it the way one would a puppy's head. "You're a good girl."

I couldn't help the laughter that escaped. "Oh, Don Abruzzi, I promise you, I'm not."

He frowned but let go of me so Tore, Frankie, and I could filter out of the church with the rest of the guests. Everyone stood in a mass as they wished the happy couple well, calling to them as they made their way quickly down the parted line of guests to the car that awaited them.

Dante opened the passenger side door for Mira, but they were sidetracked by Tore, who had surged forward to speak quietly with them. Rocco frowned beside me, muttering under his breath.

"If you're planning any funny business, I'll shoot you and your wife straight through the skull," he reminded Frankie and me before turning to one of his goons, ordering him to see Dante and Mira into the waiting car.

I watched with my heart in my throat as the thug powered through the crowd and grabbed Mira's arm.

*Cazzo.*

A moment later, Dante was punching him in the throat, the man's gurgling cry of pain discernable even over the noise of the partygoers. Someone screamed as the goon tried to swing at Dante but missed.

He'd made a mistake going for the bride.

Dante picked the man up by the neck as if he was a sack of potatoes and threw him into the open passenger side of the car. He reached for

Mira and pulled her behind his back as he faced down the struggling Italian still stuck in the car.

To this day, I don't know what happened.

If he accidentally pressed the gas pedal in his quest to get upright or if the thing was on a timer set to blow at a certain point after the door was open.

If Rocco saw the skirmish and decided to get it over with by pulling the trigger himself.

But one second later, there was a mighty *rip*, like God tearing apart the heavens.

And seconds after that, the car exploded.

# CHAPTER SEVENTEEN

## *elena*

Heat rolled out from the explosion like a mushroom cloud, singeing my eyebrows and burning my skin. Smoke followed quickly after that, obscuring the sight of the ruined car, setting everyone in the vicinity to a hacking cough as those uninjured struggled to get to safety. The fire was contained to the vehicle, but the air was waxy with heat.

Frankie and Tore both had their arms around me, shielding me with their bodies in a way that made my heart ache.

"*Andiamo,*" Tore ordered in a harsh rasp as he sucked in that acrid smoke. "Quickly, now."

"But--"

"They'll be fine," Frankie assured me when I clutched at him, paralyzed with fear. "He pushed her to the ground a second before it blew. He might be hurt, but he'll survive."

Still, I scoured the sight for signs of his black hair or her long, singed veil as Frankie tugged me along after him across the *piazza* and down a side alley.

"Did you know the car would explode?" I demanded as we came to an abrupt stop at a vintage red Vespa.

Tore was nowhere in sight, but I didn't worry. The Don could take care of himself, and he'd been with us, unharmed, after the crash.

"No, the *stronzo* obviously had it as a contingency plan if he felt Dante, Tore, and I were up to something." He handed me a little red helmet and straddled the Vespa.

I blinked at him, maybe a little disorientated from the explosion. "You look ridiculous."

He did.

Frankie wasn't as tall or wide as Dante, but he was a big guy in a Prada suit on a tiny scooter tourists and university students used to get around the city.

"*Dai,*" he ordered. "Get on, Elena. We don't have much time."

I put on the helmet immediately, taking my place behind Frankie and wrapping my arms around him.

"Try not to enjoy this too much," he teased.

Only a mafioso would joke after a freaking car bomb went off.

With a beep of his pathetic horn, he took off down the alley, sticking to the narrow streets as he wound his way from the cathedral toward the water.

"Aren't we going to the airport?" I asked because that was our original plan.

Pull off the fake wedding of the century and get the hell out of Naples. We'd talked about going to Costa Rica, where the Camorra funneled most of their ill-begotten money. I didn't speak Spanish, and I wasn't skilled with languages, but I'd learned that Dante spoke it and four others fluently. It was another new start, this one completely foreign to me, but I didn't care.

I'd go anywhere with my capo.

"Change of plans!" Frankie shouted over the rush of wind and then said nothing more.

We arrived at the *porti di Napoli* docks within ten minutes. Two cruise ships nestled in the harbor and countless little boats, luxury speedboats for the tourists and the wealthy, weathered fishing boats for the many Neapolitans who made their money off the sea.

Frankie drove straight onto the concrete docks to the very end of one vacant mooring and turned off the engine.

"What the hell are we doing?" I demanded as I got off and removed my helmet. "We need to call and see if they're okay."

"They will be."

"You can't be sure of that," I hissed, stepping forward to give his biceps a shake. "They did this for Dante and me! Don't you get that? They were never meant to get hurt."

Frankie gave me a cool look, then pulled his phone from his pocket, pressing a button before handing it to me.

I took it eagerly, almost dropping it in my haste.

As it rang, I followed Frankie's gaze to a small wooden speedboat racing in from the ocean, froth at its bow and a single captain at its helm.

It rang and rang.

My heart moved into my throat.

The boat moved closer.

A man, dark-haired and with broad shoulders stood at the wheel.

I stopped breathing.

The phone clicked then went dead.

The vessel aimed straight at the mooring, the engine so loud I almost didn't hear the phone in my limp hand ringing.

I raised it to my ear.

"Hello?"

The man on the boat bent as he brought the vehicle to a sudden, swerving stop at the dock. Only his dark head was visible.

"*Lena mia,*" my sister said breathlessly. "I'm sorry I couldn't answer. We just got away."

"Are you okay?" I demanded.

She laughed.

A high, lilting laugh like a drug addict after a good fix.

Like a villain who had just pulled off the ultimate evil plan.

"*Si, sorella mia,*" she crowed, and I couldn't help but smile. "Xan says his scalp is itching from the dye, but other than that and a nasty cut on his cheek from some loose shrapnel, we are both fine. Fine and happy because *it worked.*"

I grinned, holding the phone with both hands, about to answer when the captain of the small boat in front of us straightened and turned to face us.

It wasn't Dante, as I'd hoped, but Salvatore, his face creased into the widest grin I'd ever seen.

"Come," he beckoned, tossing a rope to Frankie, who caught it and held it taut. "Hurry, Elena."

"I have to go, Cosi," I told her even as I moved to the boat and accepted Tore's help getting in. "*Grazie mille.* Thank you for taking such a risk for me. It means more than I can say."

"Then say nothing," she suggested easily as if she hadn't just put her and her husband's life in danger to help us. "Both you and Dante have spent your life trying to protect Xan and me. It was our turn to return the favor. *Buona fortuna* and I'll see you later."

"Good luck," I echoed. "Be safe."

Frankie clapped his hands at me, so I tossed him the phone.

"Where are we going?" I demanded of either man, but they ignored me as they maneuvered a saddlebag from the Vespa onto the boat, and Tore started to push off the dock.

"Tore," I called, nearly falling into the water as he gunned the engine forward.

Frankie tossed the rope into the back of the boat and waved jauntily as if we were off for an afternoon delight and not fleeing the scene of a crime.

Tore helped me into my seat and retook his spot at the wheel.

"*Tranquilo,*" he shouted over the noise of the boat cutting through the blue waves and tossing up foam. "Be patient."

I made a face, but I didn't really have a choice in the matter.

The wind whipped over my body and through my hair, as violent as the conclusion of Dante and Mirabella's fake wedding.

It had seemed so obvious when I looked at Mira in the alleyway that day. She had a passing resemblance to Cosima that would be easy to emphasize with the right dress and veil. Dante and Alexander were almost identical when you stripped away the different coloring and wildly opposing personalities.

A little hair dye late last night and a pair of contacts procured from Capo Leonardo Esposito's wife who worked in film, and we were set.

My concern had been that Rocco would see through our ruse, but he was too simple a man to believe he could be fooled in such a way. Cosima kept mostly quiet as Mira, which fit the girl's personality and didn't alert Rocco to anything afoot.

Alexander and Cosima were the perfect stand-ins while Dante and Mirabella got the hell out of Dodge.

By the time the car bomb went off, Mira and Rosetta would have been halfway to France, equipped with enough money from Tore and Dante to set up a life for themselves and two passports with new identities.

Dante was supposed to meet me at the airfield.

Instead, I was on a boat with Tore in the middle of the Tyrrhenian Sea.

We had been driving for twenty or thirty minutes when Tore angled the boat back into the coastline, and the bright orange roofs of Sorrento came into view on the looming green mountains.

My heartbeat quickened.

"Why are we here?" I asked softly as the boat slowed and the engine quieted.

Tore turned to me, hair a windblown mess around his tanned face, and he smiled at me in a way that said he had a secret.

A secret he was dying to tell me, but wouldn't.

"You know now that I have two children I was not allowed to parent for most of their lives. Only in the past few years did Cosima find out the truth about our relationship, and Caprice has asked me not to tell Sebastian." His face spasmed with pain, then recovered its soft beauty. "But I was lucky enough to have a son by choice. A man who saw everything I was and everything I did, the bad and the ugly, yet he still chose to take my side. He chose to be my family, to be my son and my ally. I will never stop grieving for Chiara, but in death, she gave me the greatest treasure. Dante is the best man I know. It does not shame me to admit I learn from *him* every day. I am proud to be the father of his heart, so proud I could burst."

He hit his chest with his open palm and splayed his fingers, a dramatic, Italian movement that made me smile even as my chest panged with the beauty and pain of his words.

"I am very grateful now, too, that he has found his *anima gemella.*"

*His soul mate.*

I swallowed thickly as Tore slowed the boat even further, calling to a man waiting on the docks to catch his rope. Before he tossed it, he reached over to squeeze my hand.

"Only a strong woman, a fearless one, could be with *figlio mia,* and I could not have dreamed of one so perfect as you."

"I'm not fearless," I confessed thickly, watching blindly as he tossed the rope, and it was tied down to a metal prong. "I'm far from perfect."

"Ah, but that is in the eyes of the beholder," he argued, turning off the boat and turning to me with an extended hand. "And the man who believes you are his treasure is waiting for you now."

I took his hand, feeling so moved I was shaken, the tectonic plates of my soul shifting and rearranging around his words.

Because they felt very much like the blessing I told him I didn't need.

And I found, in him giving it, that I wanted it more than I could say.

I didn't ask questions as I followed him onto the dock, through the busy pier, and into the streets of Sorrento. We walked with purpose, the only sign we were living on borrowed time.

I had no doubt Rocco was looking for us and that if we stayed in the vicinity of his territory too long, he would hunt us down.

The sun was high in the sky, pale and nebulous behind thin clouds as we passed into the narrow, steep streets leading up the hills of the city.

Ten minutes later, Tore stopped at the end of the street across from a tiny piazza.

Across from us stood a small white chapel.

It was simple, unadorned but for the cross over the plain wood door.

Tore led us to the entrance.

"Tore…" I whispered because it was getting hard to breathe.

He didn't say anything as he pushed open the doors to the cool interior and pulled me inside. The space smelled of old paper and myrrh. It was basic for an Italian church, no gilt paint or carefully created murals, no glossy mahogany pews, only old, scarred wooden rows and basic white walls carved into the requisite arcs. It was beautiful, somehow pure and elegant.

And it was empty.

I frowned around the vacant space, but Tore was already dragging me into a side room.

"Get dressed and come back into the chapel," he ordered before taking both my hands in his and kissing each cheek. His countenance was so warm, I could feel the heat of his love coming off his skin in waves. *"Che la vostra vita insieme sia come il buon vino."*

*May your life together be like fine Italian wine.*

It was an old, cheesy blessing fathers often imparted at weddings in our country.

I blinked at him as he stepped away and closed the door behind him.

On the small wooden table beside the votive candles lay a box.

*Valentino* was embossed in gold on the top.

My heart stopped, then restarted with an abrupt bang that ached in my ribs.

With trembling fingers, I notched my fingernails under the lid and lifted.

Inside lay snowy white silk carefully folded in tissue paper and a note written on plain card stock.

*Wear this tonight.*

*Xoxo,*

*Your Capo*

# CHAPTER EIGHTEEN

## *elena*

Of course, the dress fit perfectly.

It was vintage Valentino, luxurious and simple silk cut exactly to my proportions, so the straight skirt skimmed my waist and hips, and the bodice hugged my minimal curves. The sleeves were long, but the material was cut, baring my shoulders and upper chest.

It was elegant perfection, and I knew without confirmation that Dante had bought it for me himself.

I had ash in my hair from the burning car, and my shoes were scuffed from my travels. There was no mirror in the small rectory, so I couldn't check my makeup, and I only had a small brush folded in my purse along with a tiny bottle of Chanel Number 5 perfume and a dying tube of red lipstick.

I was in a city I'd once condemned for the memories it harbored in a tiny chapel without friends or family or society photogs to capture the moment for Page Six.

Dante and I had only been together romantically for one month.

One month of car chases and abductions.

Of sex and exploration.

Of romance and tension.

A single month that felt like an entire lifetime.

A lifetime I never wanted to end.

So, I didn't care.

Not a single fucking bit about any of the reasons I shouldn't marry Edward Dante Salvatore.

The man who had taught me how to love and live again.

The man who had brought me back to myself.

I loved him before I even knew how to identify the feeling, and maybe that was why it happened. Because it was done before I could think to stop it.

Loving him had sparked the mass of tinder and kindling I'd stacked in my lonely soul for years, just waiting for someone to come along and ignite it. It had started in my heart and spread like wildfire through my veins, melting the tundra I'd made of myself for too long. Now, it raged within me, eternal and inextinguishable.

Everything that tried to get between us only proved to fuel the flames.

And I knew in my bones that would never change.

What happened when two villains fell in love?

Was there a happily-ever-after for people like us?

I wasn't sure, and uncharacteristically, I didn't care.

The only thing I knew for sure was that Dante made me feel so alive I burned, and I wanted to spend every single chaotic, beautiful day of the rest of my life smoldering at his side.

I smoothed my hands down the cool silk, took a bracing breath of the stale air, and opened the door.

My sister stood outside it, holding a bouquet of pure red roses.

I blinked.

Cosima had changed out of Mirabella Ianni's singed wedding dress and veil into a simple poppy patterned dress, but there was still grim on her face and a thin cut down one arm. Even though she'd told me she was unharmed, relief coursed through me.

She swept her gaze over me from the base of the slight silk train to the top of my head, a smile blooming across her face that was so beautiful, it took my breath away.

"You are perfect," she proclaimed softly as she handed me the flowers. "These are from the groom."

*The groom.*

I shivered.

"This is too surreal," I told her honestly. "I feel as if I'm in a dream."

"Good. It's about time some of those came true for you."

"I'm not going to cry," I warned her firmly, even though my throat was tight and my nose itched with looming tears. "I've been doing that way too much lately."

She laughed, reaching forward to cup my cheek in her slim hand. "Crying is the body's way of expressing emotion that's too big for words. It doesn't make you weak, Lena, and I'm happy to hear you're just *feeling* again."

"I know it doesn't. This is the first time in my life I've ever felt invincible, and it's with enemies all around us actively trying to bring us down."

"Dante's enemies," she amended with a curious glint in her eyes.

I shrugged. "So, they're my own."

She grinned again and surged forward like a stray wave to cover me in a fierce hug. *"Ti amo. Sono orgogliosa di essere tua sorella."*

*I love you. I'm proud to be your sister.*

My burning heart crackled and sparked.

*"Anch'io,"* I said, hugging her tight.

*Same.*

"I hope you know that he loves you more than I've seen any man but Alexander love another woman," she said, obviously trying to soothe whatever insecurities I felt about him once claiming to love her. "The Davenport men only love once, and they do it forever."

"I know." I kissed her smooth cheek and pulled away so she could see my certainty. "I don't have any doubts."

She pressed a finger to the corner of her eye to collect a pooling tear, then laughed lightly as she dashed it away. "Okay, enough of this. He's waiting for you."

A little shiver rattled my shoulders, sweet anticipation on my tongue.

Cosima offered me her arm and I realized she would escort me down the aisle to Dante. It was fitting that my sister would do so when she'd sacrificed and supported me through so much. Fleetingly I wished Mama was there, but then I decided she would understand better than anyone the impulsiveness of a capo.

We left the little room and moved through the archways into the main chamber before turning left to walk down the aisle.

And there he was.

My capo.

Resplendent in a gorgeous black suit and tie, the stark color bringing the vividness of his deeply bronzed skin into relief.

But all I really noticed was the look on his face as he took me in.

Awe and wonder.

He seemed struck by it as if by lightning, his gaze electric on me as I moved toward him, his fingers twitching at his sides as if he couldn't bear a second longer without touching me. Without being able to make certain I was real and not some mirage cast down from heaven.

I felt my soul crack open, light pouring out through the smile that made my cheeks hurt.

He blinked as if looking at the sun.

When we reached the altar, I finally noticed that a small but brown priest stood behind Dante with Alexander and Tore flanking him. They both smiled at me. Even Alexander's face was soft with contentment.

Impatient, Dante stepped forward to take my hand and pull me from Cosima.

She laughed. "I guess you don't need my blessing to hand her over."

"I don't need anyone's blessing but her own," he agreed easily, his eyes pinned to mine even as he spoke to her.

I stepped closer, capitulating to the magnetic force between us. There was something I wanted to say, but I was mesmerized by the depth of love and wonder in those night-black eyes.

*"Dimmi si,"* he murmured as he pressed his forehead to mine and

cupped my hips in his big hands. "Say yes."

My heart beat too hard and too slow in my chest, a heavy, aching knock on my rib cage. I realized he had been planning this for a while, since the first time he asked me to trust him, to say yes to him.

"*Si*. Yes. *Sempre*."

*Yes, forever*.

His joy cracked through his expression, his ruddy lips widening until those sharp teeth shone, and his eyes sparkled like a clear night sky with twinkling stars.

"*Farei qualsiai cosa per te*," he told me in that beautiful British, Italian accent, his hands finding my face, cupping it tight, tipping it up like a diamond to catch the light. "I would do anything for you, Elena. Men have said that to women before, but they couldn't know what it means, not really. I will kill and die for you, but I will also shop for you because I like you in the clothes I've bought, and I'll cook for you because I love to watch you rediscover the joy of indulgence. I will make love to you when your heart is aching and lonely, echoing with the past, and I will fuck you when you can't stand to be empty of me for one second longer. I am *capo dei capi* of the New York Camorra, but that is not the most important title I have anymore. In fact, it means next to nothing compared to the gift you are about to give me. The gift of being your husband and a lifetime of loving you fiercely, fucking you senselessly, and watching you awe me with your wit and beauty and drive every single day."

His sigh feathered over my mouth, his lips following it to kiss me hard then soft. The embrace fluctuated like a flickering flame, bright and dark, tender and ruthless as if he wanted to show me the two sides of his love for me, the wholeness of our unity.

When we broke apart, he said quietly, "*Resta con me per sempre*. Be my *donna* and my wife. My forever love."

*Stay with me forever.*

"Yes," I rasped through my heart beating in my throat, threatening to choke me with love and overwhelming gratitude for this man and this moment. I reached up to clutch his neck, my thumb finding his pulse as he so often did with me. "Before you, I was empty and cold, a locked room in the deepest dungeon. Now, I can breathe again, feel again, *burn* again. You proved to me that I am worthy of love, and I want to spend the rest of my life proving to you that you're the best man I'll ever know, and you made the right decision in trusting me with your endless heart."

"*Ti amo*," he said, the words too loud and forceful, two bullets fired in a holy place.

Behind us, the priest flinched, but I only smiled because I felt the power of those words throbbing in my hot heart too.

"*Ti amo*," I said in the same voice.

We laughed, foreheads pressed together, the music traveling through us both in perfect harmony. Then unable to resist, Dante leaned down and ate the laughter off my tongue. I offered my mouth to him like a sacrifice, letting him take everything he needed from me.

"We don't have time for you to make out all day," Alexander pointed out dryly. "If you want to make your plane, we need the priest to marry you formally."

Dante kept kissing me, pulling me closer so I was flush against his hard body, his hard cock pressing against my belly.

"Dante," Tore warned a moment later.

I broke away from my man, pushing him back with two hands on his chest when he tried to kiss me again. Laughter suffused my tone. "Let's get married, Dante. I want you to be my husband."

His eyes flashed, lightning through a dark sky. "Now, that sounds better than any curse or please from your lips. Say it again."

"Husband," I teased. "Husband. Husband."

A growl moved through his throat, his hands spasming on my face before one slid down to palm my neck.

"*Andiamo, padre,*" Dante ordered the priest without taking his gaze from mine. "I want to make this woman my wife."

The little priest stepped forward, opened his Bible, and in twenty minutes of compact Italian vows, I went from Elena Lombardi, the coldhearted, lonely lawyer, to Elena Salvatore, *Donna* and wife to Don Edward Dante Salvatore.

It felt like a baptism, a rebirthing, and when Dante slid the *fede*, the wedding ring, onto my finger, I knew with bone-deep certainty that every single bad thing in my life had happened as payment for the price of this colossal happiness, and I wasn't bitter anymore, I wasn't even scarred.

I was whole for the first time since I was sixteen.

# CHAPTER NINETEEN
## DANTE

It was a gamble.

A risk.

Setting up a real wedding inside the veil of a fake one.

Marrying Elena when we should have been fleeing the country.

Joining my eternally dangerous life with the life of a woman who only deserved happiness for the rest of her days. I couldn't offer her perfection, a happily-ever-after without strife and turmoil. But I could offer her the secret delights of the dark side of her soul; chaos and wonder, violence and passion, action and endless adventure. I could show her the kind of love we hadn't even known existed until we fell into each other and became two souls entangled into one.

It was selfish and reckless, but I would never regret making that incredible woman my wife, and I'd work every day to make sure she never regretted it too.

We left the church as soon as the brief ceremony was complete to return to the docks. Frankie was waiting with another boat, kissing Elena and congratulating her as I talked to Tore.

"Is everything in place?"

He nodded. "The party is in full swing. Leonardo is there. He texted to say Rocco has sent men looking for you."

"Let them find us." Marrying Elena had stirred the beast inside me. It pulled at the chains I kept it shackled in and growled so hard inside my chest I vibrated. I'd always wanted to kill Rocco Abruzzi for selling Cosima into slavery, but now I wanted to eviscerate him for daring to threaten Elena. "We have one night to clean house here, and then we're leaving. Is Damiano ready to take over?"

"As ready as he can be," he allowed, looking over at Elena as she laughed with Cosima and Alexander saying their goodbyes. "Will you tell your wife she is in for a bloody honeymoon and a long stretch without her new husband?"

"She won't care about the bloody honeymoon." My grin was savage. "If anything, she might want to put Rocco Abruzzi into the ground herself."

"Ah, young love," Tore joked before taking me in a back-slapping hug. "Be safe, *figlio*."

"And you," I ordered.

I moved away from him to collect my wife from her sister and my brother. She slid into my side like a puzzle piece, her smile brighter than the Italian sun descending quickly into the sea.

"Thank you," I told Cosima and Alexander, offering my hand to my brother. He clasped it in his own, his grip strong and sure. "The risk you took today saved lives."

"I don't care about anyone's life in this situation but yours. Though, I'm happy to have saved it," Alexander said in his blunt, cold way. "You saved Cosima when I wasn't able to save her. I'll never stop owing you for that."

"It's not a debt if I was invested too," I argued.

His golden brows rose. "Then consider this the same. Even when I thought I hated you, I never stopped loving you. Glad to see you found the best kind of woman to love you too."

"Wow," Cosima mock whispered to Elena. "This is the nicest they've ever been to each other."

Elena and I laughed.

"I'll see you soon," Cosi promised us, stepping forward to enfold us both in her arms.

She smelled of spice, of sweet autumn leaves and Indian summer nights. I held her close and felt my love for her move through me, placid and smooth.

It amused me to think I ever fancied myself in love with her when my feelings for Elena so easily eclipsed that tenderness I felt for her sister.

Our love was violent.

There was nothing soft or subtle about the way it caught my soul up in a whirlwind fury of intense longing and furious passion. I was fevered. Obsessed. So in love it felt like I was hit in the face with it every time I looked at the woman in possession of my heart.

Maybe it made me a masochist, but I fucking loved it.

We finished our goodbyes, and I helped Elena into the black speedboat I'd captain back to Naples.

"You know how to drive a boat?" she asked as I started the boat, then caught the ropes from Tore and cast off from the pier. "Is there anything you can't do?"

I winked. "No."

"You can't be humble," she said, but she did it laughing.

I watched her lean back in her seat, her hair catching in the wind as I revved the engine and took us cutting through the waves back to her hometown. She was languid, graceful as always, but heavy with contentment. Her lids were low over warm gray eyes that watched me as I steered the boat easily through the errant fishing vessels dotting the harbor.

"*Sei bellissima,*" I told her.

*You look beautiful.*

"You look like mine," she responded with a slow, wicked smile. "I don't suppose we have time to consummate the union?"

"Not yet. Later, I'll fuck you until even your teeth ache. Now, we aren't getting on a plane. We're going to end Rocco Abruzzi's reign over Napoli."

She blinked at me, her mouth a little moue of shock.

For a second, I wondered if this was too much. If my ice queen lawyer had returned and her desire to be good would stop her from supporting my plan.

Before I could curb my words, she smiled like a fox in the face of a hound, clever and sly with bad intentions. "Can I help?"

The wind caught my laughter and sent it flying around us. "*Si, Donna,* you can help if you wish."

So, I told her our plan.

We had men, some of them recruited from Rocco's own community who were tired of the fear and his fury, and Damiano's loyal crew. Thanks to Leonardo Esposito and our own investigations, we knew where some of Rocco's loyal capos liked to hang out on a Sunday night, and our men were waiting for them there.

Pietro Cavalli visited his long-term mistress in Ravello.

Paulie Gotti visited a local tanning salon to top off his color.

Tony Martinelli took a cigarette on his back patio after dinner to get away from his wife and seven children.

The rest would be at the reception for my fake wedding with Mirabella.

We'd known Rocco wouldn't reveal the truth of our misdirection to the guests because he wouldn't want people to know he'd been duped. I wasn't sure how he was going to pull it off, but Leonardo had texted to say he told everyone we were shaken from the bomb and currently reaffirming our love physically.

If Italians believed anything, it was passion.

No one would blink an eye.

"Are you going after Rocco yourself?" Elena asked, standing to join me at the helm.

I steadied her when she almost lost her balance and put her between my body and the wheel, bracketing her with my arms to secure her. My nose dipped into her hair to steal a drag of that sweet scent.

"Yes, he deserves to be ended by my hands."

She was quiet for a long time after that. I fought the urge to question her, to ask if she thought I was a monster for orchestrating the killing of so many men.

Eventually, she turned her face into my suit jacket over my heart and pressed a kiss there. "I'm glad."

"You are?"

Her sigh was lost in the wind, but I felt her shoulders move with it. "Yes. Italy is corrupted by the mafia. How can we expect him to go to prison for anything he's ever done when he can just buy off the magistrates and police? I thought America was different, and then Dennis turned out to be corrupted. I know it's much worse here. Death is the only option for someone like Rocco. He tried to kill you and a totally innocent girl today in a car bombing just because he was threatened by your power and by her love of another woman? He sold my sister to Alexander. It might be wrong to want him dead, but not as wrong as his actions have been against the ones I love."

"When I first saw you in that red dress at the San Gennaro party, I thought you looked like a heathen goddess of sex and war," I told her.

She laughed, the sound moving through her and into me like an electric current. "I still think of you like this."

"I would have thought you found me an ice queen back then," she admitted, putting her hands over mine on the wheel.

Her plain gold wedding band caught the light and winked at me.

"No, only a future *Donna*."

My words were punctuated by a strange noise.

Something like a *pfft*, a whip snapped through the air.

Elena froze against me.

"*Scendi*!" I shouted over the wind and the growl of an approaching engine.

Elena dropped to the ground at my feet instantly.

A moment later, there was another *pfft* as a bullet zigged by my torso and out into the sea.

*Cazzo.*

I looked over my shoulder to see three suited men in a small speedboat powering toward us. I recognized one of them as Rocco's best enforcer, a man they called Big Tom, because he was short but mean as hell.

"They found us?" Elena asked, peering up at me with an eerie calm in her eyes.

I reached down to stroke her head in reassurance before putting my hand on the throttle. "They found us. Hold on to me."

Her arms wound through my legs.

I gunned the engine.

The boat tipped at a precarious angle, only the stern deep in the water, the bow clearing the waves as we soared over them. It was a Wally powerboat, one of the most powerful on the market. I'd been boating since I was twelve, but boat chases were not like car chases. The water had its own obstacles, rocks hidden too close to the surface, errant waves, and wakes from other boats that could overturn a quick-moving boat as easily as a beetle onto its shiny back.

I swerved too steeply, water spraying over the edge of the port side, dousing Elena and me in salt water.

"There's a gun in my waistband and one at my ankle," I shouted to Elena.

My eyes smarted and stung in the wind as I squinted back at the boat.

They were closer.

"Fuck," I cursed, ducking as one of the men raised a gun and fired off another round.

There was a *ting* as a bullet hit a metal railing.

"You can't shoot and drive the boat!" Elena yelled, shifting into a squat with one of my guns in her hands. "I'm going to shoot back at them."

"No, absolutely not!" I ordered. "Stay down there where you're safe."

She ignored me, sliding out from between my legs on her hands and knees, crawling toward the back of the boat. The seat and back railing obscured her from vision if she stayed on the ground, but in order to shoot, she'd need to peek above the safety line.

"Elena!" I roared, my heart beating so hard I thought it would give out. "Get your arse back here."

Nothing.

Only a *crack* as a shot went off behind me and, seconds later, a volley of returning fire.

"Hold on!" I called to Elena.

I pushed the engine higher, the boat rumbling like a waking dragon beneath my feet as I swerved again, skirting the edge of a rock formation frothing just under the water before us. I hoped they wouldn't see and wreck the hull over the stone.

Moments later, there was a faint cry in Italian and a resulting splash.

"They lost one of their men!" Elena shouted. "And they're falling back a bit."

I placed one hand solidly on the center of the wheel to hold it steady and twisted my body so I could pull out the gun at my waist and fire off a few shots at them. They were too far out of range though, which was a good thing as long as we could lose them before we got to the port of Naples.

Gunfire would alert the authorities, which neither of us wanted, but they would wait until we docked to subtly corral us to a quieter place.

I had no doubt Rocco had given them orders to kill us outright.

The white rock and verdant green shrubbery of the coast loomed far to our right. I'd kept far away to avoid the hazards beneath the surface near the cliffs, but now I reasoned getting closer was our only way to escape them. Their boat had a deeper hull, potentially damaged now because of the rocks.

I angled the boat for the shore, getting so close, Elena yelled something to me that was lost in the wind. The depth sounder display showed me what was beneath us, but she didn't know that.

"They're staying farther out!"

*Bene.*

They weren't able to get as shallow as we were, and I'd use that to my advantage.

We powered along at such a clip, the cliffs were only a white smudge in my peripheral vision. I followed the ragged line of the rocks, dipping in and out of sight from our persecutors who were rapidly falling twenty, then forty, then sixty yards behind us.

Chiara had loved boating with Tore in the summer, and we'd often spent long days exploring the grottos cut into the rock near Naples and on Capri. I scrounged through the faded memories in search of one near our location and laughed like a madman with exhilaration when the dark notch of a cave peeked out from the rocks ahead of us.

"Hold on, *lottatrice mia*," I bellowed, edging the engine even faster to put as much space between us and the enemy boat as possible.

There was a curve in the cliffside just before the grotto. We'd have maybe six to ten seconds of invisibility before they rounded the corner behind us.

Just enough time to slip into the rock crevice.

"Dante," Elena called, panic finally edging into her tone as we aimed headlong at the rock.

The cave was visible from this angle. It was only a shadow, a secret tucked between two bulging stones.

"Dante!"

I didn't answer because it was a tight maneuver. One second, we were gunning toward the cove, and the next, I cut the engine entirely, twisting the wheel just enough to nose directly into the thin gap.

Elena screamed.

Two seconds later, we were between the mountains, only clearing the rock on either side by inches.

It was suddenly quiet, the outside world muffled by the white stone walls and deep, sapphire waters.

*"Dio mio,"* Elena breathed from behind me as I ducked under a low stalacite.

When I turned, she was sitting against the back row of seats, the gun held loosely in one hand, her head tipped up to look at the ceiling as the grotto finally opened up into a wide, low cave.

"How did you know this was here?" she asked in awe.

I moved to the bow to release the anchor, the chains rattling through my hands as the heavy metal fell to the depths, caught on the rocky ground and held.

"There are grottos all along the coast," I offered as I moved back to the stern, looking over her. "We used to explore them with Chiara and Tore as boys."

Her eyes were wide, pupils blown with adrenaline. If it hadn't been obvious to me before, it was now clear that my woman got turned on by danger.

We stared at each other for a long moment, the tension between us crackling and popping like blazing kindling.

We moved at the same time.

She surged up as I bent down, hauling her into my arms against my chest. Her wedding dress was sea-soaked and plastered to her form, her nipples hard as pebbles beneath the cold silk. Her lips were cold too, but her tongue was hot against mine, her mouth silken as I plundered it ruthlessly. I needed the taste of her to cool the rage biting at the back of my throat, threatening to overwhelm me. The feel of her worked strange alchemy on the fury and transmuted it into a desire that razed through me until all I knew was her.

I growled as her hands pulled my shirt out of my trousers, nails raking over my abs, then down my groin as she pulled my hard length into her palm. Trapped between my waistband and my belly, she could only squeeze her hand, just pulsing her grip in time with my throbbing heartbeat.

It made me crazy.

I licked at her lips, sucking and biting them until they were swollen and ripe with my bruising kisses. When I was done marking that mouth, I moved to her neck, down to her exposed chest in that understated but sexy as fuck gown. When I reached the fabric of the straight-cut neckline, I rolled it down her arms, trapping them at her sides while exposing her tight breasts to my scrutiny.

She let me cage her in the wedding dress, lashes fluttering as she fought to keep her eyes open and on me while I lavished her nipples with my teeth and tongue.

We didn't speak even though I loved to tell her how I would fuck her, how she was responding to me. The cave was mostly dark, lit by an eerie light that swam up through the depthless blue waters and cast the entire cave in a neon glow. It lent itself to silence, to a quiet, urgent conquest of each other's bodies underscored only by our harsh breaths and the light lap of water against the rocking boat.

Her breasts heated with my ministrations, the skin red even in the blue light thanks to my teeth and the rasp of my five o'clock shadow. I plumped both swells in my hands and alternated between the two, treating each like a decadent feast.

"*Dio mio*, Dante," she finally panted softly. "I think I could come just from this."

*"Bene,"* I growled against her trembling flesh. "This is how a man loves a woman with his body, Lena. He takes his time to pull her apart seam by seam until she is unraveled completely in his arms."

She shuddered when I finally bent to find the hem of her dress and dragged it up, up, up, to tuck the end into the fabric gathered under her breasts so it would stay up.

My hand went straight to her sex, cupping the wet, swollen mount in my palm. My thumb pressed over her clit and rolled, the wet fabric of her underwear providing hot friction. She seeped through the satin and over my fingers, thighs trembling. The other went to her throat, thumb at her pulse to feel the way it kicked for me.

*"Moglie mia,"* I whispered against her bruised mouth. "My wife."

"Yes," she hissed, shivering as I hooked my fingers in the elastic of the panties and dipped two inside her. "Please, Dante, don't tease me. I need you to fill me up. I need my husband to fuck me until my teeth ache."

I groaned, shuddering as the chains broke, and the bestial side of me emerged. Before I could think, I was tearing open my belt and trousers, bringing my aching cock into the open. Elena tried to reach for it, but I slapped her hand away and lifted her into my arms. I moved to sit on the bench seat and brought her down on top of me, pausing to wedge my head at her sopping entrance.

"Ride me," I told her, leaning back to pluck at those distended red nipples. "Ride your husband and show him how much you love his cock inside you. Filling that tight, greedy pussy."

She gasped at my words, then took her lip between her teeth, balancing precariously because her arms were still trapped at her sides. Slowly, fucking excruciatingly, she lowered her cunt inch by inch down my shaft until she was seated fully on top of me. My dick kicked hard inside her tight folds, my balls already drawn tight.

I wanted to pin her hips and fuck up into her, to bruise the walls of her pussy so they ached from me for days because I knew even though we'd conquered our Italian villains, New York still waited on the horizon.

And New York meant we would be apart.

She seemed to sense my eagerness, or maybe it was her own. Her hips set a brutal pace, thighs quivering as she rose and lowered over me, fast and hard as our boat had rolled through the waves outside the grotto. The wet sound of our coupling echoed in the small space, loud and filthy enough to make us both curse with desire.

I leaned forward to take a nipple in my mouth and ravished it unforgivingly with my tongue and teeth. She groaned and quaked, then abruptly erupted all over me, her magma a cool sluicing of cum that dripped down my dick and soaked my balls.

I reached up to put my fingers in her open, panting mouth, wanting to be inside her in every way I could. She sucked on them as she came down from her climax, eyes glazed and heavily lidded but pinned on me. My wife in her rucked-up wedding dress riding me like she'd die if I didn't fuck her harder, deeper.

"Please." The word leaked from her mouth as she tried to move faster, but the weight of the wet dress and her own exhaustion stopped her from fucking me the way she wanted. *"Per favore."*

She gasped as I moved suddenly, taking her to her back on the bench without losing our connection. I palmed her throat, took her mouth with mine, and I fucked her.

Ruthlessly, almost painfully. The slap of my balls against soaked thighs, the grunt of breath through my laboring lungs, and the sweet gasps of her pleasure as I bottomed out again and again inside her.

*"Vieni per me, moglie mia,"* I gritted out between my teeth as I reached down to pinch her clit tight. "Come for me, wife."

I released the pulsing nub, and she screamed.

The sound bounced off the walls of the cave, echoing all around us.

She clenched around me so hard I couldn't resist the tingling in the small of my back and the tightening of my balls that urged me to spill inside her. So, I did. I thrust hard every time cum shot from my balls, filling her pussy until it leaked and squelched around my still hard shaft. When I went to pull away because my bones were soggy and I was definitely crushing her into the seat, Elena held me to her with legs twined around my back.

"I love you," she said straight into my ear like a secret before she kissed the lobe. "I love you so much it terrifies me, but I'm not even mad because even that makes me feel alive. I've thought a lot about what your mama said about all our choices and the choices of our ancestors before us, leading to this moment right now. It makes me believe in fate."

"In any life I might have lived before, you were mine," I agreed, running my nose down her cheek. "And I was yours. Still, I am sorry you've had to give up so much to be with me. I promise, I will fix it so that we can go home."

"New York isn't home without you. I don't care about that."

"But the law, you must miss it?" I was pressing because I wanted to know I was about to do the right thing.

She hesitated, her eyes turning vacant as her mind traveled across the Atlantic. "I do. I love the puzzle of a good case, how to make the laws bend and contort for me. But I'm sure I will find something else to do in Costa Rica."

She wouldn't.

Costa Rica was a mirage. She didn't belong there.

She didn't even really belong *here* in Italy.

Elena was a city girl in Chanel suits and bold lipstick. I wanted to give that back to her, and I knew I'd die trying to right enough wrongs to do so, even if it was without me.

"What happens now?" she asked, so trusting when four months ago, she had been so closed off no one could reach her without a fight.

I pulled away enough to look into those gray eyes and say, "Now, we begin our bloody honeymoon."

# CHAPTER TWENTY
## DANTE

We went in the early hours of the morning just before the sun is a thought on the horizon, a smudge of burnt orange lining the horizon. We'd stayed in the cave for another hour because I had to take her again, this time with her arms free so she could touch me too. Instead of the porti di Napoli, we pulled into a private dock owned by Damiano and then took a waiting Fiat to Villa Rosa. Rocco would never dare wage a full-scale effort against the home, as fortified as it was, so we felt safe to reconvene and arm ourselves for battle.

Frankie took out Pietro Cavalli at his mistress's house in Ravello, killing him clean through the head when he went to open the window, having staked out a neighboring unit's balcony for just that moment.

Nico took out Paulie Gotti. He paid off the woman tending the front desk, opened the coffin-like lid on the tanning machine, and shot Paulie three times in the gut.

Damiano took out Martinelli on the back patio by old-fashioned strangulation.

There was more.

Nine staunch supporters and higher-ups in Rocco's organization were all killed to end his reign of tyranny and poor economic success in the Neapolitan Camorra to make room for the return of the Salvatores.

Elena and I went after Rocco himself.

She demanded she be allowed to come with me, and I didn't want to refuse my bride on her wedding night even though the idea of endangering her still made me sick. The truth was, since I'd told her about women becoming Made just as men did, I'd noticed the mad glint in her eye that implied she wanted that.

Not because she was inherently violent, but because she wanted to be with me and mine more than she wanted anything else. We had become her family, but she wanted to be a part of the Family too.

I would never let her take another life if I could help it.

Her father's life had been more than enough, even if she wasn't certain who between us had delivered the killing blow.

It wasn't that I had some fucked-up Madonna-whore complex where I wouldn't want her anymore if she became too sinful. It was both simpler and more profound than that.

I didn't want to corrupt her totally. I didn't want to eradicate those things I loved about her and those things that made her *Elena*. Her love of justice and her thoughtfulness around morality. I needed those qualities from her as much as she did, and I wouldn't see them ground to dust under the heel of my violent life.

So, we drove in the Lambo together, a gun on my console beside the gear shift and one in her hand loosely resting on the other side of mine. We both wore black, and it shocked me how goddamn sexy she looked in the absence of color.

And we had a plan.

Rocco's villa downtown was ridiculously easy to breach. The walls abutted neighboring estates on both sides so whatever security he had in place was accessible at three points. We parked the car in an alley off *Spaccanapoli* Street and walked to the neighbor's house on the left of Rocco's. The streets were empty but for a drunk man sleeping sprawled across the stoop of an apartment building down the block. No one noticed when we quietly broke into the front door using a lock pick, and no one asleep in the home stirred as we carefully took the stairs up, up to the fourth floor.

Nico knew the house well because he was sleeping with the daughter of the merchant who owned it. He'd told us about the window at the top of the stairs that opened onto a rooftop garden beside Rocco's own terrace.

A guard was watching that vulnerability, and he was somewhat alert, which meant Rocco was nervous.

Knowing that made me smile as I gestured for Elena to stay down before leaping over the wall and landing with a soft thud against the armed man. We rolled to the ground, and before he could get his bearings, I knocked him out with a clean punch to the temple. His head bounced against the ground, then he lay still.

"*Vieni,*" I whispered to her.

*Come.*

She dropped over the wall easily, graceful even in her sneaking.

I led her through the garden, keeping my eye on a guard by the door to the house, half-hidden behind a planted palm.

Elena kicked a pebble that rolled across the tile and then knocked against a planter.

*Cazzo.*

The guard pushed off the wall, gun raised, eyes sweeping through the jungle of plants. I pushed Elena down with one hand, then lowered to my belly beside her, rolling slightly onto my side to raise my weapon at the right angle.

*Click, click.*

His shoes against the tiles.

I counted until I thought he would be close enough, the leaves of a bush swaying, displaced from something just a few feet to our right. My breath was calm, a quiet stream through my open mouth.

The guard rounded a massive pot of jasmine, and I shot a single bullet straight through his chest. He fell into the post, then slowly slid to the ground, clutching his torso.

Elena didn't move or gasp beside me. She watched as I got up slowly and went to the dying man.

"You don't have to die like this," I offered him in low, seething Italian. "You can tell me where Rocco Abruzzi is right now, and I can save your life."

He spat at me, a thick glob that landed on my chin. I wiped it off, then smeared my wet hand over his face despite his struggles.

"No?" I sighed wearily. "Okay."

I stepped back and leveled my gun at him.

"In the kitchen," he grunted as blood seeped through the fingers pressed to his wound. "*Testa di cazzo*."

"Can't you see a lady is present?" I asked lightly, then used the butt of my gun across his face.

He crumpled to the ground, out cold.

When I looked over at Elena, her eyes were wide, dark, and silver like the moon in the night sky above us. She wanted me. It was in the panting breath and dilated eyes, in the way she squirmed like she wanted to spread her legs for me right there.

"Later, *bella*," I promised as I took her hand and led her to the door.

We moved silently into the house, only crossing one guard as we went down a set of stairs and rounded the corner onto the level with Rocco's office. I took him down in a chokehold. When Elena moved past him, she carefully placed his errant hand on his chest so she didn't step on it.

How she could make me laugh at a time like that was beyond my comprehension.

Voices in the office alerted us that Rocco had company. I gestured for Elena to approach carefully then wait by the door.

"Listen, you asshole," he was spitting in rapid-fire Italian. "I'm only working with your Sicilian ass because we both have a common enemy. There's no way I'm going to do a single fucking favor for you beyond this. And if this is the way you treat an associate, I gotta say, I'm surprised you're still in business."

There was silence as Rocco listened to whoever he spoke to on the phone. My gut tightened as I wondered who the fuck he was talking to.

"I'll get him, you piece of shit," Rocco shouted, slamming his fist against a surface. "You're speaking to a Don from your fucking homeland. Treat me with respect. Oh?" He paused, his breath heavy with anger. "Well, fuck you! You can forget my number. Dante Salvatore will be dead within twenty-four hours and when he is, I expect you to keep your end of the deal. Get out of *Campania* and go back to your godforsaken island, uh?"

The phone was slammed down, and Rocco cursed under his breath in Italian.

I raised a finger to my mouth and signaled for Elena to remain where she was before I pushed Rocco's door open and entered with my gun raised.

"Rocky," I said in my most American English. "Who the fuck you talking to in here?"

Rocco sat behind his palatial desk with his head in his hands. The moment he heard my voice, he froze in the act of rubbing his tired face and dropped his palms to the tabletop. One tried to drop farther, probably to reach a gun secured beneath the desk.

"Ah, ah," I chastised. "Hands up, Rocco."

"This is a mistake, Salvatore," he warned. "You don't want to do this."

"Oh?" I cocked the gun and leveled it straight between his eyes. "I think I do."

"You want to leave the Camorra crippled, huh? It'll hurt your own business in America, you do that."

"Every dictator thinks the world will fall apart without their rule." I smile ruefully. "It is the bane of all powerful men to realize that one day, they won't be needed any longer. Today is that day for you."

"I have men who will come as soon as I scream," he tried.

"Scream," I suggested pleasantly. "I'll shoot you through the mouth before you can get a single note out of that fat throat."

"You want to pretend you're some good guy, Dante?" he snapped, his viciousness coming out in the flush of his face and the gruff hatred in his voice. "You're no better than me. We're fucking *camorristi*. We fight each other to get to the top, and we kill those we count as enemies. You're a murderer and a villain just the same as me."

"Never said I wasn't."

He hesitated, scowling at his inability to rile me. "You got that slut wife of Frankie's in your bed, don't you? She make you come here and do this? She got her hands so tight around your balls you--"

I pulled the trigger.

A bullet wedged in his hand where it lay palm down on the desk, clean through the center. The exact same place I loved to plant a kiss on Elena's hand.

His scream was delayed by his shock, and before he could get more than a note out, I was lunging across the desk, slapping a hand over his gaping maw and my gun to his temple.

I seethed, my breath as hot as fire against his face. "You don't talk about her. In fact, you shut your mouth unless I ask you a goddamn question, or I'll kill you right now."

He warbled against my palm, his face contorted with pain.

There was a jar filled with pens and utensils on the desk. Carefully,

I moved my hand from Rocco's face and plucked a letter opener from the cup.

"Now, tell me who the hell you were plotting with on the phone?"

He glared at me, one small, black eye twitching.

I sighed.

The letter opened went down through the bullet wound in his hand, embedding itself in the wood beneath it.

He howled, but I cut off the noise by shoving my gun in his mouth.

"Who. The. Hell. Were. You. Talking. To?" I growled.

He mumbled something around the gun, but I didn't remove it.

"I can't hear you," I told him calmly.

He tried again, this time louder.

It was pathetic really. A *camorrista* should be strong and resilient, unafraid. Death was nothing to us because it was such a frequent bedfellow. It could find us through any means because we were in the wrong place at the wrong time, we insulted the wrong man, or our boss got on the wrong side of another capo or rival family. Rocco's sniveling lack of resolve made me sick.

"I was speaking with *la Cosa Nostra,*" he mumbled around the gun when I took it slightly out of his mouth. "Agostino di Carlo."

Fury flashed through me like a flood.

"You were working with the wannabe capo of the New York Cosa Nostra," I repeated quietly, the words so heavy they fell between us like stones.

"He *is* the capo now. Killed the *consigliere* two days ago and won the title."

"Why would you go against your people?" It was almost unheard of for a mafioso to switch clans let alone mafia affiliations entirely. Usually, turncoats like that became dispensable to either side.

"The bastards in Sicily were encroaching on Campania," he growled, referring to the Camorra territory. "Agostino promised to rein them back in."

"*Sei debole,*" I told him flatly.

*You are weak.*

"Oh, there she is," Rocco almost purred as his eyes darted from me to the door. "*Ciao puttana.*"

I pistol whipped him across the face, but he only laughed.

Elena appeared in the doorway with her gun held to a guard's temple. "He was about to ambush you."

"And you got to him first." I was impressed and more than a little aroused by the fact. "*Lottatrce mia.*"

She grinned at me as I moved forward to take him from her. "Point that weapon at Rocco for me."

She did.

I twisted my torso and landed a massive, cheek-crunching punch to the other man's face, then watched implacably as he fell like a log to the floor.

"Now..." I shook my hand out a little, spraying blood to the floor. "Rocco, did Agostino mention anything about a *traditore* in my organization?"

His eyes widened, a manic smile seizing his bloated face. "Not so clever as you think you are, Salvatore."

"Cleverer than you at least." I rounded the desk and carted him up onto his tiptoes with a hand around his throat, squeezing tight. "You're going to die now, Rocco, and I want you to know why. It's not because I am better than you because you're right, I'm not. You and I are both villains, men with corrupt souls and greedy minds. I don't deny my darkness. But I also don't deny the light. You think you can force a girl into marriage just because she loves a woman instead of a man you chose for her? You think you should kill a man because you're jealous of him? Beat someone because they disagree with you?

"I'm not better than you because I'm pure as snow, Rocco. I'm better than you because I may be a villain, but I'm not a monster. I have a heart, and I know how to use it. But again, that's not why I'm going to end up the victor here. That's not why I'm going to shoot you straight through your thick skull."

I bent closer, my mouth so close to his that the old, bigoted fool flinched and made me cackle. "I'm going to kill you because I want to live more than you do. Because I'll do anything it takes to stay alive and keep my woman at my side. I'd skin you alive and feed pieces of you to your entire crew to show them just how much I mean it when I said the reign of Rocco Abruzzi is dead and the Salvatores are taking over Naples again."

"You greedy *fuck*!" Rocco shouted.

I slapped him. Open palm with all my rage behind it. His head cracked to one side, his skin gone red immediately like instant Jell-O.

"You hit like a girl," he spat, blood-tinged saliva falling to the desk.

"I hit *you* like a bitch because you are one," I told him matter-of-factly. "You think you can force Mira into marriage, Cosima Lombardi into sexual slavery, and threaten Elena?"

"You can't," Elena cut in, her voice true and ringing like church bells throughout the room.

It drew my gaze.

She stood just to the side and behind me, her gun aimed straight at Rocco. Her eyes were as cold and gray as the metal in her hands.

"Lena, don't," I ordered.

But I knew as I said the words that she wouldn't listen. This was the truth of why she'd demanded to come with me.

She wanted revenge herself.

The gun fired, the recoil smashing back into her hands. She didn't even flinch.

I looked at Rocco who was staring at her in stupefied horror, clutching his chest with his undamaged hand. At first, I thought she'd missed, but then Rocco's chin tucked to his chest and his hand fell away from his torso, revealing a bubbling hole in his right side.

Straight through his lung.

His breath wheezed in and out, trying to gather enough air to speak.

I knew he wouldn't die for a long time with a wound like that and I was glad.

Elena wasn't meant to be a cold-blooded killer.

She was better than me in soul and spirit. I didn't want the stickiness of my depravity to transfer wholesale to her.

So I blocked Elena's view of Rocco, leaned close to his laboring face again and whispered, "May your soul burn for eternity in hell if you betray the Omertà and the Family."

Rocco gasped. "*Figlio di puttana.*"

*Son of a whore.*

I brought my Berreta to his temple and pulled the trigger.

Elena made a noise of distress for the first time behind me as his brains blew out the back of his skull across the wall, his prized Titian painting splattered with gray matter.

When I turned to Elena, it was with mild apprehension.

She'd seen me kill in the basement of that house in Brooklyn. Watched me drill three rounds into her father's head. Witnessed me burn out a man's eyeball with a blowtorch and a spoon.

But this was different.

This was mafia brutality. An execution not self-defense.

She stared at me with wide eyes, pale as silver dollars in the low light, her eyebrows cut high into her smooth forehead.

"*Stai bene, lottatrice?*" I asked her softly, moving forward as if toward an anxious colt.

She shivered then rolled back her shoulders, snagging my hand in a tight grip to drag me closer. When I stepped against her, she lunged to her toes and pressed her mouth so hard to mine, I could feel her teeth beneath the cushion of her lips.

When she pulled away, her eyes were dark again, hot like the sky during a summer storm. "You once told me, sometimes the only honor to be had is in revenge." Her eyes darted quickly over my shoulder to the dead capo and then returned to mine with even greater conviction.

"Thank you for killing the man who made my family suffer for so long."

She kissed me again, this time soft and sensual, sucking my lips, rolling her tongue over mine in a languid glide that made my blood heat. When she pulled away, she cupped my neck, her thumbs on both pulse points.

"I hope you know that since I met you, you've been the hero I never knew I needed."

Her words rocked through me, satisfying some entrenched white knight complex I'd buried deep in the ground of my soul.

I was a bad man with good intentions, but people only ever saw what they wanted to see, and a capo was a villain.

Even Cosima had seen me as one when all I'd wanted to be was her hero.

My whole life, I'd strived for that just as Elena had, to be good and strong, to protect those I loved at all costs, even if my morals didn't take a traditional bent.

I'd been the hero no one wanted.

Until, now.

And fuck me, it felt good.

So, I kissed my wife again, pouring my love for her into her mouth like water into a vase, hoping to fill her to the brim with it.

And despite everything, I thought it was a fitting wedding night for two villains in love.

# PART TWO: NEW YORK CITY

# CHAPTER TWENTY ONE

## *elena*

We were already on the plane somewhere over the Atlantic when I started to get that feeling.

The one that tightens your entire chest and floods it with acid.

The past twenty-four hours had gone off without a hitch. Rocco and his top capos were killed, Damiano and his best men had swooped in to take their place seamlessly, showing up at their various operations as if they had always worked there. One of Damiano's men had been shot, but he'd survive, and Damiano was excited in a feral, gleeful way that Napoli was his to rule.

He was filled with ideas and savage with the aggression of a young alpha just come into his own.

Dante and I agreed it would be interesting to see how he fared.

By the time we boarded the private jet to take us to Costa Rica, I was exhausted. I'd help orchestrate a fake wedding, gotten married myself, been in a boat chase of all things, and then shot another man in the chest all in the span of a day and a half.

It was a lot for anyone to handle and I fell asleep standing up while we were waiting to climb the stairs to the plane. Dante had seen me sway, dropped his carry-on to the ground, and caught me before I could go down. He swung me up into his arms and carried me easily up the steps, ignoring my protests. I was only put down in the bedroom at the back of the aircraft and then tucked into bed securely, his face annoyed as if he should have thought to secure shackles to the bed so he could force me to sleep.

It was sweet in Dante's domineering way.

I'd opened my mouth to argue with him as he pushed my hair from my face, but I fell asleep before I could figure out what to say.

Six hours later, when I woke, the feeling had started in my chest.

There was no reason for it yet.

We were on our way to start a life in Costa Rica. Dante had even bought me a Spanish phrase book from a tourist stand in Naples.

But something felt off.

I used the bathroom to splash cold water on my face, surprised when I looked in the mirror to see how much I'd changed during my three weeks in Italy. My hair was threaded with gold from the sun, my skin warmed with a tan. But it was my eyes that seemed so very different.

I blinked at the dark gray orbs, noting the smile lines pressed to their corners, the wakefulness of my expression. In New York, I'd been so unhappy and constantly exhausted from work and spiritual melancholy that it had reflected in my face in a way I hadn't even noticed at the time. My eyes were clear of dark circles and bags, my pale, indoors-only skin was rich with color and a healthy flush, my cheeks weren't as gaunt, and my hair looked shockingly nice in its natural wavy state.

I was even wearing something different than my usual neutral suits and silk blouses. The Dolce & Gabbana dress was cut simply, sleeves with an A-line skirt, but it had a bold pattern of bright flowers I'd chosen because it reminded me of Italy, and I wanted to take a piece of that with me when we left.

I looked like a new woman as much as I felt like one inside my soul.

My smile hooked one cheek and then the other until it dominated my entire face.

Momentarily, I forgot about the tight feeling in my chest and exited the bathroom into the hallway leading to the main seating area of the plane.

"You should tell her."

I froze.

"*Stai zitto,*" Dante ordered blandly.

*Shut up.*

"No," Frankie insisted. "You're being a *stronzo,* so I won't shut up. This is the woman you just made your wife, D. You exchanged *fede*. You know what that means?"

"I may not have been born in Italy, but I speak the language better than you," he countered, still mild but with a current of agitation threading through his tone.

"It means 'faith,'" Frankie continued, unperturbed. "Those rings are a symbol of faith in each other and your relationship. Don't make her doubt it when you've just begun. She's stubborn. She might not forgive you."

There was a noise like someone moving and then Dante's voice, all passivity lost. "You think you know her better than I do?"

"I think I know *you* better than you do sometimes. You're setting yourself up for failure like some goddamn martyr."

"*Basta*!" Dante snapped.

*Enough.*

My heart was a lead weight in my belly as I pressed myself against the wall and tried to breathe.

What the hell were they keeping from me?

After Cosima's reveal about Salvatore being her father, I truly hadn't thought Dante would lie to me again, even by omission.

Where was hard-hearted, skeptical Elena?

Had she been buried alive by love?

I sucked in a deep lungful of recycled plane air and moved into the living area.

Neither man looked up from their work.

I moved to Dante, who sat in a big chair facing the back of the plane working on his computer. Without asking, I moved the laptop, closed the screen, and placed it on the table beside him. He watched me with curiously flat eyes as I got into his lap and pressed my nose to his throat.

His citrus and musk scent would forever remind me of Italy now, and that wasn't a bad thing.

"Did you sleep well?"

"No, I had bad dreams."

I took his hand in both of mine, fiddling with the wide gold wedding band. It was hard to believe it was there because of me. Because he was my *husband*. It made the idea of his secret-keeping all the more agonizing.

"What were you and Frankie talking about just now?"

Dante stiffened marginally. If I hadn't been sitting in his lap, I wouldn't have noticed.

Which was why I was there.

The best lie detector was my body against his. He could lie to me verbally, but physically our bodies shared the same language, and it would be nearly impossible to hide.

"Nothing important."

"Hmm." I continued to play with his wedding ring. "I think Zacero would be a good place to settle in Costa Rica. It's not very touristic, and it's in the mountains where it's cooler. I thought it might also remind us of *Villa Rosa*."

"*Se vuoi.*"

*If you want.*

"Dante." I gave up my act and sat straighter in his lap. "What the hell is going on?"

"Well, we're currently flying over the Atlantic."

"Don't be a *sputasentenze*," I demanded. *A smart-ass*. "Frankie was trying to get you to tell me something. What's going on?"

There was something wrong in his eyes. They weren't deep and sparkling as the night's sky, but flat, almost inanimate like black marbles.

"Frankie was being dramatic."

"You're being robotic. What is going on? Dante, I'm your wife. Does that mean nothing to you?"

Something cracked in that cold gaze, fire blazing through the fissure. "Don't be *stupida.* Of course, it means everything to me. You are the motivation behind every decision I make, Elena."

"Then explain this one to me."

He looked out the oval window at the pale sky. When we'd left Naples, it had been early morning, but we were going back in time, so time seemed to freeze in place.

"Capo," I called to him, using my hands on both cheeks to twist his head to face me again. "You and I are a team. Please, tell me because if something is wrong, I can help."

The hard set of his ruddy mouth softened, his eyes a tender caress as they swept over my face. "*Lottatrice mia,* always so ready to fight for me."

"*Sempre,*" I agreed.

*Always.*

His eyes flashed, and the last of his reticence escaped him on a sigh. I echoed him when his entire body shifted around mine, finally holding me the way I'd wanted him to, the way he usually did.

"I made a decision."

That foreboding feeling grew like thorns inside my lungs.

"We're going back to New York."

I blinked, a little stunned by his words.

It wasn't that I didn't want to go back. Marco was either the mole or a friend in a coma that needed our support. Chen and Jacopo had been dealing with the di Carlo attacks all alone because Adriano was still recovering. Bambi and Aurora weren't answering my calls or FaceTime attempts anymore.

Mama was in New York and Beau.

My job.

Which was, apparently, waiting for me should I ever return.

But there was one solid, unconquerable reason we couldn't go back to New York.

Dante would go to prison as soon as they discovered he'd returned to the country.

He watched my thoughts work behind my eyes, his own face set like stone.

It made him look like Alexander. Terrifyingly cold.

"And what's your plan? Stay locked up somewhere like you're on house arrest again because the moment someone reports that you're back in the country, they'll hunt you down and take you straight to jail?"

I knew that wasn't the plan.

Dante was a wild beast of man. Voluntarily going back into a cage went against his nature.

"Not quite." His sigh was bitter against my face as he cupped my cheeks. "I'm going to turn myself in."

Every atom of my body froze.

Suspended animation triggered by the overwhelming shock and fury that hit me like a nuclear blast.

Finally, the rage cut through the disbelief.

"Are you fucking *kidding* me?" I asked quietly because it was hard to speak when anger was buzzing through every inch of me.

"It's not as bad as it sounds," he tried to reason.

As if there was anything reasonable about this stupid plan.

I lurched to my feet because touching him when I felt as if I hated him was too much. My body jerked as rage ate at me, devouring me whole.

"You are not turning yourself in."

"Lena, if you would just listen for a moment--"

"No."

"Just--"

"Absolutely *not.*"

"Elena," he finally barked, surging to his feet himself so that we were pressed nearly chest to chest. "Our Family is under attack. I'm not going to leave them to fend for themselves."

"What the hell was all that with Rocco and winning back Napoli then? We did that to get reinforcements to help out in New York."

"They need their capo," he asserted with that absolute arrogance, totalitarian dictatorship that was bred from being born the second son of a duke *and* from being an Italian mafioso.

"Well, so do *I*!" I shouted.

His fury flickered then went out as he tried to reach for me. I stepped away, unable to bear it.

*"Sono con te, lottatice mia,"* he reminded me, *"anche quando non lo sono."*

*I am with you, my fighter, even when I am not.*

"You expect me to accept the fact that my husband for all of *two days* wants to turn himself in to the police for bail jumping when there are a thousand and one ways to avoid it?"

Something was darkening the edges of my vision, pumping my heart too fast and my breath too shallowly. It took me a moment to realize it was panic.

Fear.

I couldn't fathom Dante teaching me to love him and live my life with him only to rip it all away from me just as soon as we found some degree of peace.

"This is the life," he told me. "I made it clear to you over and over again. I can't offer you anything but chaos, but I will love you through every single day of it."

"I can withstand anything if it's by your side, but asking this? Asking me to be okay with you spending months or even *years* in prison awaiting a trial that the prosecution and judge had already decided you would lose despite the fact they had no concrete evidence? You're not just asking me for some little thing here, Dante. You're asking me to live my life without you."

His eyes were dark and smoking, fissures cracked through the earth going straight down to the center of the world. "It won't come to that."

"You can't possibly know that!" I cried, hands flying like birds under attack from some greater predator. "How can you even stand there and *say that to me*?"

My entire body felt like it was about to come apart at the seams. Wildly, that bitter voice I hadn't heard for weeks reminded me that this was why I'd closed down my heart. This was why I'd resolved to feel nothing because it hurt so fucking much when the good emotions corroded and went bad.

"Because I know *you*, my fighter," he said, stepping closer, grabbing my arms even though I struggled against his grip. "I know my *donna* will hold down the fort for me while I'm away. I know you will fight every single moment to get me out of that place. I know that I'm one of the most powerful men in New York City and maybe US Attorney Dennis *stronzo* O'Malley and Judge *merda* Hartford have it out for me, but I have my own friends in high places, and I'm not afraid to call on them for help."

"If your entire reason for going home is to help the Family, how do you suppose you can do that from jail?" I argued.

"I won't be there for long," he assured me, so calm, so collected while I was on fucking *fire*.

I didn't like the role reversal.

"If you have friends that can get you out of this, why go in the first place?" I challenged. "It's possible to pay a fine for bail jumping. It would be hefty, but it's not like you can't afford it. If they can get you out of jail, then they should be able to stop you from going in the first place."

His mouth hardened to a flat, intractable line. "I have to go in, but I'll get out."

"Don't you lie to me, Edward Dante!"

"Hush, *cuore mia,* I am not lying. Do you think I want to be apart from you for even a moment? That my chest isn't aching because I've already carved out my heart to give to you for safekeeping while I'm away?"

"Away, as if you're going on vacation," I muttered, so mired in fear and fury I couldn't feel my body anymore. It was just one giant supernova of heat and mindless anger. "You're going to jail. When Yara and I worked so hard to keep you out because there are people in there who want to kill you!"

"I can take care of myself." His eyes were dark places in people's nightmares as he spoke those cold words that clicked against his teeth.

I shivered despite myself.

There was no doubt Dante was as terrifying a man as I had ever known. Of course, I knew he could take care of himself, but that didn't mean I wanted him to be in a position to have to watch his back every hour or every day.

I told him that, and he laughed grimly.

"I already do that. I'm a *camorrista,* Elena. I have eyes in the back of my head to watch for knives even during times of peace. There is no rest for the wicked because the wicked are never content with the status quo for long."

"I won't forgive you for going," I told him recklessly, lashing out with my words because he still held my arms, and I really wanted to pummel him with my fists. "I won't forgive you for leaving me like this. I left my whole life for you, and now, what, you're asking for me to take it back?"

"*Mai,*" he snapped, shaking me a little as if I was losing my mind. Maybe I was. "Never, Elena. You are mine, and I am yours. No space or time will change that."

"Death will."

"I will not die in prison. If the great di Carlo brothers and Rocco Abruzzi couldn't kill me, I doubt some two-bit criminals in prison will."

"Don't make light of this, please." Usually, I loved his levity in every situation, but this was too much.

I was scared

I was scared because he had finally found the heart of me… the real me sunk deep under layers of armor. The real me who hadn't seen the light of day in years. Or maybe, ever.

He'd found me and brought me into the light where I found I *glowed.*

And now, he was threatening to take away the two people I had fallen in love with over the past few months.

Him.

And me.

Tears rushed to my eyes, surprising me because I wasn't finished being angry. "It feels like you're abandoning me."

"I'm not," he stated firmly, bringing me into his chest where he cradled me tenderly against his body. "Just as I know you won't abandon me while I'm in there. I'll find a way to pay the fine and return to you.

Then you'll find a way to put this RICO case behind us both for good."

I stared blindly at his black shirt as he held me, listening to the steady thud of his heart against my cheek. It lulled me more than his words had, reminding me that what we had between couldn't die unless both of us did. It was in our blood and bones, in every beat of our hearts.

Even if he was in jail, we'd still belong to each other.

"I've always had to work so hard at everything. You shouldn't have to fight this hard to be loved," I whispered, feeling suddenly tired, defeated.

"Are you fucking kidding me, Elena? Fighting for love is an endless battle and it's also the most epic war you'll ever wage. I promise you, you find the right person, you'll be willing to die on that battlefield, scarred and victorious. Why do you think I'm willing to do this?" He tipped my chin up so I had to look though my tear glazed eyes into his own coal dark ones. "I want to take ownership of my actions so that you have choices. So that you don't have to spend the rest of your life as a fugitive from a country you fought hard to be a part of and succeed in. I won't take that from you because I love you."

"I'm not asking you to martyr yourself for me," I countered. "It kills me that you think I need that when I'm being honest in saying I don't. The old Elena needed the white wedding in the society pages and the nice brownstone and the office on the top floor. This Elena, your Elena, only needs you, our family, and a sense of adventure."

"This is our next adventure," he said in a way I knew he had made up his mind and would not be swayed. "I won't leave New York a bleeding wound and run off to greener pastures. You deserve more. Addie, Chen, Jacopo, Frankie and maybe Marco deserve more not to mention all the other men in the outfit. They could die because I'm their boss. How can I let them die when I'm not even there to fight with them?"

The sigh that unraveled from my lips was as long as a ball of untangled yarn. "Dante…why do you have to be the most honorable bad guy in the entire world?"

He laughed, the sound gruff with relief. I let him hug me tighter and slowly moved my arms around his waist so I could hold him too.

"It's definitely inconvenient," he agreed. "But we can do this, *lottatrice mia*. If we can take down the *capo dei capi* of Napoli, we can find a way to rid myself of these bogus charges. Do you remember? *Chi vuole male a questo amore prima soffre e dopo muore.* Whoever is against this love, suffers and then dies."

His words galvanized me as he meant them to, which irritated me, but not enough to ignore the truth in them.

I'd been planning to take down Dennis O'Malley before we fled the country; I had ideas and plans already set in motion. Maybe I could pick up those threads and continue to weave a new future with them.

I didn't doubt my own abilities as a lawyer. I didn't even doubt my resolve as Dante's wife. I wouldn't leave him, not even if the worst happened and he was imprisoned for life. My heart was his and always had been, just waiting in my chest for him to come along and activate it.

It was funny to think of love as passive, as if you could fall into it like stumbling over a misplaced shoe. Love required *work*, it didn't just happen. Like a flower it required tending to, a series of actions to make it beautiful and fulfilled. I'd always thought love just happened and then it just stayed. How wrong I'd been.

Dante was right, love was worth fighting for and I'd been fighting for it unwittingly all my life. I'd fought for my siblings in Naples, for Daniel however poorly that had ended, and now, I could fight for Dante too, for however long it took to win.

"If you feel like you need to do this," I said slowly, tipping my head up to look into the eyes of the only man I'd ever loved. "Then we'll do it. I'm just scared."

"That's okay," he murmured, drawing his thumb over my lower lip before he gently placed a kiss there. "I'm happy you care enough to be scared for me."

"I'm scared for me, too," I admitted, even though it hurt to rip that truth off my soul. "I'm afraid of what will happen to me without you. Will I go back to who I was before? Because she wasn't happy or healthy."

"Maybe not, but that version of you didn't die, Lena. You just stopped cutting yourself in two and letting one side wither and die. You're whole now, and you have much more to do with that than I do."

I scoffed. "It wouldn't have happened without you."

His palms cupped my ass and lifted, taking me into his arms so he could sit down and place me comfortably in his lap again. Only when I was perfectly arranged to his liking, our left hands linked so our wedding rings faced up, did he respond to me. "Flowers don't thank the sun for shining on them or the rain for its wet. Whatever happened to you because of knowing me was always in you to give. I think you just needed a little love to realize how magnificent you are. How magnificent you'll continue to be even while I'm gone."

"See," I said, tears in my throat but banished from my eyes. I didn't want my remaining time with Dante to be sullied by crying. "You always say the right thing. How do you do that?"

His smile was just a suggestion around his full lips, an implication and a secret all at once. It was intimate and small, not his usual full-bodied grin that he shared with everyone else. It was just for me.

"Some people have hobbies, art, music, playing sport. Mine is learning you."

# CHAPTER TWENTY TWO

## elena

If you'd asked me before, I would have said I'd miss my life if I was forced from it. I liked my routine, the neat orderly line up of activities that got me through my day. The Sunday dinner with whomever of the twins and Mama were in town, the cases I spent hours after dark working on alone in my echoing home and the frequent TV and movie binge watch nights I had with Beau. I would have said I would miss it all. Even my bitterness, that constant aftertaste like coffee breath I wore on the back of my tongue for so long I didn't know taste without it.

But I found, in that car rolling into New York City, a place I'd dreamed about my entire childhood having just returned from my birthplace I'd sworn vehemently I'd never return to, that I didn't miss it at all.

Not even a little.

I yearned for my Mama, her semolina scented arms and the soft press of her bosom against my cheek as she comforted me. I missed Cosima who was never around much and even Sebastian, though our connection was still fragile.

I missed what I always missed about Giselle. The "what if things had been different" and "if only I hadn't this, this, or that." I longed for Beau because he was mine and only mine in a way no one else could understand.

But I didn't miss my mausoleum of a house or the glass shard of a skyscraper that housed my much-worked for office. I didn't even really miss the law, at least, not in the way I thought I would. I had always wanted to be a hero, someone on the right side of justice, and in a way, being with Dante still let me do that, only now I was a vigilante instead of a stock hero bound by the limitations of the law.

I held his hand in the back of the GMC SUV Frankie was driving. Dante was on his phone, typing madly on the screen, the whoosh sound alerting me to email after email being sent. When he told me they conducted most of their business online instead of in person now, I'd been skeptical. Couldn't emails be tracked and phones hacked?

But he'd laughed and showed me Frankie's three monitor set up on the plane. They had so many firewalls and contingency plans, redirects and shell companies, it would take the most talented hacker years to crack even one of their codes or schemes.

I looked at my thin gold wedding band glinting in the sun and squeezed his hand a little harder in mine.

We'd agreed we would visit Marco at New York Presbyterian before Dante called the police and turned himself in to the authorities.

According to Chen, the small Italian man had woken up two days ago and wouldn't talk to anyone but Dante.

"You're quiet," Dante noted. "Did I tire you out?"

I smiled a little, a flush working its way into my cheeks.

After our argument, we sat down and set out a plan of attack with Tore and Frankie before removing ourselves to the bedroom.

If we only have one more day left, we had to make use of it.

I'd lost count of how many times he made me come. On his fingers, tongue, and dick, once even when I was riding his thigh as he played with my nipples.

He'd fucked me until there was no cum left in his balls, until we were both so satiated that we were boneless masses sunk deep into the mattress.

It had been amazing.

"I promise, when I get out, we will have a proper honeymoon," he continued. "Where do you want to go?"

"I don't care," I said honestly. "Just having you back will be more than enough."

His face softened, those strong, dark features suffused with warmth. "Sometimes, Elena, you know just what to say too."

"I'm learning from the best," I quipped.

"In every way," he countered with a wiggle of his brows.

I laughed, and then I shook my head because it was extraordinary how he could make me laugh even when my heart ached.

"You'll be okay," he told me. "Frankie, Chen, Addie, and Jaco will stay with you at the apartment. One of them will go wherever you go, *capisci?* Do not try to leave without them or I will go mad in prison and you don't want that."

"No," I agreed. "I won't. My life won't be very exciting anyway. I'm going to dedicate all of my time to figuring out how to end this farce of a case."

"If anyone can do it, it's *lottatrice mia,*" he said as we pulled to a stop.

I looked out the window and frowned. "This is not the hospital."

"No," Dante grinned that wide, boyish grin that had endeared him to me despite myself months ago. "It is not."

He got out of the car before I could say anything else, opening my door to help me from the vehicle. It was a nondescript shop front, the name *Gatti* scrawled on a faded red sign with the image of a cat curling its tail around the "I."

I followed him inside without question.

"*Ciao Gatto,*" Dante called as bells chimed over the door.

A portly man with jowls like a bulldog entered the room behind a row of glass counters and clapped his hands loudly. "Dante! I wondered when I will see you again and here you are."

"I brought a special woman to the only place I would ever go to buy her something as treasured as she is to me," Dante explained, tucking me into his side and leading us forward to the back.

The shop was a smallish rectangle with a U-shaped formation of glass cases holding glittering jewels and jewelry. I stared at a sapphire the size of a pistachio and blinked.

"Of course, a beautiful jewel for a beautiful lady." The man Dante called 'Cat' rubbed his hands together in glee and then grabbed a pair of spectacles from a case on the counter. "Now, what does the lady like, huh? You like rubies, pearls, diamonds?"

I looked up at Dante. "What's going on?"

He grinned, picking up my left hand to press a kiss to my plain gold band. "You didn't think I would leave it at this, did you? I am proud of my wife, Elena. I want anyone who looks at you to see that you are unmistakably mine. We need a big jewel for that so here we are at Gatto's."

"I have the best," the shopkeeper said with an immodest shrug.

I smiled at him, but not at Dante. "I don't need anything else. This is perfect."

Once, I'd wanted an engagement ring the size of a baby's fist. The bigger the better. I'd pass by Tiffany's on the way to work sometimes and look in the window, fantasizing about which gorgeous diamond Daniel might buy me.

Now, all I could focus on was my desire to see Dante a free man, unencumbered by the RICO case or bail jumping. Everything seemed trivial in comparison.

"Indulge me," he suggested with a roguish smile before turning to Gatto. "Bring us some rubies and pearls, maybe a few gray diamonds if you have any."

Gatto nodded enthusiastically and raced into the back.

"What about you, then? You want everyone to look at me and know I'm taken by my shiny ring. Shouldn't you have one too?" I asked, loving the idea of stamping him with a brand.

His eyes sparkled. "Feeling possessive?"

"Always."

"Okay. You can choose what you like and I'll wear it."

"Careful, Dante," I teased, moving away to look at some of the male rings in the display case to the left. "What if I get you a pink or purple stone?"

He leveled me with a look that dared me to fuck with him. "Then I will wear it and spend the rest of our lives punishing you for every single time someone makes a rude comment about my ring, *va bene*?"

I swallowed thickly, my thighs tingling even though I was sexually exhausted. Still, I was a tiny bit tempted to do exactly that.

"Elena…" he warned.

I laughed, hands raised in innocence. "I promise, I won't."

While we waited for Gatto, Dante took a quiet phone call and I focused on the rings in the case. My gaze snagged on a large gold band studded with a single, pristinely perfect obsidian stone.

"Ah, yes, that is lovely," Gatto agreed as he passed by with a covered tray of jewels. "Come and choose yours before you pick anything. You might want to match them."

I followed him, hooked through the heart by the sight of those beautiful gemstones.

My hand went to my mouth as I bent over the tray as he set it down for me.

There were six rubies and red diamonds in varying shades from pink to purple to deep, blood red but each of them was enormous. There were four large pearls, black, cream pink, and white along with tiny seed pearls that Gatto suggested could be arranged framing the main choice.

And then there were the black and gray diamonds.

"They can be cut into any shape," he said as Dante joined me.

My husband, I still couldn't believe I got to call him that, bent over the table with me and whistled. "Excellent selection, *amico*."

"Only the best for you."

"Which do you like, *cuore mia*?" Dante asked me, his breath tickling my neck in a way that made me shiver.

"All of them," I said honestly.

Both men chuckled.

"You have good taste," Gatto complimented me.

I smiled at him. "You're the one who picks them so that compliment should go to you."

He preened.

"What do *you* think?" I asked Dante, tucking myself further into his side, placing my hand over his heart just to feel it beat.

"Mmm," he bent closer, using a small diamond magnifier to look at the blood red diamond, the gray diamond, and the black diamond as if he was a jewel dealer himself.

"I like the gray because it is the color of your eyes," he told me, grasping my chin lightly to look into them. "I like the black because our soul shines brightest in the darkness."

I agreed with his poetry completely, entranced by his words and the way he looked at me as if I were more priceless than the millions worth of diamonds on the table.

"But it has to be the red," he declared, lifting the large wine-red diamond from the cushioned tray and fitting it into my palm. My fingers curled around it like one of his kisses. "It is the color of passion and fire. The color of you. But also," he paused to kiss me, a sudden, savage kiss that brought me to my tiptoes. "I think now you see the world in black, white *and* red, *donna mia*."

"I do," I agreed, somewhat breathless, robbed of air by the beauty of this man.

My man.

I was learning that there was nothing so romantic as a man who strived to know you as a cartographer maps new lands, always filled with a sense of wonder even when he discovered something you thought was a flaw.

"The black diamond for Dante, please," I said instantly. "I'll take the red."

Dante pressed a kiss into my hair and I knew he was happy with my selection.

"Thank you," I told him as Gatto moved to collect both stones. "It will be nice to have while you're…gone. But let me pay for your ring, at least."

His face changed suddenly, lips flat, eyes narrowed. "I know you can afford nice things, Lena. I know you worked hard for the ability and I admire it. But I will always take care of you. Always. Please indulge me in my archaic or perhaps my Italian nature and do not argue with me about this."

Maybe I would have put up a stink before, but Dante was going to jail in a matter of hours. I didn't want to spend those arguing over something trivial.

"Okay."

He squinted at me then placed his hand on my forehead. "Are you feeling okay?"

I laughed as I swatted his hand away. "I'm not that difficult!"

His smile softened. "No, no, you are not."

Marco wasn't alone.

"What do you want me to do, woman?" His voice was thin and scratchy with disuse, weak from the coma and his injuries.

"I want you to fix this." It was Bambi, her tone desperate. "I want everything to be as we said it would be."

"You told me a million fucking times not to leave Angie. You're giving me whiplash, and I already had a concussion."

There was silence.

Dante and I remained just down the hall pretending to read a bulletin board as we eavesdropped shamelessly on their conversation.

"Bambi baby," Marco's words were tender, smooth. "You gotta tell me what's going on. You've been so fucking stressed lately. I know things are hard with the Boss gone, but he'll be back soon, and he'll fix this thing with the di Carlos."

"Will he?" she whispered, sniffing. "It feels like it won't ever end."

"I didn't know you were so scared," he admitted. "Is it Rora? The di Carlo brothers are assholes, but they wouldn't hurt a random kid in our Family."

There was silence where they seemed to ponder whether this was a true assertion or not.

So did I.

As if summoned by her name, there was a sharp little squeal, and then a small body ran straight into our legs.

I twisted my body to look behind us. Jaco was striding down the hall toward us.

And Aurora was hugging us from behind, her dark head smooshed between Dante and me with one arm around each of our legs. As I looked, she tipped her face up with a beatific smile that took my breath away.

I'd forgotten what a gorgeous girl she was.

"*Zio* Dante," she cried, still shouting even though we were beside each other and in a hospital hallway. "Elena!"

"Rora," I greeted warmly as Dante turned and hauled her into his arms.

She laughed delightedly as my husband peppered her face in kisses. I watched raptly as she smashed her hands to either side of his face to hold him still, then planted a big, puckered kiss straight on his mouth.

"I missed you," she declared.

"I missed you more," he assured her. "I thought of you every day. Didn't I, Lena?"

"He did," I agreed, reaching over to smooth her tangled curls. "So did I."

Rora smiled at me, catching my hand so she could bring it to her cheek for a cuddle. My heart swelled, threatening to burst at the seams.

She was perfect.

My hand went to my uncooperative womb as it panged. I tried not to be ungrateful--I'd spent too long doing that--but I still wanted to be a mother so badly I ached for it.

I dreamed of one day having a daughter like sweet, precocious Aurora.

"Should we go see your mama?" Dante asked, carrying her easily with one large hand propped under her bottom.

Something shifted in her little face, a tremor that was there and gone. Dante's eyes snapped to mine instantly, wondering if I'd noticed it.

I nodded.

His mouth went flat, but he jerked his chin up at Jaco as he arrived before us. "*Cugino mio*, how are you?"

Jacopo looked exhausted, dark circles under his eyes, a patchy beard covering his jutting jawline. He was an attractive man usually, but he looked so haggard it was hard to believe he wasn't even forty years old yet.

He surprised me by smiling warily at Dante, then turning to give me the customary two kiss greeting, his hands warm on my shoulders as he squeezed them in silent comradery. Of all the men in Dante's inner crew, I was the least close with him, and it was pleasantly shocking to know he might have missed me while we were gone.

"*Che piacare vederti*," he murmured as he moved back.

*It's good to see you.*

I smiled at him. "We missed you."

His smile was thin but genuine. "Not as much as we missed you two, Tore and Frankie. It's been a shit show to say the least."

"You'll fill me in when we get back to the apartment," Dante ordered, reprimanding Jaco with his gaze for swearing or talking about such things in front of Rora. "Let's go in to see Marco."

Marco and Bambi were clearly aware we'd arrived thanks to the ruckus Aurora had made in the hall, and they were waiting for us placidly, as if they hadn't just been having a lover's quarrel.

"*Miei amici,*" Marco greeted, trying to be his usual robust self. "I can't tell you how good it is to see you."

"And we you," Dante said, sitting at the edge of the bed with Aurora in his lap. "You lost your good looks while we were gone."

Marco laughed.

It was amazing to watch as Dante struck up a light conversation with the man we both thought could be the mole. He was still his charismatic self, no signs of wariness or anger in his person. He didn't need an icy mask, as I did, to hide his true intentions. All he needed was his copious charm.

"Hi," Bambi said, having come up beside me. She looked shy, a thick sheet of golden hair curtaining her face. "I'm glad you survived the home country."

Despite my suspicions about her relationship with Marco, I laughed. "It was close a time or two, I won't lie."

"You seem much happier, now," she noted, her eyes sweeping over me. "Lighter somehow."

"And you?"

Her lashes flickered like a failing light bulb. "I-I'm okay."

"So, Marco is your boyfriend?" I pushed quietly as Marco, Dante, and Jaco spoke together.

She bit her pink lip, eyes darting to him. "I love him."

"Okay," I said easily enough, but something didn't add up. "Is he the man you came to me about, though? I know what it's like to be in a relationship with a man who hurts you, Bambi. If you love him, it can be hard to understand we don't deserve to be treated that way."

"I don't want to talk about that here," she whispered sharply, her big eyes narrowing. "Please. You said you would be discreet when I came to you."

"I did, but I'm worried about you and Rora. I'm worried about Dante, too. He doesn't want to have a man on his crew who abuses women, let alone a woman he loves and respects as much as you."

She made a tiny noise in her throat of distress. "Please, leave it for now."

I had to compress my lips against the tidal wave of words and worry that crept up my throat. It went against everything in me to allow a woman in an abusive relationship to continue to dig her head in the sand, but I also didn't want to alienate her. She had come to me before. I had to hope she would again.

So, I pulled her into an impulsive hug instead. "I'm here whenever you need me. For Rora too."

Bambi sniffed a little. I noticed her eyes were red-rimmed as she pulled away. "*Grazie*, Elena. She missed you, you know?"

Some of my anxiety smoothed out as I looked over at the little girl chatting animatedly with her hands to the three mafiosos who all watched her with indulgent grins. It was an almost comical sight and one that moved me straight through to my soul.

"Bambi," Dante called as he stood with Rora and moved over to us. They exchanged kisses. "Could you take Rora to get something from the cafeteria?"

He wanted to talk to Marco without the little girl around to curb his enthusiasm.

Bambi tucked her lower lip between her teeth, gaze darting from Dante to Marco and back. Finally, her shoulders sagged a little, and she nodded, taking a reluctant Rora from her uncle.

As soon as they left, Dante's casual, charming façade dissolved like pearls in vinegar. When he turned back to Marco, he seemed even taller, so broad and dark he blocked out the overhead lights and left a looming shadow over Marco's hospital bed.

"What happened?" he demanded coolly.

Marco winced as he tried to sit up straighter against his pillows. After a moment of hesitation, I moved forward to help him. He squeezed my hand when I offered it as leverage, shooting me a slender smile.

"Honestly, Boss, I don't really know. Bambi and I were out to dinner at Santa Lucia Pizzeria. We left the restaurant, and then Bambi forgot her purse, so I was waiting for her outside but facing the door. Didn't know I had company until I got shot in the chest. When I looked up, a man on a fucking scooter at the curb had a massive S&W Magnum trained on me. He got the next three shots off before I could even fucking blink, and then he took off."

Marco blinked slowly, obviously remembering the ordeal.

"Bambi came out, started screaming, and called 911. I blacked out pretty quick."

"You didn't get a look at the guy?" Dante pressed.

"He was wearing a helmet and leather. Not an inch of his skin to be seen, no recognizable marks or tattoos." Marco sighed, sinking back into the pillows like he was suddenly exhausted. "Gotta assume it's the di Carlos, though I'm shocked they'd come at me like that unprovoked."

"They got Roberto outside a McDonald's drive-through," Dante informed him. "They're coming for our clan whether we earned it or not. You wonder how they knew you'd be there?"

Marco flushed slightly, his eyes darting to me and back to Dante. I moved to the far corner of the room and took a seat, pretending to look at my phone.

"Bambi likes the pizza at Santa Lucia's," he muttered finally.

"And your wife hates it," Dante added dryly. "*Che cavolo,* Marco, what were you thinking? An affair with Bambi?"

"Didn't mean for it to happen, Boss. It just…it did. Angie was chewing me out for one thing or another one morning, and when I showed up at your place, Bambi noticed I was looking rough. She made me an espresso, and we talked it out. Happened a few more times and then…" He shrugged, but his eyes were bright with affection for the woman. "She's a good woman."

"She is," Dante agreed. "She deserves a man who isn't married."

Marco sighed, scrubbing a hand over his face even though it made him wince. "She told me for months she didn't want me to leave Angie. She fucking insisted. Ang doesn't have anyone else in this world, D. She ain't right for me, and she's a *la volpe* sometimes, but I'd be devastating her if I left. Seemed like I was doing the right thing at the time."

Dante pinned him to the bed with the weight of his dark stare, the gaze so heavy Marco seemed to sink even farther into the bed beneath the scrutiny.

"You treat her right, *fratello*?" Dante asked quietly.

Dangerously.

Marco blinked, his brow screwed up in the middle with bewilderment. "You ever known me to treat a woman anything but?"

"No, but things change."

"Not that. Bambi…I know you're mad I didn't tell you, but I love her, Dante. She makes me feel like a good man, maybe even the best."

I smiled slightly as I looked at my lap. It seemed love had the capacity to turn even the most hardened villains into heroes for the ones they cared about.

"There are no secrets from me in this family or in this *borgata, capisci?*" Dante said after a moment, his words as final as a judge's gavel strike. "You keep something from me again, you won't like the consequences."

I watched Marco swallow thickly then nod. "*Capisco, Capo.*"

Jacopo cleared his throat, pushing off from the wall beside the door to clap Dante on the shoulder. "Not to change the topic, but I hear congratulations are in order, *cugino*."

Like sun breaking through the crust of clouds after a storm, a brilliant smile overtook Dante's previously surly expression. He shifted to open an arm for me. I went to him, sliding into his side like two clicking magnets.

*"Si, miei Fratelli, vi present mia moglie,"* he announced proudly.

*Yes, my brothers, meet my wife.*

Marco gasped so hard he winced in pain, then laughed softly before hooting, *"Auguri!"*

*Best wishes.*

"Thank you, Marco," I said as Jaco stepped forward to shake hands with Dante, then kiss my cheeks again. "Thanks, Jaco."

"Happened quick," Jaco noted.

Dante shot him a look, but I didn't take umbrage. "It did."

"When you know, you know," Marco said in a dramatically wise voice.

I laughed, filled with contentment despite the unknown because it felt good to be back with men who felt like family.

# CHAPTER TWENTY THREE

## *elena*

We entered the Smith Jameson Building through a locked door in a subway station three blocks away from Dante's apartment. Apparently, a series of tunnels existed beneath the city made by abandoned metro stops and defunct railways, and somehow, Dante knew the system inside and out. We didn't want to be seen by the cops or anyone who might be watching the building before Dante got a chance to talk to his crew.

The apartment was the same way we'd left it, clean and tidy because Bambi wouldn't allow it to get dusty or stale even while we were away.

Yara, Chen, Addie, Tore, and Frankie all waited in the living room. We greeted each other like long-lost family, kissing and hugging before we took seats around the coffee table. Dante and I sat on the long couch beside Addie, who was still recovering from broken ribs, his bumpy nose even more crooked after the beating he'd taken from the

Irish mob when they abducted me.

"You surprised me," Yara said as she greeted me. "You should be proud. It takes a lot to do that."

"I'll take credit if you tell me how I did it," I quipped.

"I didn't think you had it in you to love a man like him." She seemed somber, almost melancholy as she reached out to clasp my shoulder. "I'm glad I was wrong."

"Me too," I said because her words felt like a blessing I didn't know I wanted.

We talked for hours.

There was so much to address—how to attack the di Carlo situation, how to flush out the mole, what to do about the RICO case, and how I should proceed with things as Dante's new wife. He argued that I should stay in the shadows and leave things to his men.

But I was a fighter, and no way would I sit out while others fought to protect him and our family.

He capitulated fairly quickly after that.

It was dark when we finished, only the familiar lights of the cityscape brightening the view outside the floor-to-ceiling windows. At one point, we'd ordered Chinese food and Addie insisted on Christmas music because it was December twenty-third, and Dante would be in prison for the actual holiday.

We danced to Nat King Cole's "Buon Natalie," Dante spinning me until I was so dizzy I couldn't stand without his arms around me. We drank so many bottles of Chianti that my tongue was stained red.

We celebrated.

It seemed the only appropriate way to say goodbye to the man we all loved.

Just before midnight, Dante tugged me onto the patio for some cold air. I fanned my sweaty forehead as we stood at the stone balustrade and looked out over the city lights.

"I always feel like a king up here looking at this city," he told me as he wrapped his arms around my hips and leaned his front into my back. "From the first second I stepped off the plane, I wanted it to be *my* city."

"It is," I told him. "It will be again."

"Even if it isn't, loving you was worth losing it all."

"Don't say things like that," I beseeched as I snuggled closer to him, his warmth a direct contrast to the bitter cold New York winter. "It makes it impossible to let you go."

His nose traced the shell of my ear. "It's only for a little while. Trust me, *lottatrice,* turning myself in is the right move."

I didn't say anything because emotion had clogged my throat. I wanted to clutch him to me, dig my nails into his skin and wrap my limbs around him like vines until he was unable to move, let alone leave me.

"I told you once that you reminded me of my mother," he said softly, almost distractedly as he looked over my shoulder to the artificial stars of the city nightscape. "The truth is, you are so much stronger than her. She was crushed by the weight of Noel's dark world, and you just seem to rise and rise like some star in my dark sky. I can turn myself in knowing that you are strong enough, that you have enough *coraggio,* to withstand the loneliness and worry. Not only that but to rise above it and find a way for us to be together again, free of this RICO case and Dennis O'Malley. You told me I was your hero, but I hope you know, Lena, you are my hero too."

I choked on the sob in my throat, trembling with the force of keeping my tears at bay.

He shifted behind me for a moment, something clinking as he moved, and then a moment later, he was dangling Chiara's silver cross in front of us. It was impossible to look at the man pinned prostrate on the silver and not realize how much Dante was martyring himself to give me a better life. One with family and friends and a career, one in New York, where I didn't have to be a fugitive for the rest of my life.

"I want you to hold on to this for me," he murmured as he slipped the large chain over my head without unclasping it. The heavy weight of the pendant settled just beneath my breasts. It was warm from his skin. "It will make me feel better to know that my mother and her ancestors are watching over you while I'm gone."

I spun in his arms, blindly seeking his mouth with my own. There were no words to describe the ache of love and sweet sorrow in my heart, so I fed the emotions to him on my tongue. He held me tenderly, lapping the words from my mouth as if he understood.

"I'm going to miss you so much," I admitted against his damp mouth. "I miss you already."

"I know, *cuore mia*. But it won't be long."

"You're so certain."

"I would never doubt you. My whip-smart lawyer can do anything," he stated as if it was fact.

No one had ever had such an unshakable belief in me before. It made me feel like I could do anything.

And I would.

I'd work every minute of every hour of every day to get him back to me.

"*Ti amo, Capo,*" I whispered against his lips. "*Ti amo, martio mio.*"

*I love you, my husband.*

He smiled against me, his hand reaching up to palm my throat. "*Sono con te, lottatice mia, anche quando non lo sono.*"

*I am with you, my fighter, even when I am not.*

Despite my abandonment issues and the fear that pooled like iron on the back of my tongue, I trusted him.

I trusted *myself*.

And when we said our final goodbye at the door ten minutes later, I didn't cry even though tears burned in my heart. I just gave my capo one last kiss, a stamp of ownership I hoped he would feel for the days and weeks to come, and then I let him go.

Because I knew no matter what, he would come back to me.

The headline in *The New York Times* the next morning read *The Mafia Lord Returns,* followed by a grainy black and white photo of Dante being handcuffed by police officers at the 23rd Precinct.

I stared at it for a long time as I sat at the kitchen island drinking my coffee. My thumb moved over the photo until it was inked with newsprint.

It was too early to call, but I did anyway.

"Any news?"

Yara sighed. "The arraignment is in two hours. Bail jumping is a Class A misdemeanor, Elena, and Judge Hartford is on the case again. They'll want to make an example of him. There's no question Dante will go to prison until trial for the RICO case."

"I know."

"Then why the phone call?" Yara asked coolly, and I knew she was probably raising her eyebrows on the other end of the phone.

We'd spoken yesterday about the game plan, but it was hard not to be directly involved in Dante's legal team after so long of being Yara's associate, especially now that I was in love with him. It made me feel impotent to sit there knowing there was legal work to be done.

It was legal for lawyers to represent their family under New York law, though it wasn't exactly advisable. Still, there was no way I was going to take myself off the RICO case now. I couldn't attend the arraignment because, technically, I was still on leave from work.

"I want to ask Ricardo Stavos for help."

There was a surprised pause, then, "What can he do that Frankie can't?"

"He's the best private investigator in the city. Frankie can do amazing work through the computer, but if we want someone on the ground, no one is better than Ric." I'd thought about it a lot in the past two days and decided I would reach out to him even if Yara vetoed it. "He could be invaluable in tracking the di Carlos."

"One thing at a time. Let's focus on proving Dante's innocence."

I picked at a hangnail until it bled, then cursed softly. "Dante said you would know who to speak with to get a speedy trial."

"I do."

Another pause while I tried to stop the flow of blood with the edge of a napkin.

"Elena," Yara called, her voice firm. "I know this is scary. I know it's against your nature to sit back and do nothing. But I've got this, I promise. Dante will spend minimal time behind bars while we set a date for the trial and then we'll hit it out of the park. He didn't even kill Giuseppe di Carlo."

"No, but USA Dennis O'Malley knows that, and he doesn't care. He wants to use the case to build his political career. Now that Dante's fled and come back, he won't want to lose even more badly."

"Too bad for him."

Chen came into the kitchen in his workout clothes, dripping sweat all over the tiles. "*Donna,* the cops are downstairs. Seems they think they should talk to you."

"Yara?" I said into the phone. "Do you think you have time to meet me at the police station for the arraignment?"

It was beyond bizarre to be on the other side of the table in a police interrogation room. We were at the 23rd Precinct, where Dante had turned himself in late last night. The two uniformed cops who had come to pick me up had long ago handed me over to a pair of detectives.

One of the men was an older man with a slight underbite that made him look almost feral, and the other was a gorgeous younger man with close-cropped dark hair and pale blue eyes like chips of arctic ice.

It was the latter who leaned over the metal table intimidatingly.

"Ms. Lombardi… or should we call you Mrs. Salvatore now?" he questioned as if he was clever and shocking.

I blinked at him. "You can call me whatever you like, but I won't answer until Mrs. Ghorbani arrives."

He scowled at me. "You think because you're a lawyer, you're above the law? We know you went to Italy with Dante Salvatore when he fled the country. We've got surveillance tapes that put you at the same airport."

I blinked at him again.

"He told us that he kidnapped you and forced you to marry him so you couldn't testify against him in court," he tried, giving me a mean, sly look as if his words could hurt me.

I almost told the idiot that of course we'd gotten married so quickly because of Dante's trial. Not only did I not have to testify against him, but now, I also had rights to see him and speak on his behalf.

I yawned.

The cop, a Detective Falcone, slapped his hand against the table. "You think this is funny? Dante Salvatore is one of the most dangerous men in New York. He probably wined and dined you with all his blood money and kept the truth from you. But he's a very bad man, Ms. Lombardi, and I'm telling you, a law-abiding *lawyer* like yourself doesn't want to be within sixty feet of him."

Actually, I would have given nearly anything to be within sixty feet of him again soon.

There was a knock on the door, and then Yara entered, dressed impeccably in a beautiful double-breasted suit.

Detective Falcone sighed and sat down as soon as she moved into the room, clearly aware of her reputation.

"Falcone, Whitmore," she greeted cordially as she took the seat beside me. "I trust you've been treating my client well while you waited for me to arrive."

Their silence was somewhat petulant.

"We're trying to protect you," Falcone tried again. "We got intel that the di Carlos family is after you. They make your *husband* look like a fucking kitty cat. You give us what we need to keep Salvatore behind bars, we can offer WITSEC."

I laughed.

I couldn't help it.

Giving up my entire life by giving up Dante? It was so ludicrous it made my belly ache.

"I think you should take that as a 'no,' gentlemen," Yara suggested coolly. "And unless you have actual charges to level against Ms. Lombardi, I think we're done here."

"You're in danger," Whitmore inserted sincerely. "Do you understand who you have coming at you? The Cosa Nostra has stayed strong for a reason. They take out anyone in their way."

*They can try*, I thought as I fixed an icy smile on my face. "Thank you for looking out for me, detectives, but I think we're done here."

Falcone sighed heavily, grabbing my arms as I went to walk back so he could press something into my palm. "This is my card. Something happens, you call."

I blinked up at him curiously because he seemed genuinely concerned for me, and in my experience, most cops didn't care about random suspects. "You seem invested in this case, Detective Falcone."

His lips pursed. "Trust me, I know the mafia seems glamorous, but it's a nightmare. Death is nothing to them. They eat women like you for fucking breakfast. I don't want to see a nice woman with a *good* reputation lose everything, even her life."

I patted his arm. "It's all a matter of perspective because the only way that would happen is if I took your advice."

# CHAPTER TWENTY FOUR

## elena

The first thing I did after being interviewed by the police was meet with Ricardo Stavos.

"Elena," he greeted me with a wide grin and open arms, kissing me warmly on both cheeks before he took a seat across from me. "I was so happy to hear your voice. Everyone at Fields, Harding & Griffith misses you."

I arched a brow. "Oh? I'm sure Ethan Topp is beside himself."

Ric laughed. "There's definitely no love lost there. So, maybe I'm the only one that missed you, but that counts for something, right?"

"It counts for everything," I assured him. "That's why I called you."

He gave me an assessing look, then swept his gaze over the tiny coffee shop Yara had once taken me to that was little more than a window cut into the side of a building. "Not your normal style. First, you disappear, then you ask me to meet you at a coffee shop of a known Camorra associate." His eyebrow hiked into his forehead, but his tone wasn't judgmental. "Am I right in assuming things have changed between you and Dante Salvatore?"

I took my left hand from beneath the table and presented it to him. The red diamond ring had arrived that morning courtesy of Gatto himself who made me put it on right there in the doorway to see how it looked.

It was stunning.

Four and a half carats of wine-red diamond cut into a gorgeous oval shape and otherwise unadorned on the slim gold band beneath it. Simple, unique, and one hundred percent Dante.

I loved it.

Ric stared at the ring a little gobsmacked. "You married the Don?"

I shrugged. "He was difficult to resist."

My friend blinked at me, then tossed his head back to laugh, the sharp yips like a hyena but oddly charming. "Oh, Elena, you are an enigma."

"I'll take that as a compliment," I decided, when before I might have thought he meant it as an insult.

"You should, absolutely. Now, I'm curious. Why did you call me?"

"Dennis O'Malley is corrupt. I caught him meeting with the Irish mob a few weeks ago, and when we tried to get him to recuse himself, he laughed in our faces. He has Judge Hartford in his pocket, and he's determined to use Dante's case as a springboard to state senator." I took a sip of the thick, bitter espresso in front of me, rallying my confidence to ask what I needed to ask. When I looked up at Ric again, my eyes were wide with intensity. "I called because I want to ask for your help. I want you to dig up whatever you can find on him."

He frowned. "The firm already did a background check."

I gave him a pointed look. "Not through you and not deep enough. I'm asking you to go above and beyond here, Ric. As a friend."

His mouth dropped open slightly, and I knew he was shocked I would ask him to do something unethical. The old Elena was as morally sound as they came, but I'd left her behind somewhere between Staten Island and Napoli.

He was quiet for a long time, studying me, peeling back my skin and bones to read what was written in my blood. I thought he would say no. In fact, I opened my mouth to tell him to forget it when he leaned back in his chair, affecting a casual pose with his legs crossed and fingers steepled.

"Okay."

I blinked. "Sorry, what?"

His lips twitched. "Okay, this is no big thing. Of course, I will look into him for you."

"No big thing?" I echoed, a little foolishly.

"Do you remember representing my cousin when he was busted for possession last year?" he reminded me.

I nodded, but I didn't think that had any bearing. I was just doing my job and helping out a friend. He hadn't asked me to do anything illegal or unethical like I was asking for now.

"And do you remember when my sister assaulted the woman who slept with her husband?"

Another nod. That one was hard to forget; Carmen Stavos was a firecracker.

"And do you know, we have worked together for years, and you are the only associate who never made me feel like their servant?"

Ah, well, that I could believe. Most of them were pricks only focused on their own upward mobility.

"So," Ric concluded. "This is no big thing. We are friends, Elena, I would do this for you even if you had not done so much for me. I'll look into Hartford too and let you know what I can find."

I blinked owlishly because it occurred to me that I hadn't really known if Ric and I were friends. We got along, and I enjoyed working with him, but I always assumed he just thought of me as some vaguely pleasant associate.

It said a lot about my mental state before Dante that I discounted a friendship because I automatically assumed they didn't want to be friends with someone like me.

It made me grieve for the woman I'd been and rejoice for the progress I'd made in the past few months.

"Thanks, Ric," I said, letting some of that tenderness seep into my tone. "That means a lot."

"Hey, don't forget, you're a powerful lady now. Maybe you'll be able to do a big favor for me someday," he teased.

"Well, while we're on the topic of favors, there is something else," I confessed. "Have you heard of the di Carlo brothers in the Cosa Nostra?"

He snorted. "Anyone in law, police work, or the media knows the di Carlo brothers."

"They've gone to war against the Camorra."

"Ah." He rubbed his chin as he pondered the situation. "Because they think Dante killed Giuseppe di Carlo?"

The coffee shop was on a quiet street and it was too cold to be sitting outside really, so Ric and I were the only ones sitting bundled up on the chairs in front of the shop, but I still lowered my voice. "They know he didn't. Apparently, the brothers were the ones to order the drive-by to take out their own uncle and get power for themselves."

Ric let out a long, low whistle. "I'm sure I don't have to tell you the world you just married into is violent as hell."

"You do not." I could still remember Rocco Abruzzi's brain blown out all over the back wall of his office like it happened two minutes ago. I knew I would live with that memory for the rest of my life.

"So what did the Camorra do to them?"

"Nothing so far as I can tell," I said honestly. "I'm wondering if you can look into that too? See why they've targeted this Family first. I think they have plans to take it all eventually, but there must be something personal there."

"Yeah, I'm inclined to agree." He had that look on his face he got when a good case landed in his lap, all quivering, animal excitement like a hound who's caught a scent. "I'll get going, got some leads I want to hit up before it gets too late."

He stood to go so I did too, initiating the cheek kisses for the first time in our friendship. When I finished, I kept hold of his shoulders and gave them a squeeze.

"Thank you, Ric. This means a lot to me."

He grinned at me, knocking my chin lightly with his fist. "Don't mention. I'm only too happy to help the female gladiator at Fields, Harding & Griffith."

I laughed. "I could lose my licence for marrying Dante."

He knew how much being a lawyer meant to me so he frowned. "Worth it?"

My hand went to Dante's cross beneath my bulky knit sweater. "Worth it."

My next stop was to visit my old idol and current nemesis. The Winthrop Gun Club was an exclusive, members only brick building in the Flatiron District. It was where decorated policemen, wealthy gun enthusiasts, and right-wing politicians spent their time schmoozing and rubbing elbows with the right crowd.

Happily, my woman's doctor, Monica Taylor, and her husband were members and she was able to secure a visitor's pass for my partner and I to tour the facilities in case we wanted to join too.

Frankie, my fake husband in Italy, once again donned the faux boyfriend role as we signed into the reception and were taken on a tour of the extensive building with all its amenities.

"You would have to sign an NDA if you wanted to go through with the application," the guide was explaining as we moved by the viewing windows overlooking the handgun bays. "We have many important members who value their privacy."

"Of course," I demurred. "We feel the same way."

Ric had called half an hour after our meeting to tell me Dennis could be found at the WGC every Tuesday and Thursday evening for a few practice rounds and a follow-up pint with friends at the bar across the street.

Still, the sight of him after so long, knowing that he was going to use Dante as a means to his own end, lit me up with fury like a fucking Christmas tree.

"Would it be possible at all to try one of the bays while we're here?" I asked sweetly, clutching Frankie's hand. "My husband is such a crack shot, but sometimes the bays are so narrow, he can barely move his arms!"

The woman nodded sagely. "I completely understand. If you'll wait here, I'll grab a key. I have the copy of your gun license, should I grab the gun you checked in or will you need to borrow one?"

"The one we checked in."

She scuttled away.

Immediately, I strode across the hall to the bay I spotted Dennis behind, recognizable for his thick brown hair and customary blue suit even in his protective earwear and glasses.

I rang the doorbell and waited.

He turned, frowning, his mouth already open to reprimand whoever was bothering him, but his eyes widened when he saw me through the small, square window in the door.

After a moment of deliberation, he took off his earmuffs and opened the door for us.

"Hello, Dennis," I said coolly as Frankie followed me and lingered near the closed door.

"Ms. Lombardi," he returned smoothly, as if we met here all the time. "You're looking remarkably well, given your client is behind bars."

I laughed lightly as I surveyed the four guns he had laid out on the table. Three handguns and a pistol. I picked up the smallest, a 9mm Glock, and tested the weight in my hands.

"He's no longer my client."

Dennis's eyebrows raised into his thick hairline. "Oh? Have you finally realized the error of your ways? Don't tell me you've come to beg for my forgiveness."

"Dante Salvatore isn't my client anymore because he is now my husband," I explained calmly as I raised the gun and aimed at the target down the range. "And I didn't come to beg forgiveness from a hypocritical *stronzo*. I came to warn you."

I sucked in a quiet breath and pulled the trigger.

*Bang!*

"...If you keep coming for my husband..."

*Bang!*

"...I'll come for you..."

*Bang! Bang!*

"...And if you thought my father could be cruel, you should see what kind of monster he made of his daughter."

*Bang!*

The paper outline of a human was riddled with puncture wounds, most of them concentrated around the head because I'd become a shockingly good shot. The gun smoked lightly in my hands as I emptied the chamber and clicked the safety.

When I turned to Dennis, he was oddly bemused, his expression torn between disbelief, anger, and not a little arousal.

"You think you can come in here and threaten me?" he asked with an incredulous huff of laughter. "Sweetheart, I'm the man around here. There is nothing I'm not protected from. You think I'm scared of little Red playing at being the Big Bad Wolf?"

"I think you're underestimating me because I'm a woman, and you're an entitled, greedy, lazy sinner who thinks he deserves to win simply because he's a man." I stepped closer, the gun still in my hand.

I could see in Dennis's eyes that he wanted to move away from me—something in my feral eyes scared him—but he resisted. My heels made me slightly taller than him, so I leaned down and in until my red lips were almost pressed to the corner of his mouth.

"I could have been civilized, O'Malley. I could have played fair, but if you want to fight dirty, I'm more than happy to comply. I'm going to beat you at your own game. I hope your loss is so difficult to swallow you choke on it and save me the trouble of killing you myself."

I pulled away smoothly, turning and adjusting my large purse on my shoulder as I moved toward the door. Frankie followed, more shadow than man.

"This accomplished nothing but tipping your hat, Ms. Lombardi," Dennis called to me as Frankie opened the door, and I made to follow him out. "You should watch yourself before you end up dead just like your father. Did you know they found him in a house in Brooklyn, shot to death like the criminal he was?"

I laughed lightly, pausing for a moment to say, "You are the company you keep, Dennis. I'd be careful you don't end up just like your childhood best friend."

Frankie closed the door quickly behind me and moved swiftly down the hall before the guide could come back and potentially get interrogated by Dennis. We intercepted her at the reception and politely declined the practice bay before collecting our things and leaving.

It was only when we were safely ensconced in Dante's Ferrari that I let out a triumph, angst-edged laugh.

When I turned my head against the seat to look at Frankie, he was smiling.

"Did you get it?" I asked breathlessly.

He nodded.

"So did I." I pulled my purse into my lap and pulled Dennis's handgun from its depths. "I can't believe that worked."

"High risk, high reward as the Boss always says. He'd be proud of you."

I sighed. "Let's hope he can tell me that in person sooner rather than later."

"Proud of you too," he said, shooting me a sidelong look. "All of us are. It's been damn interesting to watch you come into your own the past few months. You should know, the men love you because of *you*, not because you're D's wife. They started to fall when you hated him." He laughed. "I think for Addie and Marco, it happened the moment you refused to move into the apartment. They'd never seen anyone but Tore or me stand up to him before."

It seemed that everyone knew my chest was hollow because Dante had taken my heart with him when he turned himself in, and they were consciously and consistently filling up the empty cavity with love of their own.

It made me realize how lucky I was and even how lucky I'd always been.

It was amazing how bitterness could blind you to everything else.

As I sat there with Frankie on the way to the apartment to spend Christmas Eve without Dante, I resolved not to forget how much I had to be grateful for every single day. Even if he didn't come back to me for ages, I had so much more to be happy for, and it was Dante who had taught me that.

# CHAPTER TWENTY FIVE

## *elena*

It was strange to be in the Smith Jameson apartment without Dante. Suddenly, the stark black and white color scheme seemed mundane and lifeless without his vivacious spirit to liven the rooms. The guys seemed to sense I was melancholy and needed space, so they drifted off to wherever they went and left me in the living room staring vacantly out the closed patio doors.

The apartment held so many important memories for Dante and me—the balcony where we had our first kiss, the garage where he fucked me for the first time, where I had the first climax of my life, the piano where he'd played me as I played the keys.

I sat down at the Steinway and lifted the glossy cover. My hands fell softly to the ivories, light as a feather, a natural movement that made my soul throb.

The music came unbidden, pouring through me as if I was possessed by the spirit of it. I thought of my prayer to Apollo in the Cathedral of Naples, of my promises to play music again because Christopher shouldn't have the power to ruin it for me.

I thought of Dante as I played, letting the music express my sorrow that he was gone and my gratitude that he existed at all.

The sun shifted in the sky, falling beneath the crust of towering buildings, leaving a smudged tapestry of pinks and oranges in its wake. They faded slowly, the shadows elongating, darkness falling like a shroud over the city.

Still, I played.

I played until my fingers cramped and my wrists ached, until my belly growled louder than the notes I struck.

But I only stopped because I heard my name.

"Elena."

And the voice that called it was so dear to me it permeated my fog.

My head snapped up, eyes wide as they landed on Mama.

But she wasn't alone.

Sebastian stood beside her with a duffel over one shoulder and Beau on the other side of him, carrying grocery bags in both hands.

My breath got stuck on something in my throat.

Something that made me want to cry even though it was beautiful.

My people were there.

"Dante called," Sebastian explained when I sat there mutely. "I got on a plane. Beau, Mama, and I decided to bring you Christmas dinner." He hesitated. "Sinclair, Giselle, and Genevieve are in Paris for the holidays, and Cosima and Alexander are at Pearl Hall, so it's just us."

"Your mama wouldn't let me bring takeout," Beau explained a little beleaguered as if he was still recovering from the argument they'd had.

"*Boh!*" Mama exclaimed with a sidelong look of disappointment for Beau. "Of course, we do not eat 'takeout,'" she spat the words as if they were dirty. "I am here to cook for my *lottatrice*, so why do you need this takeout? My food is not good enough, Beau?"

His eyes widened comically. "No, no, Caprice, I told you, I love your food."

"You call me Mama," she asserted because all our friends had always been ordered to do just that. "And next time, do not talk to me about takeout."

"Yes, ma'am," he replied, giving me big eyes.

"Mama," she corrected.

He grimaced.

I laughed.

I laughed when I hadn't thought I would laugh again until Dante got out of lockup and back into my arms.

I would have said that I'd forgotten about the power of family, but the truth was, I'd never really harnessed it. I knew they were there for me, ostensibly, but I'd never really reached out to them in times of need. Even in Naples, Cosima had been the one to come to me.

Music still ringing through my blood, I thought again of that prayer to Apollo and decided tonight was as good a night as any to open up to the people who matter.

I stood from the piano and almost ran to my loved ones. They laughed, startled and maybe a little happy when I hugged each of them. It wasn't something I normally did, but it felt good to hold them after so long. They anchored me when I'd felt adrift without Dante.

"Come in, come in," I coaxed, taking Sebastian by the hand to lead them through the living room into the massive kitchen.

Mama made a noise of approval. "This is the sign of a good man, having a good kitchen."

"He's an amazing cook too."

Her mouth turned down at the corners, eyebrows raised as she nodded her head in surprised admiration. "See? I told you he was a good man. You should listen to your mama."

I laughed. "I did. I told you, we're together now."

"Together and married?" Sebastian asked, having lifted the hand he held to stare at my wedding rings.

I shrugged somewhat sheepishly, but Seb only laughed. "I have to hand it to you, Lena, when you make up your mind about something, there is no stopping you from attaining it."

When I fought a frown, trying to see it as a positive, he stepped closer to take my head in his hands. His golden eyes, so bright and thickly lashed they seemed inhuman, were utterly sincere. "You are incredible, *sorella mia*. You have always awed me. Marrying a wanted man and a mafia Don...only you would have such courage."

I smiled, thinking of Dante because I always did when I heard that word.

"For him, I've found I am much more courageous than I ever thought I could be," I admitted as Mama set to work loudly in the kitchen, ordering Beau around like he was her sous chef.

Seb kissed me on the cheek. "I think you should give yourself more credit. You were always the bravest person I knew."

His praise warmed me through like good brandy, but he moved away, calling to Mama as if it was nothing to give me those words.

Beau caught my eye from across the island, looking a little harried, but his eyes were soft with understanding.

"What's all the racket?" Frankie called as he, Addie, Chen, and Jaco entered the room from the hall to the office where they'd been doing whatever it was mafiosos did during working hours.

I looked from them on one side to my blood family on the other and had a strange moment of disconnect as the two worlds merged.

"Mama, Sebastian, Beau? These are Dante's men, Adriano, Chen, Jacopo, and Frankie," I introduced, feeling suddenly shy and a little anxious.

The new and old world Elenas were meeting, and I had a feeling it could be seamless or as disastrous as the Big Bang.

Yearning rammed into my chest, stealing my breath.

If Dante had been there, he would have smoothed over introductions perfectly with his charm and warmth.

Mama eyed the men wearily as did Sebastian. They were used to the mafiosos of Napoli, the ruthless, selfish Made Men who would beat you up just to steal a nickel.

These men were nothing like that.

I moved to the group of males and stood between Frankie and Adriano, sliding an arm around both of them. Frankie was used to physical affection from me after playing my fake partner so many times, but Addie looked shocked, then more than a little pleased.

It was a bold move, maybe, one that obviously surprised Mama and Beau by the wide-eyed looks on their faces, but I was glad I did it as soon as Chen and Jaco crowded into my back. We formed a little unit standing there in the hall, and I knew that even though Dante was there to force them to protect me, to encourage them to care for me, they already did.

"Hey," Sebastian said, stepping forward first to offer his hand to Chen. "I'm Elena's brother, Seb."

"I know," Chen admitted. "I'm actually a big fan."

"What?" I choked off my laughter. "Seriously?"

I would have expected it from Marco, maybe, who knew enough about pop culture to write a book, but it shocked me that stern and serious Chen, who was all numbers and efficiency, enjoyed my brother's dramatic movies.

Chen shot me a cool look. "What? I can't have good taste?"

Sebastian laughed, clapping the other man on the back in comradery. "You certainly can. Now, tell me your favorite movie."

The ice broke under the weight of the exchange, the other mafiosos chuckling at Chen as he easily launched into a discussion with my brother, who loved nothing more than to talk about his work.

"Come meet everyone, Mama." When she hesitated, I went to take her hand and led her back to my friends. "This is my Mama, Caprice."

Frankie stepped forward to take her hand and raised it to his lips. *"Sei troppo giovane per essere una madre."*

*You are too young to be a mother.*

I rolled my eyes at his outrageous flattery, but Mama laughed and insisted he should call her Mama instead of Caprice.

Beau appeared at my side and struck up a conversation with Addie and Jaco about the Yankees that devolved into a passionate debate about how their season was going in a matter of seconds.

Within twenty minutes, everyone was talking over each other like they'd known each other for years. I sat on a stool at the island watching Mama roll out pasta dough for the traditional Christmas *timballo* she made every year. Beau was beside her dicing tomatoes, and Addie stood on the other side of him slicing aubergine.

"It seems you're throwing a party."

Everyone looked up as Salvatore came in from the elevator holding Aurora's hand, Bambi following up the rear with bags of her own groceries.

The air in the room went electric the moment Mama caught eyes with Tore.

"Is anyone invited?" he asked in a voice that was carrying but gentle.

I could read the eager hope in his face from all the way across the room.

Even the people who didn't know the history between Mama and Tore looked back and forth between them, following the lines of tension written clearly in the air.

At first, it seemed Mama would turn him away on Christmas Eve, but then she looked at me, and her gaze was filled with fear.

It startled me a bit to think that my fifty-year-old mother could still be scared of her emotions. Of a man who so clearly adored her.

Obviously, though, I understood.

"*Coraggio, Mama,*" I said under my breath, reaching over to give her hand a squeeze even though it was covered in semolina flour. "*Coraggio.*"

"*Va bene,*" she called after taking a deep breath. "Come in, Salvatore, and introduce me to the *bella principessa* on your arm."

"That's me!" Aurora cried, putting her hand in the air. "I'm Rora."

"A strong name for a strong girl," Mama said, knowing just what to say.

Rora let go of Tore's hand, having forgotten him completely, and made her way into the kitchen. She shocked me when she stopped at my side and hauled herself into my lap. I helped her settle there, a little dazed by her easy intimacy yet more than a little moved by it.

"I'm six," she told Mama, leaning forward to put her elbows on the counter and her face in her hands.

"That's a good age," Mama agreed.

"Is it? I want to be eight. There's a boy who lives across the street who said when I'm eight, he'll give me a kiss."

"Rora!" Bambi cried.

Everyone laughed.

I rested my cheek against Rora's strawberry-scented hair as I held her in my lap and watched almost everyone I loved interact beautifully with each other. I wished fervently that Dante could be here to see our family merge, to see how gorgeous they were together and how lucky we were.

But even though my heart ached hollowly, I knew he already understood that. Dante never took anything in his life for granted, least of all his family.

"You okay?" Beau asked me, reaching across the island to squeeze my hand. "You must miss him."

"I do," I agreed. "Married for three days, and he's taken away. But I have faith. We'll figure it out."

He blinked at me. "You know, you've never looked more beautiful than you do sitting there talking about Dante with that pretty child in your lap loving you like she'll never stop. You can deny it all you want, but I know this is all you've ever wanted. Not the high-powered job or the closet full of Chanel––though admittedly, that's amazing too. Dante gave you what Daniel never did."

"What?" I asked even though I knew.

Even though I could feel it pulsing all around me as Addie laughed gruffly with Seb and Chen, as Tore spoke quietly with Mama while they assembled the *timballo,* as Rora absently took a lock of my hair and twirled it in her fingers while Jaco danced with his sister, Bambi, around the living room.

"A family," he said.

"Yeah," I agreed, laughing breathlessly because my lungs were compressed with happiness while my tears stung with sadness. "What a Christmas gift to send from prison."

We laughed together, but the poignancy of the night remained as we cooked together and sat down for Christmas dinner in the Italian fashion, on the eve before.

It seemed appropriate instead of shocking when Frankie announced that Dante had gifts for everyone and passed out presents to every single person seated at the table, even Beau. I watched Mama unearth bottles of Tore's Limoncello and olive oil, Seb unpack a signed copy of *The Godfather* DVD Dante must have paid a fortune for, Beau a Prada scarf, and Adriano new gold-embossed dog dishes for his beloved dog, Toro. Everyone had a gift, but I had four that Tore placed in front of me when everyone else had opened theirs.

I swallowed thickly as I lifted the lid from the first one and discovered a framed copy of the only photo we had from our wedding day. Cosima had taken it with my phone, her model's eyes capturing a truly beautiful moment where Dante had one palm at my throat and the other around my hips, both my hands in the back of his short hair holding him to me as we smiled against each other's lips.

I was crying, but no one teased me about it, not even Seb or Frankie.

Next was a long, slim box that I opened only to close immediately again.

"Oh my God!" I cried, but I was laughing.

Beau, who was next to me and had caught a glimpse, asked, "Is that what I think it is?"

It was.

A black dildo still in its package.

There was a note with it that read:

*Play with tua bella figa for me while I'm gone. I want to be able to picture you spread wide and wet, pleasuring yourself while you moan my name.*

*Xoxo,*

*Your capo*

My skin was burning up as I looked up from reading it, but everyone laughed, even Mama, who seemed to think the gift was hilarious.

After that was a gorgeous pair of *La Perla* lingerie with instructions to wear it for him when he finally got home to me.

And the fourth was a box embossed in black that read *Gatto's.*

Inside, nestled in a bed of tissue paper so fine it seemed to disintegrate against my fingers, was a black and white diamond necklace. Three huge diamonds were ringed in a halo of smaller black gems that glinted like the night sky around the stars.

I lost my breath to its beauty then again when I read Dante's card.

*Black and white and red, lottatrice mia. The colors of our life and our love.*

I looked up with teared-filled eyes at the dinner table filled with almost everyone Dante and I loved, Tore at one head of the table and me in Dante's place at the other. My fingers trembled as I lifted my glass of Montepulciano wine in a toast that everyone echoed robustly.

"To Dante."

*"To Dante!"*

# CHAPTER TWENTY SIX
# DANTE

There was only one reason I went to jail.

Elena was right when she assumed those friends in high places could get me off with a hefty fine for bail jumping instead of having to pay with incarceration.

But it was too good of an opportunity to waste.

Oh, I could have done it another way.

Hired someone or asked a favor.

But this required a personal touch. *My* touch.

After all, it was my wife he'd abused and turned against herself.

I owed it to all three of us to exact this retribution myself.

It took longer than I wanted it to.

I missed Christmas and New Year's Eve with my beautiful new wife and our family. Lying on a thin mattress on a metal bunk bed in a six-by-eight-foot cell as a six-foot-five man was uncomfortable as hell. The food was crap; the company was worse. My cellmate was a guy who had his tongue cut out by another inmate for snitching, and the group of Aryan neo-Nazis didn't like my swarthiness the moment they clapped eyes on me.

There were Made Men inside, a small gang of them and others who had joined up with other gangs inside. I told them not to bother with me because I didn't want to draw attention to myself. Though I pulled three of them aside that day to let them know I'd need them soon.

But none of that mattered.

I kept to myself, and no one disturbed me because I was a big guy and didn't cause problems.

I just waited.

With decreasing patience.

Because I knew it would all be worth it in the end.

Finally, two weeks after my incarceration, the transport van arrived, and four new prisoners entered B block.

One was a Chinese man with tattoos all over his face, only the tip of his nose and chin were inkless, and one was a fairly handsome Black man who was instantly welcomed by people he seemed to know in one of the drug gangs.

The last was a slim, pale-skinned brunette man who looked as green as the jumpsuit we had to wear in here.

I tried to see him as Elena had as a girl, if he was handsome or worthy of her in any way.

He was not.

A *brutto figio di puttana* inside and out.

"Ugly little guy," the inmate beside me grunted as he took stock of the new arrivals. "He'll be someone's bitch boy within the week."

I didn't argue even though I knew he wouldn't live that long.

I had a job in the carpentry shop turning chair legs. It was boring work, mundane, and normally reserved for the unconnected and new inmates to the prison. I could have had something else, but this suited my purposes perfectly.

Christopher started work on his fourth day inside.

He was responsible for loading the truck.

I knew this because I'd slipped the guy in charge of assigning tasks a wad of cash to make this happen.

On the sixth day, I found my opening.

It was almost quitting time, and most of the men fucked off to hang around and shoot the shit at the end of their shift.

Only Christopher and a couple of the meeker guys continued their tasks for fear of angering the higher-ups.

When someone asked Christopher a question, I ducked into the loading truck and crouched behind a stack of unvarnished dining table chairs. There was a metal click as he swung the door open, light flooding the interior for a moment before the door swung shut behind him. He shuffled forward half-blinded by the four-chair tower in his spindly arms.

It would be too easy to kill him.

I wished I could have taken my time.

Skinned him alive or beaten him, let him recover, then beaten him again in a vicious cycle that wouldn't end until his mind had broken alongside his body.

He'd almost ruined Elena's life.

He deserved more than a quick death.

But it was all I had to offer, so I'd make sure it was a brutal one.

He didn't notice me standing in the shadows, looming over him like some boogeyman in a children's story.

Only what happened next was considerably too graphic to be in any children's book.

I had a chair leg I'd turned that afternoon in my right hand, and I used it like a baseball bat against the side of Christopher's head.

There was a *thunk* and a *crunch* as the wood, backed by the entire force of my body, met his skull.

He crumpled, the chairs in his arms toppling over. I caught them before they could cause a clamor against the ground, carefully placing them behind me.

The pathetic excuse for a man groaned on the floor, clutching at his head.

"Hi," I said to him as I squatted beside his body, at ease because three Made Men were watching the doors while I took my time with this *cazzo di merda*. "Christopher Sallow, right?"

He groaned louder.

"I thought so."

I poked him with the bloody wooden leg until he rolled onto his back and then grabbed one of his hands, holding the palm steady so I could impale the screw of the chair leg into his palm.

He screamed.

But with the truck door closed, you would only be able to hear the sound if you stood right outside, as my fellow *camorristi* did while keeping watch.

I pulled the other chair leg from the sleeve of my jumper and pinned his other hand. It was too easy because he was made of nothing but bones, and then I impaled that too.

His scream devolved into a snot-filled garble.

"What are you doing?" he cried.

"Do you remember Elena Lombardi?" I asked, almost conversationally.

It was strange how I could modulate my voice even when I was filled with so much rage my skin threatened to peel off from the heat of it.

He stilled slightly, panting through his slack mouth.

"I thought so," I repeated.

I probably only had ten more minutes before the guards would arrive to usher us back to our cells, so I pulled out the shiv I'd made of a shard of glass stuck into the end of a melted toothbrush handle.

There was only the dim light of a solitary bulb hanging overhead, but it was enough to see Christopher's face, his pale eyes and weak chin.

In the darkness, with revenge in my heart and love in my veins, I let the beast I'd inherited from Noel and honed under tutelage from Tore overtake me.

It was wet work, filthy and loud because Christopher wouldn't stop blubbering and begging for mercy.

"What mercy?" I said. "What mercy did you show Elena?"

He mumbled words about her liking it at first, but that stopped when I cut off his ear and shoved it into his mouth. Then he just waxed on and on about how sorry he was, about how it was just a bad time in his life.

"Lies." I had one wrecked hand between my own, tracing his bones with the knife so they showed through the split skin and dripped blood. "You went back for Giselle and Elena a year and a half ago."

"Bitch bit my ear," he roared, niceties over, struggling hard against my grip, but too weak to do anything about it.

I cut off the other ear, noticing the massacred lobe where Elena had evidently bitten into him.

That was *my* woman.

My wife.

Fierce pride surged through me alongside the giddiness of retribution.

"She should have the pleasure of killing you, but you also don't deserve to look at her ever again. So, I'm the lucky *bastardo* that will send you straight to hell."

"You'll meet me there," he countered weakly, breathing too fast because the pain was massive and he was losing too much blood.

"One day," I agreed as I cut through his Achilles' heels because he was exactly the type of man to think loving a woman and treating them right made him weak. "But the difference is, I know I'm the villain. You don't think you've done anything wrong."

"They both wanted it," he snarled, twisting so hard, I almost lost my grip on him because the blood made his limbs slippery.

After that, he didn't talk anymore.

My cellmate had given me the idea really.

I cut out his tongue.

When I was finished, I went to the corner of the truck and found the change of clothes I'd slipped a guy some cash to stash there for me. I traded my bloody uniform for the new one and wiped my hands using paper towels and a water bottle.

I left the container, jerked my chin at the men who were watching it for me, dumped the bloody uniform in the incinerator, and went back to my post to churn another chair leg.

Twenty minutes later, when they found him mutilated in the truck, no one said a word about who might have done it.

And this was prison. People died every day, and no one snitched because ratting someone out was certain death.

So, the warden declared prisoner Christopher Sallow dead by suicide, and no one ever knew any different.

# CHAPTER TWENTY SEVEN

## DANTE

The trial was set for January thirty-first, which was a Monday. I'd been incarcerated just over a month, and I was about done with it. It wasn't that jail was nightmarish. Mostly, it was boring as hell, and for a man who was used to doing forty things at once, it wore on me steadily until I was irritable and snarly.

The worst of it was missing Elena.

If there was a silver lining to our distance, it made me realize the depth of my love for her. I could feel it in my bones and blood. It warmed me at night in the arctic prison cell and kept me sane after hours of mundanity while turning those infernal chair legs.

I used the memory of her like a drug to make me forget my surroundings and circumstances. Argued with myself over the right color for her gray eyes, if they were pewter or wet stone, storm clouded or clear gray skies. Thought of the first time I kissed her on my desk and the first time I took her on the hood of the Ferrari after I'd thought I might lose her in that car chase.

Our future kept me company at night while I lay in bed and stared at the ceiling, trying to ignore my tongue-less cellmate's incessant snoring. How I would marry her again in front of her entire family, get it photographed for Page Six if she wanted. How I would give her babies any way I could. If we couldn't conceive naturally, we could adopt. Elena would be an incredible mother, and I couldn't wait to have the privilege of watching that dream come true for her. Secretly, even though I hadn't in years, I prayed to God that we would be able to make a baby together. That I would be able to see Elena's smoky gray eyes in a beautiful face I could hold in my arms and call my daughter or son.

When I wasn't thinking of her, I was plotting.

I knew we were at war.

The men from Italy I'd recruited when we were in Napoli had arrived the day after Christmas, twenty of them whose single reason for being in the city was to support Chen, Addie, Jaco, and Frankie's efforts to end the di Carlo Family.

The Basante cartel was happy to help because they were currently trying to overtake the Ventura Mexican cartel in the East Coast market.

The Fallen MC pitched in, still furious that the di Carlos had ambushed them and killed the VP of the New York Chapter.

Caelian Accardi and Santo Belcante, the two sons of Dons in The Commission, were lying low but doing their own work. Caelian used his connections with the Gaming Commission and the Liquor Board to shut down two of their casinos and five of their restaurants. Santo used his particular set of skills to find and take out three of their high-ranking capos.

The tides were turning already.

As I knew they would if I returned home to set things right.

It was obvious with Marco in the hospital that the leaks from our side had stopped.

We had a man in the hospital at all times to make sure he didn't escape, but otherwise, we didn't tip our cap that we knew he was our mole.

I wanted to deal with him personally when I got out.

They'd transported me to the courthouse hours earlier and left me in a holding cell. I was doing push-ups in the cell when the door to the outer room opened, and the air went static.

Elena.

I jumped to my feet, my eyes snapping to hers like currents connecting. Electricity raced through my blood as I got my first look at her in a month.

She was beautiful.

So beautiful I couldn't fathom how anyone who saw her wasn't struck deaf and dumb by the sight. Her hair was that vivid, unusual shade of red that shone like candlelight through merlot, and her eyes were filled with smoke, dark and undulating as her emotions played through them. It wasn't that she was perfectly formed because that was boring. Her upper lip was slightly fuller than the bottom, and she had a trio of moles on her left hip in the shape of a perfect triangle. She was willowy, her curves slight and tight because she worked out every day with my men or me so she wasn't a typical bombshell.

But she was striking, arresting, someone you couldn't help but steal a second look at.

She was as interesting to look at as she was interesting to know. I'd revisited her mind and her body enough by then to know I would never get enough, know enough to claim mastery over either.

She was my ice queen and my fiery *donna.*

My very own enigma I'd spend the rest of my life unraveling.

"Capo," she said then, as if my name was God's.

"Elena." I walked to the edge of the cell and pushed my hand through. "Prove to me you aren't some golden dream."

She moved to me immediately, lacing our fingers, kissing each of my knuckles worshipfully. "I missed you so much. I can't even explain how much."

"I know," I soothed, pushing my other hand through the bars to hold her to me, hugging her the only way I could. "*Cazzo,* I thought of holding you again every day."

"Me too."

We were silent then, clutching each other like we'd drown if we let go. I smelled her hair and stroked my thumb over our joined knuckles, marking every single sensation of my body against hers.

"Never again," I promised even though it was stupid to do so. Every capo accepted the possibility of incarceration or death as almost inevitable. To pretend otherwise was foolish.

But I was a fool.

A fool in love with a woman I wouldn't let go of again.

"I won't let it happen again," she agreed, and I loved her conviction, her courage, because I knew she would face down anything that tried to come for us.

"We have a limited time to prepare," Yara said from just inside the door. "So, while I appreciate the beauty of this moment, please untangle yourselves, and let's get to work."

We ignored her.

"You haven't kissed me yet," she pointed out, tipping up her head so that red mouth bloomed open for me.

"No, I won't stop if I do," I admitted gruffly. "It's been a long month."

Her eyes crinkled at the corners, the gray flaring brightly like sunlight through storm clouds. I watched her laugh, held her to me while it moved through her, and I felt better than I had in weeks.

"Let's get to work then, and you can kiss me when this is all done, and you're free," she suggested.

"Just ignore me, that's fine," Yara called to us dryly.

We laughed together, and even though we got to work, we did it holding hands through the bars.

Yara and Elena had built a good case.

In fact, it was so iron-clad that, under normal circumstances, I would have felt positive about the outcome being in my favor.

But I knew Dennis O'Malley was not the kind of man to accept defeat lying down. He was a small man with a Napoleon complex who was never happy unless he was the star of the show.

When I was escorted into the courtroom, he was sitting behind the table for the prosecution smiling like the cat who ate the canary and then all of its brothers and sisters.

This was obviously not a good sign.

It became obvious why he was so smug when he immediately addressed the judge for a motion to disqualify Elena from remaining on my legal team because of a personal conflict of interest.

"Well, that is a serious accusation," Judge Hartford said with faux shock. "What do you have to say for yourself, Ms. Lombardi?"

Elena stood, utterly unflappable and poised. "My name is now Mrs. Salvatore, Your Honor."

There was a dead beat of silence where it seemed no one even breathed.

And then chaos exploded in the courtroom.

The clack of camera shutters falling and the snap of flashes, the rising murmur of people speculating about what the hell had happened when I'd fled the country and how had I returned married to my lawyer.

"Order!" Judge Hartford bellowed, thumping his gavel down mightily. "Order now. Anyone found talking will be held in contempt."

Slowly, the noise petered off, though in its wake was a silence so thick it seemed to buzz with anticipation.

"Your Honor, lawyers are allowed to represent their spouses as clients if there is consent," Elena pointed out calmly.

She didn't fidget or gesture when she spoke in court. Her posture was perfect, her language stripped of all traces of Italian, and her voice carefully modulate in tone. It should have been disconcerting to see my ice queen back in play, but I found it arousing to watch her cold strength and beauty, knowing I was the only one who could make her melt.

"Yes," the judge agreed. "If you had a pre-established relationship before you entered into a lawyer/client relationship."

We'd known this was a possibility going into trial. Dennis would throw everything at us to get something to stick, and he knew now that she meant something to me. I'd humiliated him by fleeing the country under his nose, and this was just a piece of his retribution.

I also knew Elena didn't care whether she was actually on the bench when she had already done all the work she could, but it made my blood seethe to think that Dennis had timed this to embarrass her.

"We did, actually," she said.

Another flurry of murmurs and camera flashes came from the gallery.

"Do not make me close this courtroom," Judge Hartford warned them before addressing Elena. "Are you saying that you had a sexual relationship with the defendant before you started to represent him?"

"I am."

I shot a look at Dennis and found his face pinch, his eyes dark with anger.

They hadn't thought of this.

"Permission to approach the bench?" Elena asked, picking up a folder. When the judge nodded, she rounded the table and went to the bench, showing him the evidence contained within.

I knew there was a photo of Cosima, Alexander, Elena, and me at *Osteria Lombardi* from two years ago before Noel had set a bomb to go off in the bathroom. There was another of us at one of Giselle's art shows that could be construed as intimate because we were standing side by side, gazing closely at a painting of a woman's naked ass perched on her heels while she gave head to someone beneath an office desk. There was a signed affidavit from Alexander explaining that we first met when Cosima was in a coma and that we started a relationship shortly after that.

There he was, the brother who had hated me for years, lying for me once again.

"Is that enough?" Elena asked, her voice saccharine even though I could see her eyes flash from where I sat.

*Merda*, but she was amazing to watch in her element.

The judge stared at the evidence unhappily, sliding a quick look over at Dennis, who was trying his best to seem unperturbed. Only his skin was flushed, and he snapped his pencil in two when he went to write something down.

He caught me looking at him, so I let one of my bestial grins dominate my face. He blinked, his chin canting in slightly in concession to his need to get away from me.

I almost laughed, but Elena crossing back to our table distracted me.

"Fine," Judge Hartford allowed. "Mrs. Salvatore will remain. As long as Mr. Salvatore knows the consequences?"

"Oh, I do, Your Honor," I assured him, innuendo ripe in my tone.

Behind us, the crowd laughed.

Elena sat beside me and surreptitiously squeezed my thigh beneath the table.

"May we move on to the matter at hand now, Your Honor?" Yara had the balls to ask.

The judge scowled but agreed. "Yes, the opening witness may take the stand."

"Point one for us," Elena murmured softly.

"Still have a long way to go, *lottatrice*."

"Oh, I know," she agreed, almost gleefully, so in her element she seemed to glow. "The fun is just getting started."

It turned out, she was right.

The first witness was Ottavio Petretti, the man who owned *Ottavio's* deli where Giuseppe di Carlo was murdered. The man Elena had gone to Staten Island to convince to testify and then been nearly run off the road by the di Carlos and the Irish mob.

Under Yara's coaxing, he admitted that he'd been paid to leave the premises by Giuseppe di Carlo's thug because they planned to do violence to the girl in the shop, Cosima Lombardi. He also confessed that he knew me on sight and had not seen me in Brooklyn the day of the shooting.

Dennis O'Malley looked annoyed but not crestfallen. He spoke to his associate, who scurried out of the room to do his bidding.

When he cross-examined Ottavio, he tore him to pieces like a carcass in the mouth of a wild dog. He mentioned the deli owner's drinking problems, his poor vision, the fact that he had never met me formally, only in passing and therefore could have been mistaken about not seeing me there that day.

By the time he was done, Ottavio's fleshy, pink face was quivering and deeply unhappy.

*Cazzo.*

The next day, we brought in the big guns.

Carter Andretti.

He was mostly healed from the brutal beating I'd given him in the abandoned subway station under my apartment building, but he still had the look of someone who fought often and not very well. His nose was as lumpy as a bad mattress due to poorly set breaks, his neck thicker than an average man's biceps and short on his big shoulders. He looked like a mafioso caricature, and I wasn't sure if that would help or hinder the case.

He wasn't there out of the goodness of his heart to testify against his own Family. We had men watching his house and his family. We'd told him that if he wanted any hope of surviving what he and his thugs had done to Cosima, he would confess.

"How many were there of you in the car?" Yara asked, deep into the interrogation, gathering speed and intensity like a runaway train.

"Uh, well, there was me, Philly, Pizza Paul, and Fedele."

"And you all had weapons?"

"Yeah," he said, like *duh*.

"Can you be more specific?"

"We used Colt 6920s. They're the best on the market."

"Good to know," Yara drawled, turning to make eyes at the media. A few people tittered with laughter.

"Can you tell us who sent you to *Ottavio's* and with what purpose?"

Carter looked at her for a moment, licking his dry lips. His gaze darted to me for just a second, but it was long enough for him to feel the weight of my threatening stare.

"Agostino di Carlo ordered us to hit up *O's* because he wanted to take out Giuseppe." He looked at the judge. "That's his uncle."

"Thank you, I'm aware," Judge Hartford said dryly.

"Why did he want to kill his own uncle?"

"He and his brother wanted to take over the, uh, the family business."

Yara smiled comfortingly. "Of course. Thank you for being so honest with us today. Could you just tell us what you did with the weapons when you were done?"

"We dropped 'em in the Hudson."

Yara turned to the screen set up to the right of the witness stand and clicked something on a remote. An image appeared of four automatic rifles in large plastic evidence bags.

"These Colt 6920s were found when we had a diver survey the area of the river Mr. Andretti recalled disposing the weapons in. As you can see, the guns match his description. They are also a match for the bullet wounds forensics found in Giuseppe di Carlo and his associate, Ernesto Pagano."

Yara smiled beautifully at the judge.

He stared back at her, unmoved. "Any further questions, Mrs. Ghorbani?"

"No, Your Honor. The defense rests."

"That went well," I murmured to Elena, but I could tell by her thigh bouncing erratically beneath the table that she didn't agree with me.

"Just wait."

USA Dennis O'Malley was given his opportunity to cross-examine our witness. He was a short man with a studied energy, as if every movement was a calculation instead of an organic expression. He approached Carter with an almost robotic calm.

"What brought you here to testify today, Mr. Andretti?" he asked casually. "You don't seem like the kind of man who values honesty or the law."

"Objection," Elena and Yara both stood to declare. "Speculation."

"Sustained. Mr. O'Malley, please refrain from adding your personal opinions," Hartford reprimanded lightly.

"Of course." He adjusted his cuff links. "Please answer the question, though."

"Uh, yeah, well, I was subpoenaed so I had to come and do what's right."

"Was it right to kill Giuseppe di Carlo?"

"Well, no, but maybe we didn't kill him," he denied, looking like a deer in the headlights.

*Merda.*

"Oh? You shot at him, but you don't think you killed him?" Dennis pressed.

"Well, I'm pretty sure he was already on the floor when we pulled up, but it happened quick. I can't be sure."

Dennis turned to face our table, his smile a slight, evil curl of lips.

I was going to kill the *bastardo.*

"It's funny you should say that because forensic evidence suggests that Giuseppe di Carlo was hit with *two* different types of bullets. Those from a Colt 6920 and also those from a Gen 4 Glock 19. Were you carrying such a gun that day, Mr. Andretti?"

"No," Carter said, effectively ruining the strength of his testimony for our defense. "No, we weren't."

When Dennis moved back to his seat after his cross-examination period ended thirty minutes later, he did it with the expression of a cat who ate the canary.

I couldn't wait to make the *stronzo* choke on it.

# CHAPTER TWENTY EIGHT

## *elena*

On the fourth day of the trial, a bomb dropped.

I wasn't surprised, but I was probably the only one because I'd been the one to make the bomb itself.

I'd decided it was time because despite our first two witnesses lending credible doubt to the assumption that Dante hadn't killed Giuseppe di Carlo, Dennis had done a fine fucking job of discrediting them.

He was a dog with his first bone, and his desperateness lent him a feral edge I'd never seen in him before.

But that was okay because I was desperate too.

Dennis was just fighting for his career.

I was fighting for my capo and our life together.

There was no other option but to win.

Hence the bomb.

Dennis was still cross-examining Carter Andretti when Ricardo entered the courtroom, striding down the crowded aisle with purpose.

He held a leather portfolio and an iPad under one arm. All the eyes in the courtroom tracked him, Carter Andretti and Dennis forgotten entirely.

Ric leaned over the partition between the spectators and our defense table so I could meet him halfway.

He whispered in my ear. "This is already working out beautifully."

We had orchestrated the entire thing.

The legal process was complex, a quick, quick, slow dance of tempo from arrest and arraignment to the slow grind on the way to trial. But the trial itself was always a flurry of steps, the tempo fast enough to keep you on your toes, anxiously anticipating your partner's next move so you could match it.

Until then, this RICO case had been entirely led by Dennis O'Malley.

But I was taking the lead now, and I was going to dictate the moves.

"I have everything cued up on the iPad," Ric continued. "Good luck."

I took the portfolio and iPad from him. There was an old wisdom in law that you should put the opponent on trial when you had a weak defense, and I intended to do exactly that.

"Is there a problem, Mrs. Lombardi?" Judge Hartford asked, clearly unamused by my spectacle.

"Permission to approach the bench, Your Honor?"

He narrowed his eyes at me. Martin Hartford was as old-school as they came. He didn't like sensationalist court drama or surprises, and he sensed I had a doozy.

Because I did.

I smiled placidly at him.

"Fine, approach the bench."

"Your Honor, new evidence has come to light, and we would like to call a recess so it can be properly entered into evidence," I explained as I turned on the iPad and handed it to him.

"What am I looking at?"

"That is a Gen 4 Glock 19," I explained pleasantly. "The same gun USA O'Malley told us was used to shoot Giuseppe di Carlo before the drive-by shooting."

Judge Hartford was seasoned, and his poker face was legendary, but I was close enough to see the way the skin beside his eyes tightened in disbelief.

"Where did you retrieve this?" he asked after a wooden moment.

"Detective Joseph Falcone discovered it in a locked locker at the subway station a block away from *Ottavio's*. Apparently, they received an anonymous tip a few days ago."

"Did they?" The weight of his stare was a tangible thing on my shoulders, but I couldn't be held down by it.

Inside my chest, I was light as air.

"We had a lab run for prints and DNA matches," I said slowly, trying not to be overly dramatic when the roar of victory surged through my blood. "Preliminary results revealed a match."

"Do not drag this out, Mrs. Lombardi," he warned.

"Of course." I grinned the same grin I'd seen Dennis give us when he decimated the validity of Carter Andretti's testimony. "The results showed a match for USA Dennis O'Malley."

Judge Hartford called the recess.

The courtroom was a flurry of questions when he stormed into his chambers to await our team and the prosecution.

Dante was taken back to the holding cell, but he went with a wink in my direction.

He believed in me.

In this plan.

As he should. After all, he was the one who had corrupted me so beautifully. Before, I never would have thought to fight fire with fire, but now I knew, in the underworld, the only way to win was by any means possible.

"Are you fucking kidding me, Martin?" Dennis exploded when he was told what had happened. "There is absolutely no way that gun could be tied back to me!"

Yara and I sat placidly in the chairs before Judge Hartford's desk watching Dennis storm around the room, bristling with hostility and disbelief. Suddenly, he turned on his heel and stalked over to me, caging me in my chair.

"Did you do this, Moore?" he seethed. "Did you and your criminal lover think you could *frame me?*"

"My name isn't Moore," I reminded him. "You can call me Ms.

Lombardi or Mrs. Salvatore. And don't be ridiculous."

He glared at me, his fury a tangible heat in the air distorting it like wax paper. "My office will conduct its own tests."

"Of course," I agreed. "That's just standard procedure."

He bared his white, capped teeth at me, then turned to the judge. "Marty, this is absurd."

"Be that as it may, I can't rightly continue the trial if the lead prosecutor is now under investigation for the same crime as the defendant."

I tucked the edges of my mouth down, fighting the smile that wanted to dominate my face. We'd counted on Martin Hartford being too entrenched in his ways to allow that to happen. He might have wanted Dennis's help for a bid at mayor, but he was still too upstanding to corrode as fully as the US Attorney.

Dennis gaped at him. "What the hell kind of motivation would I have for killing Giuseppe di Carlo? I didn't even know the man."

"No," Yara agreed, as smooth and sly as a cat toying with her mouse. "But we did unearth a *New York Times* article from the fall stating that you intended to use this case to make a run at State Senate."

"That means nothing."

"That depends on your perspective," I argued. "Sometimes, if you want something badly enough, you'll go to extreme lengths to procure it."

He stared at me then as if struck, not shocked exactly, but deeply unsettled. He was realizing that he had underestimated me. That he had assumed I hated my father enough to eschew criminality for the right side of the law. That I would never lower myself to the mud he himself rolled around in.

He didn't know that I would go to hell and back for Dante Salvatore.

It had been surprisingly easy to distract Dennis at the gun range so that Frankie could pull his prints from one of the handguns he'd left displayed on the table. Mason Matlock had taken the gun Cosima used to kill his uncle, Giuseppe di Carlo, to protect her and confessed as much to Dante and Adriano when they were interrogating him months ago. Addie, Chen, and Jaco had searched every subway locker for two weeks to find the one Mason had stored the weapon in.

But we'd found it.

The rest was easy.

Frankie had applied Dennis's pulled prints to the grip of the gun and returned it to the locker. Tore had called in the tip to Detective Falcone because I still had his card in my purse, and I knew he wouldn't be able to resist taking down a potential murderer.

And here we were.

I smiled at Dennis, that old, familiar grin that froze on my face from the force of its icy blast. "Run those tests, Dennis. Detective Falcone is on standby waiting to arrest you if they come back as conclusive as ours did."

"You filthy, fucking bitch," he snapped, stepping forward as if to hit me.

I stood, looming over him in my six-inch heels, daring him to act. "Better a victorious bitch than a scumbag loser. Call us when you have the results back, Dennis. And good luck. I have it on good authority from Dante that men like you survive in prison because they make such good little bitches."

Dennis fumed, his nostrils flaring around his hot, heaving breaths. I'd never seen him so unhinged, but it was easy to see that there was violence in his blood and an eagerness to sin. I had no doubt he'd committed his own atrocities to get to the top of the legal food chain, and I felt absolutely no compunction about taking him down with his own filthy antics.

Without another word, he turned on his heel and stormed out, already dialing a number on his phone, probably to find his own lawyer.

Yara and I didn't leave.

I sat back down and stared at Judge Hartford.

"It would be unfortunate to lose Dennis's endorsement for mayor," I began after a long moment of strained silence. "I understand it's been a dream of yours."

Judge Hartford stared implacably at me.

Yara leaned forward, the picture of powerful elegance. "He wasn't your only friend, Martin."

She dipped to reach her hand into her Gucci purse and tossed something thick onto his desk. We watched together as he used a finger to spin the paper bag so the opening was facing him. His eyes rounded at the sight of the stacks of crisp bills inside.

"A little campaign contribution," I explained with a polite smile. "Politics are so expensive these days."

"I won't accept this." His heavy brow was puckered so tight, it was hard to see his gaze beneath it. "I don't take bribes."

"I think we're beyond that, given you didn't force Dennis to recuse himself or declare a mistrial when you had the chance," I countered boldly, filled with righteous fury and the calm that came from having all the power.

"What about a nice little endorsement from Governor Mortimer Percy?" I suggested, mentioning Daniel Sinclair's adopted father. "He's an old family friend who would be happy to help a seasoned judge on his way to political success."

Judge Hartford stared at the stack of bills spilling out of that simple paper bag, the edge of his thumb sliding along the tower.

He was counting.

My blood was so hot it seared through my veins, pumping so hard through my heart I thought it might explode.

The metallic bite of victory bloomed on the back of my tongue.

When Judge Hartford looked up, his heavy jaw was tight with resolution. "When can you make the introductions?"

# CHAPTER TWENTY NINE
## DANTE

Free.

*Libero.*

Judge Hartford had returned to court looking mighty and solemn, Midas passing judgment at a tribunal in the Underworld. He knew I was guilty of crimes he had no evidence of, and he was loath to see me walk away a free man, but in the end, his greed won out.

And he declared a mistrial.

I had Elena in my arms in a heartbeat, one hand fisting too hard in her lush hair, the other pressing her lower back to bring her hips flush against mine.

I kissed her like I was drowning because after a month without her lips on mine, her scent in my nose, and that long body pressed to mine, I felt like I was dying.

I drank from her, crushing our lips together so tightly I couldn't breathe. But we didn't need air. Everything I needed was in this woman. In her grace and immutable strength, in her loyalty and her undying love. In her willingness to do anything to see me free.

"*Sei magnifica,*" I rasped against her lips as I dragged in a deep breath. "You are so fucking magnificent."

She laughed, her hands threading through my hair, stroking almost manically like she couldn't get enough of the feel of me. "I feel magnificent because you're free. We're free of this."

"Because of you." I kissed her again, hard enough to bruise, secretly hoping it would leave a stamp of my possession in its wake. "My hero."

She laughed again, tipping her head back so all that red hair went cascading over my arm and down her back. I stared into her face, blinking at the sheer beauty of her joy as it moved through me and tangled with my own keen happiness.

Around us, the clack and click of shutters sounded like crickets in a field.

"*Ti amo, lottatrice mia,*" I said, each word like a vow.

"*Ti amo,*" she responded instantly, before pulling my head down by my ears so she could kiss me herself. "*Chi vuole male a questo amore prima soffre e dopo muore.*"

*Whoever is against this love, suffers and then dies.*

I growled as I sealed our lips again, eating the victory off her tongue.

We were so close to whatever kind of happily-ever-after two anti-heroes in love deserved.

Two villains down--Rocco Abruzzi and Dennis O'Malley--and one to go.

I fucked her in the car.

It didn't matter that Adriano was driving and would clearly hear what we were doing in the back of the Town Car. It didn't matter that the windows were tinted, but anyone passing by might catch a glimmer of sweet golden flesh or raspberry nipples.

I hadn't been inside my wife in a month.

In fact, I practically tossed her into the back seat, her back hitting the far passenger door. Instead of righting herself, she rucked up her skirt and let her legs fall open, exposing the thigh-high stockings, black lace garter, and thong I'd bought her from *La Perla* for Christmas to wear for me when I was free.

"Come here, *Capo*," she said, her voice husky and her cheeks already flushed.

I moved into the car, slammed the door behind me, and fell on her like a crocodile surging hungrily from the swamp, snapping her up in my grasp.

I ate at her mouth, biting at those lush lips, one then the other before plunging my tongue into that sweet heat, rubbing it against her own, her teeth and gums. There was this ferocious, building need in me to own every single inch of her.

To remind her who made her body sing.

One hand went to her throat, needing the feel of her pulse thumping madly against my thumb. The other went between those splayed thighs to cup her pussy over the lace.

She was already wet.

The heat and stickiness seeped through the fabric to coat my palm.

A savage groan ripped through my throat. She echoed it greedily, clutching my head tightly.

"Fuck me," she begged shamelessly, eyes flashing with the demand. "*Fammelo sentire dentro*!"

*I want to feel you inside me.*

My fingers curled into the lace of her panties and *tore*. She gasped against my mouth as I cupped her mound again, sliding two fingers straight to her depths.

My hand tightened on her throat just slightly as I reared back to watch her writhe on my fingers, pumping them with ruthless precision against her sweet spot. She panted, her nails catching at my forearms as she held my hand to her throat, pressing even harder so her breath strained through her lungs.

"*Dio mio*," she cried breathlessly.

I bent down to take that swollen, pink clit between my lips and sucked hard, moaning at the taste of her honeyed juices.

She broke apart.

Spectacularly.

Completely.

Her limbs flailed against the seats, her hips jacking up into my mouth as her cum seeped down her thighs, pooling beneath her ass on the seat. I shifted my mouth to her entrance, lapping up the wet leaking from my gently thrusting fingers. She shuddered, moaning my name like a prayer.

Her taste in my mouth, her scent in my nose, and the feel of her coming for me, knowing she had never done the same for anyone else, broke my civilized veneer in two.

I surged up from her pussy, opened my pants with one hand, and fisted my cock. It was leaking, practically dripping precum like a broken faucet. I pulled hard on the shaft a few times, slicking it with the wet. I was so hard, steel under the hot, pink silk of my skin.

*"Apri le gambe."*

She opened her legs.

*"Più ampio."*

*Wider.*

She spread them as far as she could in the narrow space. Her pussy glistened in the cold winter light spilling into the car, pink and swollen as a fruit about to drop from the vine.

I notched the head of my cock at her entrance and warned, *"Ti scopero' fino a farti esplodere di piacere."*

*I am going to fuck you until you explode.*

I curled my arm around her upper back, my fingers curved around the opposite shoulder for leverage while the other found her throat. Her eyes were wide and dark as fire smoke.

I thrust to the hilt inside that snug little cunt.

She cried out, neck arching as I set a punishing pace. She was so unused, so tight that even as wet as she was, I had to drag my length in and out of her, friction on every stroke.

She felt like heaven on earth.

My mouth ran as I fucked her, telling her all the things I'd dreamed of in the dark of my prison cell.

"Love this tight pussy, Lena. You were made to take my cock."

"You feel s-so huge," she confessed on a broken sob, her hips writhing away from me.

"Take all of it," I demanded, thrusting her down on my dick, grinding into her until she yelped and moaned, then begged for it all over again. "This is my cunt, isn't it, *cuore mia*?"

"Yes," she agreed breathlessly, her legs quivering as I drove into her again and again. "Every inch of me."

"*Si, sei mio*," I growled as my heat sparked in my gut and spread like a wildfire through my veins. "You are mine. Mine to fuck. Mine to protect. Mine to love."

"*Sempre*," she cried out, eyes screwed shut as she began to shake.

*Always*.

I bent to seal my lips over her pulse, moving my hand to the other side so I could feel it on my tongue and my thumb. My teeth sank into the elegant column, and like a trigger on a gun, she exploded.

Her pussy spasmed around me, clenching like a wet velvet fist, drenching me in her cum. The wet slap and suck of our joining echoed in the car alongside her sweet cries.

Her heart beat a tattoo against me.

*Mine, mine, mine*.

I must have said the words aloud because she cried out as she climaxed, "Yours, yours, yours."

My balls tightened almost painfully, every muscle in my body contracting around the inferno of pleasure at my center.

"Come for me," Elena begged as I took her savagely, more beast than man. "Come inside me. I missed being filled up with your cum."

That did it.

"*Cazzo*," I cursed, my entire body clenched into one long muscle an instant before I came, spurting so hard inside her I could feel the hot splash of it against her womb. "My Lena, *lottatrice*," I chanted as I spilled and spilled.

I gave her my weight, unable to hold myself up after the hugeness of my climax wrung me dry. She accepted it happily, twining me up in her limbs like a wrapped present, humming contentedly to herself as she stroked the back of my head.

"*Mi sei mancata*," she told me sweetly, almost shyly.

*I've missed you.*

I braced on a hand in the seat to lever my torso off her so I could look into her face. Her features were soft, peaceful in a way they rarely were, broken up with love and pleasure to expose her fragile heart. I touched my finger to the corner of her red mouth and wondered at how lucky a man I'd become.

"Never again," I promised once more, foolishly. "Nothing will come between us again. I will kill anyone who tries."

"I know," she said simply, tracing her fingers over the edge of my jaw. "I will too."

It ached in me to know she meant that. There was nothing this fierce, loyal warrior of a woman wouldn't do for me. Having the love of a woman like that was the greatest gift I'd ever received. There was also a perverse pleasure in knowing I could show her my darkness, and she would match it with her own.

We weren't perfect, far from it, but that was why I thought we were meant to be. Our jagged edges met beautifully.

# CHAPTER THIRTY
# DANTE

That night, when Elena was passed out in a sexual coma in our bed, I left the apartment with Frankie and Adriano. The RICO charges had been dropped, and I was a free man, but that didn't mean I was going to live and let live.

Dennis O'Malley lived in a Soho brownstone on a quiet residential street. He had a security system, but Frankie made quick work of it from the car, his face lit blue by the computer screen.

Only Addie and I went to the house.

The lock on the door was pathetically easy to work open, the hinges well-oiled so it didn't make a sound when we pushed into the house. It was late, nearly midnight, but light spilled into the hall from an open door at the back of the house.

Jaco had cased the place for us beforehand, so I knew it was Dennis's office.

I knew how to move quietly in the shadows for a big guy, so he didn't detect me even when I was framed in the doorway.

He sat at his desk with his head in his hands, fingers dug into his messy hair, staring blankly at his computer screen. There was a bottle of Jack and an empty glass on the tabletop beside it, the bottle nearly empty.

"Boo."

He startled so hard, his hand swept out to knock the Jack Daniels to the floor, where it crashed and flooded the wood with booze.

"What the fuck are you doing in my house, Salvatore?" he demanded as he lurched to his feet and reached for his phone.

I pulled the gun in my hand up into view, training it dead center on his chest. "Ah, ah, I wouldn't touch that if I were you."

He frowned, his muddled brain taking longer to process the inevitable.

Then he froze as it occurred to him why I was there with a gun aimed at his ugly mug.

Because he was going to die.

"No," he breathed involuntarily.

"Yes," I countered with a smile that pulled back the curtains on the dark side of my soul. "I'm afraid so. Sit down, O'Malley."

He fell back into his chair, the wheels taking him away from the desk toward the row of shelves at his back.

"You don't honestly think you'll get away with killing me, do you?" he asked with a superior sneer. "I may have lost this case, but everyone knows what you are. It's only a matter of time before you're put away for good."

"Maybe." I shrugged as I moved farther into the room. "But not for this. You see, I'm not going to kill you. You're going to kill yourself."

He laughed.

He was a narcissistic *stronzo,* so of course, he did. The idea of taking his own life would never have occurred to him otherwise. He loved himself too much.

"How are you going to pull that off?" he asked, his words slurring just slightly.

His eyes were bloodshot, his skin clammy with cold sweat. He'd obviously had a lot to drink, which worked beautifully for me because it would only add to the tragic story.

"I've got a source that says *The Times* is writing an exposé on you," I said conversationally, picking up a paperweight in the shape of the Statue of Liberty with my gloved hand. "They're digging into your past. I also heard they got a tip that you grew up with a well-known Irish mobster by the name of Thomas Kelly and his associate, Seamus Moore. All of your cases will be invalidated because they'll be able to shine a light on what a fucking scumbag you are."

He stared at me, his left eye twitching. "I've never done anything half as bad as you."

"No, but then, you also haven't done anything half as well, or you wouldn't be in this situation," I pointed out helpfully.

"You're a fucking bastard," he ground out. "I'm not going to end myself because you think you can blackmail me."

"Did I say I would stop with you?" I smiled handsomely. "No, why would I do that? You went for my wife, so why wouldn't I go after your loved ones? Your mama up over Hoboken, your granny up in Albany. Did they raise you because your dad left when you were just a kid? I'm going to have men on every person you love, Dennis, because you set the rules for this game, and in them, family was never off-limits."

Finally, he seemed to understand I wasn't fucking around. His posture slumped in the chair, his eyes distant as he considered.

"Then there is that pretty assistant DA that's been sucking your cock every day for the past two years. What's her name…?" I snapped my fingers. "Angelica! Yeah, I got a man on Angelica right now."

"You're a monster," he breathed.

I sat in the chair across the desk from him and leaned forward with my forearms on my thighs to smile ferally at him. "Yeah, I'm a monster, Dennis. Yet you fucked with me and mine. You knew who I was, what I was, and you still thought you could get away with trying to ruin my life? Ruin Elena's life?" I clucked my tongue against my teeth. "No, no one gets away with that."

"I'll leave you alone," Dennis suggested, trying not to beg, his pride strangling him. "I won't go after you again."

I chuckled. "Cute, but too late. You made your fucking bed, and now, you can lie in it six feet under."

It was late, and I wanted to get back to my wife, to a real bed for the first time in over a month, so I stood to finish this even though I was having fun. I pulled the wrapped package from the back of my waistband and tossed it on the desk for him.

Dennis peeled the paper back with trembling hands, pale and ugly as city doves.

He gaped at what lay inside.

"Your gun," I pointed out. "The one Frankie and Elena stole when they were with you at the gun range. I brought it back to its rightful owner. I recommend using it to end your misery before it begins, O'Malley. Because if I don't hear about your obituary in the news tomorrow, I'm going to come for you and your entire family until they even beg you to end yourself, *capisci?*"

He didn't answer, but then, I didn't expect him to.

I left him staring blindly at the gun as if it held the questions to life's mysteries like some crystal ball. And for him, it did.

He had two options, and death was the least of them.

I walked back through the house, Addie joining me where he had been waiting as backup in the hall. He locked the door again behind me, and then when we got into the waiting car down the street, Frankie armed the alarm once more.

We sat there for three hours before it happened.

The bang echoed through the peaceful neighborhood and sent a black cat scurrying across the street.

We drove home, and when I crawled into bed with my wife, taking her in my arms, I had only sweet, golden dreams.

# CHAPTER THIRTY ONE

## *elena*

We decided to throw a party and invited almost everyone we knew.

I even called my sister.

"Hello?" her soft voice floated over the phone.

I hesitated for a moment, caught up in the memories it evoked, Christopher and Daniel, my self-loathing and bitterness.

Dante laughed across the room in the kitchen where he was pouring glasses of champagne for Tore and his crew.

And I remembered that I had nothing to be bitter about anymore.

"Giselle," I said. "It's Elena."

It was easy to read her shock through the phone.

"Oh, hi. Is everything okay?" There was alarm in her tone, which warmed me slightly. It felt good to know whatever our issues, she didn't want me unhappy or unhealthy.

"Everything is wonderful, actually," I confessed as I sat on the couch, staring at our chosen family. Frankie had his arm slung around Dante's shoulders while Addie pretended to fight him, throwing mock punches that made everyone else laugh. "I don't know if you followed the case, but Dante was acquitted today."

"Oh! That's so wonderful. The charges were dropped?"

"We proved the murder charge was bogus, so the prosecution's case crumbled." I would never forget the look on Dennis O'Malley's face and the resulting triumph I'd felt like David taking down Goliath. "Anyway, we are having a party tonight to celebrate. Mama, Sebastian, and Beau are coming. I wondered…I wondered if you and Daniel were free to join us?"

"Yes," she said instantly, almost without thinking. "I mean, we have Gennie, but I can see if our babysitter could watch her for a while."

"If you can't, that's fine too," I said. "I just wanted to call and, well, extend the invitation. It's a night to celebrate."

"I'm happy you called, and I'm happy he's free. I'll call the babysitter and talk to Sinclair, then text you so you know what our plan is, okay? And, Elena, thank you for inviting us. I'm excited to see you and to hear that you seem so happy." Her voice was sweet, but then, it always was because Giselle wore her tender heart on her sleeve, whereas I'd hidden my own behind layers of ice like something that had become extinct in the Ice Age.

"Thank you," I said sincerely. "Sounds good."

And it did.

If she and Sinclair could come, I would be polite but most likely a little distant. I didn't know if forgiveness was something that could manifest as soon as you wanted it to happen. It would take time, and even then, I might not ever feel the way for Giselle I did with Cosima, Mama, and even Sebastian.

But again, that was okay.

Life was messy and imperfect, and I was just a part of that.

A little resentment and bitterness didn't make me a bitch. It just made me human.

I shut off the phone and wandered into the kitchen where Dante immediately made room for me at his side.

"*Stai bene?*" he asked, checking in as he ran his nose down my hair.

"Yes," I said, wrapping an arm around his waist. "I invited Giselle tonight."

He stilled for a moment before curling me tighter into his body. "*Che coraggio.*"

*What courage.*

Frankie's phone ringing cut through the music and laughter of the kitchen, but I ignored it to roll to my toes to kiss the hinge of Dante's jaw.

"Boss."

The atmosphere in the kitchen fell flat like old pop.

Dante's head snapped up, eyes alert and predatory on his right-hand man.

"The di Carlos are at the house in Queens," Frankie relayed. "Bruno is on the phone, hiding in the crawl space. They're taking the entire load."

"*Cazzo di Merda,*" Dante cursed savagely, putting his champagne flute down so hard on the counter that the stem broke, and Prosecco went everywhere. He ignored it, looking down at me with eyes like chips of black ice. "We have to go, *lottatrice*."

"Go," I agreed, kissing him quickly before moving away to collect the glasses from the rest of the men who were already starting to move out. "Just keep me posted."

A hand snapped in my shirt and pulled me back. Dante spun me to face him and kissed me one more time, hard enough to bruise.

"I'll be back soon," he promised.

I smiled softly at him because his own anxiety about being away prompted him to say that. I'd already known he would come back to me.

*"In bocca al lupo."*

*Good luck.*

The party was in full swing, the apartment stuffed with friends, family, and mafia associates who greeted me like their queen when they arrived. Even Giselle and Daniel had shown up, though I hadn't done more than say hello and kiss them both on each cheek. That seemed to surprise them, startling a pure smile out of the usually reserved Daniel and a surprising hug from my sister that I weathered with a mixture of pain and pleasure.

Dante had texted to say not to cancel the party, but they wouldn't be back for a while. The lawyer in me wondered if he was using the party as an alibi, but I tried not to worry.

"They'll be fine," Yara promised when I looked at the clock for the four hundredth time. "They're big boys."

"I know, but that doesn't mean I won't worry about them."

Her hard face softened slightly. "You know, I wasn't sure about you at first, Elena, but I'm happy to say I've grown to care for you very much."

I blinked at the woman I'd admired for years, completely caught off guard by her compliment. "Well, thank you, Yara. Coming from you, that means everything."

"Have you considered what you are going to do about your career now that you're married to one of the most infamous mafiosos of our time? It might hinder your job prospects at Fields, Haring & Griffith slightly."

I winced because I'd thought about that. "Honestly, everything has happened in such a whirl. I'm trying to take it one day at a time right now and be grateful for what I have."

She nodded, but her gaze was sly, considering. I watched as she took a sip of her martini because I could feel her gathering the words to speak. "Have you ever considered starting your own firm?"

My heart stopped. "Fleetingly. I never thought it would be a real possibility, at least not anything close to short term."

"Well, now you are one of the most famous lawyers in the country. Most fourth-year associates don't end up on the front page of *The New York Times*," she pointed out.

I blushed slightly. The paper had featured a photo of Dante lifting me in his arms and kissing me savagely in the middle of the courtroom after Judge Hartford had declared the mistrial. The heading read *Mafia Lord & Lawyer Claim Victory And A Happily-Ever-After.* It was stupid and cheesy, a gimmick to sell copies, but it worked.

Apparently, today's issue was one of the bestselling in the past two years.

I guessed everyone loved a good love story.

And I had to admit, ours was the best.

"I only ask because I want you to consider opening a firm with me," Yara continued calmly as if she wasn't blowing my mind. "I want to focus on female lawyers and criminal law. We just defended a notorious mafioso, so we have to go into this knowing we would attract a certain kind of clientele…" She studied me with her rich brown eyes. "But I have the feeling you don't see life in such stark black and white as you used to."

I laughed because it was absurd to think of how much I'd changed in the past four and a half months. It didn't feel as if I was a completely new person, only that the secret things I'd kept hidden in the darkness of my soul had finally burst free like a black butterfly from its chrysalis.

I felt more like me than I ever had before.

"I hope you aren't laughing at the idea," Yara drawled with an arched brow.

Immediately, I sobered. "No, no, far from it. I'm sorry, I was just overwhelmed by how much life has changed in the past few months. Opening a firm together would be more than a dream come true. It was a dream I never even thought to form because it seemed so outlandish."

She graced me with a small smile, stepping closer to squeeze my hand even though she wasn't a tactile person. "Sometimes, the darkness in someone else brings out the best in us. That's what my Donni did to me, and I can see it's what Dante has done for you. I'm in no rush, but let's talk about it further sometime next week after you're settled. I'd like to strike while the proverbial iron is hot and people are still talking about us."

"I agree. Okay, thank you, Yara." I hesitated, then decided to go for it, following my mandate to be more open with people. "It means a lot to have a woman I highly respect believe in me."

"I hope it will teach you to believe in yourself even more," she countered. "I really believe the sky's the limit to the success you can achieve in this field, Elena. You're truly a talented lawyer."

She moved away then, leaving me with an enigmatic smile as I tried to digest the beauty of that moment.

I'd thought that in loving Dante, I would have to give up my second love—

my career. It wasn't a hard decision to make, though I knew it would be a painful one to see out.

There was an Italian saying, *non si può avere la botte piena e la moglie ubriaca,* which roughly translated to "you can't have a full cask and a drunk wife" or in English, "you can't have your cake and eat it too."

But it seemed after a lifetime of injustices and heartbreak, I had the opportunity to have exactly that.

I stood there beaming with joy for a few minutes before I thought to look for Mama to tell her the news. I spotted her in the kitchen because, even at a party, that was her domain, but she was backed against the corner of the cabinets by none other than Salvatore, who had stayed with me at the apartment while the younger men went to take care of business. She looked angry as she spoke to him about something, but when he lifted his hand to tuck back a lock of loose barely graying black hair, her entire face softened.

"Uh..." My brother shuddered as he stepped beside me. "Are you watching our mother be seduced?"

It was surreal and a little uncomfortable to know that I was watching his father attempt to seduce his mother, but I didn't say anything because I understood it wasn't my place to.

For now, I smacked him in the chest. "Now who's the prude?"

He grinned at me, slinging an arm around my shoulders to pull me in close. "Not you anymore. You seem much more relaxed than ever before. I'll have to buy Dante a bottle of whiskey to thank him for the attitude adjustment."

"Hey!" I protested, but I did it laughing because he loved to tease, and I was finally comfortable enough with myself to take it. "You're disgusting."

He shrugged. "I've been called worse."

My phone buzzed where I'd tucked it into the pocket of my black Prada wrap dress.

"Excuse me a moment," I murmured as I pulled it out to see Bambi's name on the screen.

"Bambi?" I answered, moving away from Sebastian out onto the patio so I could hear her better. "I thought you and Aurora would be here already."

"Lena, I'm scared," came a frightened whisper. "I did what you said and met with your friend Tilda when you were gone. She helped me get a restraining order against the man I told you about, but he won't leave me alone."

Everything in me stilled. "It's not Marco?" He was still in the hospital in the long-term care ward getting rehabilitation because one of the bullets had shattered his femur.

"No!" she cried. "Marco would never hurt me. But I'm beside myself. I don't think there is any way we can stay here and be safe. I have to go."

"Go where?" I demanded, cupping the phone to my cheek as I left the cold patio and returned inside, powering through the party to the foyer. I used the code to open the lockbox for the car keys and grab the set for the Ferrari. "Listen, Bambi, I'm going to come to you, okay? I'll pick you and Rora up and bring you to our house. Pack enough for a long stay. We can figure this out as a family, *va bene?*"

She burst into noisy tears through the phone.

*Cazzo.*

"Bambi? Bambi, listen, I'm coming. Don't freak out, and do not leave. Where is Rora? Don't startle her, okay? I'll be there in ten minutes." I hung up on her wails, hoping that she would try to calm down for Rora's sake at least.

I stepped into the elevator and pressed the button for the garage. As the doors closed, I saw Tore spot me from the kitchen, his face a stern mask.

I texted him while I descended, letting him know where I was going.

The streets were fairly empty for Manhattan, the sky dense with snow clouds that threatened to fall at any moment. I pulled up in front of the house that had been split into eight apartments in Queens where Bambi and Rora lived and sprinted up the stairs, shivering because I'd forgotten a coat.

I knocked on the door for a long minute before it creaked open, and Rora appeared. Her face was tearstained, her hair a tangled mess around her pouting face. She was fully dressed even though it was long past her bedtime, even a pair of pink sneakers on her feet.

"Are you here to save us?" she asked me, sniffing through it.

My heart constricted. "Yes, *gattina mia,* I'm here to save you. Where is your mama?"

"She's crying in her bedroom."

I sighed as I stepped into the house and closed the door behind me, locking it and pulling the deadbolt across the frame. Rora grabbed my hands in both of hers, squeezing tightly as if she was afraid I'd let go.

"Are you scared?" I asked her gently, bending to push her messy hair back from her sweet face. "What are you scared of?"

"My papa," she whispered so quietly, I almost missed it. "He says he loves me, but he scares Mama."

I hadn't realized the man who'd been stalking them was her father, and I couldn't understand why Bambi hadn't just told me. But I smiled at the little girl and stood to let her lead me back to the bedrooms.

"Bambi?" I asked as we rounded the corner, and I found her sitting on her bed among a pile of strewn clothes and two open suitcases.

She was sobbing so hard it sounded like she was choking.

I went to her, sitting beside her hunched form so I could pull her into my arms for a tight hug.

"Hush," I urged, stroking her back. "It's okay. Calm down. *Calmati.*"

I held her for a few minutes with Rora standing there tugging on a lock of her hair, watching us with wide, frightened eyes.

"Can you talk now?" I asked Bambi, moving back to look at her. I pushed her hair from her face and *tsk*ed at her swollen eyes and red face. "You've made yourself sick crying. Everything will be okay, I promise. Dante and I will make it better."

That set her off again.

My patience was a fraying rope. Aurora absolutely did not need to see her mother going to pieces, not when she was obviously frightened herself.

I gently shook Bambi by the shoulders and cooled my voice, hoping it would shock her like cold water. "Georgina! Listen to me, okay? You're making yourself sick, and you are scaring your daughter. Take a few deep breaths with me, *si?*"

She gave me a shuddering nod, hiccoughing through three deep breaths. Finally, she seemed to regain the ability to speak because she whispered something to me.

"*Scusi?*" I asked because I didn't catch it.

"I'm sorry," she repeated again, her voice wrecked. "I'm so sorry."

"For what?" I asked, still so focused on comforting her that I almost missed the niggle of premonition in my gut.

Slowly, disbelieving, I pulled back from her.

She sobbed, catching it in her palm as she slapped it over her mouth.

"Bambi?" I asked, each word tightly bound with control so I wouldn't lash out before I knew for sure. "What have you done to be sorry about?"

"H-he told me he would take Aurora," she explained, her voice wet and thick with snot. "He told me he would take her away and never let me see her again."

"Who did?" I snapped so hard she flinched.

"Auggie," Aurora chimed in sullenly. "My papa."

"Auggie?" I racked my brain trying to think of who the hell Auggie was, but then I didn't have to.

"Agostino di Carlo," Bambi explained, tears squeezing out the corners of her eyes. They fell off her chin in a steady stream. "Agostino is Aurora's father."

## Chapter Thirty-Two

**Elena**

She told me everything then, a voice like a guttering candle, about her history with the Cosa Nostra's new Boss.

They'd met when she was only seventeen, and he was older, handsome, and wealthy. He found her at a bodega in Little Italy and chatted with her about which candy was better, Smarties or Reece's Pieces. When he asked to take her for a drive, she went without question.

They only saw each other for two months before Bambi got pregnant. Apparently, Agostino was pleased.

Bambi's father, when she told him, was not.

Emiliano had been the Capo of the New York City Camorra for years, and he knew immediately who Agostino was when Bambi described him. His rival's firstborn son.

Bambi winced as she told me about being cast out by her family and then abandoned by Agostino.

She was alone for years until Dante offered her help.

Apparently, it was a double-edged sword because it brought her to Agostino's attention again. He tried to blackmail Emiliano by threatening Bambi and Aurora. Even though he'd cast his daughter out as many old-school Italians would have done, he still loved her, so he tried to make the money to pay Agostino off on the side.

Which had gotten him killed by a Mexican cartel.

I hauled Aurora into my lap as Bambi continued to relate her horrors in a voice stripped of all emotion. The little girl was disturbingly unperturbed hearing about her family's past, and it ached in me that she had been exposed to the horrors of mafia life in much the same way I had been as a girl.

"When Papa died, Agostino left us alone for a while. I guess he was just patient. Then Dante got arrested, and he showed up the next day on our doorstep wanting to see Rora. He really just wanted to threaten me." She sobbed for a few seconds, then valiantly tried to swallow them down. "I couldn't tell Dante because he didn't know about him being Rora's father. He would have cast us out or started a war."

"The war had already started, Bambi," I pointed out coolly even as I cuddled Rora closer when I noticed she'd fallen asleep. "You should have told him."

"I know that now," she admitted miserably. "But I told my brother instead."

A chill slid down my back.

Of course, Jacopo would have known about this.

"He said we shouldn't tell Dante, that it would ruin everything he'd worked for in the Family. He said he'd take care of it, but Agostino wouldn't listen to him. He made Jaco tell him stuff too."

"You've been spying on the Camorra for him," I surmised in a dead voice. "You and Jaco."

She started to sob again, but I felt little compassion for her.

Of course, I understood the difficulty of the situation. I had no doubt Agostino would have taken her daughter from her without any qualms, that Bambi truly felt she was between a rock and a hard place.

But she had Dante in her corner.

A man who lived and breathed loyalty. Who gave a woman a job because she was a single mom with no prospects, and he was just that good a man.

A man who had become a pseudo uncle to her daughter and called her the love of his life.

I couldn't fathom why she had thought Agostino was the better of those two options.

Rage rose in my throat and then abruptly cooled.

Because I thought about Mama.

She had the choice between Seamus and Tore, and she had made that decision based on fear. That fear had led her to choose the worse man who might have appeared artificially better, especially through the skewed eyes of terror. She had assumed Tore was the greater of two evils just as Bambi had, and they'd both been proven wrong.

I sighed so long it hurt my chest.

"Okay, Bambi, please stop crying and listen to me. You're going to pack up what you and Rora need as quickly as you can, and then we are going to leave here. I doubt you'll come back, so take the essentials. I'm going to take you home and put you both to bed, but in the morning, you're going to have to answer for yourself. What you did...I can't pretend it doesn't make me see red. But I know you've been in an impossible situation, and I can't fathom how hard it's been for you to live with this."

"It's driving me insane," she whispered. "Lying to the sweetest people I know. To Dante, to Marco, to you."

"I can't promise there won't be consequences," I warned. "But no matter what, I promise we'll find a way to make you safe."

Bambi used the soggy tissue in her hand to blow her nose, then smiled at me weakly. "Thank you, Elena. You really are a beautiful *donna.*"

I sighed again, standing up with Rora. "You pack quickly, okay? I'm going to lie her down on the couch and come back to help."

The blonde nodded eagerly, her eyes already a little clearer now that we had a plan.

I moved into the main room and went to put Rora on the couch when there was a click at the door.

Just that.

A click.

But it set the hairs on the back of my neck on end.

Slowly, quietly, I crept away from the living room and its front door back into the shadowed kitchen.

*Bang.*

Something pounded on the door.

My back pressed against the kitchen cabinets with Aurora a heavy weight in my arms.

Bambi appeared in the bedroom doorframe, her hair a haloed mess, red-rimmed eyes wide as blue saucers.

"Is that him?" I mouthed.

She nodded hysterically.

"Where can we hide?" I asked as there was another bang at the door, and a voice yelled Bambi's name through the wood.

She jerked her chin at the long, narrow wooden door next to the fridge. I opened it to find it mostly empty, only a mop, dustpan, broom, and vacuum inside. It was just big enough to fit us both if we squeezed.

"Go," she whispered harshly, moving to us.

I folded myself inside, ducking my head and pressing Aurora tight to my body. Bambi took a long look at us folded in the enclosure before she closed the door on us.

My breath was loud in the dark space.

Aurora didn't make a sound, out like a light.

Carefully, I fished my phone out of my pocket and sent a group text to Dante and his crew.

*Come to Bambi's. Agostino di Carlo is here. We need help.*

I prayed fervently that they were done with whatever they'd been called to do, and they'd get here soon.

Next, I typed in 9-1-1 and pressed send.

It was too late to speak, but I laid the phone on mute next to the crack in the door.

"Why the fuck didn't you answer the door?" Agostino's cold, cruel voice emanated across the room like dry ice.

"I was cleaning," Bambi tried to explain in her sweet voice. "And I'm a mess. If I'd known you were coming, I would have made myself presentable."

His laughter was harsh. "You know I have no interest in you that way, Georgina. I'm in this for the intel. You didn't show up at the shop yesterday. You know I get irritated when you miss our dates."

*Dates.*

What a fucking psychopath.

"I'm sorry," she said meekly. "Dante got out of jail yesterday, so I spent the day cleaning his apartment. It's my job."

"I don't give a fuck if it's your job. Your job is to keep me fed with intel about the Salvatore's, or I'll take our daughter away somewhere you'll never find her." There was a pause and then, "Where is she?"

"At a friend's house."

The response was too quick. I could feel the suspicion in the air between them.

There was a clack of shoes against the wood floors, and then his voice was closer.

"Aurora?" he yelled.

In my arms, his daughter jerked awake.

I clamped my hand gently over her mouth so she wouldn't scream, but she only looked up at me, her eyes wide in the thin stream of light cutting in from the living room. She trembled slightly, so I held her even tighter.

"She isn't here, Agostino," Bambi insisted. "And you shouldn't be either. If you want me to be your precious rat, you can't keep showing up where they could find you."

"Dante come to your house much?" he asked in a low, dangerous hiss.

"N-no, but he has before to pick up Rora or drop her off."

"The filth near my daughter is disgusting. He's not even Italian, you know that? The British *figlio di puttana*. The sooner I end him, the better. That's why I came. I want you to tell me what he's planning now that he's on the outside."

"I don't know." Her words were immediately followed by a shriek as he hurt her somehow. "Please, Agostino, I really don't know anything. I'm his housekeeper and his cook. He doesn't speak freely around me very much."

There was a pause filled with the sounds of her struggling. "You're right. The only useful thing you've done is given us Jacopo, who has value to Salvatore. You're nothing. Not to him and not to me."

"Please," Bambi whispered. "Please just leave us alone."

"You're pathetic, Georgina, you really are. A pathetic liability. If I don't need you, what are you good for, huh?"

"I'm the mother of your child," she tried.

In my arms, Aurora whimpered, ducking her head under my armpit to block out the noise. It was impossible to stem my own panic, both remembered and real. Hiding in the kitchen felt too much like a nightmarish déjà vu waiting for the Camorra to beat up my father.

"You've been a waste of my time since the moment I met you." He hummed as if in consideration, and then there was a *bang* as he slammed something against the wall.

From the feminine gasp, it was obviously Bambi.

"I don't need you anymore," he decided in a cold, detached way as if assessing a stock risk. "And I don't need you running your mouth to your precious Camorra men. You saw what happened when you got too close to Marco, didn't you?" he teased cruelly. "Stubborn *bastardo*, I thought for sure he would die."

Bambi started to cry, soft sobs that rolled through the room like a fog of despair.

Adrenaline pumped through my veins. I couldn't just let him hurt her or kill her or whatever he was gearing up to do. But I was also stuck in hiding with Aurora, and I didn't want to put her in danger.

The choice was taken from me when I heard the cock of a gun.

Gently, I shifted Rora off my lap, encouraging her to curl up in the depths of the cabinet under the mop handle. She shook her head frantically, clutching at my hand as I tried to peel her away from me.

"No, stop," Bambi screamed, the cries followed by thumping as if she was kicking at him. "Please, Auggie, think about your--"

Three things happened at once.

One.

I burst from the door of the cabinet, slamming it behind me to shield Aurora and startle Agostino.

Two.

He fired the gun.

Straight into Bambi's sternum.

I shouted wordlessly and raced across the twelve feet between Agostino holding her up against the wall and my hiding place.

Three.

There was a knife lying on the counter, a paring knife to cut fruits or vegetables. I gripped it in my fist and lunged at Don di Carlo.

I impacted with him as he was turning to look at the commotion I'd made. I was lucky to catch him off guard because he was almost as big as Dante. He staggered as I hit him, loosening his grip on Bambi who fell to the floor clutching her chest, leaving a big wet, red smear of blood on the white wall.

Fury turned my vision blood red.

I jammed the knife into the first place I could reach, Agostino's upper right chest. It slid in deep enough to hit bone then got stuck.

At that moment, I wondered madly if I was going to die.

He flipped me so quickly, I wasn't even aware I was moving until my back slammed into the floor and the air expelled entirely from my body.

"Elena Lombardi," he greeted with a sneer, pulling the knife from his chest as if it was only a minor inconvenience. "What a pleasant surprise. Did this bitch enlist your help to get away from me?"

His hands found my neck, strangling me just enough for black spots to prance across my vision, but not enough to kill me.

Not yet.

I was grateful to have long legs.

I kicked the right one up and notched my foot against his belly where he crouched over me, pushing with all my might to get him to budge.

He didn't.

So, using the last of my energy, I kicked him in the kidney again and again.

Finally, he cursed in Italian and shifted away from me, taking the pressure off my neck for just a second.

One second was enough.

I threw my right arm up and punched him straight in the throat.

He gurgled, his hands loosening. I rolled away and to my feet, grabbing for the knife on the floor again because the gun had fallen under the couch behind him.

He staggered to his feet with a growl. "*Puttana.*"

*Whore.*

I didn't care what he called me. My focus was on his hands. He aimed a punch at my right cheek, so I tucked my shoulder and rolled under it, then came up and sliced at his belly with the knife. I'd learned my lesson about stabbing him, but the thin wound that bloomed on his stomach was hardly enough to stop him.

He came at me again.

And again.

And again.

Sweat dripped into my eyes and made them burn. There was no way I was going to be able to defend myself forever. He was bigger, stronger, better than me.

Maybe it was the defeatist thought, but on his next punch, he caught me on the chin and sent my head snapping back. The white ceiling whirled with black and white constellations as my knees turned to jelly.

He let me fall to the ground, my forehead bouncing against the corner of the chair at the dining room table before thumping to the ground.

I fought to stay conscious.

Which was why I missed the cacophony at the door as my Family arrived.

I groaned as Agostino carted me to my feet and pressed my back tight to the front of his body. A second later, the cold bite of metal met my temple.

He'd recovered the gun from under the couch.

But my vision cleared enough to see the hero who stood in the doorway.

Dante.

His face was thunderous as he glared at us over the barrel of his gun. His expression was so terrifying, so without mercy, that I could finally understand how he got the nickname The Devil of NYC.

He'd come for me.

"Dante," I croaked, just needing to say his name and hear his voice.

"*Stai zitto, trioa,*" Agostino snapped in my ear, grinding the gun deeper into my temple.

*Shut up, whore.*

Across the room, Dante coiled tighter, the air around him buzzing with potential energy.

"Speak to her like that again and I won't hesitate to put a bullet in your brain," he threatened.

Agostino laughed, moving the gun from my temple to my lips, pushing until my teeth tore the inside of my mouth, and I was forced to open around the barrel. For the second time in my life, I knew the taste of a gun. "You would never take the shot. She's too close. You could end up killing her."

There was a noise in the hall, and then Jacopo appeared in the door, gun raised, face set to stone.

My heart turned to ash when I looked at him. I knew he was just protecting his sister, but I couldn't believe he'd turned on Dante. They were cousins and friends, comrades.

"Bambi?" Jaco whispered as his eyes blew wide and his mouth dropped.

He'd spotted her.

In the commotion, with an obvious concussion, I had almost forgotten her.

Jacopo dropped his gun to his side and raced through the standoff between Dante and Agostino to drop to his sister's side. Blood had pooled in the center of her chest, but not much. It gave me a brief flare of hope before Jacopo shifted, moving her slightly so that I could see the lake of blood staining the ground beneath her.

One look at her angelic face lost to repose, and I knew she was dead.

Jacopo burst into tears, hauling her onto his lap.

Neither man shot him.

Dante seemed to realize this, his eyes narrowing. He didn't seem to mourn Bambi at all, but I knew his entire focus was on getting both of us out of here alive.

"Jaco," Dante called, his voice like smoke, dark and acrid. "Jaco!"

His cousin didn't respond, still bent over Bambi, watering her with tears.

"You didn't suspect, did you?" Agostino gloated. "You had no idea your dear sweet Bambi was reporting to me. What, Jacopo, huh? Did you suspect?"

Dante's face didn't give anything away. He only stared into my eyes, trying to communicate that everything would be okay.

I had a gun shoved between my lips, a dead friend at my feet, and Aurora witnessing it all from the kitchen cabinet, but I trusted him.

I had to.

This couldn't be the end when we'd only just started our life together.

"You're pathetic, really," Agostino continued, and I had to wonder if this *stronzo* was actually a psychopath. "You think you can rule a Family with love? This is the mafia, Salvatore. The only way to rule is through power and fear. Bambi and Jacopo didn't fear you as much as they feared me, so they became mine."

On the floor, Jacopo stopped crying.

"Big words for a man who lost $227 million dollars' worth of cocaine in one night," Dante said calmly, so coldly I almost shivered. "The refrigerated container at the Port of New Jersey? The one filled with about 140 packages of premium grade coke from the Ventura Cartel."

Agostino went still behind me.

Dante's lips curled like a villain's moustache, eyes dark as tar. "Yeah, Don di Carlo, if you were going to make it out of here alive, how would you ever explain that one to the Venturas? It's better really that I'm going to put a bullet through your brain right here."

Agostino reanimated, his pride wounded so, like an animal, he attacked because he couldn't flee. "*Vaffanculo a chi t'è morto,*" he cursed savagely before taking the gun from my mouth and aiming it at Dante. "I'm going to kill you, and your woman, then take your entire fucking empire, Salvatore."

He fired the gun.

*Bang!*

*Bang!*

*Bang!*

The first shot grazed Dante's shoulder, and the second embedded itself in his left bicep.

My husband barely flinched, firing off his own shot as Agostino shot his third.

Only, Dante was no longer in his line of fire.

Jacopo was.

He'd surged to his feet between the two men with his gun raised. Agostino's shot found its way through his throat.

Dante's in his low belly.

But Jacopo didn't go down.

His face clear and cold, eyes filled with pain that was more spiritual than physical, he fired a shot straight at Agostino.

At me.

He was a turncoat. A traitor. And it was clear that he'd never totally approved of me.

So I felt one moment of fear that would haunt me for the rest of my life.

Because the bullet didn't touch me.

It went straight through Agostino's skull.

He collapsed to the ground behind me.

In front of me, Jaco swayed, his free hand going to the base of his throat where the wound bubbled grotesquely.

When he fell, Dante was there to catch him, lowering him to the ground gently, going to his knees beside him.

"*Cazzo,* Jaco," he cursed, pressing a big hand to the wound in his neck.

I dropped to my knees and pressed both of mine to the one in his belly.

"Are you okay?" Dante demanded, his eyes wide and matte black. "Tell me, *merda,* are you all right!?"

"Yes, yes, focus on Jaco. I'm fine."

Adrenaline had eradicated whatever damage Agostino had done to me. I was pure energy, all of it focused on the dying man who had stood between Dante and a gun.

"Why?" Dante murmured, pressed his hands even harder around the seeping wound. "Why didn't you just tell me, you stubborn *stupido?*"

Jaco's lids fluttered, his breath a wet rattle. "Family shame. Started with my father. D-Didn't want to hurt you, D."

"*Stai zitto,*" he ordered. "Shut up. You can explain when you are healed."

Jaco tried to laugh, but blood spurted from his mouth like a mini geyser. "'Fraid not, *fratello.* 'S okay. I go to Bambi and Papa."

"Jacopo." Dante's voice was ravaged with tears, his face so taut in anger that I thought it would crack in two. "You idiot. I would have protected you all."

A little smile teased the bleached edges of his mouth, but Jaco didn't open his eyes again. Blood leaked from the corners of his lips and trailed down his chin.

"Call me your brother before I go," he whispered, hardly any sound. "Forgive me."

*"Fratello,"* Dante murmured, pressing a kiss to his forehead. *"Ti amo sempre, fratello mio."*

*I will love you always, my brother.*

Tears dripped down my own face as Dante held his cousin in his lap and watched him die, choking slightly on his blood, then going still. His face relaxed with peace, and Dante kissed him again on the forehead as he murmured a prayer for the dead in Italian under his breath.

Sirens wailed in the distance.

I knew they were coming closer because I'd left my phone in the closet.

My heart stopped, then restarted with an awful electric shock. I shoved to my feet and sprinted to the kitchen cabinet to throw the door open.

Aurora sat huddled in the shadows at the back, hugging her knees to her chest as she rocked herself, tears dripping from her cheeks.

*"Vieni, gattina mia,"* I murmured, bending into the cabinet to pick her up. "Come here, sweet girl."

She clutched at me, her nails breaking the skin of my arms as she practically crawled up my body into my embrace. I held the back of her head and bottom as I stood, careful to keep her from seeing the dead bodies in the living room.

Although she had just spent the last half an hour in a closet listening to her mother, father, and uncle die.

She was so quiet, crying silently in my arms until Dante stalked forward, his face like a thunderclap. She didn't flinch as he approached even though I almost did, he looked that ferocious. Instead, she turned in my arms and launched herself into his, sobbing the second she hit his chest.

He curled her against his big torso, curving his shoulders inward, wrapping her tightly in his arms as if he could shield her from the pain.

He couldn't.

Neither of us could.

I moved into them, wrapping one arm around Dante's waist and the other around Aurora, who grabbed my hand and lifted it to her cheek, cuddling it desperately.

We stood there together, silently, mourning, as the sirens grew louder, and finally, a red and blue block of light spiraled through the bloody crime scene.

# CHAPTER THIRTY THREE

## elena

*Six months later.*

Dante didn't like it.

It was the only way, but I understood his reluctance. I never wanted to be within ten feet of another di Carlo ever again.

That Family had worked their asses off to ruin Dante's Family. To ruin mine.

Now the New York Salvatores were a unit of four; Tore, Dante, Aurora, and me.

Which was why Dante eventually agreed with my plan to parlay with Gideone di Carlo, the new Don of the Cosa Nostra.

If we wanted to adopt Rora, it was the only way to do it.

Technically, Gideone had legal rights to be her guardian as he was her only surviving blood relative. If we wanted to make her ours, we needed him to surrender those rights.

Surprisingly, Gideone had reached out to me after the massacre at Bambi's house. The crime was all over the news, throwing Dante and me into the spotlight again in a way I could have done without. Thankfully, it was obvious because of Bambi's restraining order against Agostino and her records at the hospital proving his abuse that he was to blame for the circumstances of Jacopo's and Bambi's deaths.

We were free from blame legally, but not morally.

All three of us had been shell-shocked by that night.

Dante couldn't sleep most nights for the guilt he felt about not realizing their situation sooner, for not pressing Jacopo about his strange behavior or forcing Bambi and Aurora to live at his place.

Aurora, of course, was the most deeply affected by it. She couldn't stand to be away from Dante or me at all, so we had to work our lives around one of us being with her at all times for the first month she lived with us. She didn't trust strangers, and she didn't want to go back to school where she felt exposed and vulnerable. Sometimes, at home, when I couldn't find her, she was hiding in a cabinet in the kitchen or the bathroom. She told me it made her feel safe.

She broke my heart every single day.

Thankfully, we took her to see the best childhood psychologist in Manhattan, an old friend of Dante's from his days at Cambridge, and within four months of bi-weekly therapy, Aurora was starting to be more like her old self again. She'd even agreed to have a sleepover at Mama's house last weekend.

It was a process, and I knew it would be a long one.

I hadn't had the same childhood trauma, but I'd had my own, and it had taken me twenty-seven years to get over the brunt of it.

I hoped that the love and affection of the rest of her family would go a long way to healing her much more quickly than I had.

Which brought us back to the little café Yara had first taken me to nearly a year ago to tell me her own mafia story.

I was close with the shop owners now, Andrea and his wife, Guilia, and they greeted us with big smiles and kisses as we turned up that Friday morning to meet with Giuseppe.

"I still don't like that he had your number at all," Dante grumped as we accepted our little white cups of thick espresso from Andrea and moved to one of the three tiny iron tables on the sidewalk.

I rolled my eyes because we had been over this one hundred times. "It was my work number, Capo, which has since been terminated because I don't work for Fields, Harding & Griffith anymore."

He didn't say anything, his silence churlish.

Again, I couldn't blame him.

We'd healed a lot in the past six months, but losing two of his dearest friends had made Dante moodier than usual. He was such an alpha, such a protector that it killed him believing he had let Bambi and Jaco down.

"Hey." I reached across the table to grab his hand and pressed a kiss to its center the way he did with me. "*Ti amo, Capo*. Everything is going to be okay."

"Sorry to interrupt."

I looked up and over to see Gideone di Carlo standing a few feet away. I'd forgotten how handsome he was and also how unlike his deceased brother he looked. I'd been worried about seeing the ghost of Agostino, how it might trigger the feeling of that gun in my mouth again, of the terror I felt fighting for my life.

He was dark-haired and green-eyed, broad and burly, while his brother had been fair-haired and dark-eyed, tall but lean. And there in the swampy depths of those green eyes was something almost human.

There had been nothing human about Agostino.

"Thank you for coming," I said, standing up to gesture to the chair across from us. "Please sit down."

Eyes on Dante, who was coiled like a predator about to pounce, Gideone took the offered seat, keeping almost a yard of space between himself and the table.

This was how two alpha lions met without violence. Lots of space and a woman between them.

"Let's get straight to it," Dante declared, pulling papers out of the bag he had at his feet. "We want to adopt Aurora. Technically, you have a right to object to that as her blood uncle. We're hoping you have some decency in you where your brother did not and sign your rights away."

Gideone blinked at him.

I winced. "My husband *meant* to say that we would be honored to make Aurora part of our family officially, and we need your consent to make that happen."

His firm mouth softened. "How is she?"

A smile took my mouth before I could stop it. "She's beautiful. We had her seventh birthday party last month. It was only family and a boy she's had a crush on for years." The very same eight--now nine--year-old she had mentioned to Mama when she first met her. The one she wanted a kiss from.

*"Bene,"* Gideone murmured, looking across the street as if he was picturing it. "I am glad for that. What she saw…it would be hard on any child."

"She didn't sleep for weeks," Dante growled.

I put my hand on his hard thigh and squeezed. "She's making progress. We're going to therapy with her once a week, and she has her solo sessions too."

Something flexed in his face, some muscle he seemed surprised still worked. "You're good to her. She should be okay."

"She'll be better than okay," Dante asserted, his hand curling into a massive fist on the tabletop, a territorial threat display.

I felt like I was in the middle of a David Attenborough documentary.

"She's perfect," Dante finished, looking down at the hand he kept in his lap where his fingers fiddled with a pink beaded bracelet she made him that read '*il eroe*.'

*Hero.*

I'd cried for an hour after she'd given it to him.

Gideone studied us both for a long moment, then reached into his suit jacket to pull out a folded stack of papers. He tossed them on the table between us and our coffees.

"I already had my lawyer send me the documents. They're signed," he explained as I pulled them toward me and opened them up.

"You could have emailed them," Dante pointed out with narrowed eyes, his whole body tense. "Why did you want to meet?"

I sensed that Gideone was a considering man because he stared at Dante for a long second before he responded, his eyes cutting to me. "I wanted to see what kind of parents you'd make. This is *le mafie*. There aren't many good ones to go around."

"Thank you," I whispered, holding the signed papers to my chest as it glowed with warmth. "That's very…sweet."

He smiled flatly at me, the expression more menacing than anything pleasant, but I appreciated that he tried. Abruptly, he stood, but our business was finished. We would never be friends, so I understood his haste to leave.

He hesitated though, knocking his knuckles against the table before he finally locked eyes with me to say, "You should know, that day in the coffee shop, I wanted to take your measure. See what kind of woman you were because I knew Georgina was going to you for help." He hesitated. "She came to me, but I couldn't do shit. When I called later, I wanted to warn you that Agosto had gone *pazzo,* that he'd been talking nonsense about taking her out." He shrugged tightly, his jaw jumping. "No excuse. I should have tried harder. Georgina didn't deserve to die that way."

He rapped his knuckles against the table again, turned on his heel, and strode away, disappearing into an alleyway half a block down the street.

"I should have taken his calls," I said woodenly.

I was shocked by his show of decency, but then, wasn't I a prime example of a good person who could do bad things? Why couldn't Gideone be a bad person capable of good?

"He was just trying to make you feel badly," Dante grumbled, shooting back his coffee and standing to take my hand. "*Andiamo, lottatrice mia*. Let's go home to Rora."

We didn't adopt her right away.

She needed time to mourn her parents and her uncle, and we didn't want to pressure her. We wanted her to choose us just as much as we were choosing her.

I woke up on my twenty-eighth birthday to a heavy weight on my chest.

When I opened my eyes, Rora was lying on her stomach on top of me, her chin propped on her hands, her elbow digging painfully into my beasts.

"*Buon compleanno*!" she shouted in my face as soon as she saw I was awake. "Happy Birthday, *Zia*!"

I grinned, wrapping her in my arms to roll her off me and onto the bed at my side so I could tickle her. "*Gattina*, you dare to wake me up on my birthday?" I teased over her squeals of laughter.

I looked over at Dante, who stood in the doorway holding a tray.

My eyebrows raised. "Breakfast in bed?"

"Only the best for *donna mia*," he explained with a little shrug as he sat on the edge of the bed and put the tray beside me.

I stopped tickling Aurora so I could lean over to accept his warm kiss. He cupped my cheek in one hand and brought me back for more.

"Gross!" Aurora yelled, rolling back onto my legs so she could watch us kiss with her tongue sticking out.

Dante pulled away and bopped her on the nose. "You're gross. I bet you didn't brush your teeth this morning."

"Yes, I did!"

"If I check your toothbrush, will it be wet?" he questioned with narrowed eyes.

I lay back against the pillows, snagging a piece of bacon from the tray to watch their normal morning routine.

"*Si.*"

"Because you splashed water on it or because you actually brushed your teeth?" He raised a brow. "Come here, let me smell your breath."

Rora glared at him for a second, then huffed, rolling off the end of the bed to stand and stalk sassily from the room.

"You better wait for me to open her presents!" she shouted on the way to her bedroom.

Dante stared after her bemusedly. "*Dio* help me when she becomes a teenager."

I laughed, fisting my hand in his black tee to bring him closer to me for another kiss. "Her papa is an infamous mafia Don. I don't think you have to worry about boys around her until she's fully grown."

"It's not the boys I'm worried about," he muttered, moving the tray over my lap so he could sit beside me, curling an arm over my shoulder and taking the ends of my long hair between his fingers. "She's enough trouble on her own."

I laughed again because this was undoubtedly true.

"Happy Birthday, *cuore mia*," he murmured, drawing his nose from my forehead to my ear. "Are you a happy twenty-eight-year-old?"

I beamed at him. "I don't think I could be happier. I barely recognize myself sometimes."

He chuckled as Rora came sprinting back into the room in her pajamas and dived onto the bed at my side.

She snagged a piece of my bacon and chewed it noisily as she asked, "Can we give her our presents now?"

"I think so." Dante leaned over the bed and handed me a long, wide, flat-wrapped present. "This one is mostly from Rora."

My sweet girl grinned at me, propping her arm and chin on my thigh as she watched me open it.

I tore the paper off without an inkling of what might have laid beneath it, so I wasn't prepared when I saw the adoption papers signed and notarized in my hands. I had signed them months ago when we first got the papers back from Gideone, but we hadn't asked Aurora yet how she would feel about being our daughter.

My mouth hung open, my wet gaze snapping between Dante and Rora.

"What?" I whispered.

"Rora came to me a few weeks ago and asked why we hadn't adopted her yet," Dante explained, as he reached across the bed to draw his big hand over her hand. "She thought we didn't want to keep her."

My eyes darted to Rora, horrified. "How could you ever think that?"

She shrugged a little weakly. "You guys could have your own babies one day. Maybe you wouldn't want me then. I just wanted to know where I would go if that happened so I could be prepared."

My heart tore inside my chest with an audible ripping sound that echoed in my ears.

"Rora, *gattina,*" I murmured through the tears in my throat. I cupped her sweet face, staring into those big brown eyes that were much too worldly for a seven-year-old. "We would never want you anywhere but at our side, *capisci*? We didn't want to rush you into becoming our daughter legally. You've been through so much."

"I never had a dad, not really. I loved my mama," she whispered brokenly. "I love her today and always. But she's gone, and I love you too. I want to be your daughter. You both saved me. I don't feel safe anywhere but here at home with you."

I moved the tray of food off my lap and fitted my arms beneath her pits to draw her up between Dante and me, her thighs straddling each of our laps.

"I always wanted to be a mother all my life," I told her softly, tracing the line of her nose and her soft cheek, the curve of her eyebrow and the corner of her jaw. Every inch of her was as dear to me as every inch of Dante was. "It was my biggest dream in life to have a family. It might not be possible for Dante and me to make a baby together, but do you know what? That doesn't matter because even though I never ever would have wished what happened to Bambi and Jacopo to happen, my dreams came true when you came into our home. You just made them real by giving me this." I shook the papers in my other hand. "How many people do you know whose dreams really come true?"

She pursed her lips adorably. "*Zio* always says his dreams came true when he met you."

My gaze shot up to Dante who was smiling at us both like he couldn't believe his luck.

"Yeah, okay," I allowed, swallowing the emotions clogged in my throat. "Both your *zio* and I had our dreams come true, and you are a massive part of that. I hope you never doubt how much we love you."

"*Siamo con te,*" Dante told her, leaning forward to kiss the top of her head. "*anche quando non lo siamo.*"

*We are with you, even when we are not.*

"That's like what you always tell Elena," she murmured, eyes wide.

"Yeah, because I love you two most of all," he whispered. "But don't tell *nonno* Tore."

She laughed in a way that said she was totally going to tell Tore.

Dante smiled at me over her head and leaned in to kiss me softly. "Happy Birthday," he repeated. "And happily ever after. Let's enjoy the peace while it lasts."

I laughed, and Rora laughed with me because she loved our mirth tangled together like a song. Then Dante joined in, and my heart almost burst in my chest with joy.

There was no ice left in me.

No walls.

Because I had a mafioso to protect my heart better than I ever could.

# EPILOGUE

## *elena*

I was thirty-three when it happened.

Older than I'd thought I would be as a girl before everything happened.

Now, my age didn't matter.

Miracles existed outside of time, and that's what this was.

A miracle.

I took a test.

Then two more from different brands.

But that wasn't enough.

I'd learned a long time ago that hope was a fickle bitch.

So, I made an appointment with Monica just to confirm.

If I was going to tell Dante, it had to be true. Feeding him a false dream would be worse than swallowing it down myself.

For once, I wanted to give the man who had gifted me his world something worthy of his love.

When she confirmed it was true, I almost panicked because I wanted to give him the news like the gift it was.

Like a treasure.

So, I waited two weeks and told him on his fortieth birthday.

"*Svegliati, cuore mio,*" I murmured as I got back into bed that morning, straddling his prone hips so I could press a kiss to his face. "Wake up, my love."

"Mmm, I'm an old man now," he grumbled without opening his eyes. "I need my rest."

I laughed against his stubbled cheek. "Too old to open presents?"

Immediately, those olive-black eyes I adored snapped open. "I could wake up for presents."

I rolled my eyes as if I wasn't almost jumping out of my skin with excitement. "You're ridiculous."

"Well, where is it, *lottatrice*? Or…" He waggled his brows and sat up to push his face into the valley between my breasts. "Are you my present?"

I screeched with laughter as he held my breasts together and motorboated me. "Okay, enough! I'm going to have to sit over there if you can't control yourself."

"That might be best," he admitted, eyes sparkling like an entire universe built just for me.

I scooted over to the other side of the bed and retrieved the small box I'd wrapped. He took it eagerly, making love bubble up in my chest. He was a killer, a mafia Don, the scariest man I'd ever known. But to me, he was just this, boyish and charming and so handsome it hurt.

He frowned when he opened it to reveal a key.

"*Grazie?*" he asked.

*Thank you?*

"It opens something in the house," I told him, getting out of bed and grabbing my robe in case Rora was already awake. "I wonder if you can find it."

His eyes lit with the challenge, and he took my hand to practically drag me out of the room. I laughed as he searched, trying to open drawers in the office and the kitchen.

When he got to the second floor, my stomach erupted with butterflies.

I held my breath as he tried to open the door to my old room, the one I'd first stayed in when he'd blackmailed me into moving in.

It didn't open.

Dante turned to look at me with raised brows before he slid the key into the lock and turned.

I followed him as he stepped inside, then came to an abrupt stop when he did. I slid between his body and the wall so I could look at his face as he took in what I'd done with the room.

It was a nursey now.

The walls were the same light gray like we were inside a cloud and the furniture made to match the theme. The cribs were white with thick cushions, the rocking chair in the corner a dark gray boucle, the carpet beneath that a silvery blue. Giselle had even come over to paint clouds on the ceiling, a beautifully detailed mural of a twilight sky dotted with fat clouds and the first twinkling stars that came out at night.

It was like being on the inside of a tiny universe.

But I wasn't arrested by the room.

I was fascinated by the look on my husband's face.

He was a big man, a brutish one in build and sometimes, in action, but nothing about him was intimidating at that moment, nothing spoke of violence or harshness in any form.

The planes of his strong face were soaked in the dawn sunlight pouring in through the windows, highlighting the soft, open set of his mouth as if he had opened it to say something but immediately forgotten the words. His brows were heavy, almost compressed as if in confusion, but it was his eyes that stole what breath was left in my lungs.

Because they were lacquered with tears that brimmed precariously in the troughs of his lower lids, catching in his thick lashes.

"Elena," he called roughly, clearing his throat but otherwise still as a statue.

"Yes, Capo."

*"Vieni."*

I obeyed, stepping close enough so that he could reverently corral me into his embrace. When he tipped his head down to look at me, the tears spilled like diamonds from his black velvet eyes. One fell on my cheek and felt like an anointment.

"Are you really?" he asked, his voice so ravaged it was almost hard to discern the question. "Are you having our baby?"

I didn't notice I was crying until one of his rough-tipped thumbs brushed across my cheekbone, collecting the wet there.

I nodded because my voice was lost somewhere in the chaos of emotion storming my chest.

He closed his eyes then, slowly as if in pain, or maybe, as if his prayer had finally come true, and he couldn't believe it was real. Gently, he pressed his forehead to mine and cupped my face as if it was fragile like an eggshell.

"You're pregnant," he confirmed on a shaky sigh. "With our baby."

"I am, but there is a second part of your present." I pulled away, but he wouldn't let me go, so I lead him with an arm around the waist to the other present I'd wrapped and placed on the ottoman before the rocking chair.

He sat down in the seat, tugging me so I fell onto his lap. I grabbed the gift on the way, passing it into his hands as I curled up safe against his big body.

His hands shook as they opened the box.

Inside was a small black and white photo of the ultrasound Monica had given me two weeks before.

A photo of two tiny, perfect bodies curled up together like yin and yang.

"We're going to have twins," I whispered, in case he couldn't tell from the ultrasound photo.

Dante stared at the photo with such intensity it was palpable in the air around us. Tears fell from his eyes and sluiced down his cheeks, quick and silent. He seemed transfixed, unable to bear the amount of emotion coursing through his body.

I pressed my cheek to his heart and felt its racing beat.

"I always said I wasn't a lucky man," he finally murmured, his throat sticky with tears so his words were rough-edged. "I won't ever say that again."

Tears burned so hot in my eyes I had to close them as I curled even tighter in his lap, wrapped my arms around his neck, and clutched him to me.

We cried then, silent and strong, for a long time.

We'd been trying for years, from that first time on the hood of the Ferrari in the garage, and nothing.

So we'd gone to Monica two years ago and started hormone treatments.

Still nothing.

We had Aurora, who was everything, so we didn't let it depress us as much as it could have, but it was hard when I'd always wanted to carry my only child, when I wanted so badly to see a baby with Dante's black hair and lightly dimpled chin.

Last year, we tried IVF.

It didn't take either time.

So we stopped.

I was tired. Dante was tired.

Even poor Aurora was tired of praying for a baby brother or sister that didn't seem to want to come.

We stopped trying, and then, somehow, it happened.

I'd asked Monica about it, and she said it was actually fairly common. That the stress of trying to procreate could keep it from happening. When we gave up, we released that tension.

I had a slightly more romantic theory.

Our babies were always meant to be ours, but like their dad and mum, they were stubborn, and they took their time coming to us.

I didn't care about the heartaches we'd endured to get to this point. Dante had taught me that every single decision in your life was leading to something, was leading to exactly where you needed to be at the moment.

And this moment, for us, was a miracle.

"Good luck topping this birthday present next year, *cuore mia,*" Dante quipped after we'd both composed ourselves and just sat quietly rocking back and forth in our babies' room.

I laughed a little wetly as I tipped my head back to look up at his handsome face and scratch my nails down his bristly jaw. "I had to try to top yours when you made Rora our daughter legally, but I think this one might take the cake."

"I'm okay with that. More than okay." He dipped down to kiss me, our lips salty from tears, his soft and firm as they parted my mouth for his tongue. He kissed me sweetly, but thoroughly, until I ached for him. "Do you know how much I love you, *lottatrice mia?*"

"Yes," I said because I did.

Because Dante proved to me every single day that I was worthy of love, and he showed me just how much he had of that to give not only to me but also to Aurora and our entire family.

"Do you know how much I love you?" I asked him.

His face creased into that small, closed-mouth smile that was just for me. It wasn't his flashy grin or showstopper smile, just this intimate little curl that he only gave to me.

"Yes," he echoed. "Enough to change your entire life for me."

"I changed it for the best thing that ever happened to me," I corrected. "It wasn't as horrible as you make it sound."

"I would live with the guilt if everything hadn't worked out as well as it did," he admitted as he palmed my still-flat belly. "Ghorbani & Lombardi has been massively successful, so I didn't completely ruin your dreams of being a lawyer."

I laughed. "Not at all. I never thought I'd be famous for representing criminals and mobsters, but I can't complain. Most of them are good men."

This was true.

I never took a case if I truly felt the person a harmful criminal, but most of the time, I had no problem taking on clients in the mafia or other gangs. I'd recently represented the Prez of The Fallen MC in New York on trial for manslaughter and got him off on self-defense.

Maybe I wasn't the hero I'd always thought I'd be in the courtroom, but I represented the kind of people I'd come to know and love. The kind of person I'd become. The anti-hero. And that was infinitely more interesting than anything I could have dreamed up in my youth.

"They'll be proud to have such a gladiator for a mother," he told me, splaying his big hand entirely over the width of my belly. "Just like Rora is."

"She will be over the moon about the babies."

"*Certo*, she might not leave your side again."

I hoped not.

We still took Rora to therapy six years from her mother's death, which helped, but we'd also given her a cell phone so she could keep in touch with us all the time. It helped alleviate her worries, and it was a simple fix.

Often, she would just text us one word. A word her *zio* Sebastian had taught her.

*Insieme.*

Together.

The same word that had banded my siblings and me together as kids.

"I was thinking Chiara or Georgina for girls," I suggested, thinking of Dante's mother and Bambi. "And maybe Amadeo or Jacopo for boys."

If it was possible, Dante's eyes grew even warmer on my face. "*Bellissima.* Those are perfect."

"For the record, capo, you have nothing to feel guilty for, ever. You gave me the only two things I ever really wanted." I threaded our fingers together on my belly. "True love and a family."

"Cheesy," he teased, and then he kissed me.

And I didn't care if it was cheesy because it was the truth.

Most of my life, I thought success meant money and a career, that rigid structure and adherence to societal guidelines would make me happy and beloved.

The truth was, the only thing that brought me peace was chaos.

A lot of people would have said loving Dante condemned me to hell. The truth was, loving him saved my life. Because he reminded me what it was like to be alive.

What really mattered.

I pressed our tangled hands to my belly, tucked my chin into his neck to breathe in his lemon grove and ocean brine scent, and enjoyed this moment of tranquility before our new brand of chaos was born.

# DANTE

Watching Elena Lombardi give birth to the children we created together after years of trying and failing was the single most incredible experience of my life.

My woman was a fighter, so even when the babies took twenty-eight hours to enter the world, she didn't complain. In fact, she took every moment as a gift, her face suffused with gratitude that she could ever have this experience with them and with me. I fed her ice chips, stroked back her sweaty hair, and let her hold my hand to the point of breaking.

Because I felt the same way.

Nothing about this was anything less than perfect.

I'd done a lot in my forty years on the planet.

Gone to the best schools, reinvented myself three times into three very different men, and until then, the greatest thing I'd ever done was love Elena Lombardi.

When those tiny little humans entered the world, screaming at the top of their lungs like the fighters they were born to be, that became the single best accomplishment of my life.

Creating them and giving Elena her dreams of motherhood.

She looked at those dark heads of hair, into those red, scrunched little faces as if the entire universe was embedded in every pore. There was so much awe in her tear-glazed eyes, so much wonder. A blind woman discovering sight, a mute her voice. It was an expression of waiting finally relieved, a miracle she had been waiting for all her life finally actualized in her arms.

In the perfect forms of a tiny boy and girl.

"*Ciao, mio piccolo capo e mia piccola donna,*" she whispered in a threadbare voice worn with the weight of her emotions. One knuckle reached up to feather against our baby boy's flushed, silken cheek, and she gasped at the sensation of feeling our son under her hand. "Welcome to this mad, bad world, little bosses. We are so grateful to have you."

A sob wrapped firm fingers around my throat and throttled me. Instead of trying to find meager words to explain the tumult of emotions rioting through me, I leaned against the side of the bed and carefully wound one arm around my woman, the other gently cupping the head of our newborn son, the fingers extended to brush our daughter's petal-soft cheek.

"They are so beautiful," Elena breathed, dazed and awed. "How did we create such perfection?"

My laugh was almost a bark of disbelief. "*Lottatrice,* you just gave birth to twins, and you look like a goddess. It is no wonder to anyone but you."

"I'm not perfect," she murmured as she stared at our children nestled in her arms. "I stopped trying to be a long time ago, and look what it got me."

She tipped her head up, a sweet, exhausted smile on her face. There was so much love in her eyes, I couldn't look at her without feeling like I couldn't breathe.

"A man better than I could have ever dreamed of," she told me. "And three children when I thought for years I wouldn't have any."

I kissed her soft mouth, tasting her joy straight from the source.

A moment later, the door creaked open, and Tore, Mama, and Rora appeared.

"Someone wanted to see their siblings," Tore explained, holding Mama's hand as they moved into the room.

"Come meet them," I encouraged, opening my arm for my thirteen-year-old daughter who stepped into me, leaning over with an expression of awe that almost rivaled her mother's.

"They're so beautiful," she breathed. "And we have one of each."

Elena and I laughed.

"What do we call them?" she asked as she softly reached out to run a finger over the boy's silken cheek.

"What do you think of Amadeo Jacopo and Chiara Georgina?" I asked her, squeezing her against my body because I could feel her still as soon as I spoke the names.

She turned those beautiful brown eyes to me, her gaze full of pure, unadulterated hero worship aimed at, as always, of all people, Elena and me. Two people who had never thought they would be anything but villains.

"They're perfect," she whispered.

And they were.

Just like she was.

I bent to kiss her head and then the heads of our two new babies and finally my wife's upturned mouth, waiting for me.

And I knew this was exactly the kind of ending we deserved.

# THANKS, ETC.

I was so nervous to write Dante and Elena's love story. Not only because they played a role as villains in The Evolution of Sin Trilogy about Giselle and The Enslaved Duet about Cosima, but because they are very different characters in general. Dante is a ruthless capo, but he also has a tender heart and isn't afraid to communicate his desires. Then there is Elena, my ice queen, my fighter. She is broken and bitter, lonely and cold, and so tired at the beginning of the Anti-Heroes in Love duet. But through the lens of Dante's unconditional love, she comes into a version of herself that she always secretly longed to be: strong, passionate, courageous, and, most of all, happy. I was worried people wouldn't enjoy her brittleness or bitterness so imagine my surprise when so many readers reached out to tell me they fell in love with Elena for her flaws as well as her strengths. It means so much that readers have loved reading about her evolution and about my two villains who become heroes to each other.

Now, on to the people who make everything possible for me.

Annette, you are the *consigliere* to my *capo*! Thank you for always supporting me, looking out for me, and keeping me on track. I love you endlessly.

Allaa, talking to you sparks my creativity like a lit match to tinder. Thank you for your advice, support, and friendship.

Michelle, my dirty soul sister and ride or die, thank you for being my friend through everything and for always knowing exactly what to say to make my heart happy.

Ella, you mean everything to me. We've been through it all and come out the other side closer than ever. I'll never stop loving you and being grateful for your presence in my life.

Candi, thank you for being not only an amazing PR boss lady, but for also being a steadfast, fun, and loving friend.

Jenny, I will always and forever be grateful for you putting up with my messy manuscripts and short turnaround times. Thank you for turning my dirty words into gold.

Sarah Plocher, thank you for being such a sweet friend and support while also being incredibly proficient and professional when proofreading for me. I value you so much.

Ramzi, thank you for bringing my visions for the Anti-Heroes in Love paperbacks to life! They are utterly gorgeous just like you.

Giana's Poppies Street Team! You shout about my word across the webosphere and I'm so grateful for every single post, comment, like, and share you give and garner for me. Thank you for being such incredible supporters.

My ARC team, I am honored you love my words enough to read them no matter the subject matter. Your confidence in my storytelling buoys me when I doubt myself.

Giana's Darlings, thank you for being excited about my books, spreading the word about them, and always being down for new content.

Najla Qamber, you are the queen of graphiclandia and I am so blessed to have found you at the very beginning of my author journey. You bring my visions for book covers and aesthetics to life so brilliantly, I am in awe of your talent.

Thank you Veronica for providing invaluable perspective on Italian language and culture. I would have been lost without your expertise!

Thank you to Jennifer Severino for being my legal expert and answering my myriad of questions. Your guidance was crucial to the success of this story.

There are, as always, countless bloggers, Tiktokers, and Instagrammers to thank for their support of this release, but I can't possibly name them all so please know, I am grateful for every post and share about my work. In addition, a special thanks goes out to my girls: Tish from @bookthief28, Mary from @makeupandmary, Jess from @peacelovebooksxo, Weronica @littlesteamyreads for her love and graphics, Pang @shereads_pang for her support and gorgeous edits, and last but never least, Emilie from @fansofgianadarling who is CEO of my fandom and one of the sweetest souls ever.

Fiona and Lauren, we've been friends since we were just girls with braces and bad skin and it has been an honor to grow and evolve alongside you both. Thank you for always being supportive, for hyping me up and celebrating my successes even when I forget to.

Armie, you are a constant light in my life and like Dante with Elena, you can always make me laugh even when I'm sad or stressed out. Thank you for being the best friend I always dreamed of.

Albie, you taught me about the beauty of male/female friendship. Thank you for inspiring me to write about found families and how wonderful friendships like ours can be.

To my fur babies, Romeo and Persephone ,who bring me joy every single day and keep me company during my solitary hours of writing.

As always, I saved the best for last. To my gorgeous man, H, who is better than any hero I could ever write because he's real and he's mine. I am grateful every day that I found the love of my life. Thank you for teaching me how to love and for being with me since we were fifteen even when you were not. *Io sono con te sempre.*

# OTHER BOOKS BY GIANA DARLING

The Evolution of Sin Trilogy

Giselle Moore is running away from her past in France for a new life in America, but before she moves to New York City, she takes a holiday on the beaches of Mexico and meets a sinful, enigmatic French businessman, Sinclair, who awakens submissive desires and changes her life forever.

The Affair
The Secret
The Consequence
The Evolution Of Sin Trilogy Boxset

The Fallen Men Series

The Fallen Men are a series of interconnected, standalone, erotic MC romances that each feature age gap love stories between dirty-talking, Alpha males and the strong, sassy women who win their hearts.

Lessons in Corruption
Welcome to the Dark Side
Good Gone Bad

After the Fall

Inked in Lies

Dead Man Walking

A Fallen Men Companion Book of Poetry:

King of Iron Hearts

The Enslaved Duet

The Enslaved Duet is a dark romance duology about an eighteen-year-old Italian fashion model, Cosima Lombardi, who is sold by her indebted father to a British Earl whose nefarious plans for her include more than just sexual slavery… Their epic tale spans across Italy, England, Scotland, and the USA across a five-year period that sees them endure murder, separation, and a web of infinite lies.

Enthralled (The Enslaved Duet #1)

Enamoured (The Enslaved Duet, #2)

The Elite Seven Series

Sloth (The Elite Seven Series, #7)

Coming Soon

Fallen King (A Fallen Men Short Story)

# ABOUT GIANA DARLING

Giana Darling is a USA Today, Wall Street Journal, Top 40 Best Selling Canadian romance writer who specializes in the taboo and angsty side of love and romance. She currently lives in beautiful British Columbia where she spends time riding on the back of her man's bike, baking pies, and reading snuggled up with her cat, Persephone, and dog, Romeo.

Printed in Great Britain
by Amazon

16365552R00271